Iris Gower was born in Swansea, where she now lives with her husband in a house overlooking the sea she loves. The mother of four grown-up children, she has written more than sixteen bestselling novels, and has been awarded an MA in English at the University of Cardiff. This is the fourth novel in her *Firebird* sequence, and *Kingdom's Dream*, the fifth novel in the series, is now available from Bantam Press.

DAUGHTERS OF REBECCA

Iris Gower

CORGI BOOKS

DAUGHTERS OF REBECCA
A CORGI BOOK : 0 552 14450 9

Originally published in Great Britain by Bantam Press,
a division of Transworld Publishers

PRINTING HISTORY
Bantam Press edition published 2000
Corgi edition published 2001

1 3 5 7 9 10 8 6 4 2

Copyright © Iris Gower 2000

Set in 11/12pt Plantin by
Kestrel Data, Exeter, Devon.

Corgi Books are published by Transworld Publishers,
61–63 Uxbridge Road, London W5 5SA,
a division of The Random House Group Ltd,
in Australia by Random House Australia (Pty) Ltd,
20 Alfred Street, Milsons Point, Sydney, NSW 2061, Australia,
in New Zealand by Random House New Zealand Ltd,
18 Poland Road, Glenfield, Auckland 10, New Zealand
and in South Africa by Random House (Pty) Ltd,
Endulini, 5a Jubilee Road, Parktown 2193, South Africa.

Printed and bound in Great Britain by
Cox & Wyman Ltd, Reading, Berkshire.

*To Tudor, my husband,
for all his love and patience*

CHAPTER ONE

The sun was shining on the narrow, cobbled road outside number 13 Fennel Court, highlighting the motes of dust that grimed the windows so that the light failed to penetrate into the small kitchen at the rear of the house.

In the heart of Swansea Town the chapel bells were ringing for evening prayers but only the rich could spare time for the Almighty. The grand copper barons would take their seats in St Mary's and offer thanks to God for all their riches. And all that the Sabbath gave Shanni Price was a few hours to spend with her mother.

Shanni brushed the damp red curls from her brow and stirred the thin stew with more enthusiasm than expertise. She heard a stifled moan and looked up from the cooking pot. 'Soon be ready, Mam.' Shanni bit her lip, staring anxiously at her mother who was lying on the narrow bed in the corner of the room. 'I've done some nice *cawl*, Mam. This will make you feel better.' She attempted to smile, though fear clenched her heart. Her mother was sick, had been for months, and the talk around the courts was that widowed

Mrs Price was 'in the way'. Shanni had tried to ask her mother if she was expecting a child but even as the words formed in her mouth her courage failed her.

'Bryn the butcher has given us some ham bones,' Shanni said. 'He's even left a bit of meat on them. Kind man, Bryn.' If she talked, perhaps everything would be normal: her mother would sit up and smile and she would be well again.

Shanni tasted the stew and grimaced. She was no cook – in fact, she was not adept at anything, which was why she worked in the heat of the copper sheds fetching beer for the furnace men. Once the copper, red and liquid like hot blood, had caught her arm and she still had the scar. It was a hard job and it might be lowly but at least it brought some money into the house.

Shanni threw more salt into the pot. The handful of carrots, cabbage leaves and a few old potatoes did not make for a tasty meal but with the last of yesterday's bread it would do; at least they would eat today.

Her face was hot from the fire and Shanni paused to wipe the beads of perspiration from her face with her arm. She looked up as her mother moaned again, a low moan that seemed to start deep in her throat.

'What is it, Mam? Are you worse?'

'I think it's started. My pains are getting regular, see.' Dora Price was sweating and her knees were drawn up to her stomach. Shanni stood silent, unable to ignore the truth of their situation any longer. Her mam was about to bring a bastard child into the world and all Shanni could think of was the shame of it, of another mouth to feed and not enough money to go around.

'Oh, Mam, how could you?' She started to move towards the bed but she stopped suddenly, her head lifted in an attitude of listening. '*Duw*, Mam, what's that?'

The crash of tin kettles, the beat of wood against wood, the howling of human voices shattered the stillness of the evening. Shanni put down her spoon and wiped her hands on her apron. Her heart was thudding and she could hardly breathe.

The sounds grew louder and Shanni began to tremble. She stared around her in panic. She knew what the noise meant and she was terrified. She dragged the heavy pot to the side of the grate, careless of the soup splashing into the fire. 'Mam, what are we going to do?'

Dora Price pressed her hand across her swollen stomach and lifted her head wearily. 'Sounds like the *Ceffyl Pren*. They're bringing the wooden horse to punish me. Run, Shanni. Get out the back now, don't let them see you.'

Shanni ignored her mother and hurried to the small front window. She pushed aside the torn curtains and rubbed her fingers over the grimy glass. She took a ragged breath as she saw a crowd of women rounding the bend. They were carrying tin buckets, brandishing sticks and screaming abuse as they marched into the narrow, filthy court off Potato Street.

'Go on, girl.' Her mother had made an effort to rise from her bed. She stood swaying beside

Shanni, holding her swollen stomach. 'No sense in them getting you as well.' Though she spoke with studied calm, Dora Price was terrified and it showed in the pallor of her face.

'I'm not leaving you, Mam.' Shanni stood in the doorway, forcing the rotting wood into place. She propped a battered chair against the planking and picked up a broom ready to stand guard over her mother. 'They are not putting you on the *Ceffyl Pren*! That wooden horse was made to punish cheats and liars and loose women, and you're not going to be dragged through the streets like that, not when you're so sick.'

'Let us in, Dora Price!'

One voice, more raucous than the rest, rang out stridently into the sudden silence. Trembling, Shanni peered through a crack in the door and stared into the bulging eyes of May O'Sullivan. 'Where's your mam?' the woman demanded, kicking the frail door in her fury. 'Let us in, Shanni Price. There's no stopping us and our quarrel is with her, not you.'

'She's very ill!' Shanni called. 'Why do you want to punish her? She's done nothing wrong.'

'Nothing wrong? The woman is a harlot, a stealer of husbands. We'll show her right from wrong.' May O'Sullivan began heaving and kicking at the battered door. She was joined by others from the crowd and, in a few moments, the frail door splintered and swung on its hinges, broken beyond repair.

May O'Sullivan pushed past Shanni, sweeping the broom from her hand with little effort. 'Out of the way! You're only a child. You must pray you don't grow up a wanton like your mother.' She confronted the sick woman. 'You know the charge, Dora Price, that of tempting a married man, making him be unfaithful to his wife.'

Shanni looked at her mother. Dora's face was white and her lips trembled so much she could not answer. 'It was the other way round!' Shanni shouted. 'Mam has done nothing. That Spencer man has been round here telling my mother he loved her, that he would leave his wife for her. I've heard him myself!'

'Lies!' May pushed her aside and hauled Dora upright. 'That's my poor sister's husband you're talking about and her crying her eyes out over a weak man.' She spat on the floor. 'You're a whore, Dora Price, and we're taking you out to make an example of you – and don't think that your belly will save you. Spawn of the devil you got in by there, see?' She prodded Dora's stomach with spiteful fingers.

'Don't do that! My mam is having the pains – you can't take her out of her bed.' Before she had finished speaking Shanni was knocked to the ground by the rush of women fighting to get their hands on Dora Price.

'We'll teach the whore a lesson she'll never forget,' May shouted.

Shanni struggled to her feet and screamed in anguish as her mother was dragged outside into the dusk of the evening air.

Shanni stared through the shattered door at the roughly made *Ceffyl Pren*. It was made of old wood and bits of cast-off clothing with a carved head jutting from the front, painted eyes rolling. Beneath the hangings at the back four legs were visible, men's legs. Shanni recognized the polished boots of one and pushed her way forward. 'So, Dan Spencer, you would carry my mam to her shame, would you? After you coming here lying and cheating, telling us what a harridan your wife was. You evil devil, you!'

Her attempts to lift aside the rags were obstructed by May O'Sullivan's meaty arm. She smacked Shanni in the face and she fell backwards on to the filthy ground. She stared up at her mother, white and pleading, her lips forming the words 'Help me.'

The procession wound out of the court and on to the main street. The throng of women shouted abuse and May laid into Dora Price's back with her own broom. Other townsfolk joined the procession, anxious to see an example made of a loose woman. More than half of the women in Swansea had suffered the same fate as poor Mrs Spencer, that of a wicked woman taking advantage of a married man. But not all culprits were found out in their sin and this was the first time a woman pregnant by a bewitched husband had been exposed.

Shanni followed at a distance, tears running down her cheeks. She knew what came next for she had seen such acts of vengeance before. Her mother would be stripped naked, her shame exposed for all to gaze upon. She would be tied to a horse post and pelted with mud. The mud would be rubbed into her skin and chicken feathers daubed all over her. Her mother would be forced to stand there until she dropped from exhaustion.

When the women reached the square, the procession halted. Spoons were rattled against the sides of pots and kettles; the noise was deafening.

Shanni cried out as her mother was dragged from the horse and tethered like a beast. She saw her mother moan and hang her head as the ragged clothes were torn from her and she was made to stand silent and bowed.

May O'Sullivan was the first to throw a clod of earth; it caught Dora squarely on her protruding belly. Other women joined in the sport of tormenting a fallen woman, and all the time Dora stood silent, her long greying hair hanging over her face.

'Stop it!' Shanni cried, as her mother's thin legs buckled under her. Dora lifted her head and her eyes met Shanni's.

'Get off her!' Shanni picked up a piece of wood that had fallen from the *Ceffyl Pren* and laid into the nearest women with it. She was almost at her mother's side before a straight blow to her head felled her.

Half-conscious, Shanni slumped to the ground, clutching the gritty earth beneath her fingers with a feeling of despair. 'You'll kill her!' she sobbed, but no-one was listening.

Shanni was struggling to her knees, shaking her head to clear it, when she heard a voice, cultured and strong, ring out over the heads of the women.

'Stop this obscenity at once!' Mrs Mainwaring, pottery owner, was pushing her way through the crush. 'What in the name of heaven is going on here?' Shanni got to her feet and a faint stirring of hope began to burn within her as she saw the richly dressed woman make her way to the front of the now silent crowd.

'You.' She pointed a riding crop at May O'Sullivan. 'Release that poor woman at once before I have you thrown in jail!'

'This is no business of yours, Mrs Mainwaring, if you'll pardon me saying so.' May O'Sullivan had lost some of her bluster. 'This is a matter for we working folks to settle.'

Mrs Mainwaring took no notice. 'My coachman and his boy are gone to fetch the constable so I would advise you to go about your business, if you do not wish to be flung in the castle dungeons. Now, go before you find yourselves in deep trouble.'

Grumbling, the crowd thinned and when the coachman came swinging round the corner of the square, a huge stick in his hand, even May O'Sullivan thought it politic to move away. 'That'll teach you to act the whore, Dora Price.' Her parting shot was emphasized by a lump of mud that caught Dora's cheek.

'Come on,' Mrs Mainwaring said, breathlessly, 'let's get you home.' She untied Dora and put a cloak around her shoulders. 'Can you manage to climb up into the coach?'

When Dora was seated, Mrs Mainwaring wrapped a warm rug around her knees with gentle hands. Shanni sat on the opposite seat, sunk in misery, hating the barbarism, the injustice in punishing a woman for loving the wrong man.

The coach manoeuvred its way through Potato Street but was too broad to tackle Fennel Court. The coachman lifted Dora and carried her gently into the tiny kitchen of number 13.

'Fetch some water, Graves.' Mrs Mainwaring was rolling up her sleeves. 'Is there any left in the kettle, child?'

Shanni nodded and poured the water into a bowl. Mrs Mainwaring took it from her and gently washed the mud from Dora's swollen stomach. 'Come on, now, get into bed. Try to rest and to forget this dreadful day.' Mrs Mainwaring pulled up the thin blankets as tenderly as if Dora had been a child herself.

'I'll get more water, Mrs Mainwaring,' Graves said, and went out into the yard. When he returned, he pushed the kettle on to the fire, his head discreetly turned away from the woman on the bed.

'Thank you, Mrs Mainwaring.' Shanni stood awkwardly in the gloom of the kitchen, not knowing what to say. 'Thank you for being kind to Mam. She's not to blame for any of this. It's Dan Spencer who should be punished. He's a liar and he led her astray.'

Mrs Mainwaring nodded and touched Shanni's shoulder. 'Look, I shall bring this to the attention of the magistrates. It's rough justice and should not be tolerated in our society, not in these enlightened days.'

Shanni nodded, but she did not hold out much hope that Mrs Mainwaring's intervention would do any good. She was about to say something when the silence was shattered by her mother's terrified cry. 'The waters have broke. The baby is coming – oh, Lord above, help me.'

Mrs Mainwaring took charge. 'It's getting very dark so light some candles, find clean cloths – is that water hot yet? Graves, fetch the doctor. Tell him I need him at once.' She turned to Shanni. 'We'll both have to help your mother until the doctor comes. I can't manage alone.'

Shanni fetched the tin bowl and some pieces of rag from the clothesline. Her heart was still beating rapidly and she felt sick. She hated people, she hated the whole world, and one day she would have her revenge on them all.

Mrs Mainwaring worked hard, encouraging, admonishing, as Dora struggled to bring forth her baby. Shanni built up the fire, boiling more water, but in her heart she knew it was useless. Today the heavens were against them and nothing good would come from the birthing of the infant conceived in shame.

Graves returned and stood in the doorway, shaking his head. 'The doctor is out, Mrs Mainwaring, but I've left a message with his wife. He'll come as soon as he can.'

'We'll just have to manage till then.' Mrs Mainwaring glanced at Shanni. 'I don't suppose the local midwife would come, would she?'

Shanni shook her head. No-one in the vicinity of Fennel Court would help them, not now. The moon was gliding across the sky by the time the child slid into the world, white and dead. Dora Price sighed wearily. 'It's for the best,' she whispered. 'The little mite wouldn't stand a chance.' Her eyes closed and her lips were pale.

Her hair was plastered to her forehead with sweat, and a streak of dirt still darkened her cheek.

'Where's the damned doctor?' Mrs Mainwaring said tersely. 'Go to Graves, Shanni. Tell him to try again to fetch a doctor or a midwife – anyone will do.'

'It's too late to help me.' Shanni heard her mother's voice, thin and threadlike. 'But, please, take care of Shanni, my lady.' Her hand fumbled for Shanni's. 'You must forget all this and have a good life, Shanni. May God in his mercy take care of you.'

Shanni clung to her mother's hand for a long time until, at last, Mrs Mainwaring drew her away from the bed. 'Let's go now,' she said softly. 'Graves will come back here and see to everything, so don't worry.'

Dumbly Shanni allowed herself to be led back along the silent court towards where the coach was waiting. She sank into the cold leather seat and closed her eyes. Her mother was dead and nothing Shanni could do would bring her back to life.

Llinos Mainwaring stared across the breakfast table at her husband. 'I'm so sorry for Shanni Price, deprived of her mother in such dreadful circumstances.'

Joe Mainwaring put down his paper. 'I know. The barbarism of the wooden horse was a terrible thing for you to see, my love, and you must try to put it out of your mind.' His dark hair was streaked with a ribbon of silver and hung to his shoulders. He looked noble and proud, every inch a man of mixed race. His American-Indian blood showed in the gold of his skin, and his inheritance from his white father was the bluest eyes Llinos had ever seen.

And the years had been good to him, Llinos thought lovingly. She felt her heart swell with joy. He was her husband, and though he was past his fortieth birthday he was as dashing and handsome as the day she first met him.

'You did your best for the poor woman,' he said. 'You ensured she had a decent Christian burial and you found the little girl a position in service.'

'I worry about Shanni Price, though,' Llinos said. 'She's so young, so vulnerable. What effect will her mother's death have on her, I wonder?'

'She'll survive,' Joe said. 'You suffered a great deal of hardship when you were young too and you survived, didn't you?'

'I suppose you're right, but then I had you.' Not always, insisted a small voice inside Llinos's head. Once Joe had left her for another woman. He had fathered an illegitimate child, a child growing up even now somewhere on the plains of America. As always, it was the woman who bore the consequences of an affair, and Joe had come out of it unscathed. Like the awful Mr Spencer. She pushed the unpleasant thoughts aside.

She took a piece of toast, ignoring the dish of devilled kidneys and steaming bacon. Whenever she thought of Joe's mistress her appetite left her. She forced her mind on to other matters. 'Perhaps we'll hear from Lloyd this week.'

'Our son is growing up now,' Joe said. 'He is

becoming a man. We must stand back from him, let him mature in his own way.'

'But he's still very young.' Llinos protested, 'and I hate him being away. I'm sure a local school would have served just as well as one in England.'

'He's at my old school,' Joe said. 'I received an excellent education there and I wanted Lloyd to have the best.'

'I still think of him as a baby,' Llinos said softly. 'I know he's into his teen years now but I still want to hug him close, to feel his arms around me.'

'Llinos, my love, to you Lloyd will always be a child. That's the way of it with so-called civilized people. In the animal kingdom a newborn matures fast or dies.'

'Don't start on your American-Indian philosophies!' Llinos said lightly. 'Not over breakfast – you'll give me indigestion.'

Joe helped himself to more toast. He ate silently, his whole being contained. Anyone would think he was still on the plains of his homeland, wary lest an enemy creep up on him. He looked up, and Llinos was comforted by the love she saw in her husband's eyes. Would she ever understand this man who, after years of marriage, was still an enigma to her? She doubted it.

'Why the scrutiny?' Joe asked. 'Not thinking about the past again, are you, Llinos?'

She shook her head. 'I try not to, Joe, but sometimes I'm overwhelmed with the pain of it.' She looked down at her hands, hands that had moulded clay into shape, had toiled long hours in the pottery in an effort to make the business the success it was today.

Joe regarded her steadily. 'I know you were hurt, my love, and I'm so sorry for betraying you, but all that is past. We can't let it affect our future.'

'I do realize that, Joe. But how would you feel if I was unfaithful, if I had a child by another man?'

He sighed heavily. 'I would want to kill you both,' he said simply. He threw down his napkin and got to his feet. 'I'd better get some letters written,' he said more easily. 'I, too, have a business to run.'

His words seemed like a reproach and Llinos sighed. Would she and Joe never fall back into the easy, loving relationship they once had?

She drank her tea in an effort to clear the obstruction from her throat; she would not cry the bitter tears that were always present whenever she thought of Joe in the arms of another woman. She would have to be brave like any other woman forced to swallow the pain of infidelity. 'I think I shall take a look at the order books,' she said, to his retreating back.

Her days were empty now: she was not needed in the flourishing pottery; she was not needed in her own house, come to that, not without her son. There were servants to cook and clean, and book-keepers to see to the financial side of her business. She was adrift, a woman without purpose. Suddenly her life seemed futile. Biting her lip, Llinos Mainwaring watched her husband leave the dining room and disappear into his study.

The idea of looking over the order books had lost its appeal. Instead, Llinos climbed up the broad staircase to the bedroom she shared with Joe. The windows were open and the breeze brushed the curtains into a frenzy of dancing. Llinos was restless; she stared out into the grounds where the lawn was sun-scorched. She felt downcast, her heart heavy with the knowledge that Joe, ensconced in his study, would be writing a letter for his mistress to read to their son.

She would go out, she decided, take a ride in the carriage, walk in the park and get some fresh air into her lungs. Then, maybe, she would go visiting. She paused before the mirror, examining her reflection. She was slim still. Her hair was dark with hardly any silver running through it, her complexion smooth, yet there was a sadness in her eyes that never left her.

Later, as the carriage took her along past the promenade Llinos looked out at the sea. The flow of the tides always made her feel calmer, as though the world was so big that her worries were diminished by the grandeur of the ocean, spreading away to merge with the sky. Beyond the bay the rocky head of Mumbles formed a sheltering arm around the town of Swansea. How she loved it here where she had been born and bred and where, doubtless, she would die.

The coach pulled into a long driveway and as Llinos leaned out of the window to stare at the house, large and mellow in the sun, she saw a familiar figure on the step. He stood tall, his hair pale and shining, her dear friend Eynon Morton-Edwards.

As soon as the coach stopped, Eynon opened the door and held out his arms to lift Llinos on to the drive. 'Llinos, my lovely girl, you grow more beautiful every day.'

He kissed her cheek and she clung to him for a moment. Eynon had been her friend through the good times and the bad. He had always loved her and never had that love been needed so much as the day Joe left her.

'Come inside. I must tell you about the season in London, the theatres, the brightly lit streets. It was such a sight, so much pomp and splendour. You would have loved it.'

He led her into the house and Llinos felt the coolness of the old mansion wash over her. 'It's always so peaceful here,' she said softly.

'Not when my beloved daughter is at home!' He opened the door of the drawing room with a flourish. 'Jayne is back at school now and I was glad to have her off my hands.'

'I don't believe that for one minute,' Llinos said. She pulled at the tips of her gloves and handed them to the maid who hovered, waiting to take her coat.

'Shanni, how nice to see you again. Are you well?' She studied the girl, who was sombre in a long black skirt covered with a pristine apron. 'You're certainly looking very grand.'

She felt in that moment that she shared a common bond with the girl: they had both been orphaned, had struggled to survive. Llinos remembered the old days when her father had gone to the war against Napoleon. Her mother had been feckless, unable to control her own life, let alone keep a business afloat. After her mother died, Llinos had tackled the future with courage – courage that seemed to have deserted her now.

She watched as Shanni left the room. She was so pretty with her red hair, tied back in a knot now and covered with a cap as befitted a servant girl.

'How is she settling?'

'Shanni, you mean? She's done very well in the few weeks she's been here. Now, let me tell you all about London.'

Eynon was bent on talking about his trip and Llinos smiled indulgently. It would be good for her to listen: the trivia of court life would be a distraction from her own, often uncomfortable, thoughts.

Shanni Price returned to the kitchen and sat down near the window. She had taken to occupying this particular chair when she had some time off from work. From it she could look down at the sea rolling away below her, and think of things more important than being lady's maid to the precocious Jayne when she was at home and maid-of-all-work when she was not.

'Don't sit there dreaming, girl!' Mrs Pollard was the housekeeper and wielded her power over the other servants with great enthusiasm. She glanced at the cook. 'Any tea going spare, Mrs Davies?'

'I'll warm the pot,' Mrs Davies said obligingly. It paid to keep in with Mrs Pollard.

'It's my day off,' Shanni said. 'I shouldn't be working at all, though I don't suppose Mr Morton-Edwards even notices I'm here.'

'Why on earth should he notice a jumped-up little serving wench?' Mrs Pollard's tongue could be acid on occasions. She turned her attention to the cook. 'I just do not understand the young people of today, Mrs Davies, do you?'

The woman uttered something unintelligible and Shanni hid a smile. Mrs Davies was quite old, of course, almost thirty-five, and a widow, but even so she was far younger than the housekeeper, who would not see fifty again.

'Going to meetings, talking about violence.' Mrs Pollard was on her soap-box. 'Decent women should know their place. Didn't we have enough trouble in 'thirty-four when the Poor Law came in? A riot there was in Brecon, and the Swansea Yeomanry sent to sort it out. Brought back dead, some of them.' She shook her head. 'I don't know what the world is coming to, these days.'

Shanni remained silent. What did the old woman know of injustice? She had spent her life waiting on rich folk. She had not known the shame of poverty or of being alone in the world. Shanni was not so fortunate: she had been born in a hovel, had learned to hate the way society treated the poor in general and women in particular.

'Well, what have you to say for yourself, Shanni Price?' She sniffed. 'Who would call a girl Shanni, I ask you? A fancy enough name for a child from the slums, wouldn't you say?'

Shanni remained silent. What use was there in talking? Action was needed: action against the rich, action against the men who wielded power. She had heard only yesterday about poor Sally Jones. The girl was only twelve years old and a

24

prostitute. She had been dragged to the sessions not because of her trade but because she dared to take away a copper kettle from an alehouse. For that small crime she was sentenced to transportation to some far-flung country. It seemed to Shanni that there was one law for the rich and quite a different one for the poor.

'Take your mam,' Mrs Pollard said. 'I hear she was fooling around with Dan Spencer and carrying his babba.' Mrs Pollard had a spiteful gleam in her eyes. 'Lying in the bed of a married man is disgusting. What that man's poor wife had to go through is no-one's business.'

'It's none of yours either.' Shanni stood up and stared at the older woman. 'But, then, no man married or single would take you to his bed and that's why you are so bitter!'

For a moment Mrs Pollard was silent then she screamed and held her hand to her brow. 'Oh, Mrs Davies, fetch me some water quick, I've come over all faint-like.'

Mrs Davies obeyed, helping the older woman into a chair. 'Go to the master, Mrs Davies, there's a dear. Tell him Mrs Pollard can't work today because of this dreadful girl. He must dismiss her. It's her or me. I won't stay under the same roof as her.'

Mrs Davies hesitated, but Shanni smiled slowly. 'Don't worry, I'm leaving! I can't stay here with you, Mrs Pollard. You've an evil tongue and I hope you rot in hell!'

Shanni ran upstairs to her room. It took only a few minutes to put her clothes into a bag. She would have to take her maid's skirts with her. It might be stealing, but the rags she had arrived in had been burned in the brazier in the garden.

Shanni felt the cool of the day on her cheeks as she left the house. She was half-way down the drive when she heard the sound of carriage wheels behind her.

'Shanni Price, where do you think you're going?' Mrs Mainwaring was leaning over the side of the carriage, her eyes alight with amusement. 'I hear you told poor Mrs Pollard a few home truths.' She laughed, a pretty, ladylike sound.

'Come on, climb in. I suppose I'll have to take you in myself.' Mrs Mainwaring moved over to make room on the seat and, after a moment's hesitation, Shanni climbed aboard.

'You're a bright girl, Shanni Price. How would you like to read and write and do figures?'

'I can read – a bit,' Shanni said defensively. Then she relaxed. 'I would like very much to be clever, to figure out sums and to write proper words.'

'Then that's what you shall do.' Mrs Mainwaring smiled. 'No more cheeking your elders, though. Is it a bargain?'

Shanni looked into the face of the older woman and saw only kindness. She remembered how gentle Mrs Mainwaring had been with Mam, how brave she had been to send the crowd of howling women packing.

She wanted to thank her but the words would not come, and for the first time since her mother died Shanni gave way to the hot, painful tears that she had long wanted to shed.

CHAPTER TWO

Shanni sat in her bedroom at the top of the house in Pottery Row and looked around her. The curtains on the windows were of heavy material, clearly expensive, and the cotton sheets on the bed were spotless. She hugged herself in pleasure. She had a room to herself, not like the kitchen-maids who huddled three together.

Shanni put down the book she was trying to read. Sometimes she thought she would never learn to be fluent with her words the way that Mrs Mainwaring was. Still, she was getting better every day, even she could see that, and Shanni tried hard to learn. She wanted to please Mrs Mainwaring, to show that she was grateful for being taken into her home. Shanni had no idea what she would have done if Mrs Mainwaring had failed to notice her rapid departure from the Morton-Edwards household.

Shanni had come to admire Mrs Mainwaring; she was a woman who knew her mind, who took no cheek from anyone. Shanni had heard how bravely she had run the pottery when she was little more than a girl, and here she was now, a rich, successful businesswoman. It was an achievement Shanni dearly wanted to emulate.

Shanni moved to the window and stared out at the neat gardens below. A fountain spiralled water that fell like diamonds back into the stone bowl; the birds were singing in the trees and the sun dappled the lawns. Beyond the walls and to the left of the house stood the pottery. The kilns were always in use, shimmering with heat, but from her window Shanni could see nothing but beauty and greenery.

Whenever she thought of the past weeks, she comforted herself that she was not the only one to lose her mother in tragic circumstances. It had even happened to Mrs Mainwaring. She had not given in to an unfair fate but had worked night and day to make a success of the business that had once belonged to her father.

And just look what she had now: a place in society, a handsome husband and a fine son. Lonely and alone, Mrs Mainwaring had found the courage to flout the unwritten rules of polite society and marry an outsider.

Shanni could never imagine herself living with someone so different, a man from a land far away across the sea. But Joe Mainwaring was a good man, as far as Shanni could judge. He had strong features and lovely blue eyes, and he would never betray his wife the way some of the other rich folk did. Poor folks, too, come to that.

Her eyes narrowed as she thought of the way Dan Spencer had made a fool of her mother. He had ruined the lives of two families and escaped unscathed. No-one in Swansea blamed him for

Dora Price's humiliating death yet the towns-folk had poured scorn on Llinos Mainwaring's marriage to an American-Indian.

Shanni sank into the window-seat and rested her head against the cool panes of glass, fighting back the tears. She was lucky to have found a benefactor who cared about her and wanted her to get on in the world. And she would prove that Mrs Mainwaring had acted wisely, whatever effort it took. She would make her so proud, make her glad she had taken in a poor girl from the slums. Mrs Mainwaring had no daughter, only one son who was away at school in England. Shanni would not presume to imagine she was the daughter Mrs Mainwaring had never had, but she came damned close to it.

She was startled out of her thoughts by a knock on the door. She brushed the tears from her eyes and patted her hair into place.

'Miss Price, you're wanted downstairs.' The voice of Flora, the youngest of the maids, sounded shaky and timid. Shanni felt angry with the girl: she should not be humble; she should not believe herself beneath anyone.

'Coming, Flora.' Shanni opened the door and the girl stepped back respectfully. 'Sorry to disturb you, Miss, but there's visitors and Mrs Mainwaring wants you to meet them.'

'Flora, straighten up!' Shanni said firmly. 'You do not have to bob a curtsy to me. I'm just a girl from the slums, remember?'

'Right, Miss.' Flora stepped aside and made way for Shanni to pass her on the stairs.

Shanni sighed. It was no good: Flora had the

mentality of a maid and nothing would ever change her.

In the drawing room Mrs Mainwaring was waiting for her. She smiled and raised her hand, gesturing for Shanni to come forward. 'This is Madame Isabelle.' She nodded at the well-padded lady who stood tall and statuesque, dominating the room. 'She will be giving you singing lessons and will teach you to play the pianoforte.'

Shanni nodded dutifully, but she was not sure she wanted to learn music. What good would playing the piano be to her in the outside world?

'I would much rather learn about government and the running of the country, Mrs Mainwaring,' Shanni said softly.

'First things first, my dear.' Madame Isabelle took charge, her voice echoing around the room. 'A young lady needs refinement if she is to procure for herself a good husband.'

Shanni did not want a husband and she was not sure she wanted to be refined. What she really wanted was to alter the world for the poor, to make sure everyone had enough bread to eat and coal to keep them warm in the winter.

She bowed her head. 'Thank you, Madame Isabelle,' she said respectfully. She regarded the woman steadily. Madame Isabelle had some sort of foreign name but she was as Welsh as Shanni was, and she was putting on an act for the benefit of Mrs Mainwaring.

Shanni glanced at Mrs Mainwaring, who was smiling encouragement. She meant well: she wanted Shanni to be a lady. She had explained that she was often lonely, with Mr Mainwaring and their son being away so much. And she had lost her daughter at birth so in some ways Shanni felt she was there to make Mrs Mainwaring happy, not the other way round.

Mrs Mainwaring rose to her feet and walked elegantly across the room. 'The lesson will take about an hour,' she said, smiling, 'and then we shall have some tea.' She went out and closed the door behind her.

Madame Isabelle took Shanni's arm and led her to the piano that gleamed with beeswax polish and pressed her down on to the stool. 'Now, let us see what you are made of. This is middle C. Play it for me.'

Shanni did as she was told and the key responded to her touch. The sound pleased her and she smiled.

'Now you run along the keys thus,' Madame Isabelle demonstrated, 'and so you complete an octave.'

More to humour Madame Isabelle than because she really wished to learn Shanni made an attempt to understand what the teacher was telling her. But she was bored and her eyes strayed to the fine paintings on the walls, to the heavily draped curtains on the windows.

The scent of beeswax polish reminded her of poor Flora, who rubbed at the furniture endlessly, eager to please. The girl was so grateful to be given a good position and have enough food to eat that she would have laid down her life for her mistress. And no-one should be made to feel like that.

Shanni forced herself to concentrate on her lesson but her mind was becoming filled with a confusion of quavers and semi-quavers, and with major and minor keys.

'It's all so difficult,' she said, rising from the stool.

Madame Isabelle inclined her head. 'It is now but after a few months it will become clear to you.' She smiled. 'You have a good ear and you will learn very well under my tuition.' She sat on the stool and lifted her hands, her fingers gleaming with jewellery. Then, as she began to play, the music soared into the room, fine and stirring.

Shanni felt her heartbeat quicken. 'That's so beautiful,' she said, when Madame Isabelle at last lifted her hands from the keys.

Madame Isabelle turned to face her. 'What are you really interested in, Shanni?' she asked quietly. 'I can see you like to hear me play but your heart is not with music, is it?'

Shanni frowned. Should she speak her mind? She looked into Madame Isabelle's clear brown eyes and decided to tell her the truth.

'I want to make the world a better place for the poor, especially for women,' she said. 'I want to put right injustice, to get rid of poverty.' She was unaware that she was spreading her hands wide. 'I want to educate women, to give every girl the chance of a better life.' She sighed. 'I've explained all this to Mrs Mainwaring but I'm not sure she understands.'

'I'm sure she does, my dear,' Madame Isabelle said. 'Mrs Mainwaring is a remarkable lady. She took a failing pottery and made it the success it is today. Don't underestimate her, Shanni. It would be a mistake.'

Shanni supposed Madame Isabelle was right: Mrs Mainwaring was a very special person. She must be to have taken Shanni into her fine home.

'I would like to see the downtrodden of the world seek their rightful place in society,' Madame Isabelle said. 'I believe it wrong that a husband owns his wife as though she was little more than a chattel. But, my dear, education is required to achieve such aims.'

She stood up. She was a tall woman and towered above Shanni. 'To start on that road you must learn your lessons well. You must learn oratory and for that your voice must be improved. You will lose the cadences of your forebears, you will speak like the gentry and then, only then, will you be listened to. Do you understand?'

Shanni did. Her coarse speech had become apparent once she was settled in her new home. Listening to Mrs Mainwaring's cultured, gentle voice had emphasized that Shanni sounded rough and uneducated.

'I will bring you some books to read, my dear,' Madame Isabelle said, 'but by some they would be considered subversive, so you must make this our little secret.'

Shanni nodded and Madame Isabelle smiled in approval. 'And in the meantime you will practise the scales just as I have shown you.'

'I will,' Shanni said, delighted at the prospect of learning more than the intricacies of music. 'I will try my best to master them by the time you come again.'

'Ring for the maid to bring in my hat and gloves, there's a good girl.' Madame Isabelle was once more in charge. 'I will forgo tea as I have another appointment.'

Shanni obeyed, storing away in her mind the fact that the music teacher was not the martinet she had first thought her but an intelligent, educated woman who seemed determined to show Shanni a better way of life.

Together, Mrs Mainwaring and Shanni watched from the window as Madame Isabelle rode away in her coach. 'Well, what do you think of her?' Mrs Mainwaring asked. 'Is Madame Isabelle as strict as she appears to be?'

Shanni shook her head. 'She is a very interesting lady,' she said quietly. 'I think I will learn a great deal from her.'

It was on the following day that Shanni first met Lloyd Mainwaring. He had come home on holiday from his college and Shanni watched from the window as he climbed out of the coach and stepped outside on to the dried earth of the forecourt.

He was a handsome boy, whose hair clustered around his face in tight curls. He was tall, his limbs slender like those of a newborn colt. He looked every inch a gentleman in his fine suit of clothes yet he did not stand aside as the coachman lifted down his luggage but pitched in to help him.

He looked up suddenly and his eyes held fire as he saw her framed in the window. He smiled and Shanni smiled back at him, knowing instinctively that in Lloyd Mainwaring she had found a friend.

34

★   ★   ★

'He needs feeding up.' Llinos sat beside Joe in the garden and stared at her son as he walked through the lawns with young Shanni at his side. The girl's head was bent and her shoulders turned away from the boy in an attitude of shyness. Llinos laughed. 'I do believe that Shanni is falling for our son, Joe.'

'No, I think this is simply her first real friendship. She likes Lloyd and he likes her, but love? No, I don't think so.'

'I suppose you're right,' Llinos mused. 'It's good for her to learn to mix with all sorts of folk and, in any case, she will probably fall in love several times before she becomes mature.'

Joe took his pipe from between his teeth, his eyes thoughtful. 'I think she will fall in love only once,' he said, 'and her love has not yet entered her life.'

'I only fell in love once,' Llinos said, 'and I have stayed in love with the same man all my life.' There was a break in her voice.

'Llinos, I have always loved you. Why do you keep on reproaching me with what is past?'

'Because it still hurts,' Llinos said honestly. 'And in any case, it's not past, is it? You write to her often enough and sometimes you make the trip to America to visit her.' She bit her lip, forcing down her anger, but when she spoke again her voice trembled. 'I hate to think of you lying in the arms of that woman, of fathering a child with her. How can you expect me to forget all that, Joe? You are asking the impossible.'

He sighed heavily. 'It was something I could

not control,' he said heavily. 'I felt I was doing the right thing by my mother and by her people. My son will grow up as a leader in the Americas. He will restore stability to the Mandan peoples.'

'Your son is there, before your eyes,' Llinos said flatly. 'The other one is a by-blow, an illegitimate child with no name.'

Joe was silent, retreating into himself as he did whenever anything displeased him. He did not seem to feel shame that he had betrayed his wife, that he had left her for an Indian squaw. Joe was a man who had different values from the other men, she knew. Eynon would never have acted in that way.

But then, in thinking of her friend Eynon, she realized that Joe was not so different, after all. Eynon Morton-Edwards had tasted many women. He claimed he would have been faithful if he could have married Llinos but did she believe him? Could she believe any man capable of faithfulness? She sometimes doubted it.

'Don't think about unpleasant things now, Llinos.' His voice was forced. 'The sun is shining, the sky is filled with light, and bitterness is always destructive to the one who feels it. Forgiveness heals.'

'That's easy to say.' Llinos looked down at her hands. 'To ask someone to forgive such a betrayal is asking a great deal. Why shouldn't I feel bitter sometimes? Isn't it natural?'

She waited for Joe to speak again but he was silent for a long time. That was his retreat, his silence. When she cornered him, when she forced him to confront her feelings, he went into his own little world.

She looked at the figures of Shanni and Lloyd close together, talking animatedly, and felt a sliver of comfort. She was making a difference to the world if only in the rescue of Shanni from poverty and shame. The girl was becoming more confident, her eyes were not so haunted these days, and the company of another youngster of her own age was sure to do her good.

'Perhaps it would be wise to discourage Lloyd from seeing too much of Shanni,' Joe said.

'Why?' Llinos said. She grimaced: Joe had deftly diverted the course of the conversation. But she was surprised at his words. Joe had never been bigoted: a foreigner in Swansea, he had often been the subject of prejudice himself. 'It's not like you to be a snob, Joe.'

'I'm not a snob, Llinos, but the young are hot-headed, and I do feel there is something of the rebel about Shanni Price. She has need to right the wrongs of the poor. I'm sure she will make her mark on the world one day.'

'Oh, is that all? I thought you were saying she's not good enough for your son.'

'He could do far worse.' Joe took her hand and smiled. 'I have heard that the local maids have a strange courting ritual, don't they?'

'You mean bundling?' Llinos asked. 'Well, I don't believe Shanni would be happy with that sort of behaviour. She's a respectable girl. In any case, the practice of courting by sharing a bed at night is not widespread. It's just that rich folk like to find a way to blame the poor for what they are.'

37

Llinos's voice was clipped. 'Then we don't have to feel guilty about our luxuries.'

'Oh, I see, you're still a bit of a rebel yourself, aren't you?' Joe's voice was teasing. 'My Llinos, my firebird.'

It was a long time since her husband had called Llinos by her pet name. Once it had been an indication of his love and admiration but that was a long time ago. She took a deep breath. 'Look, Joe, if more young girls were educated they would realize that to allow a boy liberties is to give away something precious.'

'Are you saying it doesn't happen?' Joe asked, and Llinos read him well. It suited him to discuss the morals of others and so distract her from his own failings.

'I'm not saying that at all.' Llinos decided to play along: she was weary of going over the same ground with him. She had lost count of the times she had begged him to give up contact with his mistress and all to no avail. 'The practice suits young men, of course it does. They can sow their wild oats with the benefit of parental approval.'

'Poor Shanni,' Joe said. 'Her mother didn't set her much of an example, did she? I'm surprised the girl is still pure.'

'I think you do Shanni and her mother an injustice,' Llinos said sharply. 'Mrs Price thought the man loved her. She allowed him to father a child on her and for that she was made the scapegoat. And, in any case, I think your own views on morality are more than a little suspect.'

Joe was staring into the sky. 'Will you never let the past lie, Llinos?'

'How can I when you are incapable of forgetting it yourself?'

A butterfly landed on a branch of the lilac tree and Llinos watched it, focusing her attention on the beautiful things in her life. 'I'll make life good for Shanni.' She spoke as if it was a vow. 'I'll try to teach her about life, about feelings and about pride.'

'She seems very adaptable,' Joe said. 'I think she will learn her lessons well.' He turned to look at Llinos. 'You are very good to take her into our home and treat her like a daughter. Perhaps she makes up a little for the daughter we lost.'

Llinos was suddenly angry. 'Don't be absurd!' She rose and stared down at him. How dare he hurt her like that? She left Joe sitting in the garden his head in his hands.

Once inside, she hurried upstairs, feeling tears burn against her eyelids. She wanted to cry for the daughter she and Joe had lost; for the trust she had lost when he left her to live with an Indian squaw. She wanted to shed tears for the sweetness of first love when Joe had been her hero and life was a wonderful thing.

'So you are to be a radical, are you?' Lloyd said, and his hand brushed hers.

Shanni moved slightly away from him. 'I wouldn't say that.'

'But you think people of that sort are right to burn down barns and pull down toll-gates, do you?'

'If that is the only way to achieve justice, yes, I do.' Shanni felt uncomfortable. Lloyd was so well

39

educated, so nicely spoken that he made her feel rough and ignorant.

'Well, in the end they will destroy their own livelihood,' Lloyd said. 'Folk should work with their masters not against them.'

'It's easy for you to say that.' Shanni forgot her shyness. 'You were born to privilege, born to eat good food, to read books and wear clean clothes.'

'And you were born to poverty,' Lloyd said. 'Were conditions really as bad as you describe?'

Shanni looked up at him. 'I tell you what,' she said. 'Shall we dress up as street urchins? Then you can see at first hand what poverty really looks like. That's a challenge. You can't refuse me or I'll think you a coward.'

She saw Lloyd smile. 'I don't think I'd have the courage to refuse you anything, Shanni Price.'

She glanced at him covertly, wondering if he was teasing her. 'Will you come with me, though?'

'Yes, but for heaven's sake don't let Mother know.'

'Tonight?'

'Why tonight?'

'One of the maids told me the *Ceffyl Pren* is riding tonight.'

'What on earth is that?'

'*Duw!* For a Welshman you are very ignorant, Lloyd Mainwaring!' she chided. 'I suppose your English schooling has taken away all your pride in your country. Anyway, the wooden horse is a custom the poor have. It's used when the assizes and judges can't be bothered to punish the wrongdoers – and sometimes as a means of revenge.'

The bell rang out across the garden and Lloyd relaxed and smiled. 'Tea is being served. Come on, we'd better go indoors and wash our hands like good children.'

Later, under the cover of darkness, Shanni met Lloyd near the back gate of the house. She smiled at his too-short trews and the ragged shirt that hung on his thin shoulders flapping like the wings of a bird.

'This all right?' he asked, with a grin that lit up his eyes and illuminated his face.

'Wait.' Shanni bent, grasped some soil between her fingers and rubbed it into his face. 'There! That's more like the street urchins I know.'

'You look pretty awful yourself.' He took her hand and together they left the house.

Once in Pottery Row, the narrow street leading towards the town, Shanni breathed more easily. 'Your mother wouldn't thank me for this, you know.' She looked up at Lloyd. His head was high, his eyes shining. Clearly, he was enjoying himself.

'Mother will never know, will she?' He winked at her, and Shanni felt warm, as if she had found a real friend. But she began to doubt the wisdom of bringing Lloyd to town during a march of the *Ceffyl Pren*. Much as Mrs Mainwaring liked her, she would not approve of Shanni taking Lloyd into the slum streets of Swansea.

The town was alive with people. The doors of public bars stood open, candlelight gleaming on to the roadways. The sounds of laughter and drifts of smoke from fires and pipes gave the evening an atmosphere of jollity.

'I've never seen the town like this before,' Lloyd said.

Shanni drew her hand away from his. 'Be quiet!' she said warningly. 'Or your voice will give you away.'

'Yes, Miss,' he whispered, and Shanni felt a sudden urge to giggle. She must be mad to bring him here, yet Lloyd had no such qualms. He evidently thought this a huge adventure, something of a joke.

'Where are we going?' Lloyd whispered in her ear.

Shanni pushed him away. 'All in good time, boy!' she said. She drew him into a small court, near where she had lived with her mother. 'It's one of my old neighbours, Dan Spencer, a married man.' She felt the bile rise in her throat. 'He was the one who dishonoured my mother, gave her a baby then blamed everything on her.'

She felt Lloyd look at her. 'And now he is to be punished also?'

'Not for what he did to my mother.' She heard the bitterness in her voice and caught her breath. 'He has seduced a young girl, ruined her.' She looked up and met Lloyd's gaze. 'The daughter of the woman who led the mob to my mother's house.'

'Divine retribution, wouldn't you say?' Lloyd took her hand again. 'You've had a damn' awful time of it. I'm sorry, Shanni.'

'Hush, they're coming for him.'

The cacophony of sound echoed through the mean courts leading to Potato Street. The beat of a drum, then the clash of sticks against tin buckets

42

rang through the alleyways. Shanni drew Lloyd into the shadows, crouching against the doorway of the saddler's shop.

The sound came closer, the jangle of tin against tin, the crack of wood against wood. The voices raised in anger sounded almost inhuman in the clear air. Shanni held her breath as the *Ceffyl Pren*, followed by the procession of men and women, came around the bend.

'There's the wooden horse!' Shanni whispered. She felt Lloyd's arm close and protective around her shoulders and did not move away. He was comforting her: he felt for her loss and she warmed to him.

One of the men beat on the door of Dan Spencer's house with a hammer, splintering one of the thin planks. The door was thrust open and some of the crowd were swallowed up in the darkness of the house.

A woman began to scream as Dan Spencer was dragged into the street. He was hauled unceremoniously on to the back of the *Ceffyl Pren* where he slumped, head on chest, in an attitude of abject terror.

Egged on by the jeers of the women, the men berated him for his misdeeds. He was repeatedly beaten with sticks and all the time he sat there, on the back of the wooden horse, not moving or speaking out in his defence.

'We can't let this go on.' Lloyd made a move to leave the shelter of the doorway but Shanni put both arms around him and held him back. 'Don't interfere. You'd be beaten to a pulp by the crowd. In any case, this is what he deserves. It's

43

often the only sort of justice given to people like us.'

They remained quietly in the shadows and Shanni's heart pounded as Spencer was castigated, beaten and humiliated. She felt no pity, only triumph: she would have been the first to strike a blow if she had had the opportunity.

At last the procession moved out of Potato Street and, gradually, the noise died away. Lloyd seemed subdued. He walked back the way they had come, a few steps ahead of Shanni. Miserably, she followed him, knowing he was horrified by what he had seen.

At the back gate to the pottery, she caught his arm. 'Try to understand, Lloyd. No magistrate and certainly no visiting judge would condemn Dan Spencer for what he's done.'

'He slept with a young girl,' Lloyd said. 'Does that act deserve such primitive barbarism?'

'He ruined her!' Shanni said. 'Took her maidenhead. No man will want her now. Can't you understand that?' He stood there shaking his head, and suddenly Shanni wanted to slap him. 'I suppose you think that poor girls do not deserve respect, is that it?'

'No, but—'

'But a man's a man and will pluck any flower he chooses, is that it?'

'No, that's not what I think, but the blood is strong, the urge to mate is always there. Can't *you* understand *that*?'

'I'll *never* understand it.' Shanni left him there and walked rapidly back to the house. She let herself in at the back door, crept along the passage and up to her room praying that no-one had seen her. She threw off her clothes and washed quickly, hating the feel of soil on her skin. She made a face at herself in the mirror – she had soon become used to cleanliness, to freshly washed and ironed clothes, to all the comforts of the rich.

She sat on the bed and put her head in her hands. She must forget her feelings of friendship for Lloyd Mainwaring: they were poles apart, they could never truly be friends, not now, not ever. And yet she had hoped for so much from him. A young man with Lloyd's advantages, his compassion, would one day have the power to put right many wrongs.

'Fool!' she said, as she climbed beneath the blankets. She would remain single all her life. Never would she trust any man – they were all ready to rut and plunder and she would do well to remember it. Yet tears, hot and bitter, flowed on to her pillow. Her triumph vanished and all she was left with was sadness.

CHAPTER THREE

Llinos stood in the warmth of the pottery yard, looking at the bottle kilns and feeling the heat emanating from them. Watt Bevan, her manager, scratched his head worriedly. He was younger than Llinos by several years but his hair was prematurely tinged with grey. Llinos loved Watt like a brother: he had come to the pottery as an orphan when he was about nine years old, and together they had struggled to wrest a living from the clay. Looking around now, she was proud of the success they had made of it.

'I can't leave the pottery right now, Llinos,' Watt was saying. 'There's trouble brewing. The men are agitating against the rise in toll charges again, and you know as well as I do what hardships it's brought them.'

'I do understand all that, Watt, and I sympathize, but you are supposed to be bringing Rosie home.' Llinos looked up at him anxiously. 'This is your future we're talking about. Rosie is your wife, after all, and you should feel responsible for her.'

46

Watt sighed. 'I know, but it's difficult to concentrate on family matters just now.'

'Well, that's your choice, I suppose, Watt,' Llinos said. 'But Rosie needs to come back to Swansea now, and I do feel it's your place to go and fetch her. You never know, it might be the beginnings of a reconciliation between you.'

'I doubt that!' Watt said. 'We've been apart for too long. In any case, Rosie is an independent woman – she has been left a small fortune. How would it look if I tried to patch things up with her now?'

The sound of raised voices from one of the sheds caught Watt's attention. 'Look, whatever my personal feelings I can't leave, not now when we could have a dangerous situation on our hands.'

Llinos sighed resignedly. 'I'll go and bring Rosie back to Swansea.' She rested her hand on Watt's arm. 'Go on, sort everything out as you always do. What would I do if I didn't have you to run the pottery for me?'

'You'd run it yourself,' Watt smiled, 'I've no doubt of that. Still, I'm grateful to have done a good job here. At least I can say I've made a success of that even if I failed in my marriage.'

'Go on with you, and get the men back in line!' Llinos watched as Watt strode purposefully towards the sheds. He was right, of course: she would have run the pottery without him but it would have been a lonely task.

She began walking towards the stables: she had better tell Graves to prepare the carriage for the journey. Perhaps it would be a good idea to take

47

Shanni with her for company – the girl seemed lonely now that Lloyd had returned to college. The two had formed a bond while he was at home, and whenever a letter came from him, Shanni read it avidly. But Joe was probably right: Shanni saw Lloyd only as a friend, which was just as well. In the meantime, she was wonderful company for Llinos.

She thought of Joe's words about Shanni being almost like the daughter Llinos had lost and a pain caught her heart. She bit her lip. Would her little girl have turned out to be fiery like Shanni, full of the will to put the world to rights? She sighed. That was something she would never know. And Joe was right: she must live in the present and try to forget the past, but sometimes the past had a nasty habit of creeping up on her. Llinos took a deep breath. It was time she put her mind to the matter at hand, that of bringing Rosie home to Swansea.

Rosie Bevan closed her bag and looked around her bedroom for one last time. She was leaving the elegant house where she had lived with Alice Sparks for the last long months of the older woman's life. It had been a strange sort of life to a girl used to the poorer streets of the east of the town. Because of Alice, Rosie had enjoyed the luxury of living in a grand house with plenty of money at her disposal. Alice had trusted her implicitly, and Rosie felt she had earned that trust.

She stared at the large window, the heavy curtains, the well-polished furniture, and felt a pang of regret. Alice had been a difficult employer but the two women had grown close, especially in the last few months. Now Alice was dead, and Rosie missed her as much as if they had been sisters rather than friends.

She brushed away the tears. She must not mourn but do as Alice had instructed and live her life to the full. No-one knew what lay around the corner and happiness was to be treasured.

Poor Alice, she had not known a great deal of love in her life. Her marriage had been forced on her: her tyrant of a father had threatened to disown her if she did not settle down. But Alice had survived it all. Even to the end she had fought for life, had styled her hair, rouged her cheeks and presented a brave face to her friends.

She had never ceased to be grateful to Rosie, not even in death. She had made a will instructing her solicitor to place a large sum of money in the bank in Rosie's name. It was enough to buy a modest house and for Rosie to live in ease for the rest of her life. If Rosie used her inheritance wisely she would want for nothing.

Her heart lightened, she must look to the future: she now owned property. She would love her house, make it a home, fill it with warmth. Rosie left the room and hurried down the gracious staircase. She was trying to be brave, to be optimistic. But what did the future hold in store for her? Would she always be alone? The thought frightened her.

She paused at the door. Watt would be outside. Her husband would be waiting with a carriage to take her back to Swansea. It was strange to think of Watt as her husband. Their marriage had been one of convenience – at least, that was how Watt Bevan had looked on the arrangement.

Rosie, like a fool, had loved him, adored him, wanting only his love, but it had not taken her long to realize that Watt did not love her. He took her to his bed, made love to her and she had cried with joy, but when her dreams vanished, like mist in the sun, she had left him.

Rosie stood for a moment in the silence of the elegant hallway and stared around at the familiar staircase, the jewel-bright colours of the drapes, and smelt the warm aroma of beeswax. She would miss all of it, but most of all she would miss Alice.

She heard the sound of hoofbeats on the fore-court. Taking a deep breath she opened the door then locked it carefully behind her. It was no longer her home. Outside, the coach was just drawing to a halt and Rosie recognized Graves, the coachman, as he tipped his hat to her.

She felt excitement burn in her heart. Would Watt have changed? Did he regret the past? Or had he met a new woman, one to whom he could give his love? Her head buzzed with questions. She knew Watt had comforted himself with other women from time to time, and in her heart she could not blame him. Everyone needed love and Watt was no exception.

Her heart plunged with disappointment when she saw that Watt had not come for her. Llinos Mainwaring was leaning through the window of the coach, and at her side was a young girl, her face fresh, eyes bright. Of Watt there was no sign.

Her husband could not even spare the time to bring her home.

She climbed into the coach and sat opposite Llinos. 'Thank you for fetching me,' she said, her eyes on her hands. 'I suppose Watt couldn't be bothered to make the journey.'

'Watt sends his apologies,' Llinos said quickly. 'He wanted to come but there was trouble and I needed him to stay at the pottery. I'm sorry, Rosie, I wouldn't have had this happen for the world.'

'It doesn't matter.' Rosie settled more comfortably into the seat and folded her hands on her lap. It did matter. It hurt. It hurt very badly indeed.

'Anyway,' Llinos said gently, 'this gives me the opportunity to see your new house.'

Rosie felt warmer as she thought of the small but elegant house set on the headland of Sgeti, looking out over the craggy Mumbles Head. It was built of mellow stone, it had a small garden and was within walking distance of the town.

When Rosie began to buy furnishings for her new home, Alice, on her good days, had helped. She had given Rosie advice on what was tasteful and good value for money. A pang of loneliness brought tears to Rosie's eyes. Alice had been such a comfort and now she was dead.

'You'll miss Alice Sparks, Rosie,' Llinos said, picking up on Rosie's thoughts. 'I know you became very good friends.'

'We were close.' Rosie smiled but there were tears in her eyes. 'She was a real lady and so generous.' She bit her lip for a moment, deep in thought. 'My wages, when Alice remembered to pay them, were always much more than I needed. I tried to tell her that often but she would never listen. I grew to love Alice like a sister and though I never told her I think that she knew.' Rosie dabbed her eyes impatiently. 'I cried buckets the day she was buried but I did what she would have expected of me.'

Rosie remembered every detail of the funeral; it had been a fine sunny day, absurdly bright with blossoms on the trees. Alice had left instructions that she was to be buried alongside her father in the graveyard on the hills above Swansea. She requested a simple headstone with a brief inscription, and Rosie had ensured her wishes were carried out to the letter.

Alice, poor Alice, had taken a long time to die. At the end she had clung to Rosie. 'Pray for me, Rosie,' she had whispered. 'You are the only friend I've ever had and I've loved you for it.'

Those words would ring for ever in her mind. Rosie swallowed hard. She knew it was best not to dwell on the past but who would she talk to now? In whom could she confide her deepest feelings?

'Look, there's the sea, it looks so wide from here. Oh, and there's a dear little house on the hill. Is that where you are going to live, Mrs Bevan?' The young girl was leaning closer to the window, peering down from the track to where the bay curved in a glistening arc around the coastline of Swansea.

Rosie really looked at the girl for the first time. She was very young and very pretty, but where did she fit into the Mainwaring household? She sounded so confident. Her voice was a strange mixture of the gently nurtured young lady and an ordinary Welsh girl. Her eyes were bright with the love of life, and Rosie envied her. 'Please, call me Rosie,' she said.

'Oh, I'm sorry, I should have introduced you right away,' Llinos said apologetically. 'This is Shanni. Shanni, this is Rosie Bevan, Watt's wife.'

The girl held out her hand. 'I'm very pleased to meet you.' She pushed back the curls of dark red hair that sprang from beneath her bonnet. 'If that's where you are going to live I envy you.' She pointed to the house standing out from the cliffs. 'What a wonderful view.'

Rosie warmed to her. The girl had a pleasant manner and a friendly smile. Without knowing anything about her she felt drawn to her too – perhaps it was because of the sadness that lurked at the back of Shanni's eyes. 'You're welcome to visit any time you like,' she said. She glanced at Llinos. 'Though after the luxury of living in the Mainwaring household my home might be a little bit small and insignificant.'

'I'm from the slums,' Shanni said frankly. 'I'm an orphan and Mrs Mainwaring was good enough to take me in.'

Rosie was taken by the girl's honesty. 'You don't look like a maid. Oh, I'm sorry, that was rude of me.'

'Shanni is not a maid,' Llinos said easily. 'She's more a companion – a lively and energetic one at that!'

'So we have something in common, then,' Rosie said. 'I was companion to Alice Sparks. She

53

cared for me and looked after me and I'll always be grateful to her.'

A silence fell, but it was a comfortable silence. Rosie stared out of the window at the passing scenery, feeling calm and even content for the first time in weeks. She was going home.

When at last the coach drew to a halt, Rosie's heart lifted as she alighted on the boundary of her own front garden. She looked at the house, and a smile transformed her face. The windows gleamed with polishing; the door was surrounded by roses, the small garden neatly kept. 'You've had someone up here working,' she said to Llinos. 'It looks lovely and I know I'll be happy here.'

'It was Watt who did the garden,' Llinos said quietly. 'And Watt who brought in a local woman to clean for you.'

Rosie felt a brief sense of happiness. So her husband cared enough to prepare the house for her. That was something small to cling to.

'Come on, then,' Llinos said. 'Let's have a conducted tour. I can't wait to see inside.'

Rosie led the way through the short passage to the front parlour. From the light, sunny room the view was breathtaking. The land in front of the house slanted away and there, below, was the sea with a ship's sails outlined hazily against the horizon.

'It's lovely!' Shanni said. 'It's really lovely. Anyone could be happy here.'

'You must come and stay with me sometimes,' Rosie said, 'if Mrs Mainwaring can spare you. Come, let me show you the rest of the house.'

A small book-lined room led off from the parlour and from there, too, the view was splendid. The kitchen was compact with a carefully cleaned grate over which hung a large stew-pot. Behind that was the scullery, with a cold slab running the length of the room.

'You'll have some staff, won't you, Rosie?' Llinos asked. 'I think the woman Watt brought in is looking for a position. Otherwise it will be lonely for you up here on your own.'

'I'll get someone in I expect,' Rosie said, but she knew that the first few days in her new home were hers and hers alone.

'So in the end it was me who had to go to fetch Rosie,' Llinos said softly. She was standing at the window in the bedroom she shared with Joe, watching the moon make patterns on the lily-pond. 'I was so sorry for her. She just couldn't hide her disappointment.'

Joe came up behind her and put his arms around her waist, bending his head into her neck. 'That's your trouble, you feel for everyone.' He turned her to him and kissed her throat, his lips warm. Llinos knew he was roused, he wanted her, needed her, and she wanted him. 'I love you, Joe Mainwaring.' She felt gladness fill her heart. He was here, wasn't he, right here at her side? He was still her husband and even though he had fallen from grace once she could not punish him for ever.

'I know you do, Mrs Mainwaring,' he said softly. 'And I love you more than life itself.' He nuzzled his head against her breasts and she heard

55

his ragged breath with a feeling of joy. Even now, after years of marriage, she had the power to make Joe desire her.

'Let me take you to bed.' Joe drew her across the room and laughing, they fell together on to the silk quilt. 'You look like a young girl,' he said, the laughter vanishing as his hand cupped her breast. 'As beautiful as the day I first met you.'

He made love to her with all the vigour of a young man. His body was still lean and well-muscled, his skin like silk as she ran her hands over his back. He murmured sweet words of love and Llinos closed her eyes, swept away by the passion they shared.

Later, as they lay naked, entwined in each other's arms, Llinos kissed Joe's shoulder. She was so happy to lie in bed with him, feeling his warmth close to her.

'What are you thinking?' he asked. 'You're very quiet.'

'I'm happy with my life,' she said. 'That's what I was thinking.' She felt his hand smooth her hair from her face and she caught her breath, loving him so much it hurt.

After a while, she sat up and drew the sheets over her breasts. 'I'm worried about work, though, Joe,' she said. 'There's trouble in the pottery. The men are resentful about the ongoing effects of the Poor Law and the farmers are arranging public debates to argue about why the price of the toll-gates keeps rising all the time. These are troubled times.'

Joe leaned on one elbow, his dark hair swinging

forward. 'I can see why the people are angry,' he said. 'With the farmers being charged such a lot of money to pass the gates, with the tolls increasing almost monthly, the result is that the price of flour and other necessities must rise. The people just can't afford it.'

'But men dressing up as women because the Bible says, "The daughters of Rebecca will storm the gates", where is that going to get them? Why can't they deal with their grievances in a civilized manner?'

'That's been tried and it's failed.' Joe sat up and propped himself against the wooden headboard. 'I suppose the workers feel the need to take matters into their own hands.'

'I can understand that, but I do worry about Lloyd growing up in a hostile world. He has ambitions to go into politics. Has he spoken to you about it?'

'I knew.' Joe smiled. 'But don't worry, Lloyd has plenty of common sense. He realizes nothing can be achieved overnight and by the time he leaves college the matters with the farmers and the toll-gates will probably be settled. He might even have changed his mind about what he wants to do.' He touched her cheek. 'Now, stop worrying about things that might not happen. Live for the present. It's all we really have.'

He extinguished the lamp and Llinos felt him warm against her. 'Come, I'll hold you until you sleep and in the morning all your troubles will have vanished.'

Llinos closed her eyes, knowing Joe's reassurance was well-intentioned but nothing would be settled easily: that much was becoming clearer every day. Still, he was right about one thing: that she could do nothing about the problem now, perhaps not ever. She curled against him and slept.

CHAPTER FOUR

The fair had come to town, and the streets of
Swansea were thronged with revellers. Shanni
felt excitement blossom as she pushed her way
towards World's End. She wished Lloyd were
here to share the moment: she felt in need of
company and Lloyd was very good company
indeed.

During Lloyd's holidays from college he spent
as much time with her as he could. They shared
the same ridiculous sense of humour. He never
put on airs and graces and never acted like
a spoiled rich boy the way some offspring of
the gentry did. He was handsome, very Welsh-
looking with his strong features and his thick hair
curling around his forehead.

Had things been different, Shanni might have
married a man like Lloyd Mainwaring. She knew
he was far above her socially and that one day he
would find a wife among the high-society ladies
who lived on the west side of Swansea but, still, it
was nice to dream.

Shanni grimaced. Lloyd would probably marry
someone like Jayne Morton-Edwards. Now, she

was a spoilt brat. As for Shanni, she would never marry, never give herself into the keeping of any man: they simply weren't to be trusted.

Shanni had once believed that Llinos and Joe Mainwaring were a couple made for each other until one of the maids had told her differently. One night, in a talkative mood, Flora had claimed that Mr Mainwaring had foisted a bastard child on some Indian woman. Shanni had been shocked. If a wonderful lady like Mrs Mainwaring could not hold her man, what hope would she have?

She was startled out of her thoughts by a hand touching her arm. 'Shanni! It's me, Rosie Bevan. It's nice to see a familiar face in the crowd.' Rosie stood smiling at Shanni's side. 'I was supposed to meet my brothers here but they have let me down and I've been feeling so lonely and self-conscious all on my own. Would you mind if I walked around the stalls with you?'

Shanni shook back her dark red hair. 'I'd like some company too,' she said. 'I know what you mean about being alone – it's as if I'm here just to get myself taken up by some young man or other.'

It was not that she felt lonely, Shanni was happy in her own company and more than capable of dealing with anyone forward enough to talk to her, but half the fun of the fair was sharing the excitement with someone else.

Rosie linked arms easily and, for a moment, Shanni was surprised – she was not used to such familiarity. Shanni and her mother had loved each other dearly but Dora Price had never been demonstrative.

'Oh, look!' Shanni drew Rosie to a stall hung with ribbons in a variety of bright colours. 'Aren't they lovely?'

She watched as Rosie ran her fingers through the silk and selected a ribbon in shiny olive green and one in gold. 'One for you,' she said, 'and one for me.' She handed the green ribbon to Shanni. 'It should be a sweetheart giving you ribbons for your hair,' Rosie smiled, 'but there's time enough for that and, anyway, it gives me pleasure to buy you a small gift.'

Shanni was pleased. She held the silk ribbon, knowing it would suit her red hair. 'You are so generous!' she said. It was not that the ribbon cost a great deal of money but it was a gift from a lady Shanni hardly knew. She immediately tied her hair in a loose bun away from her face and Rosie, watching her, laughed. 'Now you look even younger and more innocent than ever. Have you got a beau, Shanni, or are you still looking?'

'I'm not going to get married.' Shanni spoke with determination. 'I don't want to be any man's servant.'

'Oh dear.' Rosie led her to the cordial tent. 'You get us a seat and I'll order us a drink. It's so hot I think I'll faint if I don't have some refreshment.'

Shanni sat on the roughly made wooden seat and stared round at the groups of people laughing and talking, enjoying the fun of the day. Some ladies were well dressed, with parasols and fine gowns of silks and satins. Shanni looked at her own muslin dress, pretty enough and sprigged with bright cornflowers but marking her lowly place in society none the less.

She watched as Rosie came back across the dried grass lifting her skirts clear of the dust. Rosie was an enigma: she spoke like a girl from the poorer quarters yet she appeared wealthy – left money, so downstairs gossip had it, by her late employer Alice Sparks. Still, Shanni could not hold that against Rosie even though she believed a woman should fend for herself. Rosie was a sweet, generous person, and it was no wonder Alice Sparks had wanted to show her appreciation.

As Rosie came towards her Shanni realized she was very beautiful. What was wrong with Watt Bevan that he did not choose to live with his wife?

'The man is going to bring our drinks in a moment.' Rosie sank into her chair. 'You're staring. Have I got a spot on my face or something?'

'Sorry!' Shanni smiled. 'It's none of my business but I was just wondering why you don't live with your husband.'

She saw Rosie look away, a blush spreading over her neck and cheeks, and Shanni was ashamed. 'That was rude of me!' she said quickly. 'It's none of my business. My tongue sometimes runs ahead of my thoughts.'

'It's all right,' Rosie said. 'I don't mind telling you about Watt and me. We married for all the wrong reasons. Watt felt he had to look after me and my brothers because my mam fell sick.'

'Well, that was good of him, wasn't it?' Shanni asked.

Rosie shook her head. 'My mother Pearl

worked at the pottery for years and Watt admired her, wanted to do his best for her family.' Rosie sighed. 'So he married me. And, yes, it was kind of him. But it wasn't right, and when I realized that Watt had married me out of pity I left him and found myself a job as a companion to Alice Sparks.' Her voice faltered a little. 'I miss Alice so much. We were such good friends in those last months of her life.'

'I'm sorry,' Shanni said. 'I shouldn't have asked. I have no right to stir up all your past worries like that. I mean, I don't really know you, do I? But you're so pretty and so well dressed I think any man would be a fool to let you go. And do you know something? I envy your independence, Rosie.'

'You envy me?' Rosie sounded incredulous. 'But you're young with all your life before you. You have lovely red hair and such a creamy skin, you're a beautiful girl.' She paused. 'And so far you haven't fallen in love with the wrong man.' She rested her hand on Shanni's arm. 'Use your youth wisely, Shanni, and don't be blinded by love because those loving feelings can play you false.'

'Good afternoon, ladies.' Watt Bevan had stopped beside his wife and Rosie's colour deepened. She bowed her head staring at her hands in her lap. The silence was embarrassing.

'Good day to you, Mr Bevan,' Shanni said quickly. She looked up at him, evaluating him afresh. She had seen him only as the manager of the pottery, a stern man who laughed seldom. Now she knew that he was compassionate, that he

63

had felt duty-bound to take care of a young girl and her brothers.

'Watt, how nice to see you.' Rosie had regained her composure. She spoke formally, the Welsh vanishing from her voice. 'Please sit down, have some cordial with us.' She looked towards the table at the edge of the tent. 'The man was supposed to bring it to us ten minutes ago.'

Watt turned and lifted his hand. As if by magic a boy appeared, eager to serve him. No doubt he was hoping for a few pennies to put in his pocket for waiting on such a powerful man as Watt Bevan, pottery manager.

'Three jugs of cordial, please.' Watt delved into his pocket and brought out some coins. 'And have a drink yourself. You look all hot and bothered.'

The boy touched his scruffy hair and hurried away. Watt sat next to Shanni and she felt uncomfortable – it was as if she formed a barrier between husband and wife.

'I didn't expect to see you at the fair, Watt,' Rosie said. 'I thought my brothers were coming but they are probably off courting some girl or other.'

'Probably,' Watt said. 'Anyway, I wanted to see you, I owe you an apology for not being there to fetch you back to Swansea. Things were difficult, the men were in a bad mood – still are, come to that. Half of them are ready to tear the town apart.'

'But they have good reason,' Shanni said slowly. 'The tolls the farmers have to pay will raise the price of everything we buy from meat and drink to fripperies like this.' She flicked at her

64

ribbon. 'I'm surprised you're not with them, Mr Bevan.'

Watt glanced at her. 'And I'm surprised at your cheek, young lady!' He smiled, his tension vanishing. 'I think our Llinos is teaching you to be a little rebel or is it Madame Isabelle we have to blame for your radical ideas?'

'My thoughts are my own,' Shanni said heatedly. 'I see injustice all around me. My mother was killed by it and the poor are kept down to serve the rich.'

Watt leaned forward. 'Lower your voice, little Shanni, otherwise the wrong ears will hear. Your thoughts may be your own, but keep them to yourself. That's my advice.'

Shanni stared at him for a long moment then nodded. 'I understand,' she said, 'and you're right.'

Rosie touched her arm. 'Come on, Shanni, we're supposed to be enjoying today. All this talk of rioting and violence worries me.' She rose and shook the creases from her skirts. 'We'll doubtless see you around, Watt.'

'Rosie,' Watt pushed himself from his chair, in a swift easy movement, 'Rosie, I would like to talk to you.'

'Not now,' Rosie said sharply. 'I just want to enjoy the sunshine and the music of the fair. Another time.'

'Look, I'll go and have my fortune told,' Shanni said quickly. 'I'll meet you back at the tent in ten minutes or so.' She hurried out into the sunshine and glanced back to see Rosie arguing with Watt, and doubted her wisdom in leaving them alone.

There was a queue of grand ladies waiting to have their fortunes told and Shanni turned away in despair. In any case, she knew her future: work, learn and keep her mouth shut until the time was right. Speak like a lady, as Madame Isabelle had instructed her, and remember to tread carefully rather than rushing into things like a fool.

'Shanni!' Rosie's voice startled her and Shanni turned round. 'Wait for me.' She slid her arm through Shanni's. 'I know you were trying to be tactful but I don't want to be alone with Watt, not yet. It's too soon after losing my dear friend. I can't take any more upheaval just yet.'

She drew Shanni towards the hoop-la. 'Come on, let's have a go at winning a rag doll, or a bead necklace. It'll be fun.'

Shanni smiled. Rosie was older than she was by several years but here she was like an enchanted child, drinking in the fun of the fair.

It was Shanni who won the prizes, a black bead necklace and a matching black fan, painted with ladies of the royal court of Queen Victoria.

'I wouldn't like to see you with a firearm, my girl,' Rosie said. 'Your aim is deadly!'

'Well, that's not likely,' Shanni said. 'At the moment I'm learning ladylike things, the piano-forte, deportment and elocution.' She chuckled. 'Not that I'll ever think like a lady, mind.'

'Gentility comes from inside you, Shanni,' Rosie said. 'Money, position, these things can be earned, but a kind heart and a sense of fair play are born in folks.'

Shanni sobered. 'Are you being fair-minded

66

with your husband? Was it so wrong of him to marry you to take care of you?'

'I wanted love,' Rosie said. 'Is that asking too much?' She turned towards the edge of the park. 'Come on, let's have fun.'

She hurried away and Shanni saw her step up on to the carousel. She climbed on a carved horse tucking her skirts around her legs. 'Come on, Shanni, don't get left behind!'

Laughing, Shanni straddled a fierce-looking animal with white wooden teeth yellowed by the sun. The music began, loud and discordant, but Shanni did not care about that: she was here, with a friend and she intended to have a good time.

It was Rosie who weakened first. 'It's time I went home,' she said breathlessly. 'I feel so tired.'

Shanni looked at her closely. Rosie was very pale. 'Your spirit is weary, not your body,' she said. 'Here, have these beads and the fan too. I wouldn't have won them if it wasn't for you. And thank you for a lovely time.'

Before Rosie could reply, Shanni was running across the dry ground her skirts flying. At the edge of the field she turned to wave but Rosie was nowhere in sight.

Watt stood in the smoky taproom of the Castle Hotel and stared at the angry faces of the men seated around him. 'Try to stay calm,' he urged. 'Rioting is the wrong way to go about things.'

'It's all right for you, man.' Tom Levinson had been a sailor until his eyesight failed. Now he ran errands for the potters and painters, fetching beer from the public bars knowing his way instinctively without the aid of sight. 'You has your pay whatever you does, and you don't have to bow the knee to anyone. Tell us, Watt Bevan, why should men of pride have to suffer so that the rich can get richer?'

'Burning and plundering is not the answer,' Watt insisted.

'Don't talk daft, man!' Bill Brazil lifted a beefy arm. 'It worked in the thirties, didn't it?'

'Bill, you might be a good potter but you're not very good at reading the signs, are you?' Watt said, in exasperation. 'Men were killed in the thirties, good men, and what did it achieve? Nothing!'

'It showed we was together, though, didn't it?' Bill Brazil said. 'Showed we had strength and wasn't going to take no nonsense from anyone. Now, Watt, are you with us or agin us? If you're agin us, leave now so you can't carry tales back to the bosses.'

Watt shook his head in despair. 'I'll leave, then,' he said. 'I can't talk sense into you so it's best I go. As for carrying tales to the bosses, you're talking out of the seat of your trews, Bill Brazil. You should know me better than that.'

Watt left the hotel and walked towards the river. He was tired of arguing with the men. They would do what they wanted in the end so what was the use of talking? In any case, how could he be sure he was right to advise caution? What good had caution done them in the past?

He sat near the river watching the moonlight playing on the swiftly moving water. He guessed the tide must be full in because the river was high against the bank and small eddies made gurgling inroads into the lower grassy areas. The weather had turned colder now: the Indian summer that had come with autumn had spent itself at last. Soon, the cold winds of winter would drift in with the tide, the seas would be rougher and the hills covered with misty rain. Many folk hated winter but Watt would have welcomed it, had he been able to spend his time with Rosie.

It was silent on the bank except for the rush of the water. The birds had nested for the night and sensible people sat around their own fireside. He thought of Rosie alone in her cottage up on the hill. Why had he been such a fool as to lose her when he had held her in his arms?

When he saw Rosie at the autumn fair, she looked so cool, so unattainable, it was hard to believe they had once slept in the same bed. He had longed to kiss her sweet lips, to touch her fresh skin. And when Rosie had walked away from him it had hurt him deeply.

But could he blame her? He had not even been the one to bring her back to Swansea. As always, he had been too wrapped up in pottery business to think of himself and his relationship with his wife.

'All alone, Watt?' The cultured voice of Joe Mainwaring cut into his thoughts. Joe sank down beside him and rested his hand on Watt's shoulder. 'Been down at the Castle trying to talk sense into the men, have you?'

'Aye, and a fat lot of good it did,' Watt said. 'I might just as well have saved my breath. They are hell bent on some scheme or other and I'm best out of it.' He glanced at Joe: the man's profile was strong, handsome even in the dim light of the moon. 'Who am I to try to talk sense to anyone else when I can't even sort out my own problems?' he said ruefully.

'You haven't had a chance to talk to Rosie, then? She is still your wife after all.'

'I think she's forgotten all about our marriage and I can't say I blame her for that.' Watt picked up a pebble and skimmed it into the water. Dark ripples moved in restless circles across the surface of the water. 'Perhaps I should have made my life in America, like my old friend Binnie Dundee. Binnie was like me once, a lowly worker at the pottery, and now he owns a huge business. He has a wife who loves him and sons to bear his name after his days. Binnie's had two wives who adored him and I'm wondering what his secret was.'

'Who knows? It's a brave man or a liar who claims to know the mind of a woman,' Joe said.

Watt frowned. 'I thought if anyone understood women it would be you.'

'No! I'm as big a fool as the next man. I did wrong by Llinos and now I'm paying for it. To tell you the truth I'll be glad when my business takes me away from Swansea again. Sometimes I think I can't bear the reproach in Llinos's eyes.'

Watt sat in brooding silence. He knew what Joe meant because he, too, had broken the vows he made at the altar. He had taken other women but only as release from the unbearable desires of a man alone. If he had Rosie's love he would be faithful to her till the day he died.

Joe seemed to pick up on his thoughts. 'When I

took another woman, an American-Indian squaw, and fathered a son on her I thought it was fated for me in the stars but was it all an excuse, Watt?' For once Joe sounded uncertain. 'Was I fooling myself that it was my destiny to enjoy the delights of another woman's passion? Llinos and I lost something then, Watt, something we might never reclaim.'

'So you are telling me that you enjoyed the love of the Indian lady?' Watt said. 'That duty soon gave way to pleasure.'

'I was lusty then and I know it,' Joe said. 'Like any man I wanted to taste other fruit. It does not pay in the long run, Watt. A man should sow his wild oats before he marries and afterwards keep all his love for his wife. I will try to teach Lloyd to learn by my mistakes, but I doubt if I'll succeed.'

Joe pushed himself upright with ease. He was as lithe and fit as he had been when he first came to Swansea as a young man. Watt had been very young then, and had looked in awe at the stranger who was batman to old Captain Savage, master of the Savage pottery.

Watt got to his feet and stood beside Joe. He was younger than Joe by eight years or so and was putting on weight. His shoulders had grown broad, his muscles hardened by hours of labour in the pottery. Beside him Joe was as lithe and slim as a boy. No wonder women found him irresistible.

He stared up at the night sky, forcing his mind back to the present difficulties that plagued the pottery. 'There will be bloodshed before long,' he said, 'and I can't find any way to stop it.'

'Life will work its pattern without our help,' Joe said. 'Just be true to yourself and pray that God spares us all to live to see our grandchildren.'

Joe vanished as soundlessly as he had come, disappearing into the darkness. What had he meant by his cryptic words? He was as much of an enigma as he had ever been. Watt shook his head. It was time he was getting home to his bed. There would be work to do in the morning.

Then he lifted his face to the stars, wishing that Rosie would come to him, forgive him, give him a second chance of love. But that was a dream and it was about time he faced reality. Briskly, feeling the chill now, Watt began to walk away from the river and uphill to his home.

CHAPTER FIVE

The books Madame Isabelle brought for Shanni were difficult to read but the message was clear enough. It was time women took possession of their own souls as well as their bodies. One of the books was about the law regarding married women and Shanni felt angry as, finger pressed to the page, she laboriously read every word.

Once a woman married she was her husband's chattel, his to do with as he wished. He could beat her and abuse her, in some cases he could even offer her for sale or exchange if the mood took him. Shanni had believed ill-treatment of that sort happened only to the 'lower orders', the women who had no education, who had been subjugated all their lives. From what she read, nothing could be further from the truth.

The door opened and Flora stood back to allow Madame Isabelle to enter the drawing room. Madame glanced at the piano and then at Shanni, who closed the book marking the page carefully with the piece of ribbon Rosie had bought her at the fair.

'Have you been practising your scales?'

Madame Isabelle asked easily, as the maid closed the door behind her. 'Or have you been too busy reading?'

'These books you brought me, they make me so angry!' Shanni said, keeping her voice low. 'How can women allow themselves to be treated worse than the cattle in the fields?'

'It is because many of them lack education, which you are privileged now to receive, thanks to Mrs Mainwaring.' She looked at Shanni and smiled. 'I know you won't forget to whom you owe a debt of gratitude for all you have here.'

Shanni nodded but she felt she owed as much to Madame as she did to Mrs Mainwaring.

Madame Isabelle sat at the piano and ran her fingers over the keys. The music swelled softly into the room and Shanni felt her heart lighten with joy. She listened in silence for a while, then Madame Isabelle rose from the stool, twitching her skirts into place. 'Shall we begin?'

'Before I start to play for you, may I ask you something?' Shanni said meekly.

Madame Isabelle smiled. 'Yes, indeed. I'm not saying I shall have the answers you want to hear, but ask away.'

'Was I wrong in believing only working women get shabbily treated by men? From what I've just been reading rich ladies have to put up with infidelity, and worse, just like the poor. Aren't they well enough educated to complain?'

'Women can be well educated in the niceties of life,' Madame Isabelle shook her head and her combs threatened to fall loose from her thick hair, 'but that does not mean they are educated realistically or politically. Not everyone is given the opportunity to study the economy of the place in which they live, and any woman may fall foul of a wicked man who vowed before God to love and cherish her.'

Was Madame Isabelle talking from experience? Shanni glanced at her tutor's hand; she wore no wedding ring.

'Rich women with a fortune inherited from their fathers give up everything when they marry. They are owned by their husbands, most of whom treat a mistress better than a wife.'

'Why do women marry, then?'

'Some, like me, do not.' Madame Isabelle shrugged. 'But for others who are unequipped to look after themselves, what else is there? A spinster is expected to stay with aged parents, to tend and care for them until they die. Then she is forced to live on charity with relatives often reluctant to take her.'

'It sounds such an awful fate,' Shanni said. 'I will never let that happen to me.'

'Well, then, you must learn all you can,' Madame Isabelle said. 'Beginning with your piano lesson. Did you learn the little tune I set you?'

Shanni sat on the stool and played the simple piece without faltering. Madame Isabelle watched in silence until Shanni lifted her hands then smiled knowingly.

'Ah, I see you have a good memory! You did not once look at the music, my dear, and you must learn the notes if you are to read music correctly.'

Shanni played some scales and glanced over her shoulder. 'We both know I will never be any better than adequate as a pianist,' she said. 'What I'm really interested in is putting right the wrongs inflicted on the poor, women in particular.'

'Well put! Your vocabulary has improved greatly. And such high ideals, Shanni. I hope you keep them.' She paused, her brow furrowed in thought. 'Perhaps you would like to come to a meeting tomorrow. I shall ask permission for you to have tea with me, if you wish. I'm sure Mrs Mainwaring wouldn't mind. And as I live so far out she might even allow you to stay overnight. After the meeting you shall be introduced to some of my friends.'

'Oh, please, I'd like that!' Shanni said.

'Very well, it shall be done. But now, back to your task. Show me how you transpose the little tune you've memorized from the key of F to the key of G.'

Madame Isabelle sank into a chair and closed her eyes. There was a satisfied smile on her face.

'This pattern is selling well.' Watt held up a plate decorated with daffodils with trails of green leaves around the border. 'At least there are not so many problems with potteryware as there were with the porcelain.'

'Good heavens, Watt, it's years since the Mainwaring pottery produced porcelain.' Llinos took the plate to the window of the paint shed and Watt watched as she held it to the light. 'The colour is a little intense, don't you think?' She returned the plate to Watt. 'Perhaps you can tell the artist to mix the colours a little more subtly.'

Watt nodded. 'I'll speak to him before the next batch is painted and fired but we must remember that this pottery is designed for general use, not special occasions. Perhaps extra expense on painting would not be justified.'

'Still, the product we sell should be of the best quality we can manage, and that means in the painting department as well as in the potting.'

Watt followed as Llinos moved to the door. 'May I take the afternoon off, Llinos?' he asked. 'I would like to visit Rosie. I've sent her a letter so she will be expecting me.'

'You go and see her at any time you like, Watt,' Llinos said. 'I know the pottery runs like silk because you have organized the workers so well.'

'Thank you.' Watt was thinking how beautiful Llinos was. She still looked as fresh and lovely as she had in the old days when together they had struggled to make the pottery survive.

'Why are you staring at me?' Llinos asked, standing in the yard, hesitating. 'Was there something else?'

'No, I was just thinking you've never changed since the day I first saw you. Straight from the orphanage I was, and terrified of your mother.'

'Aye, and even more terrified of that awful Mr Cimla! Why my mother let herself be taken in by a good-for-nothing like him I'll never know. Poor Mother, that awful man was the death of her.'

'Far-off days, Llinos,' Watt said. 'We've both come a long way since then.' He put his arm around her shoulder. 'I'll always be grateful to you. You gave me a new start, hope for the future and a job I love.' He kissed her cheek and she flapped her hand at him.

'Go on with you!'

'Right, then, I'll go home, get washed and changed, then go up to see Rosie.'

'Give her my love and tell her she's welcome to visit any time she wants.'

Watt watched as Llinos went back towards the house and then he turned towards the gates of the pottery. His heart fluttered as he thought of seeing Rosie. How he loved his wife! It was just a pity he had taken so long to realize his true feelings. Now it might be too late.

He had meant well when he married Rosie, not understanding that a girl of her tender years needed love and care. That was something in all his reasoned reckoning he had not taken into account: how Rosie would feel. Watt had seen only that Rosie's mother was in trouble. Pearl had been very ill, she had two young sons to bring up and she needed a man's wages coming in. Wages he could provide.

And Watt had admired Rosie for some time. He thought her a lovely girl, with the glow of youth and health about her. He was a man alone, with many sad memories, and marrying Rosie seemed the ideal solution to his own problems as well as those of Pearl's family. How could he have been so wrong?

Watt walked alongside the river winding its way towards the town and felt the chill of the coming winter in the air. The leaves were turning brown, the smell of mist was in the air and Watt breathed it in with a sense that life, if he was not careful, would soon be passing him by.

Shanni climbed from the carriage and stared in amazement at the tall, terraced house where Madame Isabelle lived. She had not expected anything so grand. A brass plate on the wall beside the door declared Madame Isabelle's credentials. There were letters after her name that had no meaning for Shanni but she could tell from them that her tutor was a woman of some importance.

The hallway was compact; the smell of beeswax permeated the air. A maid in a pristine uniform took Shanni's coat and Madame Isabelle led the way into one of the airy rooms.

'We are having some of my cook's special egg sandwiches for tea, and then we shall indulge ourselves with delicious cake.'

'Where is the meeting going to be?' Shanni asked.

Madame Isabelle closed the door before replying. 'Here, of course.' She frowned. 'Shanni, to all intents and purposes this is just going to be a social evening, a meeting of friends, and I shall expect you to keep very quiet. I don't want any airing of opinions, I just want you to listen.'

'I understand,' Shanni said. 'I will stay very quiet, I promise.' She sat on the edge of the plump sofa and studied the contents of the room. A heavy cloth obscured all but the carved feet of the table. On the walls pictures proliferated: scenes of country life alongside portraits of well-dressed women, presumably Madame's ancestors.

A large oil lamp with a rich pink glass shade dominated the window-ledge.

'This is a lovely room,' Shanni said softly. 'One day I will own a house like this.'

'Well, to achieve anything in life you must be clever – and work exceptionally hard into the bargain.'

'I am willing to work day and night, Madame Isabelle.' Shanni sank back against the soft cushions. 'And when I am rich I'll help the poor. I won't turn up my nose at street beggars the way some of the gentry do.'

The door opened and the maid brought a tray of tea into the room. 'Put it down on the table there, Sarah,' Madame Isabelle said. 'And bring me more hot water, there's a good girl. You always make the tea too strong for me.'

Shanni was hardly conscious of eating the tiny sandwiches; she was staring at the bookshelves where some volumes were covered with brown paper concealing the contents. These, she guessed, were Madame Isabelle's private books.

After tea, Sarah showed Shanni to her room. 'There's hot water on the stand, Miss.' The girl bobbed a curtsy, and Shanni opened her mouth to explain she was nobody of importance and did not warrant a curtsy but thought better of it.

'Thank you, Sarah,' she said. 'Would you open the hooks at the back of my dress for me, please?'

Sarah obeyed at once and Shanni felt a dart of pity. 'Do you like working here, Sarah?'

'Well, yes, Miss. I was lucky to get a position with such a fine lady and I thank the Lord every night in my prayers for Madame Isabelle's kindness to me.'

Shanni sighed. It seemed that some girls had no ambition but were content with their lot.

'Is that all, Miss?' Sarah asked meekly. She stood with her hands folded, waiting for Shanni to speak.

'Will you always work here?' Shanni asked curiously. 'I mean, don't you want to be mistress in your own house?'

'I'll marry one day, Miss,' Sarah said, 'but even then I'll be lucky to have a house of my own. Folk like me rent rooms in other people's houses, more often than not.'

'Well, is that enough for you? It doesn't seem right to me.' Shanni frowned and Sarah stepped backwards towards the door.

'I can't stay and talk, I have work to do, Miss.' She managed a small smile. 'I'd better be going downstairs. There's not many good jobs going in Llanelli, so I must look after my place here.'

Shanni followed the girl across the room and closed the door after her. She stood for a moment before the window and stared out at the street below. Llanelli was not a very large town but it had charm. The small twisting streets that led out on to green pastureland were, for the most part, cobbled. The houses looked well kept with neat gardens. The perimeter was dotted with the occasional isolated cottage, the roof thatched, the windows mullioned. Yes, Shanni thought, she would be happy to live in Llanelli.

When Shanni had washed and dressed in fresh clothes she sat on the bed, not knowing if she should go downstairs or wait until she was sent for. In someone else's house it was difficult to know how to behave. She heard the clock in the hall chime seven and, almost at once, the doorbell rang out stridently, echoing through the house.

After a moment voices filled the hallway, masculine voices. Words spoken in the Welsh tongue reached her, and Shanni listened shamelessly at the door, trying to pick up any hint of rebellion, of the wish to put the world to rights. All she heard were the usual pleasantries exchanged between visitor and hostess.

A knock on the door startled her and Shanni stepped away guiltily. Sarah's soft voice called, 'Miss, Madame Isabelle would like you to come downstairs.'

Shanni waited a few seconds then opened the door. 'Thank you, Sarah. It's kind of you to fetch me.'

'It's just my job, Miss.' Sarah led the way down the carpeted stairs, her hand barely touching the well-polished banister. Shanni smiled to herself. It was Sarah who did the polishing and she was not above saving herself the pain of fingermarks ruining all her hard work.

The sitting room was filled with smoke and the smell of wine. Men stood around in good cloth coats and heavy twill trews. Gold watches hung at expansive waists and, to Shanni's critical mind, it seemed these rich gentlemen were only playing at reform.

'Ah, Shanni,' Madame Isabelle drew her into the room. She introduced the gentlemen one by one and chuckled as Shanni pulled a face. 'Don't worry, dear, I don't expect you to remember all the names, not at once anyway.' She drew Shanni away from the others.

'But there's one name I guarantee you will remember, and that's the name of our speaker for the evening.'

As if on cue the door was opened by the maid. A tall, well-set man, younger than the rest, stepped into the room, and a silence fell on the gathering. With him he brought an air of contained excitement. His dark hair fell in unruly curls over his forehead and his eyes gleamed almost with the light of the fanatic. He was a man of great presence.

Instinctively Shanni took a step back as, beckoned by Madame Isabelle's slender hand, the visitor came closer. She felt it then, the magnetism of the man, the power of him as he loomed over her.

Madame Isabelle rested her hand on Shanni's shoulder. 'This is Shanni, our newest convert,' she said. 'Shanni, I want you to meet our speaker, a man I admire greatly, Mr Dafydd Buchan.'

Shanni took a deep breath and looked into a pair of the deepest brown eyes she had ever seen.

CHAPTER SIX

'Oh, Watt, come in. I forgot I was expecting visitors. Isn't Llinos with you?' Rosie pushed back her hair, tucking a stray curl behind a pin. Her cheeks were flushed, and she wondered if it was the heat of the oven making her hot or the presence of her estranged husband.

'I'm sorry. Didn't I make it clear that I was coming alone?' Watt sounded a little disgruntled and Rosie hid a smile. She was far from mean-spirited but it would serve Watt right to feel his visit was an unimportant event in Rosie's life.

'You'll have to forgive my appearance. It's the maid's day off and I was making bread.' She smiled a little ruefully. 'I suppose I was reminding myself of the old days when I was just plain little Rosie with chores to do around the house for my mother.' She gestured towards the back of the house. 'Will you come through into the kitchen?'

She was conscious of Watt behind her as she pushed open the door. Her heart was beating uncomfortably fast but she concealed her feelings by bending to untie her apron.

The aroma of freshly baked bread filled the

room and Watt sniffed appreciatively. He stood beside her and she forced herself to smile pleasantly, as if his visit was simply that of an old friend. But Watt was not just a friend. She had lain in the same bed as him, shared the intimacies of married life with him, and she blushed now at the thought of how much pleasure his touch had given her. Still, all that was before she found out he had married her out of pity.

'Sit down, Watt. I'll just take the bread out of the oven and then I'll make us a pot of tea.' She glanced to the dresser where a cake was cooling on a stand. If Watt were an observant man he would realize that she had been fully prepared for his visit, but how many men were that perceptive?

He sat awkwardly on the wooden kitchen chair, his long legs jutting out from under the table. Rosie, glancing surreptitiously at him, thought he was more attractive than ever. When they married he had been slim with the boyishness of youth still in his face. Now he had filled out, his features had hardened, he was a man.

A wave of regret washed over her for what might have been, if the marriage had been a love match on both sides.

'How are things at home?' she asked. 'You must have tired of living with my brothers. Are they behaving like men, these days?' She smiled.

'They're hardly ever home if the truth be told,' Watt said. 'I am on my own most of the time.'

Rosie pretended his words had not registered. She was on her own, too, and she did not complain. 'And the pottery?' She bent over the oven and slid the loaf on to a tray. Steam rose from the oven misting her eyes. Or were those tears she could feel on her cheeks?

'Rosie . . .' Watt began, and she stiffened, knowing he wanted to talk about their marriage. She pushed the kettle on to the fire, scraping the bottom noisily against the hot coals. Then, struggling for composure, she sat down opposite him.

'We have to talk,' Watt said.

'No, we don't.' Rosie shook her head. 'All the talking in the world won't change anything. I fell in love with you, that's why I married you.' She sighed. 'But you didn't love me, did you?'

He did not deny it, and Rosie's spirits fell. 'Have some tea with me, Watt. Let's try to be friends before we think of anything else, shall we?'

She rose and clattered the cups as she put them on the table. As she fetched the milk from the pantry she took a deep breath, trying to slow the beat of her heart.

'Good thing I'd washed the table down before you came, otherwise there'd be flour all over the place.' She spoke lightly. 'I never was the fussiest of women but living with Alice certainly taught me to be both neat and thrifty. If left to her own devices she would have ruined her good clothes by leaving them around on the floor and she would most certainly have squandered her inheritance.'

She fussed over making the tea then sat down again. 'Would you like to try some of my cake? I'm not the best of cooks but it won't poison you.'

'I just want to talk to you, Rosie,' Watt said. 'Aren't you lonely up here on your own?'

'Of course not.' But Rosie was. She craved even now to throw herself into Watt's arms. She was a woman with a woman's needs. Why did he always fail to see that?

He sipped the tea, and stared at her over the rim of the cup. 'You grow more beautiful every day,' he said. 'Where did I go wrong, Rosie? How did I lose you?'

'It was probably my fault.' She did not look at him. 'I was too young and ignorant to know that you married me simply to make things easier for my mother.'

'I can't argue with that. I'm sorry, it's the truth.' Watt rubbed his cheek. 'Pearl was a good friend and I had worked with her for a long time. I thought what I did was for the best. Can't you at least allow me that much credit?'

'It was very worthy of you,' she said, with a hint of sarcasm that he did not miss.

He reached across the table to take her hand. 'Rosie, when you left I soon realized what a fool I'd been.' He ran his fingers through his hair and Rosie noticed a silver thread or two. Somehow her heart was moved.

'I knew when you'd gone, when my bed was empty of you at night, that I was in love with you.'

'You didn't learn that lesson soon enough,' Rosie said. 'It's probably too late now, Watt. How can I ever trust you again? You could change your mind and go off with another woman for all I know.'

'I wouldn't do that. Just give me a chance to prove myself, Rosie, please.'

'No, I can't think straight, not yet.' She drew

her hand away, unwilling to show him how much his touch affected her. 'I have only just come back here to live. I have lost my great friend, Alice, and I don't know what I want, not right now.'

Watt rose to his feet. 'Well, you are rich and independent,' he said. 'Perhaps you're setting your sights higher than a mere manager of a pottery.'

Sudden anger surged through Rosie. 'That was not worthy of you, Watt.'

He moved to the door. 'Maybe not, but I'm only human and I can't come begging you to forgive me for ever, can I?'

'I am not asking you to!' Rosie's voice held a bitter note. 'I never had you, not really, did I? When we married you were mourning Maura Dundee, the woman you promised to love with all your heart. I was such a fool not to see that I was second best to her ghost.' She glared at him. 'How could you do that to me, Watt? You took my dreams and crushed them. Oh, what's the use of talking? Go away and leave me alone!'

All the hurt and pain of the past welled up inside her. Rosie stared at her husband and saw a man growing older alone. He wanted her now and it was he who had raised the subject of her inheritance. Was that the attraction now? That she was a woman who could take care of herself?

'I can't find it in my heart to forgive you, Watt,' she said. 'I still burn with anger whenever I think of the grief you caused me. Don't you see how humiliated I was? A girl you married out of pity and everyone but me knowing it?'

'You have to keep bringing up the past, don't you?' Watt's face was white. 'I was a fool to come here. Well, I won't bother you again, you needn't worry about that.' Watt strode through the passage and let himself out into the growing darkness.

Rosie followed him, wanting to cling to him, to beg him to stay. But a hard knot of anger stopped her. 'Goodbye, then, Watt,' she said lightly, to his retreating back, 'and good luck.'

She closed the door and leaned against it. Suddenly it was as if the light had gone out of her world.

'We need to fight our cause with actions as well as words.' Dafydd Buchan stood in Madame Isabelle's parlour, fired with enthusiasm. 'We must stamp out the tyranny, abolish the impossible charges put on the gates. All we're after is justice.'

Shanni sat listening quietly to Dafydd. She was intrigued by him: he was well dressed and spoke in cultured tones but he really cared about the poor.

'The tolls are monstrously unjust! A farmer pays more to pass through the gates than he does for the lime he transports.'

Madame Isabelle spoke in well-modulated tones: 'And what are we going to do about it, Dafydd?'

'We have already attacked some of the gates where the tolls are excessive and we must continue to do so. We'll burn them to the ground and the toll-houses with them. We'll teach the traitors working for the idle rich where their loyalty lies!'

'But that was tried in 'thirty-four without a great deal of success,' Madame Isabelle said reasonably. 'I don't know that violence achieves anything in the end.'

'Eighteen thirty-four was a different matter.' Dafydd sounded impatient. 'The men protested against the Poor Law then, not the tolls, and they were without leaders, without weapons. Now we are better prepared. We can fight to the death if necessary.' His eyes were shining with zeal.

'I don't know.' Madame Isabelle seemed unconvinced, and Shanni watched her covertly.

'We have organized bands of men,' Dafydd went on talking, 'men not armed with pitchforks but with pistols. We have drawn up our plans and we are ready.'

Shanni was suddenly afraid. She thought of the *Ceffyl Pren*, of the rough justice that could so easily turn to violence and even death. The police and the yeomanry would turn out, better armed and in greater numbers than the rebels.

Shanni had been a small child when the men of Swansea had been sent to Brecon to stamp out the rioting, but she had heard the lurid tales of the conflict many times. Men had been killed, women beaten and all to no avail. The laws had been reinforced and the people left worse off than ever before.

'We have to strike at the oppressors before they become too powerful,' Dafydd was saying. 'We let them get away with a rise in tolls this time, and within a few months the price of passing through the gates will rise again. We must stand and fight or all is lost.'

'For that to happen we need money to buy more arms.' Another man spoke up roughly. 'Are you trying to tell us that we few can beat the might of the police and the militia with one or two pistols? They'll shoot us down without mercy, man, and hang a few of us, no doubt!'

'With that attitude, Thomas Carpenter, you are asking to be exploited,' Dafydd said cuttingly. His shoulders were tense. He was a man capable of great anger.

Shanni glanced at Madame Isabelle, who looked worried. She watched as Madame smoothed back her elegant hair and, as if on an impulse, rose to her feet.

'I suggest we all relax and have a drink to celebrate our unity.' She rang for the maid, and Shanni knew that the offer of refreshment was a ploy to take the heat out of the argument.

Shanni felt the tension ease as Dafydd sat down and loosened the buttons on his coat. He glanced across the room at her but it was as if he did not see her. His eyes were hot with anger and Shanni shivered.

Glasses of wine were carried in on a tray and the maid handed the drinks around, bobbing curtsies to the men. A tray of comfits was produced, and the talk became general.

'I shall play for you,' Madame Isabelle said and, lifting her skirts, she settled herself on the stool in front of the piano. Her fingers ran lightly over the keys, bringing life and warmth to the room. The melodious sound of Madame singing brought foolish tears to Shanni's eyes.

'I see the music moves you, Shanni.' Dafydd had crossed the room and seated himself beside her. He was calmer now. She shivered a little as she felt the warmth of his arm against hers. 'You are a delicate flower and perhaps our words are too strong for you.'

'I hate violence,' Shanni replied.

'Sometimes violence is the only answer, don't you think?'

She glanced up at him. He was smiling and the anger had gone from his eyes. He seemed kindly, a champion of the poor, and she wondered if she had been mistaken about his fanaticism.

'I can't see it myself,' Shanni said. 'I would think that cunning might achieve what outright action would not.'

He touched her hair. 'Such an old head for one so young,' he said. 'What has made you like this, Shanni?'

'I have seen violence close to,' Shanni said, her voice low but hard with anger. 'Violence which takes the name of justice can kill.'

She saw a glimmer of amusement in Dafydd's face. 'Go on,' he said humouring her.

'No, I don't want to think about it.'

He took her hand in his and smoothed her wrist. 'Sometimes it's better to talk about something painful. It's like lancing a sore and allowing the poison to run away.'

She took her hand away. 'The past is dead and gone, buried like my mother and her baby.'

'Then I'm sorry, Shanni,' he said, 'but sometimes good comes from pain. Look where you are now, a beloved friend to Madame Isabelle. Indeed, you are a privileged friend and trusted too, otherwise you wouldn't be here.'

Shanni bowed her head. 'I have been very fortunate.' She looked up at him. 'But at what cost?'

'Come along, Shanni!' Madame Isabelle's voice cut into the conversation. 'Let's hear you play your little piece, shall we?'

Shanni recognized the request for what it was: an attempt to get her away from Dafydd Buchan. Madame's next words confirmed what she was thinking. 'You are too old and intense for our little Shanni.' She tapped Dafydd on the shoulder. 'She is young yet, and needs to form her own opinions.' She took Shanni's hand. 'Come along, I want everyone to know what a talented pupil I have.'

Reluctantly, Shanni sat at the piano. She looked at the music and saw that Madame Isabelle had chosen the piece she knew best. Her fingers hovered over the keys. She must not let her teacher down by giving a poor performance.

She played hesitantly at first, then with growing confidence. It was as if the presence of an audience brought out the best in her. The simple music sounded rich and tuneful. Her fingers no longer faltered but struck the notes with confidence. And when the piece was ended, she rose and curtsied to a burst of clapping. Shanni smiled, but was wise enough to know that the shouts of 'Bravo' were meant as encouragement to a young girl, not as an accolade to an inexperienced pianist.

Later as she lay in bed in the unfamiliar room, she stared at the patterns of light on the ceiling and thought about the evening. Dafydd Buchan was a powerful man, a strong leader, but was his zeal just a little too ardent to be healthy? And yet when she remembered how close he had sat, how powerful he was and the way his eyes had searched hers, she felt thrilled, wanting to be more to him than just a silly young girl.

She was almost asleep when she was wakened by a muffled noise downstairs. Something crashed to the floor and then there was a shot. Shanni sat bolt upright and tried to see through the darkness. She slipped from her bed, pulled on a robe and carefully opened her door.

From the landing she saw a man lying on the floor, his arms splayed, another figure crouching over him. Someone brought a candle and, to Shanni's horror, she saw blood seeping into the pale boards of the hallway.

Shanni hurried downstairs and stared at the man on the ground. She recognized him at once: it was Thomas Carpenter, the man who had shouted down Dafydd's attempts to enthuse his listeners.

Madame Isabelle came to the foot of the stairs. 'Go back to bed, Shanni,' she said sternly. 'There's been a dreadful accident and I don't want you involved.'

Shanni hesitated, then returned to her bedroom. She lit a candle and sat on the bed staring at the flame. There was a dead man downstairs and his shooting might be called an accident, but Shanni knew that Dafydd Buchan's fight for justice had claimed its first martyr.

CHAPTER SEVEN

'Well, what are you looking so miserable about?' Llinos rested her hand on Watt's arm. 'Is it Rosie?'

Watt nodded. 'She's turned me down again. She had even forgotten I was coming to see her.' His face was tight with anger. 'Well, it's the last chance she'll get. I'll not go cap in hand to her again.'

Llinos crossed the room and stood at the window, staring out at the pottery kilns beyond the garden. It seemed to her that Rosie was playing her own little game, giving Watt a taste of his own medicine, and who could blame her? There was nothing worse than the pain of knowing your man did not love and cherish you as he should.

The heat from the bottle-shaped structures shimmered in the bright winter sunshine, and Llinos breathed in the sights and sounds of the potting industry she had grown up with. 'Don't be too hard on her, Watt.' She turned to face him. 'Rosie is a good girl and she needs time. She has just lost her best friend after all.'

'Anyway, I didn't come to talk about my own problems,' Watt said.

'I know. Sit down, Watt. Let's talk in comfort, shall we?' Llinos sat back on the large sofa and pushed a cushion behind her back. She might not look as if she was past forty but sometimes she felt it.

'It's about Ceri Buchan. He's asked if he might come to see how we work things here. I've told him he can call today.' Watt sat on the edge of one of the high-backed chairs and rested his hands on his knees. 'He's the chap who founded the Llanelli pottery with his brother Dafydd.'

'I know who he is,' Llinos said. 'I'm not so out of touch that I don't read the papers. What does he want exactly?' She was a little angry that Watt had not consulted her sooner.

'I think he just wants to ask our advice about a few things, the patterns we use, the transfer printing. I don't really know, to be honest.'

'He had better curtail his brother's activities if he wants to succeed in business.' Llinos spoke sharply. 'Dafydd Buchan is one of those leading the fight against the toll rises. That's not good for business, is it?'

'Llinos,' Watt looked grave, 'you *are* out of touch with the people. The men calling themselves Rebeccarites are fighting injustice.'

'Maybe I am out of touch, but what good is anarchy?' Llinos felt the colour rise to her face. 'I care about the people of Swansea, you know I do, but pulling down gates and burning toll-houses won't achieve justice for anyone.'

Watt shrugged, and Llinos knew by his

expression that he did not agree with her. 'It will all end in the death of some innocent,' she said. 'You know as well as I that the insurrections of the past were swiftly put down. Men were shot and killed, women left without a provider. Is that good in your opinion?'

'I seem to have lost the Llinos I once knew,' Watt said sadly. 'You have changed so much over the years. You've become like all the rest of the wealthy folk who hide their heads in the sand.' He stood up. 'Any minute now you'll be telling me that it's better to pass on the other side.'

'Watt!' There was a lump in Llinos's throat. 'I do care, of course I do. I took Shanni in, didn't I? I've tried to educate her and make a lady of her. I'm not one of the heartless, idle rich, and you know it.'

Watt nodded slowly. 'I'm sorry, Llinos. I may be airing my views too bluntly. I know you're a good woman at heart but you are oblivious to what's really happening on your own doorstep. Open your eyes, Llinos. See what's really going on around you.'

Llinos felt a moment of fear. 'What do you mean?'

'I'm just trying to warn you that the world is changing, values are changing. Ordinary folk want more out of life, a decent standard of living and the chance to earn an honest crust. The dissatisfaction of the poor has culminated in the need for a stronger voice and that's why houses are burned and gates hacked to pieces. It might not mean much to you, but those with little money are being penalized for needing to pass through the roads of their own home town.'

Llinos was about to speak when there was a rapid knocking on the door. Flora peered into the room and the angry words died on Llinos's lips.

'Your visitor is here, Mrs Mainwaring.' The girl stood aside. 'Mr Dafydd Buchan.'

Llinos glanced at Watt, who frowned. The man who entered the room was about thirty. He was tall and dark, with an imposing air of authority. His hair was thick, and curls clung to the collar of his immaculate shirt. He bowed politely. 'Thank you for taking the time to see me, Mrs Mainwaring,' he said. 'I apologize for my brother but he is indisposed and I've come in his place. I do hope it's not inconvenient.'

'Come in, and let Flora close the door,' Llinos said. 'There seems to be a draught in here.' For some reason she was breathless. She could almost believe her pulse was fluttering in excitement, but that was absurd. 'I'm sorry I'm unprepared but your visit was sprung on me by my manager.' She gestured towards Watt. 'I was unaware that such an eminent gentleman was visiting today.'

'Shall I go away again?' There was a hint of laughter in his eyes.

As they met hers Llinos felt the magnetism of the man. She held her head high, unwilling to be persuaded by his obvious charm. 'My husband is away on business at present or I'm sure he would have been delighted to meet you.' Now, why had she said that? Was it defence against Dafydd Buchan's rudely familiar stare?

'What can we do for you, Mr Buchan?' she

asked sharply. The two men waited politely until Llinos had sat down and had arranged her full skirts. 'Please, take a seat.'

'I do hope this is not an imposition, Mrs Mainwaring.' Dafydd Buchan's voice seemed to ring through the room with power and strength. 'I wondered if you would allow me to observe the processes you employ here in Swansea.' He spread his hands deprecatingly. 'I am a comparative newcomer to potting, as you doubtless know.'

'But your brother Ceri, he is the businessman, is he not? His name is always in the newspapers.'

'Ah, my brother, yes.' His tone told Llinos that he was not impressed by the way his brother conducted his life. 'He is a very clever man but sometimes he's . . . something of a pacifist shall we say?'

'I find nothing wrong in that,' Llinos said. 'Now, I'm sure Mr Bevan will be delighted to show you around our pottery. You do realize that we are not the biggest potters in the vicinity? Next door to us is the largest, most productive pottery in all of Swansea. Have you been to see the owners there?'

'I have indeed,' Dafydd Buchan smiled, 'but in my humble opinion the Mainwaring pottery is by far the most artistic and innovative.' His tone belied his words. There was nothing humble about Dafydd Buchan.

Llinos raised her eyebrows, thinking that the honeyed words were just so much flattery. 'Watt, perhaps you'll show Mr Buchan our methods.'

'Yes, of course.' Watt got to his feet. 'If you'll

come this way, Mr Buchan, I'll be happy to give you a tour.'

'And in return,' Llinos said, 'I hope I might be allowed to look around your pottery in Llanelli some time.'

'It would be my greatest pleasure to see you there.' Dafydd Buchan took her hand, bending towards her, his eyes on hers.

She stepped back unconsciously and took a deep breath. 'Right, then, I have work to do. I will speak to you later, Watt.'

Llinos followed the men to the hallway, her heart beating absurdly fast. As the maid opened the front door Shanni swept into the house bringing the chill of the wind with her. Her cheeks were flushed and her eyes bright. She stopped abruptly, almost cannoning into Dafydd Buchan.

'This is my impetuous ward, Shanni.' There was a smile in Llinos's voice: Shanni seemed as struck as she was by Dafydd's magnetism. 'Shanni, this is Mr Buchan. He's come to see how our pottery works.'

'Oh, good day, sir,' Shanni blinked rapidly. 'It's nice to meet you again.' She stood in the hall twisting her fingers together, and Llinos sensed that Shanni was discomfited by the presence of the visitor.

'I'm happy to see you, too, Shanni. I hope you've been practising your music.' He was smiling as he walked away, standing a head taller than Watt. Shanni stared after him, her mouth open.

'You've met Mr Buchan before?' Llinos asked, as she led Shanni into the drawing room.

'I think I might have met him at Madame Isabelle's little tea party.' She spoke hesitantly, as if wondering at the wisdom of her words.

Llinos's curiosity was aroused: if Madame Isabelle was inviting a known troublemaker to her home perhaps she was not a good tutor for Shanni after all. She watched from the window as Watt led Dafydd Buchan across the yard and into the first of the painting sheds.

'Strange man, Mr Buchan,' Llinos said. 'He's very full of himself. Tell me all about him, Shanni. How does he know Isabelle?'

Shanni shrugged. 'I don't know. They live in the same area and I suppose that's how they know each other. Apparently he's a wonderful orator.'

Llinos was surprised. A short time ago Shanni would not have known the word 'orator', let alone understood its meaning. 'Go on.'

'He cares about poor folk. He wants social justice, a more equal society. That is what we all should be striving for.'

'Is that your opinion, or the opinion of this Dafydd Buchan?'

'It's wrong what is happening to people who are just trying to make an honest living for themselves,' Shanni said. 'The farmers can't earn enough to pay all the tolls demanded of them. It's no wonder there's discontent in the world.'

Shanni was saying almost the same words as Watt had spoken earlier. Was she getting too insulated in her own comfortable home, Llinos wondered, too wrapped in her own bitter memories of the past? Was she out of touch with the people?

'I shall have to come with you to one of Madame's *soirées*,' Llinos said. Anger was building inside her: everyone was treating her as if she was against justice for the poor. That simply was not true.

'It's so hard for the farmers,' Shanni said quietly. 'They sometimes have to pay three tolls to pass along a mile of road and it's ruining them.'

'I'm just a little tired of hearing about the lot of the poor,' Llinos said, in a hard voice. 'I was poor once and I worked my own way out of it. I faced great hardships when I was your age, and I had enough spirit not to let it dishearten me.'

'But you are well educated, Mrs Mainwaring. Your father was a captain in the army. He was respected and well known for his cleverness and his bravery. You were never of the lower orders.' She paused. 'I was, and it's a pit with sheer sides, too difficult to get out of.'

'I do believe you're turning into a poet, Shanni,' Llinos said, forcing a tone of lightness into her voice. She took a deep breath. 'I agree with what you say. I had all the advantages you talk about, but they vanished into thin air and I had to work until my fingers were raw.'

She looked down at her hands, soft and white now, showing no evidence of how she had worked the clay. 'I had to grow up fast, to manage a business that was falling apart. It takes more than education and more than an accident of birth to make a success out of chaos.'

'I think you are wonderful to have done all that.' There was genuine admiration in Shanni's voice and a little of Llinos's tension vanished.

'Come, let me hear you play. Let's see if Madame Isabelle is deserving of the money I pay her.' There was an edge of sarcasm in Llinos's voice that was not lost on Shanni, but she sat obediently at the piano and placed her fingers on the keys.

Eynon stared at his daughter and smiled. She was turning into a beautiful young lady. She looked nothing like her dead mother – now that her features were maturing she favoured him more. It was a pleasing thought.

'So you are going out with Lloyd Mainwaring today, then, are you?' He took Jayne's hand and held it lightly. 'I think you youngsters spend far too much time away from your studies. In my day we had to work hard at our lessons.' He grimaced, thinking how old-fashioned he must sound.

He rested his hand on the girl's shoulder. 'I hope you don't bowl Lloyd over with your beauty. Poor lad wouldn't stand a chance against your wiles.'

'Father, you might just be a little biased, don't you think?' Jayne asked.

'No, I don't. Come here.' He held her in his arms and kissed her silky, sweet-smelling hair. 'You are a lovely-looking girl with a fine education and a rich dowry to offer. Any man would jump at the chance of getting you for a wife.'

'You are jesting with me, aren't you, Father? I have no intention of marrying anyone for several years yet.' She drew away and stretched her arms above her head. 'I want to be free to enjoy myself.

I want to be presented at Court – you know that's what Grandmother would have wanted for me.'

'We'll see about that, Jayne, but I do not want you living in London. It's a racy place and your grandmother had some strange friends.'

Jayne smiled. 'I know. Wasn't she a courtesan to a royal personage at one time?'

'That's just idle gossip.' Eynon looked at his daughter, whose eye held a wicked gleam. He realized suddenly that she also had a will of her own. No-one would deceive Jayne Morton-Edwards: she was far too sharp.

The sound of carriage wheels crunched along the gravel outside the house and Jayne looked up expectantly. 'That will be Lloyd,' she said easily.

Eynon followed her into the hall where the maid was already holding out a warm coat and a thick scarf. Jayne scarcely looked at the girl, and Eynon shook his head; his daughter had grown up to expect a privileged lifestyle, good food on the table and servants to cater to her every whim. It was the natural order of things. Eynon himself had never known poverty. What he had known was the sharp edge of his father's tongue on more occasions than he could recall. Phillip Morton-Edwards had been a selfish man, who considered his only son a failure. Anything Eynon had attempted was met with ridicule.

Eynon pushed away the unpleasant memories of the past. At least he could claim he had built up the pottery founded by his father, and when he had sold it, he had made a huge profit.

'I'm going now, Father, so stop daydreaming

and kiss me goodbye.' Jayne stood on tiptoe to plant a kiss on Eynon's cheek.

'Take care, now.' Eynon watched as his daughter stepped out of the house and waved to Lloyd Mainwaring as casually as if he had been an underling, a servant to obey her command. If Lloyd was anything like his mother, he would be too spirited to put up with any nonsense from Jayne. From behind Lloyd, Eynon caught sight of Shanni Price, her red hair peeping out from beneath her bonnet. Eynon smiled. His daughter would not like to be seen in the company of a girl who had once been her maid, especially as that girl was so pretty. Shanni looked composed and held herself like nobility. She was finely dressed in an outfit of warm red with a bonnet covered in feathers. She looked every inch a lady born to riches. What did Llinos have in mind for Shanni's future, he wondered. The girl was neither fish nor fowl, educated like a lady but with all the disadvantages of the mean slums from which she had come. Her health might suffer from the effects of living in a hovel, eating little food – and poor food at that. Many of the inhabitants of Swansea drank water from the canal into which the filth of the town had settled. No, the girl would not be sturdy and healthy as his daughter was. What he really worried about, if he was honest, was that Shanni Price would take Lloyd's attention away from Jayne. But that could never happen: Lloyd was a most discerning young man.

He stood waving until the carriage was out of sight, then returned to his fireside and to the glass of rich red claret waiting for him on the side table.

He was happy with his lot. As he sipped the fine wine he thought that all he needed to make his life complete was a good wife. What a pity the only woman he had ever wanted was Llinos Mainwaring, who was married to a man she loved very much. Eynon rested his head against the soft cushions of the chairback and closed his eyes. His feet were warmed by the glowing coals and his stomach by the wine. All in all, it was a good life.

Shanni moved aside reluctantly for Jayne Morton-Edwards to sit next to Lloyd. He smiled at Shanni as if to beg her tolerance.

'This is Shanni,' Lloyd said. 'Shanni, this is a childhood friend of mine, Jayne Morton-Edwards.'

'She knows who I am,' Jayne said sharply. 'Perhaps you've forgotten she used to be my maid.'

Shanni had taken a dislike to Jayne when she first set eyes on her. The girl's haughty, unpleasant remarks did nothing now to make her change her mind. She was of the breed of gentry who looked down their noses at ordinary folk. Thank goodness she did not have to work in the Morton-Edwards household any longer. Shanni suddenly realized how grateful she should be to Llinos Mainwaring for taking her in and treating her so well.

Jayne was studying her, and Shanni straightened her shoulders. 'Don't you know it's rude to stare? Are you sure you'll recognize me next time you see me?' She knew her tone was impudent but Jayne brought out the worst in people.

'Well, you do look different now you're not wearing a cap and apron,' Jayne said. 'And it's a good thing you've left service – you were a dismal failure and it takes little intelligence to wait on your betters.'

'Especially those so-called betters who have no intelligence at all,' Shanni replied.

'Hey!' Lloyd intervened. 'Come along, you two. I thought you would be friends.'

'I'm sorry,' Shanni said. 'I just can't help being sensitive, which Miss Morton-Edwards is not.'

'We're going to the Assembly Rooms,' Lloyd said, breaking the uncomfortable silence that followed Shanni's words. 'There's a discussion about the toll-gates. The prospect of raising the tolls is being debated and I think it should be a lively discussion.'

Shanni frowned. 'It's stupid to propose yet *another* rise in tolls,' she said. 'What do you think, Lloyd?'

Lloyd met her eyes. 'I think it's hard on the ordinary folk who are trying to make an honest living.'

'Rubbish!' Jayne broke into the conversation with a burst of righteous indignation. 'The lower orders have no conception of the way the country is run. Do they think that the government of Britain comes without cost? Roads have to be maintained, and who is going to pay for it?'

'I'd be quiet if I were you,' Shanni said innocently. 'I hardly think you're qualified to judge affairs of this magnitude.'

'Why not?' Jayne demanded, her face flushed.

'And how is it that you class yourself an expert? Are you one of the rebels?'

'That is beside the point.'

'No, it is exactly the point.' Jayne was leaning forward in her seat. 'You happen to be of the lower orders yourself. Is that why you are such a hot-head about paying what is due?'

Shanni tried to keep her voice calm. 'It might just mean that I have more compassion than someone like you, brought up to live on your father's bounty.'

Lloyd took Shanni's hand. 'Look, we don't have to go to this meeting. I'm sorry I suggested it now.'

'No, no,' Jayne said. 'We must attend such an important debate. Who knows? I might even learn something about the rights of the poor.'

Shanni studied Jayne's face, searching for signs of sarcasm, but there were none. Perhaps Jayne Morton-Edwards was not such a stuck-up prig after all, or perhaps she was good at hiding her feelings.

The meeting at the Assembly Rooms was well attended. Shanni caught sight of Dafydd Buchan and thought with a sudden shock of the night she had stayed with Madame Isabelle. Had Dafydd been responsible for the death of Mr Carpenter? He had been angry that the man dared to disagree with him. But, no, it must have been the tragic accident Madame Isabelle claimed it to be.

Dafydd saw Shanni and acknowledged her with a slight tilt of his head. Shanni responded, hoping that Jayne had not noticed the discreet action. Her hope was in vain.

'Ah, you know him. He's one of the rabble-rousers, I assume,' Jayne said. 'Isn't he one of the speakers, Dafydd Buchan?'

'Yes, and he is a very powerful man, too. Remember that.' Lloyd ushered them into a seat near the front row.

Shanni wished he had chosen somewhere near the back where she did not have to meet Dafydd's eye. She was having feelings for Dafydd that were not appropriate in a girl of her station. But, then, what exactly was her station? She no longer knew.

Lloyd leaned closer to Shanni and whispered in her ear, 'Do you know Buchan, then?'

'I have met him once,' Shanni said. 'He might be unpopular but he has common sense on his side, Lloyd.'

'It all depends which side of the argument you support,' Lloyd replied, settling back in his seat.

Shanni listened as the first speaker, a member of the planning committee, outlined the proposals for increasing the tolls at the end of the year. His tone was reasonable and his arguments convincing.

'You surely understand,' he said, 'that we who are responsible for the smooth running of our fair town impose these tolls with the best of motives. We have to improve roads, attend to proper sewerage, but this costs money and we all have to pay to ensure a better future for ourselves and for our children.'

'But what about the poor sods who have to dig into their pockets?' The protest came from someone at the back of the room. Someone called for the man to hold his tongue and uproar broke out.

Chairs were sent flying and one hit a man sitting close to Shanni. He got to his feet bellowing in outrage, and lifted his chair above his head.

'What bastard did that?' he shouted, and Shanni put her hands over her ears. Jayne began to scream.

'We have to get out of here.' Lloyd tried to force a way for them between the crowd, but bodies heaved and fell and a missile spun past Lloyd's head missing him by inches.

Shanni became aware that Dafydd Buchan was suddenly at her side. He caught her arm in a none-too-gentle grip. 'Tell your friends to hold on to each other, form a chain and I'll get you out of here.'

Shanni was dragged through the crowd towards the doorway with Jayne clinging to her skirts like a frightened child. Lloyd followed in the rear as Dafydd pushed and beat his way through the morass of fighting men.

Outside in the cold winter air, Shanni took a deep breath. She looked up at Dafydd fearfully. She knew he was right that the meeting was no place for her and certainly not for a hysterical girl like Jayne.

'Get off home, Shanni,' he ordered. 'You shouldn't have come here. I would have thought you had enough intelligence to expect trouble over such an emotive issue.'

He disappeared back into the hall and Shanni realized that she was trembling. 'Come,' she said. 'Let's do as he says and leave while we can.'

'That awful man knew you!' Jayne said, weakly.

'I might have known you'd be associated with rabble.'

'Be quiet!' It was Lloyd who spoke. 'It was that same rabble who got us out of there alive.' He led the way to where the carriage was waiting, the driver sitting in his seat shivering a little in the cold.

'Sorry, Graves,' Lloyd said, 'I didn't think to tell you to go into one of the inns and warm yourself. Take us home, there's a good man.'

Jayne climbed into her seat, her face white. For once she seemed subdued, her eyes wide with shock. Shanni suddenly saw how frightening the experience had been for a girl who had never seen violence before.

'It's all right, Jayne, we'll be safely away from here and nearing home in just a few minutes,' she said.

Lloyd sank into the seat beside Jayne and put his arm around her. 'Come, come, there's no harm done.' He glanced across at Shanni. 'I was foolish to take you girls to the meeting. I might have known there would be trouble. But, then, you would think folk who attend the Assembly Rooms would be more respectful of each other.'

Shanni sank back against the leather seat and closed her eyes. Between those who were born rich and those born to poverty there was a great divide, and Shanni wondered if it was too great ever to be breached.

CHAPTER EIGHT

Llinos stared out of the window, her hands clasped. A light powdering of snow covered the yard, melting rapidly as it reached the heat of the kilns. The trees were brushed with light, the bare branches tipped with frost. It was going to be a hard winter, and somehow Llinos felt very alone. But, then, she was alone.

Lloyd had gone riding and he intended to spend the night with some friends at the gentlemen's club in the town. Shanni was staying at Madame Isabelle's house and Joe, her dear husband, was away on business yet again.

She bit her lip, wishing he would come home. She was missing him but, worse, she was worried that she was thinking too much of Dafydd Buchan.

Dafydd had called to see her only yesterday. He had told her of the near riot at the Assembly Rooms and his tone had been stern. 'Keep your son and his companions away from political meetings in future. It's for their own good.'

Llinos had reacted frostily. How dare he talk to her like that? And yet, even while she argued with him, told him to mind his own business, she was aware of her attraction to him.

She sighed, bringing her thoughts back to Lloyd. He was balking at returning to college. It seemed he wanted to travel to America to see the place where his father had been born.

Llinos was at a loss as to how to deal with Lloyd. Her son seemed wilful, rebellious, even. When he had returned from the fracas at the Assembly Rooms Shanni had been trailing behind him, looking wretched. Lloyd's clothes were torn and he had a bruise on the side of his face. But he had still been defiant. His father should have been here to give him a good dressing-down.

Llinos lifted her head as she heard the crisp beat of hoofs against the frozen earth and her heart quickened. Perhaps Joe had come home. She heard voices in the hall, but when the maid opened the door it was Eynon who came into the drawing room, his face red from the easterly wind.

'Llinos, I am so angry with Lloyd,' he said, without preamble. 'What was he thinking about, taking my daughter to a meeting of rowdies and villains? I don't want Jayne mixing with such people. She is just a child and innocent in the ways of the world.'

Llinos held up her hand. 'You don't need to lecture me. I agree with you wholeheartedly. In any case, I've already had one lecture from Dafydd Buchan. Please, Eynon, sit down, you're making the room look untidy!' She paused. 'Look, Eynon, I'm as angry as you are about the disgraceful way Lloyd behaved. It was irresponsible of him to take the girls to such a meeting.'

'It's Lloyd who should be apologizing, Llinos,' Eynon said, as he sank into a chair. 'I know they went without your knowledge or consent but, for heaven's sake, impress on the boy that such behaviour is unacceptable.'

'I have spoken to him most severely, Eynon,' Llinos's shoulders were tense, 'but I can no more control Lloyd than I can his father.' She felt a sudden flare of anger: Joe seemed to care more about the son who was living on another continent than he did about his legitimate son in Swansea. He should be here now dealing with the problem, not leaving it all to her.

The front-door bell rang again. Llinos sighed. 'Oh dear, I don't want any visitors at the moment.'

The maid knocked on the door of the sitting room. 'Excuse me, Mrs Mainwaring, there's a gentleman to see you, a Mr Dafydd Buchan, pottery owner from Llanelli.'

Llinos hesitated. She did not want to see Dafydd now. She had thought far too much about him since his last visit.

'Show him in,' she said, reluctantly.

Dafydd entered the room and seemed at once to dominate it. She thought afresh how handsome he was, with his hair just a little long to be fashionable. He glanced briefly at Eynon and nodded, but then his penetrating brown eyes turned to Llinos. She felt transfixed by his gaze. 'Please, won't you join us, Mr Buchan?' Llinos forced a smile. 'I was just going to order tea.' She looked at him. 'Unless you've come to scold me again, have you?'

'I came to apologize for that, Mrs Mainwaring.' He spoke formally but his eyes were filled with laughter now. 'I realize your son is a young man – he no more listens to his mother's words of advice than I would.'

He seemed quite at ease as he sat down and spread out his long legs before him. 'That's a splendid fire, Mrs Mainwaring.'

Llinos glanced at the ornate grate. The fire was blazing with freshly placed logs and the aroma of applewood was pleasantly refreshing. She realized suddenly that Eynon was very quiet.

'I am sorry. Do you know each other?' She made the introductions as brief as possible, and she could tell by the look on Eynon's face that he did not altogether approve of the unexpected visitor.

'Your husband is away again on business, I understand,' Dafydd said. 'How unfortunate that I always seem to miss him.'

He looked her over, his dark eyes taking in every detail of her appearance, and Llinos was absurdly pleased that she had dressed with care. She was aware that her figure was slender still, with the look of a young girl, but there were lines around her eyes and a silver streak in her hair that clearly did not escape Dafydd's shrewd eye.

'Yes, he is still absent. I'm sorry about that, but if there are any specific questions you wanted to ask about the pottery perhaps I would do?'

She saw a tiny smile twitch the corners of Dafydd's lips. 'I think you will do very nicely, Mrs Mainwaring,' he said.

Eynon got to his feet abruptly. 'I think your

tone over-familiar, sir,' he said curtly. 'It would do for you to remember your manners in the presence of a lady.'

'Are my manners lacking, then, Mr Morton-Edwards?' Dafydd's eyebrows were raised. There was a hard edge to his voice.

'Eynon,' Llinos said quickly, 'do you have to leave so soon? Come along, I'll see you to the door.'

If he was surprised by her words Eynon hid it well. 'Yes, I must go. Good day to you, Mr Buchan.'

When they were in the hall Llinos put her hand on Eynon's shoulder. 'Don't worry about Mr Buchan, I can deal with him.'

'I hope so. The man doesn't seem to know his place.'

Llinos smiled. 'Come, Eynon, do I detect a touch of jealousy?' She kissed his cheek. 'You are my dear friend and I know you want to protect me, but I'm not a little girl any longer.'

'Don't let the man stay too long, Llinos,' Eynon said. 'His sort needs discouraging. He's too bumptious by half.'

She watched as Eynon rode away, then returned to the drawing room.

'Your friend is very protective,' Dafydd said. 'I think he doesn't much like me.' He smiled widely. 'He's in love with you, of course. That's why he was so aggrieved at my sudden visit.'

Llinos sat down and clasped her hands in her lap, aware that they were trembling. Eynon had been right: Dafydd *was* being familiar for a man she had known only for a few weeks, yet she was not irritated by his interest. Rather, she was intrigued. 'Eynon is a very old friend,' she said. 'He took it upon himself to look after me when my mother died. When the pottery was in a bad way, Eynon was always on hand to help in any way he could.' She smiled wryly. 'In those early days, when I was trying to get the pottery back on its feet, it was hard going, believe me. It was a case of sink or swim.'

'And you, very bravely, chose to swim.'

Llinos looked at Dafydd from under her lashes and wondered if he was being patronizing, but he met her glance with a switch of his eyes and she felt herself grow tense. She sensed that Dafydd Buchan could be dangerous as well as attractive.

'Did you come to look round the pottery again, Mr Buchan?' Llinos asked.

He stared at her lazily and Llinos felt the heat come into her cheeks. There was a long silence, and then he smiled. 'I would much prefer to stay here and talk with you, Mrs Mainwaring. You are charming and intelligent, and such ladies are rare, I've found.'

He was smooth-tongued, a flatterer with charisma and good looks. Llinos knew that, and yet she warmed to him. She felt like an attractive woman again, not a wife of many years' standing. She realized that it was a long time since Joe had made her feel that way.

'Then, by all means, stay and talk.' She hoped her voice did not reflect her excitement. She wanted him very much to stay, to talk to her about potting, about anything that came into his head. He was an exciting man, intelligent too, and she relished the time spent in his company. That was all that attracted her to him – she needed companionship and the mental stimulation of good conversation.

He talked. His enthusiasm for his work was boundless. He was now producing pottery, he told her, good tableware with colourful patterns that would be exclusive to the Llanelli pottery. He described the designs: some would be stylized flowers and others would be gaily painted farm animals.

Llinos found herself enraptured by his energy and enthusiasm. These were feelings she had lost, the pleasure in the pottery work and the challenge of new ideas.

'Perhaps I will come soon to see your pottery.' Llinos leaned forward in her chair. 'Your patterns sound so exciting.'

'That would be a delight,' Dafydd said, his face revealing nothing. 'I know you would be most appreciative of what my brother and I are trying to achieve.'

'I hope your brother won't mind if I visit. Have you any other family?' Llinos could have bitten her tongue. He would know exactly what she was really asking.

'I have no wife as yet,' he said, and his mouth twitched at the corners.

Llinos felt like a young, untried girl, and as the colour spread hotly from her neck to her face she lowered her head, as if plucking a piece of cotton from her gown. 'I'm sorry,' she said. 'I am being far too personal and we are practically strangers.'

But he did not feel like a stranger. It was as if she had known him for ever.

He echoed her thoughts. 'No, I wouldn't call us strangers. We have the beginnings of a fine friendship, I think.'

'Yes, you're right.' She spoke breathlessly. What was it about Dafydd Buchan that made her feel like a lovely young girl again?

'My brother is married,' he offered. 'Ceri has a pleasant wife and three infants.'

Llinos tried to think of something sensible to say. 'You have met my son,' she said. 'He's my only child. But Lloyd has a half-brother somewhere in America.' Now why on earth had she blurted out what was in her mind?

'I see.' Dafydd looked into her eyes. 'Well, I expect many a married man has dallied a little before the knot is tied. It is no great sin for a man to take a woman before he takes a wife.' He smiled suddenly, and dimples appeared in his cheeks. 'Some even say it is beneficial.'

'Oh, yes? For whom?' Llinos said sharply. 'Not the poor wife, I think. In any case, my husband did his dallying not before our wedding but after.' She paused to gather her wits. 'How did we come to this? I'm mortified to be talking so intimately with you, Mr Buchan.'

'Please call me Dafydd, and there's no need to feel embarrassed. I am pleased that we can talk in this way.' He gave a little laugh. 'Before I met you I was led to expect that Mrs Llinos Mainwaring was something of a dragon. That was far from the truth because here you are, a beautiful lady with fire in her eyes.'

Llinos was suddenly fearful. She was getting into an intimacy that was dangerous. Yet she felt rosy and warm and happy, a woman in the presence of an attractive man who showed a real interest in what she had to say. 'You'll stay for tea?' she asked, and heard without remorse the note of entreaty in her voice. She wanted him to stay; she felt she could have talked with him for hours.

'Alas,' he glanced at his pocket watch, 'my time is short. But may I call again at an arranged time more convenient to us both?' He rose to his feet and Llinos felt a dart of disappointment. 'Then we can talk to our hearts' content.'

She smiled. 'That would be very . . .' she searched for an appropriate word '. . . enjoyable. I hope it will be soon.'

She got up reluctantly, and went with him to the door of the drawing room. He stood for a moment, his hand on the latch, and she was very conscious of his nearness, of the breadth of his shoulders, the power in his dark eyes.

'I will make the visit a priority,' he said. 'It's a long time since I enjoyed the company of a woman so much.' He took her hand and bent to kiss her fingers.

The brush of his lips against her skin sent a thrill of desire through her, and Llinos snatched her hand away. 'The maid will see you out,' she said, in a low voice, afraid to meet his eyes. 'But please call again, soon.'

When he had left, Llinos closed the drawing-room door and stood looking at her reflection in the mirror over the fireplace. She saw a woman with animation in her face, an expression that could almost be described as radiant. It was the look of a woman highly attracted to a man. Had Dafydd noticed? Somehow Llinos felt sure that he had.

'Dafydd.' The name escaped softly from her parted lips. Dafydd, the Welsh for David. A strong name for a strong man. Llinos pressed her hands to her hot cheeks; she was being silly, wicked, lusting after him. And yet, and yet, she just wanted to savour the memory of Dafydd Buchan for a little while.

Llinos sank into her chair and stared at her hands. His lips had touched her skin and she had enjoyed the sensation more than was proper for a mature, married woman. But he liked her, Dafydd really liked her, and she could not wait to see him again.

The next morning Joe arrived home, and Llinos felt a pang of guilt as he took her in his arms and kissed her. But thoughts did not constitute actions; being unfaithful in her mind was not the same as putting those thoughts into practice. If only Joe had been as circumspect.

'I'm glad you've come home,' she said, disentangling herself from his arms, 'although you should have been here sooner if you were to be of any help. It's a bit late now that Lloyd's back at college.'

'Why? What has he done wrong?' Joe asked. He seemed more interested in poking the coals in the grate than in listening to her and her voice rose.

'Your son needs a good talking-to. He's been attending political meetings in the town.'

Joe turned to look at her and she saw afresh that he was a very handsome man. But not as handsome as Dafydd Buchan – or was that thought disloyal?

'That's surely not such a bad thing.' Joe moved to the sideboard and poured a glass of rich red wine. 'What was the meeting about?'

'What else but the price rise at the toll-gates? It seems there was a riot. He might have been hurt.'

'He's spreading his wings. It's what the young do,' Joe said.

'But he was silly enough to take Shanni, not to mention Jayne Morton-Edwards, with him. Eynon was very cross about it.'

'Ah, well, that was unwise. I'll speak to him.' He seemed abstracted, as though his thoughts were elsewhere. Llinos bit back the angry words that rose to her lips, knowing he was thinking about Sho Ka and the son she had borne him.

They sat on opposite sides of the fireplace, Joe in the chair that yesterday had been occupied by Dafydd. Llinos wondered if she should mention his visit but decided against it. The pottery was her business; it was nothing to do with Joe.

'Lloyd's talking about leaving college. Joe!' Her voice was sharp. 'I had to talk him into going back at least until he had had the courtesy to speak to you about it. You are interested in your son's welfare, aren't you? Your legitimate son, I mean.'

Joe looked up at her over his glass. 'Llinos, I'm tired and worried, I can't argue with you now.'

She was suddenly concerned. 'Are you ill, Joe? What is it? What's wrong?'

He rubbed his eyes tiredly. 'It's Sho Ka's child. My child. The boy is sick. I'll have to travel to America. There's nothing else for it – they need me.'

Llinos got to her feet, walked towards the fireplace and stared at the glowing coals without seeing them. How dare he? How dare Joe talk about his other woman and his child as though they were the most important people in the world?

'And how did you find out about this? Come to think of it, how do you know anything about your other family? We never get any letters from them here.'

'That's unimportant.' Joe sounded impatient. 'What's it to you where my letters go to?'

'I am your wife,' Llinos said bleakly. 'Are you keeping the house in Neath in case Sho Ka comes back?'

'Let it rest. I'll have to go to America.'

'Well, go, then!' Llinos spun round to face him. 'Since this squaw woman needs you so badly, you must run to her as you always do.' She longed to tell him that she needed him, too. She wanted a proper husband, who put her first in his life. She stared at Joe. He refused to meet her eyes. Was it over? Was their marriage a sham now?

'Llinos,' he spoke quietly, 'try to be reasonable.'

'Oh, no!' she said. 'I have been reasonable for too long. I am your wife. Lloyd is your son, your *only* son as far as I'm concerned. This other child is growing up in another culture, in the American-Indian culture. He is nothing to do with me or my life here in Swansea.'

Joe sighed heavily. His head was bent and the long dark hair brushed his golden skin. She felt bitter regret for the days when she had been Joe's only concern. He had waited patiently for her and she had married him against her father's wishes. They had shared the rapture of first love, of what Llinos had believed was an all-consuming love. Now he was a different man, a middle-aged man with a mistress, just like all the other men of the town.

'I thought you so fine once,' she said brokenly. 'I loved you with all my heart, Joe, I believed in you.' She swallowed her tears. 'But you are no better than the men who keep doxies, and I am no better than the wives who pretend not to care.' He remained silent with his head bent. 'But I *do* care, Joe, I care very much. So much that I can't bear to think of you in the arms of another woman. If you go to her now, Joe, don't come back.'

She left the room and swept upstairs to her bedroom, her heart thumping with anger and fear. Surely Joe would follow her, would take her in his arms and tell her he would stay, tell her that he loved her and would put her welfare above all other considerations.

Llinos lay in bed for a long time, hope burning in her heart and tears burning her eyes. But Joe did not come.

*   *   *

It was almost a week after Joe had left for America that Dafydd Buchan called on her again. She had been anxious, wondering if she had imagined the interest in his eyes. She need not have worried. The moment she saw him again she knew she had imagined nothing.

Llinos wrapped herself in a shawl and led him around the pottery sheds herself, talking animatedly about her work. 'We have changed our patterns yet again,' she said. 'The people of Swansea seem to like variety.'

'Ah, this is good.' Dafydd held up a newly decorated plate and examined the border of sea-shells with interest. 'I like this sepia tone.' He replaced the plate carefully on the table. 'Once it's fired it will be ready for use, I take it?'

'That's right,' Llinos said. 'We often use transfer prints but occasionally we branch out into something more imaginative.'

'At Llanelli we've acquired the services of a very good artist, a Mr Bartlet. He's using a rose decoration, and very fine and colourful it looks with the soft, loose brushstrokes of the talented artist.'

'I'm sure it will be a great success,' Llinos said, striving to speak calmly, but she was feeling unsettled, wanting something she could not have. Dafydd affected her that way but surely it was just that he engendered the old enthusiasms in her. After all, it was a long time since she had taken a real interest in the potting business.

He followed her to watch the potters at work. He stood close as one of the men threw a freshly kneaded lump of clay on to the wheel.

Miraculously, the pot began to take shape and Dafydd nodded in appreciation. The potter shaped the neck of the vessel with a damp cloth and the lip of a jug began to form.

'I never cease to be surprised at the skill you men have,' Dafydd said.

The potter did not look up from his work. 'It all comes with practice, sir,' he said easily. 'And it's a trade I've followed since I was nothing but a *boy bach*, you see.'

'A small boy,' Llinos translated, forgetting that Dafydd was as familiar with the Welsh as she was. 'Roberts followed his father into the trade. Potting is in the blood, isn't that right, Roberts?'

'Aye, that's right.' The potter slid a wire beneath the jug and separated it from the wheel. 'Now she goes to be baked and eventually we'll have a fine jug and bowl set for some lady's washstand.'

'What about the decoration?' Dafydd asked. 'Will the piece be hand-painted?'

Llinos shook her head. 'We usually use transfer prints on the bigger pieces.' She smiled up at Dafydd. 'That's a skill all of its own, and things can easily go wrong. If the pattern shifts when it's being pressed on to the surface the piece is ruined. Then the kiln has to be just the right temperature or the colour will slip and the decoration will look blurred.'

She made to move on and collided with Dafydd. He put out his hand to steady her and his touch seemed to burn her skin. By the time the tour of the pottery was completed Llinos wondered desperately how she could shake herself free of the obsessive need she had to be with Dafydd. She was a woman of past forty, and she judged that Dafydd was at least ten years her junior. To think there could be anything between them was foolishness.

He needed no encouragement to stay. They took tea together, and before Llinos realized it, dinner was being served. Over the meal they talked about so many things that her head was reeling. She was so happy that she scarcely ate a thing.

At last, with night closing in, Dafydd decided reluctantly that he must go. His horse was brought to the yard but before he mounted he took Llinos's hand. She stood close to him oblivious of the cold.

'You will come to visit me in Llanelli?' Dafydd said.

'I would love to,' Llinos replied at once. 'When is it convenient?'

'Tomorrow?' he asked, his eyes holding hers. 'Make it tomorrow. I don't think I can wait any longer.'

'Tomorrow, then.' She watched as he swung gracefully into the saddle. He was a well-made man with a good breadth of shoulder, a small waist and fine legs beneath his breeches. Llinos felt a stirring of desire, and was as startled by it as if she had made physical contact with Dafydd.

'Until tomorrow, then,' Dafydd said quietly. His dark brows met over his deeply set eyes, his gaze seemed to hold her and she nodded, her heart beating swiftly. 'I'll expect you around four.' Then he was riding away from her. Llinos felt lonely. It was as if a light had gone out. As she returned to the drawing room, she thought of his face, his eyes, his magnetism, and her pulse quickened. She would not sleep tonight, she would think of Dafydd. Tomorrow she would be with him again.

Once indoors, she stared out of the window and smiled. It was a happy chance that Shanni was staying with Isabelle. Llinos had been given the opportunity to be alone with Dafydd, to cement their budding friendship.

Llinos covered her face with her hands. Oh, no, she knew that what she felt for Dafydd Buchan was something far deeper than mere friendship.

CHAPTER NINE

Snow fell in powdery gusts, drifting into pristine shapes against the walls of the garden. Llinos shivered, wrapping her shawl more closely around her shoulders, feeling the bite of the frosty air through her boots. Was it only since she had grown older that the cold had affected her so much?

She watched Shanni as the girl brushed the steps to the house vigorously and with a great deal of laughter as she called comments to Llinos about her progress. Shanni's cheeks were glowing and she looked very beautiful with her hair bright against her white woollen scarf. Llinos wished for spring to come to warm the earth. It would be wonderful to see the glowing daffodils replace the virginal white of the lovely *lily wen fach*. '*Lily wen fach*.' The Welsh name for the snowdrops that grew profusely at the bottom of the garden rolled off Llinos's tongue. As she spoke, her breath misted before her in the chilly air. Winter seemed determined to hold the land in its icy grip. As yet there was no break in the heavy leaden clouds and the ground remained frozen beneath the light fall of snow.

Llinos returned to the house, picking her way carefully up the newly brushed steps. 'These steps are like glass.' She tapped Shanni on the shoulder. 'Get some salt from the kitchen and scatter it over them so it will be safe for anyone who calls.'

And who was she expecting to call? Dafydd? Llinos entered the hall and took off her shawl. Hanging from the stand, the woollen cloth immediately began to drip freezing droplets on to the polished floor.

In the drawing room she pulled off her boots and stretched her feet to the blaze of the fire. She smiled as she heard her mother's warning voice in her head telling her she would get chilblains, putting her feet so near to the flames.

Stubbornly, her thoughts turned again to Dafydd. Llinos had been seen with him on so many occasions now that people were starting to notice. Well, let the gossips talk, she was doing no wrong. In any case, she was only human and needed the warmth of someone who cared. Did Dafydd care, or was she deluding herself seeing more in a relationship than was actually there? But no, she had not misread the signals in Dafydd's eyes. He was falling in love with her.

It was becoming abundantly clear that Joe no longer loved her. He had been gone for almost a month now and still no letter from him. Llinos pictured him with Sho Ka and the child and jealousy burned within her. Joe seemed to think he was above the vows of marriage, he believed he could do just as he wished, even betray his wife with impunity. She stared into the fire, wondering when her husband would come home or even *if* he would come home, and anger began to grow in her.

He should be here, dealing with his legitimate son. Only yesterday a letter had come from Lloyd telling her he was tired of college life but he would put up with it until he had spoken to his father.

Llinos heard the voice of Madame Isabelle in the hallway and popped her head around the door. 'Good day to you, Isabelle. You managed the trip from Llanelli, then?'

Isabelle nodded ruefully. 'It was slow going in this weather but I was glad to get out of the house. The man who supplies me with coal has failed to deliver and the place is freezing.'

Shanni came into the hallway, unlaced her boots and kicked them aside, with little thought for Flora who would have to mop the floor.

'Come along, then, Shanni, let's get to work, shall we?' Isabelle said briskly.

The door to the parlour, grandly renamed the music room, closed and Llinos returned to the warmth of the fire. She listened for the sounds of the piano but all was silent. Isabelle must be instructing Shanni in theory.

She had wondered briefly about Isabelle's suitability as a teacher for Shanni, but if Dafydd Buchan respected her, and he clearly did, then Isabelle must be a woman of great integrity.

Llinos sat up sharply in her chair and her pulse quickened as she heard the clip-clop of hoofs on the driveway. She hurried to the window and her heart leaped as she saw the unruly dark hair and the lithe figure of Dafydd Buchan.

He dismounted from his horse in one smooth movement and handed the reins to the groom. He looked towards the house, as if aware of her gaze, and Llinos darted back into the shadows. She must never show him how eagerly she waited for him to call. He was a young man, he had a business to run, and she understood she could not monopolize his time. But, if she was truthful, she had been aching to see him again.

Llinos sat at her table and picked up a pencil pretending to adjust some designs. She tucked her shoeless feet under her skirts and tried to steady herself.

She heard his voice in the hall and held her breath until the maid knocked at the door. 'Mr Buchan to see you, Mrs Mainwaring.' The girl bobbed a curtsy and Llinos inclined her head, hoping she appeared composed.

'Show him in, please.'

Dafydd came into the room, bringing the cold air of winter with him. He was so alive, so eager to see her that he scarcely waited for the door to close before grasping her hands.

'Dafydd, I'm glad you've come.' Her good intentions to appear composed vanished as she clung to his hands.

'I couldn't stay away.' Dafydd looked down at her for a long moment, then released her. He seated himself in one of the armchairs and stretched his feet towards the blazing fire. 'Am I interrupting anything?' He gestured towards the table and the scattered papers. His dark eyes met hers, and it was as if time stood still, as if they were wrapped in a world of their own, where no outsiders could penetrate. Once she had thought she would always feel like that with Joe. Where had the joy of her marriage gone?

'I've missed you,' she said softly. It had been only a day since they were together but the hours had dragged interminably.

'I've missed you, too, Llinos, my lovely. Will you come out to supper with me?' He sat forward, his face eager. 'You see, Llinos, we have so much in common, and in any case I would be honoured to have such a beautiful woman on my arm.'

Llinos ignored the warning bells that rang in her head. 'Where would we go?' She strove to keep the tremor of excitement out of her voice.

'How about the Grand? I hear they do a fine hot supper with *cawl* to start the meal, made with beautiful Welsh lamb and the finest vegetables from the farmlands in Gower.'

'Delicious!' Llinos said, not caring about supper. What did food matter so long as she was with Dafydd?

'Then to follow there will be fresh cod in butter sauce and for the main course the speciality of the Grand.'

'And what is that?' Llinos asked, her eyes meeting his and holding.

'Beef stuffed with oysters.' He kissed his finger-tips. 'A meal fit for a queen.' Llinos smiled. He was telling her that only the best was good enough for Llinos Mainwaring. It made her feel desirable and beautiful.

'How could I refuse such a wonderful offer?' She glowed, drinking in the attention with such eagerness that it frightened her. Was she being foolish? Was she allowing her heart to rule her head?

'Good!' Dafydd said. 'I shall call for you at seven thirty prompt, then.'

She nodded just as Flora opened the door and brought in a tray containing a jug of steaming chocolate. Llinos glanced at the maid, wondering if she had overheard the arrangement. Even if she had, did it matter? All Llinos was doing was joining a neighbour for a meal in a very public place.

'What do you think of the growing storm about the toll charges, Llinos?' Dafydd seemed at ease, his conversation impersonal, as Flora placed the tray on the table.

'I think the continued rises at some of the toll-gates are scandalous,' Llinos said. 'The prices have shot up in the past months, and I know what it's like to struggle to make a living.'

He nodded, as though well satisfied with her reply. Llinos stared at him, wondering how far Dafydd would go to help the protestors. Did he dress as a woman and attack the gates himself?

'I don't think violence ever achieves anything, though,' she said slowly. 'I can't condone the rebellion by the Rebeccarites.'

'Sometimes words will not suffice.' Dafydd tasted the chocolate and changed the subject. 'This is delicious. You must give me the recipe for my housekeeper. It certainly warms the body on a cold day.' He leaned forward. 'And the company warms the soul.'

Llinos caught her breath. Dafydd had a

compelling way of speaking and there was always a glint in his dark eyes. Was he an anarchist? But that was none of her concern.

'How is the pottery doing?' she asked. He put down his cup and there was a line of chocolate across his moustache. Without thinking, Llinos took up a napkin and moved closer to him, dabbing away the chocolate with a gentle touch.

He caught her wrist and held it. Llinos felt as though his fingers were scorching her flesh. His face was close to hers and they stared into each other's eyes. Llinos held her breath, wanting so badly to press her lips to his.

A sudden loud chord from the piano broke the spell. Dafydd released her hand and she rubbed her wrist unconsciously.

'Shanni is practising her music,' she said, trying to gather her wits. 'Isabelle is a good teacher but she must tell Shanni to use the soft pedal.'

She returned to her seat, her legs trembling as if they had lost the strength to support her.

Dafydd rose abruptly. 'It's high time I got back to work.' He smiled down at her. 'Don't come to the door with me, it's far too cold.' He paused as he reached for the latch. 'Just be ready for me tonight.'

Llinos watched from the window as he rode away, wondering about his words. What was he really asking of her? She smiled as, at the end of the driveway, Dafydd lifted his hand in a farewell gesture. He was so conceited: he had known she would be watching him.

When he was out of sight, she returned to her chair and leaned back, closing her eyes. Was she a

136

fool to dine with Dafydd? Was she playing with fire?

But she would go, of course she would. It was what she wanted, to be with a man who admired her, who found her beautiful and desirable. She felt hot suddenly. The chocolate had brought warmth with it, or was that the effect Dafydd's presence had on her?

She clasped her hands, unaware of the dreamy expression on her face. Tonight she would bathe, dress in her finest clothes, make sure her hair was brushed and silky. She would be at her best when she met Dafydd.

She opened her eyes sharply. She was thinking like a woman enchanted, a woman about to embark on an affair. And, she decided, that was exactly what she was going to do.

'So, you see, Shanni, you must never discuss what we talk about together with anyone else.' Madame Isabelle was pulling on her gloves, preparing to leave. 'The safety, even the lives, of the men could be in danger if the plans were leaked.'

'I know when to remain silent,' Shanni said. She smiled at Madame Isabelle and tucked the piece of paper into her pocket. 'And don't worry, I'll be there.'

'For heaven's sake, keep in the background. Young girls are not usually allowed to be present at the storming of a gate.' She frowned. 'And remember, it's not a tea party, so don't go thinking it's excitement all along the way. Sometimes people get hurt and, though violence is not something I condone, unfortunately it occasionally happens.'

In spite of her warnings, Shanni felt exhilarated at the thought of witnessing at first hand the rebellion of the farmers. Many of the ring-leaders were like Dafydd Buchan, businessmen, well-to-do but with a fire in the belly and the courage to stamp out injustice. Shanni admired Dafydd so much. She wished sometimes that she was older, more sophisticated. Then he might look at her as if she was a woman.

'If there's a challenge of any kind,' Madame Isabelle said, 'if constables arrive, or even if a landowner brings so much as a walking-stick to the scene just run for your life. Do you hear me?'

'Yes, I do understand, Madame.'

'See that you do.' Madame Isabelle moved to the door. 'I shall collect my hat and coat and I shall be off home.' She rang for the maid to see her out. 'Dress warmly, mind. I don't want you catching a chill.'

After she had gone, Shanni sat staring at the piano. She was not thinking of the music but of the meeting to come, the burning of the toll-gate on the Swansea road. Excitement flared within her – she would be seeing Dafydd again. Even if she had no chance to speak to him or even approach him, she would be able to look at him from a distance. He was a hero, a strong man with a fighting spirit that was a joy to behold. He was determined to make the world a better place for the people who could not speak out for themselves.

Shanni felt her face grow hot with anticipation.

It was high time that women took a hand in the affairs that affected them deeply. If money was short it was the women who made ends meet. It was the housewife who boiled up bones to make broth, and dug potatoes out of the meagre soil in back gardens to feed the family. Often, it was the woman who went without. It might take a lifetime to bring about change but at least the revolution had begun and she, Shanni, was part of it.

Llinos felt a flutter of nerves as the carriage drew to a halt outside the Grand. The new young footman jumped from the driving seat and opened the carriage door. She thanked him with a smile. She lifted her hand to Graves. He was a good driver but he was getting old now, and he was training Merfyn in the art of handling a coach and pair.

'Stable the animals and get yourselves a hot toddy in one of the taverns,' Llinos said. 'I might be here a few hours.' She paused outside the shining doors of the hotel, wondering just what she would do when the moment of decision came.

The doorman doffed his hat and swung the door wide, and the warmth of the coal fires encompassed her. At least, that was how she accounted for the blush that seemed to spread over her from head to toe.

He was waiting for her. Dafydd was elegantly dressed in a good coat and narrow, striped *trwsus* that came to the ankles of his good leather boots. He looked so handsome, so self-assured. Llinos smiled. That was one of the things she admired about Dafydd, his assurance that what he was doing was right. She had the feeling that this was going to be one of the most memorable nights of her life.

He came towards her, his hands outstretched. 'Llinos, I've found a nice quiet corner table where we can sit and talk to our hearts' content.' He kissed her fingertips, and Llinos caught her breath. She knew what she wanted and that was to be alone with Dafydd, to play with fire and get burned. She wanted him so badly she could scarcely contain her emotions.

She did not know what she ate. She picked at her food, pushing it around her plate. It was undoubtedly delicious but she was too fascinated by Dafydd's dark Welsh looks to pay any attention to it. She loved the way his brown eyes warmed as they looked into hers. Once, he covered her hand with his own and she looked away, suddenly shy.

'Llinos, will you stay with me tonight?' His voice was little more than a whisper. 'I have booked a room here and, before you ask, yes, I know exactly what I'm doing.'

She took a deep breath. 'Yes, I'll stay.' She swallowed hard, her heart fluttering like a thousand butterflies as Dafydd ordered wine to be taken upstairs.

Llinos stared at the cut of his jaw, at the thick eyebrows marking a strong arch above those wonderful eyes. What was she thinking of? Was she prepared to betray her marriage vows and go to bed with a man she hardly knew?

She almost panicked. Could she really betray Joe? But, then, where was Joe? He was far away in a foreign land with his mistress and his illegitimate son.

Was this an act of revenge, then? No. She wanted Dafydd – she needed his warmth; his desire fed her faltering ego. She would lie with him and she would think of nothing but her lover, at least for tonight.

The bedroom glowed with the light of many candles, and warmth emanated from the blazing fire in the hearth. The heavy drapes were drawn together and it was like a secret world, Llinos decided, a world removed from everyday life. This room would become her universe, just for a few hours.

Dafydd took up the bottle of wine and abruptly put it down again. 'I can't wait any longer, Llinos, I must have you or I'll die.'

He took her in his arms and kissed her, and she was aflame with desire. He kissed her over and over again, then led her towards the bed. Llinos turned for him to undo the hooks on her gown and as she felt his fingers against her skin all her doubts vanished.

Dafydd was a skilful lover. He teased her breasts with his tongue, caressed her belly and all the time he murmured of his passion in sweet Welsh words.

'*Cariad*, sweetheart, I love you.' He took her with passion. She felt desire flood through her limbs, through her belly, through her senses. She clung to his broad shoulders, arching her body, feeling the strong thrust of him, anticipating the glorious moment of release.

When it came, Llinos shuddered, her body

taut, even her breathing still. The waves of pleasure encompassed her, her mind emptied of thought. All she could experience was a sense of rapture and fulfilment.

Afterwards she lay quiescent in his arms. Over the curve of his shoulder she could see the bottle of wine reflecting red in the candlelight. It was unopened. They had needed nothing but each other. Llinos fell asleep in Dafydd's arms.

As the morning light crawled weakly into the bedroom, Llinos opened her eyes and saw Dafydd beside her, lying on his back, his broad chest rising and falling with the even breathing of the sleeper.

The candles had burned out, the fire was grey ash in the grate, and she wondered if, when Dafydd woke and looked at her, she would feel that this was no more than a tawdry affair.

Abruptly, as though sensing her thoughts, Dafydd opened his eyes. He moved swiftly and, in a moment, his body covered hers. Then he was within her, possessing her, making her feel alive and glorious. She forgot everything but the aching flame that only Dafydd could extinguish.

CHAPTER TEN

Joe sat in the lodge with his son lying limp in his arms, tears furrowing his cheeks. He had held Sho Ka this way a few days ago. He had sat with her for hours, moistening her fevered brow, murmuring words of endearment to her. The tribe doctor came and danced around them waving feathers, putting down pouches of dried herbs close to her fevered body, but she was fated to die and Joe knew it. He held her until the spirit of life left her, until he knew she had gone to her final rest.

Their son would soon join her. The boy was still, his eyes closed, the lids almost transparent. He lay inert in Joe's arms, his breathing shallow and his head lolling to one side.

The lodge grew dark, and the flames faded from the fire. Moonlight silvered the doorway and still Joe kept vigil with his son. He sent up prayers to the Great Spirit and to the God Llinos worshipped in her grey stone church on the hills of Wales. But the boy was not destined to grow and thrive: his short span of life was almost at an end. The plague that had ravished the tribe had now claimed him.

Joe was still holding the boy long after the breath had left the child's body. He sent up wordless prayers for the soul of his child. When the dawn light crept into the lodge the women came and took Joe's son from his arms. He sat still, his head bowed as his child, the son he scarcely knew, was borne away.

With the sunrise, the burial ceremony took place. The small boy was laid to rest beside his mother near the flowing river. Long after the women and the braves had paid their respects, Joe remained beside the grave until the light died and the moon returned to spread silver over the river. He continued to pray for the souls of his son and Sho Ka to be taken into the Great Spirit.

He sorrowed as he prayed. His life here with the tribe was gone, dust to dust, as the Welsh preached. So what of the great prophecy his mother had spoken of, that one day his son would rule the Mandan? Had it been merely the rantings of an hysterical old woman?

He stayed in the lodge of mourning for another week, watching the sun rise and set, clearing his mind even though his heart remained heavy. And then as the sun rose on a new morning, Joe packed his possessions, took his leave and began the long ride to the coast.

It was hot, even with the sun sinking beyond the horizon. Joe, seated on the porch of the elegant house, closed his eyes against the dying light. He was grateful to Binnie Dundee for allowing him to break his journey there and rest.

In the past weeks Joe had scarcely closed his

eyes. He had mourned and prayed, and now he felt the need to talk to people who were full of the joy and strength of life. He hoped he could put the past behind him and return to normality. He would still grieve for Sho Ka and the boy, perhaps he would grieve for the rest of his life, but for now he needed the comfort of the living, the comfort he had taken for granted for many years.

Binnie Dundee was a generous host. He was a genial man and yet there was an air about him of success. He had once worked for Llinos at the pottery but had come to America a long time ago to make a new life. He owned huge tracts of land and was proprietor of several productive potteries. He was happily married with fine, growing sons and a wife who adored him. And he was happy to share his good fortune with Joe.

But the time came, late one night as he lay in bed, hearing the sounds of creatures abroad in the dark, when Joe allowed himself to think of home. He let the picture of Llinos, his wife of many years' standing, fill his mind. She was a good woman, a beautiful woman. Would she still want him?

How would his wife feel when he told her that the prophecy had proved wrong, that Joe's son would never rule the Mandan tribe? Unless, a startling thought entered his mind, it was Lloyd, his first-born, who was meant to rule the Mandan. Surely that was impossible.

Thoughts whirled around in his head and he was relieved when the morning light came creeping into the house, filling the corners of the large rooms with warmth. Joe rose and washed, then stood naked at the window of his bedroom, staring out at the new day. A cloud of dust rose on the horizon and he shaded his eyes against the sun to see more clearly. Gradually, the dust gave way to the figure of a man on a horse. And as horse and rider drew closer, Joe saw Binnie lift his hat and wave it in the air.

Joe dressed and made his way downstairs. The maid was cooking breakfast and the smell of food filled the room. Joe never ate breakfast so he took a glass of juice and sat with it on the porch.

Binnie was already seated on the porch swing. He smelt of horses and fodder, and Joe knew he had been about since sun-up seeing to his animals. Binnie scarcely worked in the potteries these days: he left that to the men he employed. His stables were his interest, filled with thorough-bred horses for show and for stud.

Joe glanced at Binnie. His skin was almost as bronzed as Joe's and he looked well and healthy, a man content with his life. Binnie was the sort of man who would never take another woman to his bed: he loved his Hortense with a burning passion, and Joe envied him his uncomplicated life.

'Joe, man, you've hardly slept a wink and you look dog tired. I know the death of your woman and your child is painful for you. Life can be hard sometimes.' He leaned over and rested his hand on Joe's shoulder. 'Go home to Llinos and to your son. They need you.'

How could Joe tell Binnie his inner thoughts? How could he explain that in the darkness of night he feared he had ruined his marriage and lost the love and respect of his wife? 'I'll pack up my belongings tonight and start back first thing in the morning,' he said. 'You're right. It's time I took charge of my life again and settled things at home. I'm grateful to you and Hortense for allowing me this resting time, peace to gather my wits and accept that the death of Sho Ka and the boy was meant to be.'

'It's been great to have a visitor from back home,' Binnie said. 'I love my life here in America but I still think of the old town of Swansea sometimes. And look, Joe, don't think you're obliged to leave. You can stay with us for as long as you like, you know that.'

'Thanks, Binnie.' Joe smiled. 'But I have to get back, I'm longing to see Llinos. I need to see if I can make up for the unhappiness I've caused her. Do you think she'll understand, Binnie?'

Binnie rubbed his tanned cheek. 'Some women need to know the truth.' He spoke thoughtfully. 'My wife is one of them. I was slow in realizing that I should have told her about my first marriage to Maura, how I ran away from my responsibilities.' He shrugged his big shoulders. 'I thought it best to keep quiet, but it nearly cost me my marriage to Hortense.'

'And you think Llinos is a woman who needs to know the truth?'

'Llinos is a brave lady, and I admire her with all my heart. Tell her you're sorry you hurt her. Try to explain that the past is over and the future with her is all-important to you. I expect she will be angry, hurt, and perhaps unforgiving for a

147

time, but Llinos would prefer the truth to any shilly-shallying, I do know that.'

Joe sighed. 'I expect you're right.' He stared up at the sky. 'Perhaps I had better make a start early in case the weather changes.'

'Well, if it rains you must wait. It's no good to man or beast to ride out in a storm.' Binnie got to his feet. 'I'm going to wash the dust off me. See you later.'

Joe nodded, but still he sat looking out into the bare plains dotted with dried brush. It would rain, he could feel it in his bones, and that meant a delay of another few days. All he could hope was that, once she saw him, Llinos would forgive him. But even he knew that it was a faint hope.

Darkness was falling on the streets of Swansea. Low, heavy clouds threatened rain. Shanni shivered, edging close behind the crowd of men. A few other women straggled along, dressed as Shanni was in hooded cloaks. She felt her excitement mount: she was eager to see at first hand what Dafydd intended to do by way of protest. Madame had changed her mind at the last minute and forbidden Shanni to go out. 'On second thoughts it's far too dangerous for you and for me.' Madame Isabelle had been frowning. 'If you were seized by the police where would they come? To me, of course. No, better you stay in your bed this night.'

That was where Isabelle thought she was now, safely in bed. Shanni smiled, remembering how she had climbed from the window of her bedroom and made her way to the place where the men were to meet.

The moon trailed across the sky, dodging in and out of the clouds, and Shanni caught sight of Dafydd Buchan, strange in horse-hair wig and petticoats. And yet, in spite of the clothes, he looked menacing. Some of the other men were wearing women's clothing, 'Daughters of Rebecca', they called themselves, and Isabelle had explained that the name was taken from a quotation from the Bible. Dafydd had a different story: he said that a woman called Rebecca, a huge woman, was the only one in the neighbourhood with skirts big enough to fit a man.

The crowd had reached the gate on the Carmarthen Road at last, and Shanni heard Dafydd shout for the keeper of the gate to come forth from his bed. After a few minutes a startled woman with hair loose to her waist opened the window of the toll-house peering over the sill, her face white in the glare of the torches. 'Go away!' she called feebly, but for an answer, one of the men began to hack at the gate, tearing at its hinges. The cracking of timber echoed through the darkness.

Once the gate was down, a torch was set to it and the wood began to blaze fiercely, sparks shooting into the sky like fairy-lights. The woman inside the toll-house began to scream, and Shanni looked over her shoulder, afraid the noise would attract attention from the wrong quarter. Perhaps the police would come and drag every one of them off to the prison. It was a fearful thought.

One of the men shouted above the noise,

'Justice for the people!' Someone threw a burning torch through the window of the toll-house and immediately the flames sprang upward, smoke billowing from the window. Justice for the farmers, if it came at all, was going to cost some people their lives.

Shanni heard a terrified shriek and the woman ran from the house, her skirts aflame. 'You'll kill me!' she wailed.

A torch was lifted high into the air and Shanni heard it crack as it caught the woman a blow to the side of her head.

'No!' Incensed by the mindless violence, Shanni pushed her way through the crowd but Dafydd was there before her. 'Stop this!' he shouted above the noise of the flames. 'The Daughters of Rebecca want justice not revenge on the innocent.'

Shanni pulled her cloak closer around her, shivering in spite of the warmth of the evening. Dafydd stood before the crowd of men, his arms raised. 'Get to your homes!' he shouted. 'Our work here is done.'

Slowly, the men began to disperse, muttering protests but afraid to disobey. As the crowd thinned, Shanni saw the woman from the toll-house crouching on the ground holding her head. Shanni took a quick breath, the picture in her mind of her mother being shamed by the *Ceffyl Pren*. Anger against this woman who was betraying the cause mingled with pity as she watched her limp back towards the toll-house.

Shanni heard the sudden crack of a pistol and

broke into a run. Breathless, she made her way back across the fields to Isabelle's house. There had been nothing heroic about the action tonight. A defenceless woman had been hurt, her belongings burned. Was that how justice was achieved?

Climbing back into the bedroom was more difficult than Shanni had imagined. The rough stonework tore at her stockings and by the time she swung herself over the sill she was breathless. She dropped through the window into the bedroom, gasping for breath.

'I needn't ask where you've been!' Madame Isabelle was standing in the doorway, a candle in her hand. Her face was white in the pale light, and her voice had a hard edge to it. 'I expressly forbade you to go to the gate.'

Shanni sank on to the bed. 'I'm sorry.' She was still struggling for breath. 'I didn't know there was going to be so much anger and violence or I wouldn't have gone.'

'I told you it would be rough. The men are tired of half-hearted efforts to make landowners see sense, and that is why I changed my mind about you going tonight. Do you realize that if you had been discovered you would have been traced to my house? I would be questioned about how a young lady from Swansea came to know of the movements of the rioters.'

Shanni nodded. 'I do understand and I'm sorry, Madame. I was very foolish and I won't ever do it again.'

'You won't be given the chance!' Madame Isabelle said. 'At least, not from my house.' She sat on the bed. 'I won't allow you to stay here until I have your solemn oath that you will not disobey me again.'

'I'll give it freely,' Shanni said. 'I swear I will never go to a meeting from your house without your consent.'

Madame Isabelle nodded. 'Very good.' She held the candle high. 'Well, now that you have seen what happens to the gates, what do you think?'

'The energy of the men was wasted. Why don't they attack the people who impose the tolls instead of picking on poor defenceless women?'

'The women you speak of, they should not betray their fellows by manning the gates in the first place. It's often their own families who suffer when the tolls are imposed.' Madame paused. 'As for the landowners, their day will come.' She got to her feet. 'Now, try to sleep, or you will be too tired in the morning for your music lesson – and then what will Mrs Mainwaring have to say?'

She closed the door quietly and Shanni was left in darkness. As she undressed she could smell the smoke on her clothes. She grimaced and draped them across the chairs to allow the air to freshen them.

She washed quickly in the cold water from the jug and basin then crept into bed. But she could not sleep. Shanni kept seeing the frightened face of the woman at the gate, and deep within her she knew that, however just the cause, nothing good would come of this night's work.

'So the gate on the Carmarthen Road was burned last night, then?' Llinos sat in the hotel bedroom with Dafydd and pulled on her boots. 'Thank goodness you got back safely. But how did Pedr Morgan know where to find you?'

'I left word with Isabelle,' Dafydd said. 'I should have held the men back, kept them in check.'

But he had been thinking of her. She was more important to him than the burning of a gate. The thought made her feel young again, beautiful and desirable. But it was a dangerous feeling, and a dangerous situation she had got herself into. Llinos felt a pang of guilt: she was a married woman and she was committing adultery, she should be ashamed. But all she felt was happiness.

'Do you know if anyone was injured?' she asked, although her mind was scarcely on the rioters – not when she had her own worries. Joe would be home one day, and how then would she manage to meet Dafydd, with her husband keeping his eye on her?

'According to Pedr, the woman from the toll-house was hit,' Dafydd said, 'but she wasn't badly injured, thank God. I wish the men would show a little restraint. I'm all for the rights of the privileged but last night's violence was unnecessary.'

Llinos felt suddenly anxious. 'Isn't this danger-ous, Dafydd, this rioting and burning down gates?' She answered her own question: 'It must be! Oh, Dafydd, be careful.' She turned to him, rested her head against the warmth of his back. 'I hate to think of you going out there on dark nights. What if the men of the constabulary catch you? And surely the militia have guns? You might be killed.'

'Don't worry.' Dafydd took her in his arms. 'I'm like a cat – I've got nine lives. Now, come along, Mrs Mainwaring, I'd better get you home.'

Yes, home. But for Llinos home was no longer the happy place it had once been. Home in the pottery house took her too far away from Dafydd.

'We'll see each other again soon, won't we?' she asked.

A smile softened Dafydd's face. 'Of course we will. Nothing could keep me away from my little darling.' He kissed her, and the gentleness of his touch, the look of love in his eyes, made her heart swell with happiness. Whatever happened in the future, she would always be glad she had spent this time with Dafydd Buchan.

Joe stared miserably through the window at the rain-drenched plains. There was little chance of continuing his journey if the weather did not change. Even when the rain stopped, the ground would be muddy and the animals would find the going heavy.

'Hey, Joe, come and have a drink of my father-in-law's fine whiskey with me.' Binnie was intentionally cheerful. He was a kind man and Joe knew he would far rather be sitting round the log fire with his family than drinking with him.

'I think I'll have an early night,' Joe said, 'but I'm obliged to you for the offer.' At the door he paused. 'I know I must be outstaying my welcome but I'll be off in a few days and leave you in peace.'

'Nonsense!' Binnie said. 'You're no trouble around the place. Hortense likes you, and the boys enjoy your tales of the Mandan. It all sounds like an adventure story to them, you growing up with the Indians then going off to a fine college in England.'

Joe nodded. 'I suppose mine was an unusual upbringing to say the least. I hardly knew my father. I spent more time with him when he was on his death-bed than I ever did as a child. I used to think he was ashamed of me because he was white and I was of mixed blood.'

'And you were proved wrong?' Binnie asked.

'Yes. He left me his fortune. But, more important than that, we became quite close at the end.'

'Well, now you've got your own little family and I can understand your impatience to get home to them.' Binnie handed him the jug of whiskey. 'If you're determined to go to bed at least take some of this to help you sleep.'

Joe took the whiskey and walked soundlessly up the stairs to his room. He put down the jug and fell back against the pillows. He wanted to sleep but all he could see was his wife, his own Llinos, and clouds of mist wrapped round her, closing him off from her embrace. Had he lost her? The heaviness in his heart told him that something was wrong at home. The sooner he set sail for Swansea, the better he would be pleased.

CHAPTER ELEVEN

Rosie glanced up at Watt Bevan and her heart missed a beat. Even now, after all this time, he was so familiar to her. The cut of his jaw, the way his hair would never lie flat, even the scent of him was enough to remind her of the time she had spent as his wife.

'I vowed to keep away from you, Rosie,' Watt took her hand, 'but I just couldn't. I had to see you, to try again to make it all up to you.' He glanced up at the sky. 'Come on, let's run. It's going to rain.'

It felt good to be linked to Watt, fingers entwined as he drew her towards the cottage. This man was her husband. She had made love with him, slept beside him and woken to find him next to her when the sun rose. But had he ever loved her? He professed love now, but was that just his conscience bothering him? How could she trust him, and how could she trust her own instincts?

'I want you back as my wife, Rosie.' He pushed open the door to her small home. Below, the sea swept into the shore, the clouds raged over Mumbles Head. They had ended their walk just in time because all the signs indicated that a storm was brewing.

Inside the house the fire glowed in the grate, the smell of baking bread emanated from the kitchen and all was welcoming. Could she give this up? Now that she had become independent, how would she adapt to being a wife again? On the other hand, did she want to live out her life alone?

'Sit down, Watt.' She pushed open the door to the sitting room. 'I'll just get changed. The hem of my dress is covered with mud.'

He sat like a visitor on the edge of his seat. He stared miserably at his boots, and Rosie wanted to run to him, to hold him close and tell him she loved him, she had always loved him. She restrained herself, this time. She must be really sure of Watt or she would always be insecure and afraid.

In her bedroom, with the beams cutting across the corners of the room, Rosie studied herself in the mirror. She was still young: her hair was bright, her skin had a bloom of health. She was young enough to bear children, to fulfil herself as a mother. Was that what she wanted?

She sat on the edge of the bed and pulled off her boots, remembering when she had first noticed how handsome Watt was. It had been her birthday and her mother had invited Watt to join them in the small celebration she had planned. Rosie had seen Watt before: he was a manager at the pottery where her mother worked. Then she had never really looked at him as a man, but as he sat opposite her at the table, his face scrubbed, his linen fresh and clean, she had known he was a man she could love.

She sighed. It was all in the past now and she had changed a great deal from the dewy-eyed bride she had once been. Living with Alice Sparks had seen to that.

Dear Alice, she had clung to Rosie in her dying days, the gulf between them breached by friendship. Alice had been born to riches, had enjoyed the best that life could provide, at least until she had married Edmund Sparks. And Rosie, well, she was simply the daughter of a pottery worker.

Rosie changed her petticoats and drew on a clean gown. She found her house slippers near the window and pushed her feet into them. She looked out across the bay: the storm clouds had become blacker and the Mumbles Head was shrouded in mist. Even as she watched the rain began to fall in heavy bursts, flaying the window, driven by the winds coming in from the sea.

'Rosie, are you all right?' Watt's voice startled her. She glanced once more in the mirror before hurrying down the stairs. She knew Watt would want an answer, but was she ready to give it?

He was seated on a chair in front of the fire his head in his hands. He sat up as she entered the room and there was such longing in his eyes that Rosie knew beyond doubt that he wanted her. But would it work this time? She was so unsure of her own feelings and needs, how could she deal with his?

'This would be an ideal time for us to try again, Rosie,' Watt said, watching as she took a seat on the opposite side of the room. 'Your brothers are independent now. My job of bringing them up was over and done with long ago.'

'I'll always be grateful to you for that,' Rosie looked into the fire, 'but I won't make the mistake you made.'

'What do you mean?'

'You married me because you felt you should, not because you loved me. Please don't try to make me feel obligated to you – that's no basis for a marriage.'

Watt made to rise but Rosie held up her hand. 'I have to think everything over very carefully,' she said. 'I'm not sure I'm ready for marriage right now.'

'But you *are* married!' Watt was becoming impatient.

Rosie lifted her head and stared directly into his eyes. 'In name only,' she said calmly. 'And I will decide if and when that is to change.'

Watt got to his feet. 'Very well, Rosie, you win, but don't blame me if I find someone else. I'm only a man, after all, and I need a woman beside me.'

'You need, you need! It's always you, isn't it?' Rosie was on her feet, her hands clenched into fists. Suddenly she was furious with him. 'What about my feelings? What do I need to make me happy? Have you asked yourself that?'

He took a deep breath, but she shook her head at him. 'Just go away and leave me. Find someone else if you haven't done so already.'

'I have been faithful to my vows!' Watt seemed outraged. 'I have led the life of a monk since you left me.'

Somehow Rosie knew he was lying. 'I don't believe that of you for one minute! You can't even tell me the truth now.' She opened the door of the sitting room. 'Go home, Watt. Make what you will of your life. I'm not sure that I have a part in it any more.'

'But, Rosie, can't we just talk?'

'It doesn't seem like it, does it? Just give me time, Watt. I've got a lot to sort out in my mind. Now that I'm back home in Swansea I don't seem to know what I want any more.'

'You've grown up, Rosie.' Watt stood in the doorway. 'You've grown into a fiery, beautiful woman.' As he opened the front door, the rain lashed inwards and he stepped back. 'Lord!' he said. 'I think the heavens have opened.'

'Wait a while,' Rosie said quickly. 'You can't go out in that – you'd be soaked to the skin before you walked half-way down the hill.'

'I'll be all right,' Watt replied harshly. 'In any case, I can't trust myself to stay here any longer. I might forget to behave like a gentleman.'

He stepped outside and closed the door behind him. Rosie hurried to the window and watched him disappear over the brow of the hill. Suddenly she felt lonely. Had she done the right thing in sending him away?

Gloom settled over the house. Darkness had come early because of the lowering clouds. Rosie sank into a chair in front of the fire and it was only then that she realized her eyes were full of tears.

*　　*　　*

Llinos opened her fingers and allowed the letter to fall on to the table. So Joe was coming home. His ship had docked in Bristol several days ago and his first thought had been to visit Lloyd, not to rush to his wife's side. Llinos stood before the window and stared out at the drizzle. It had rained for almost a week now: the bushes in the garden drooped miserably and droplets fell from the overhanging branches of the alder trees. The landscape was grey, misty, and Llinos shivered.

In his letter, Joe had not mentioned Sho Ka. Was he coming home to settle his affairs and to tell his wife he was leaving her?

He would know about Llinos's altered feelings. Joe, in the mystical way he had of knowing everything about her, would know she had been unfaithful. What would she say to him? Did she want to leave him for Dafydd? She had asked the question of herself more than once, but as yet she had no answers.

Was it possible to love two men at once? Llinos bit her lip. She could not give up Dafydd: he was like an addiction. She wanted him badly, wanted his lovemaking, but did she love him? She was confused, uncertain, but one thing was clear: life was never going to be the same again.

'Excuse me, madam, but there's a visitor. Mr Morton-Edwards would like to see you. Are you at home?'

Llinos turned at once. 'Of course, Flora, I'm always at home to Mr Morton-Edwards, you know that.'

Eynon swept into the room and took her hands in his. 'You smell of rain,' she said accusingly.

'So would you if you'd just ridden miles on a reluctant horse, my love. Now, instead of insulting me, get me a good hot toddy, there's a darling.'

'Flora, fetch some glasses and a jug of hot whisky, and tell the cook to put some herbs in it this time.

'Sit down, Eynon, and tell me what's been going on in your life. I've scarcely seen anything of you these past weeks.'

'Well, I've been courting.' Eynon smiled wickedly. 'She's a very polished lady – and this is not one of my usual dalliances.'

'Tell me!' Llinos smiled, even though she was somewhat taken aback by his revelation. Eynon had always been in love with her, or so he claimed. 'Who is this special lady?'

'I met her here, actually, Llinos,' Eynon said. He paused as the maid returned with a tray.

'Just put it down there.' Llinos was impatient for Flora to be gone. When the door closed behind her Llinos prompted him, 'You met her here? Who could that be?'

'Who else but Isabelle?' Eynon leaned forward in his chair. 'Shall I pour the drinks, Llinos?'

She nodded, trying to hide her sense of shock at his words. Isabelle was a cultured lady, there was no doubt about that, but she was hardly Eynon's social equal.

He seemed to know what she was thinking and smiled. 'I know she's not rich but what does that matter? I have more money than I can ever spend. Isabelle has a brain.' He tapped his forehead. 'She can talk about serious matters, affairs of state, that sort of thing.'

Llinos attempted to see Madame Isabelle as a woman to be courted. She was a mature woman . . . but there was fire behind her eyes that belied her calm exterior. 'So are you serious about her?' Llinos asked. 'I mean, serious enough to ask her to be your wife?'

'Yes,' Eynon said. 'Llinos, no-one will ever replace you in my heart, but I'm a man, I have needs, and I'm tired of chasing women who have only fast living on their minds. No, Isabelle will suit me very well, I think.' He lifted his glass and Llinos sank back in her chair, trying not to show how much his words had shocked her.

They sat in silence for a while, and Llinos reflected that nothing remained the same. People changed – even she had changed. Once, long ago, when she stood beside Joe in the little church and made her vows she would never have imagined she would be unfaithful to him.

'What do you think of the troubles, then, Llinos?' Eynon asked. 'It seems another gate was burned and the toll-keeper badly injured. How do the people expect to get justice that way?'

'I suppose there's no other way for farming folk to express their anger,' Llinos said mildly. Being with Dafydd had shown her the injustice of the continued toll rises. 'No-one will listen when they complain that the tolls are ruining them.'

'You sound just like Isabelle,' Eynon said. 'She's on the side of the underdog too.'

'Is she?' Llinos asked. 'I suppose I have never really talked to her. She is simply here to teach Shanni the pianoforte.'

'I told you she was intelligent, didn't I? She tells me that the discontent goes far deeper than the injustice of the tolls. Even in eighteen thirty-four there was unrest among the people because of the Poor Laws.' He sipped his drink. 'But they have to accept that there is a price to pay for progress.'

'A price that they have to pay, not people like us with money in our pockets. Do you think that's just?'

'I have no intention of getting into a debate with you, Llinos. Come, now, tell me what has happened to put the sparkle in your eyes. Have you taken a lover?'

The unexpected question brought rich colour flooding into her face and Llinos looked deeply into her drink. 'I don't know what you mean,' she said. 'I'm just happy because Joe is coming home.'

'Oh, I see. Your beloved Joe has had enough of his foreign mistress and is returning to his wife. I don't know why you put up with it,' Eynon said. 'I've always liked Joe, always thought what a wise man he is, but for him to treat you this way makes me so angry. You are a woman of spirit, Llinos. Don't put up with being used.'

Llinos tried to think of some excuse for Joe's behaviour but there was none. What he was doing to her and to Lloyd was unforgivable.

'So, are you looking elsewhere for comfort, then?' Eynon asked. 'I don't believe you're so bright and sparkly because your faithless husband chooses to pay you a visit.'

Llinos had a high regard for Eynon. He respected her, even loved her in his own way. How would he feel if she admitted to her infatuation with a younger man?

'Just leave it be, Eynon. Tell me more about you and Madame Isabelle.'

He touched his lips with his index finger, and Llinos smiled, knowing him well enough to understand his need for privacy.

'Well,' she said, 'it's about time you settled down with a good woman.'

'I'm not so sure she's a good woman.' Eynon laughed. 'She's certainly got a fiery temper!'

'And yet she always seems so serene,' Llinos said. 'She's a dark horse – a *very* dark horse.'

Eynon nodded. 'She is that. Now, Llinos, tell me what you are doing in the pottery these days. Any new designs in mind?'

She was on safer ground now. She would be quite happy to talk with Eynon about the affairs of the pottery.

'Settle back, Eynon, this could take a long time!'

It was dusk when Joe arrived home and Llinos had been taken unawares. She was dressing for her meeting with Dafydd. Her hair was coiled and pinned, and she was wearing a gown of the blue shade he liked on her.

She heard Joe walk lightly up the stairs. The bedroom door opened and then he was standing before her. 'I feel it in my bones that you have taken a lover,' he said flatly.

Llinos swallowed hard, she had no intention of lying to Joe yet she dreaded hurting him by telling him the truth. 'I am not going to lie to you, Joe. There is someone else but I don't really think it wise for you to know his name,' she said, in a low voice.

'Do you love him?' Joe stood, tall and magnificent, in the dying rays of the sun slanting in through the window. He was bronzed from the sun of the American plains and the white streak in his hair made a sharp contrast with the dark locks hanging over his shoulder.

'I don't know,' Llinos said honestly. 'I enjoy being with him.' She wanted to add that she thrilled to Dafydd's touch but how could she hurt Joe in that way? Men were so protective of their manly image.

'He has a good mind?' Joe asked, thrusting his hands into his pockets. 'I know you would not spend time with a fool.'

'Joe, don't probe too deeply.' She turned away, unable to bear the look in his face. She had to remind herself that he had just come from the arms of his beautiful mistress. Then why did she feel so guilty?

'He makes passionate love to you, does he?' There was a hint of scorn in Joe's voice that set Llinos's teeth on edge.

'Don't ask such questions, Joe, there's no point.' In any case she did not want her relationship with Dafydd to be cheapened by Joe's obvious disgust.

He caught her shoulders abruptly. 'Face me! Tell me you prefer him to me!'

'Take your hands off me!' Llinos pushed him away. 'How dare you treat me in this way? Have you forgotten you've recently come from Sho Ka's bed?'

'I have not,' he said.

'Joe, you have never lied to me before. Why start now?'

'Sho Ka is dead and so is my son.' He walked towards the window. 'I buried them myself near the river my son was named for.'

'I'm so sorry, Joe.' Llinos meant it. She might resent Sho Ka and her hold over Joe but she had never wanted her dead. A thought struck her. 'But that can't be. I thought your son was to be the next ruler of the Mandan tribe.'

'That's what I believed.'

'So all this, all my suffering, my humiliation, was in vain?' Llinos asked. 'I could at least excuse your behaviour on the grounds you were doing what was best for your people but now you tell me it's not to be.'

She sank on to the bed. 'And you have the nerve to lecture me! How dare you, Joe?' She wanted to hit him, to beat at his face with her fists. 'You left me to go and live with Sho Ka, you gave her a son and I accepted it all as your "destiny".' She gave a short laugh. 'That must be the most original excuse for the crime of adultery that I've ever heard!'

'It was what I believed,' Joe said tautly. 'It was what needed to be done, Llinos. At least, that's what I thought.'

'It's your turn to face me now.' Llinos spoke with a calmness she did not feel. Joe turned reluctantly and she saw the glint of tears in his eyes. 'Tell me that you didn't enjoy sleeping with Sho Ka, that you only did it out of a sense of duty.'

He sighed heavily but did not speak. He looked so beaten that Llinos felt sorry for him in spite of the anger raging through her. 'So you did enjoy making love with her, then?' She paused. 'I think I hate you, Joe.' She took a deep breath, determined not to cry. 'I'll have Flora remove your clothes to another bedroom. Unlike you, I cannot switch my affections from one man to another, whoever I happen to be with.'

'Are you saying our marriage is at an end?' Joe asked.

'I don't know. Now leave me. Go to visit Lloyd at his college for a few days. Do anything, but don't stay here looking at me as if I've plunged a knife into your heart.'

Joe walked silently from the room and Llinos sank on to the bed, her face in her hands. She was so confused. She loved Joe, didn't she? She was angry and jealous about the way he had treated her. But her heart raced with excitement as she thought of Dafydd waiting for her to join him at the Grand Hotel.

Should she stay with Joe, try to sympathize with him over the loss of his woman and her child? Anger filled her again and she stood up abruptly. He had never considered her feelings the times he had left her alone to imagine him in another woman's arms so why should she worry about him?

She heard her carriage pull up outside and patted her hair into place. She would go downstairs, take her coat from Flora and soon, in less than half an hour, she would be in the arms of her lover.

CHAPTER TWELVE

Dafydd Buchan stared around him at the industry he had created. The Llanelli pottery was flourishing: kilns were full of pots and the throwers were working long hours to meet demands. Orders were coming in from Carmarthen to Cardiff, and Dafydd, standing in the throwing house, felt a glow of excitement.

'*Sit mae*, Pedr? How are you?'

The potter slid a length of wire under the pot he was making and neatly sliced the clay from the wheel. '*Dda iawn*, sir. Very good,' he repeated in English. 'Damn good clay this last batch, sir. Come from Poole, did it?'

'That's right. Got some pots ready for drying, I see.' Dafydd looked at the row of small vessels that, when turned, would look more like the cups they were intended to be.

'I'd better check on the saggar-maker's house. No good running out of saggars, not with the workload we've got on.'

'Good news for us, sir.' Pedr smiled, and Dafydd nodded to him watching the skilful way the man took command of the wheel, shaping so naturally that the process looked deceptively easy.

Pedr was little more than a boy at eighteen, one of the youngest men in the pottery. He had fiery dark looks and a temper to match. He was an honest man and had brains, too, and that was something Dafydd respected.

'Anything happening tonight with the Daughters, sir?'

Pedr was one of the rebels, a young man with a burning passion to change the world. Changing Llanelli and the surrounding countryside was a difficult enough task, but Dafydd refrained from saying so. 'No, not tonight, Pedr.'

'Right, sir,' Pedr said. 'Pity that the other Mr Buchan won't join us in the fight.' He placed another pot on the table. 'It would add to the strength of the movement.'

'Just be grateful he is not working against us.' Dafydd was well aware that his brother disapproved of the rioting. He deplored the violence done to the gate-keepers, and so did Dafydd, but there was no holding a man with the fire of injustice in his belly. He smiled ruefully. His old nurse used to say that omelettes were not made without breaking eggs. In this case she was right.

'This lot is ready for the hot-house now, sir.' Pedr's voice broke into Dafydd's thoughts. 'Shall I send one of the boys to fetch in some saggars?'

'Aye, do that, Pedr, and come to see me later.' Dafydd left the potting-house and stared up at the kilns. He could feel the heat from where he stood even though the doorways were bricked up neatly to keep the maximum amount of heat inside.

Later the bricks would be taken away and the kilns would be filled with fresh pots waiting to be baked.

Business was good and getting better. Soon he would be taking trade from some of the bigger Swansea potteries. Still, Llinos was doing well. The Mainwaring pottery was a going concern – small, like his own, but with growing distribution facilities.

His face softened as he thought of Llinos. She was a lovely Welsh woman, as passionate as he was. Together they made a good team. Maybe one day it would pay to amalgamate the two businesses. It was something worth thinking about. As for the larger pottery, the one that once belonged to the Morton-Edwards family, its glory days had vanished with the ending of the porcelain production and the return to sturdier wares.

He was going to see Llinos tonight and the thought warmed his heart. He thought of the last evening they had spent together. Llinos had been so eager for him that she had clung to him as if they were never going to meet again. He hated it that she was married to an arrogant foreigner who had no respect for her. The man was half American-Indian and had nothing of the Welsh culture in his blood, none of the poetry of the Celtic nations running through his veins.

Dafydd had never met Joe Mainwaring, had never set eyes on him, let alone spent time with him, but he had no doubt that Llinos had married the man in haste and now was regretting it.

He walked back to the house he had built for

himself a mile out of the small township. It was a fine day and the sun was warming the earth now. There was a speckling of spring flowers: daffodils waved golden heads at him from the grassy slopes. The world seemed full of light, and he knew exactly why that was: he was going to see his beloved in a few short hours.

Shanni stared around the meeting room in the old church on the outskirts of Llanelli. Madame Isabelle had taken charge of the proceedings in the absence of their leader, Dafydd Buchan.

'I have called this meeting because news has come to me of a higher charge to be imposed on the toll-gates.' She stopped speaking as a murmur of anger rose from the roomful of people. 'I know it's unjust, and I know it makes all of us fearful for our livelihood but we must bide our time and wait to see what Dafydd has to say about it.'

'We can't wait. We have to do something about it now.' A young man stood up and Shanni stared at him. She had not met him before and she felt her heart beat faster as his eyes met hers. 'Or are you all content to sit here doing nothing?'

'Keep calm, Pedr,' Madame Isabelle said slowly. 'Mob rule never accomplished anything.'

'I disagree.' Pedr's voice echoed through the room. 'I think we should strike at once, tonight. Don't let the gentry think they have frightened us into submission.'

A chorus of assent rose from the body of the hall. Madame Isabelle raised her hands. 'I know you are impatient for action, but without Dafydd

173

to lead you anything could happen. What if any of you were apprehended by the militia?'

She paused. 'Times are getting harder for people like us. The landowners are greedy for more money but we can't beat them just by force. To make headway we need to be organized. What we don't want is for people to go off alone and make small protests that will scarcely ripple the surface of the rich folks' lives.'

Shanni watched as Pedr returned to his seat. Somehow she knew he would not listen to Madame. He was going to do something tonight and, with a rush of excitement, Shanni knew she would be with him.

As the meeting disbanded, Shanni made her way towards Pedr, who was talking quietly to some of the men. He stopped speaking when he saw her and his eyes met hers questioningly. 'I want to help,' she said breathlessly.

Pedr smiled, and he looked even younger and much more handsome when he was not scowling. 'What? You'll fetch us a brew of beer or something, is that it?'

'No!' Shanni was indignant. 'I want to come with you tonight.'

'What makes you think we're going anywhere tonight?' Pedr folded his hands across his chest. 'And, even if we were, why should we take a slip of a girl?'

Shanni glanced over her shoulder and saw that Madame Isabelle was deep in conversation with one of the older men. 'If anyone has a horse for me to ride back to Swansea I can get hold of some pistols,' she said.

'Your father can afford pistols?'

Pedr was laughing at her, and Shanni wanted to smack his face. 'Don't patronize me!' she said. 'I live with Mrs Mainwaring, pottery owner, and I happen to know there are good pistols and shot kept in the cabinet in the hallway.'

Shanni had heard the gossip about the reason for those pistols, how once Mr and Mrs Mainwaring had been attacked and almost killed. Now the guns were kept where they could easily be reached.

'Oh, Mrs Mainwaring, is it? We've all heard of her, haven't we, boys? Dafydd knows her very well – very well indeed.'

A laugh went up from the others in the group and Shanni frowned at them, puzzled by their reaction. 'Are you interested or not?' she asked sharply.

'Aye, we're interested.' Pedr leaned closer. 'Look,' he said quietly, 'I'll provide a horse – better still, I'll get two horses and I will ride with you to Swansea. What time?'

'Make it about an hour. I'll have to make an excuse to go home to Swansea so that Madame Isabelle won't suspect anything. Remember, when we get to Pottery Row you must pretend you're going home to Llanelli,' she said.

'That's settled, then.' Pedr turned to the other men. 'Meet me at the Dwr Coch gate at midnight. We'll show the owners they can't put up the tolls whenever they feel like it.'

Madame Isabelle was too wily not to be suspicious. 'I don't like the idea of you travelling to Swansea with only a young man for company,'

175

she said, when Shanni told her she was going home.

'I feel I should get back, though,' Shanni said. 'I noticed Mrs Mainwaring was not looking well when I left this morning.' She lowered her voice. 'I think she and Mr Mainwaring have quarrelled.'

'Hm!' Madame Isabelle looked at Shanni. 'I can't say I'm surprised at that.'

'Why? What do you mean?' Shanni was intrigued. What could Madame Isabelle know that she did not?

Madame Isabelle changed the subject. 'Very well. If you're so concerned I suppose you'd better get back before it's dark. When Pedr calls for you I'll have a word with him to make sure he sees you safely home.'

'I'm sure he will,' Shanni said.

'Well, I'm not!' Madame Isabelle said. 'I've heard of the ways of some of the local boys. This idea of "bundling", for example, it's not proper, not for a young lady like you, and I don't want that handsome scamp Pedr leading you astray.'

'I'm not that foolish, Madame.'

'We are all foolish when the blood is hot.' Madame Isabelle looked away.

Shanni hid a smile. Living in the heart of Swansea as she did, Shanni had heard the gossip about Madame and Eynon Morton-Edwards. It seemed that bundling, or sleeping together while courting, was not restricted to the lower orders. 'I'll behave, I promise,' she said. 'You know I wouldn't let Pedr or anyone else lead me astray. I won't even let him close enough to kiss my hand.'

'Do I have your promise on that?'

'You have my solemn promise,' Shanni agreed. 'I have no intention of spoiling my life by falling into the arms of the first good-looking boy I see.'

'Right, then, I accept your word that you will abide by a strict moral code.' Her voice softened. 'I have seen too many young girls ruined by unscrupulous men, and I have no intention of seeing you become a fallen woman.'

Shanni's heart missed a beat as she thought of her mother, dragged out to be shamed on the *Ceffyl Pren* before all the neighbours. 'I saw my mother die from trusting with the wrong man,' she said, thickly. 'You have nothing to worry about where I'm concerned. I will not let any man near me until I have a ring on my finger.'

Madame Isabelle, usually undemonstrative, took Shanni in her arms. 'I know. I'm sorry, that was thoughtless of me.' She held Shanni away and looked into her face. 'I only have your good at heart,' she said. 'I know it's not easy to take control of your feelings when love strikes you for the first time, but remember, it does not always last. Some gold turns out to be fool's gold, remember that.'

'Thank you for worrying about me.' Shanni moved away. 'I'd better get dressed for the ride back to Swansea. As you said, it's better to travel before it gets dark.'

Later, as Shanni allowed Pedr to help her up into the saddle of a young gelding she looked back at Madame Isabelle standing in the window and waved. She hated deceiving her, yet Madame would go crazy if she knew what Shanni was really up to.

It was good to ride beside Pedr, to feel the breeze brush the curls from her hot face. He was a silent young man and, glancing at him, Shanni decided that she liked him. She liked him very much indeed. But, then, he was only a potter and both Mrs Mainwaring and Madame Isabelle wanted her to have the best in life. That meant finding herself an affluent husband.

'You'll know me next time,' Pedr remarked. He did not look at her, he was scouring the surrounding hills and fields as though fearing an attack of some kind.

'I'm coming with you tonight,' Shanni said.

That made Pedr turn sharply in her direction. 'You are certainly not coming with me,' he riposted roughly. 'I'll have enough to do without looking after you.'

'You won't have to look after me!' Shanni cried indignantly. 'I am more than capable of looking after myself.'

'No.' Pedr was obdurate.

Shanni drew her pony closer and looked up at him, her eyes full of laughter. 'No Shanni, no pistols,' she said evenly.

'Look, do you really think Mrs Mainwaring will allow you to go with me?' he said. 'She might believe that you changed your mind about staying in Llanelli the night but not that you are just making a hasty visit home. That is bound to make her suspicious.'

'She won't be in,' Shanni said.

'How do you know?'

'I just do. Now, are you going to agree to my terms or do we just forget the whole thing?'

'All right, then,' he said. 'But don't get in the way and don't start crying if anyone gets hurt, right?'

'Right.' She halted her horse as Pottery Row came into sight. 'We'd better lead the horses along here,' she said, 'or we are likely to run over a couple of children.'

She waited for him to lift her from the saddle and pushed his hands away as soon as her feet touched the ground. Pedr was an attractive man and he knew it. It would be just as well to keep her distance from him. 'Come round the yard to the back,' she said. 'One of the grooms will feed and water the horses. You can have a bite to eat in the kitchen, if you like.'

Pedr touched his forelock. 'Yes, Miss, anything you say, Miss.'

'Funny!'

The cook stared at them in stony silence when Shanni led Pedr into the kitchen. 'Who is this young man and what is he doing here?'

'His name is Pedr. He's brought me on a message for Madame Isabelle,' Shanni lied glibly. 'Will you give him something to eat? He's got a long way to go back home tonight.'

'Aye, I suppose I can find something in the larder. Go on, Flora, get some bread and cheese for the young man, and stop staring at him as if he's been sent from heaven especially for you.'

'I'll see you outside later,' Shanni said, glancing at Pedr. He had settled himself at the kitchen table as if he owned the place.

'You haven't got a nice bowl of *cawl*, have you?' His smile was devastating. 'I've got just the right appetite to appreciate good soup, and I can see right off you're a wonderful cook.'

She looked coy. 'I suppose I could heat some up, if you'll wait a minute.'

Smiling, Shanni left them to it, walked through the passage and into the sitting room. She opened the desk drawer and took out the bunch of keys: one of them must fit the cabinet in the hall.

It took only a few minutes to locate the right one and it slid into the lock easily. Carefully, Shanni took out the pistols. They had been cleaned until they shone and, no doubt, they were ready for action. In any case, Pedr would only use them as a threat: he was far too sensible to shoot anyone.

She went outside to where the groom was brushing down the horses. Without looking up at her, he continued his work. 'Poor beasts haven't been brushed in a long time. Look like tinkers' animals, they do.'

Shanni put the pistols in the saddlebag of Pedr's mount then went through the back door into the kitchen.

'I've put the things Madame wanted into your saddlebags,' she said. 'I'll see you outside before you go to give you some instructions.'

She hurried upstairs and changed into her darkest clothes. Her black bonnet had feathers on it but they were darkest green and it was doubtful that they would be noticed. She tied back her hair and twisted it into a knot at the back of her head.

Then, with her bonnet swinging from her hand, she left her room and hurried downstairs. She skirted the kitchen and left by the back door. She had no intention of allowing the cook or anyone else to question her movements.

Outside, it was growing dark and, soundlessly, Shanni made her way to the stables. She peered into the darkness, trying to focus on the yard. There was no sign of the groom or the horses, and no sign of Pedr Morgan. She had been fooled! He had taken the pistols and gone back to Llanelli without her.

'Damn you, Pedr Morgan!' Shanni whispered. She looked into the stables. The horses were unsaddled and settled for the night. One moved restlessly, rustling the straw and whickering softly. Shanni knew that, alone, she would be unable to deal with the complicated tack. She had no idea how to attach the bit and bridle, let alone how to secure the saddle. Slowly, she turned away from the stables and let herself into the house through the back door.

'Llinos, my lovely, I want to have you with me always.' Dafydd was surprised at the tension in his voice. Only weeks ago he would never have believed he would utter those words to any woman. 'Now that your husband is back you can tell him you want to be with me.'

Llinos looked up languidly. 'Don't talk now, Dafydd. Just hold me and kiss me and tell me you love me.'

Dafydd slid his arm under her neck and felt the sweet heaviness of her hair against his arm. 'I do love you, and I want you so much I don't ever want to let you go.'

She snuggled into the warmth of his body and Dafydd took a ragged breath as he felt the softness of her breasts against his chest. He kissed her, and as the passion began to grow in him he knelt above her, lifting her closer so that he could take her with ease.

He heard her moan and knew that she was as hungry for him as he was for her. He made love to her slowly, teasingly, until she begged him for release. He heard her small cries of passion with a feeling of power. He, Dafydd Buchan, was bringing this lovely woman beneath him to the heights of pleasure – pleasure she had surely never experienced before.

Later, they lay side by side and he closed his eyes. 'I love you, Llinos Mainwaring,' he said softly. 'And you are the first woman to hear those words from my lips.'

'I know, I believe you, my love.'

'And you? How do you feel?' Dafydd rose on to his elbow and looked down into her face. 'Do you love me, Llinos?'

'I don't know, Dafydd,' Llinos said. 'I'm so confused I don't know what I feel any more. I only know that I want to be with you, I long for your touch and I love the way your hair curls around your face.'

'Will you tell your husband about me?' Dafydd waited with bated breath for her reply.

'He knows,' she said. 'He has no idea who you are, but he does know I have a lover.'

'Am I more than just a lover, though?' Dafydd

knew he was asking for reassurance, like a small child wanting approbation from a difficult parent.

'Of course you are.' Llinos sat up against the brass rail of the bed. Her breasts were firm white globes in the dimness of the candlelit room. 'I have never had any man except my husband.' She touched his cheek, and he took her hand and kissed her fingers. 'I know I thrill to your touch, Dafydd, I know that I can't wait to see you again. Is that love? I don't know any more.'

'It will do for now,' Dafydd said, pleased at the warmth in her voice. 'And you are not making love with *him*?'

'No, Dafydd, I've sent him away for a while until I can decide what to do with my life.'

'Good.' He kissed her mouth, sending up a prayer of thanks that the unknown husband had gone away. A sudden urgent rapping on the door broke the silence. He slid out of the bed and pulled on a robe. He glanced back at Llinos, his finger on his lips, warning her to be quiet.

He opened the door cautiously. Only one other person knew he was at the hotel and that was his brother.

'Pedr!'

The young boy was white-faced in the light of the lantern he held above his head. 'You must come, Mr Buchan. It's your brother – he's been hurt.'

'Ceri hurt? How?' He saw Pedr shake his head. 'Wait for me.'

Dafydd closed the door and began to dress. 'I'll have to go and see what's happened to Ceri,' he said, 'but I'll be back as soon as I can.'

He paused at the door, looking back, absorbing the vision of the tangled hair and flushed cheeks of the woman he loved. The pain in his heart at the thought he might lose her was like a knife thrusting through him.

CHAPTER THIRTEEN

As soon as Shanni stepped into the hallway of Madame Isabelle's house she knew that something was wrong. Madame was pale, her eyes had dark shadows under them and her usually immaculate hair was tied carelessly in a loose knot at the back of her neck.

Shanni looked at her in alarm. 'What's happened?' She followed the other woman into the parlour and waited until the door was closed. 'Something's wrong. What's upset you, Madame?'

'Everything is wrong.' Madame Isabelle spoke in lowered tones in case any of the servants overheard the conversation. 'That's what comes of the men going out without a leader.'

'The men went riding without Dafydd? Why wasn't he with them?' Shanni remembered to keep her voice low.

'Dafydd had other things on his mind.' There was an edge of sharpness in Isabelle's voice. 'Still, the men should have waited for his orders and then all this trouble wouldn't have arisen.'

'So there was a fight, then, at the gate?' Shanni could have bitten off her tongue as soon as the words left her mouth.

'What do you know about it?' Madame Isabelle caught her arm. 'Did you know of the plans to burn down the Dwr Coch, then?'

'I just heard some of the men talking, I didn't know when they were going out, though.'

'You should have come to me!' Madame Isabelle said tightly. 'We could have avoided all this upset.'

'I didn't know much about it,' Shanni said quickly. 'I thought it was a normal meeting. Was anyone hurt?'

'Pedr Morgan has a fine black eye and a fat lip for his pains.' Isabelle sank into a chair, her hand over her eyes. 'Worst of all, Ceri Buchan was badly injured. The poor man was taken to the infirmary with gunshot wounds.' She sighed. 'Heaven knows what will come of it.'

'What was Dafydd's brother doing there?' Shanni asked in surprise. 'I thought he didn't agree with the protest.'

'He doesn't!' Isabelle said sharply. 'The good, brave man was trying to bring order. He might be on the wrong side of the fence, so to speak, but Mr Buchan is a fine man.' She took a deep breath, rather like the ones she took when she was about to demonstrate with her fine voice how a note should sound. 'Look, Shanni, I think it best if you don't visit me here at Llanelli, at least for the time being. I don't want to involve you in anything dangerous.'

'Oh, please, Madame, don't stop me coming,'

Shanni said. 'I promise I won't get into any trouble.'

'You knew more about the movements of the men than I did,' Isabelle said. 'You could so easily be in trouble right now. Come, Shanni, tell me the truth. What did you know about the raid?'

Shanni hesitated. 'I knew what the men were planning but only because Pedr and I are friends and he told me about it.'

'Don't get ideas in that direction, my girl,' Madame Isabelle said warningly. 'Pedr is a good lad but he's a firebrand.'

'Oh, I know that,' Shanni said. 'Pedr is all right but I have more in common with Lloyd Mainwaring than I do with Pedr Morgan.'

'Well, perhaps you are aiming too high if you have a fancy for the Mainwarings' boy.' Madame Isabelle's tone had softened. 'I think they would prefer a bride like Jayne Morton-Edwards for their son.'

Shanni was piqued. Madame Isabelle was saying she was not good enough for Lloyd. On the other hand, it would hardly do for her to know that Shanni had fallen in love with Dafydd Buchan. 'Don't worry, I'm not chasing after Lloyd, he and I are just friends. In any case, I know Mrs Mainwaring has plans for me to meet some of the boys from the better families of Swansea. Not the gentry, of course, but tradesmen's sons and the like.'

'Well, then, you've clearly got your head screwed on the right way. I tell you what, I'm expecting a visitor so what if I give you a basket of goods to take to Pedr Morgan and his mother?

Mrs Morgan would welcome some fresh butter.' Madame Isabelle pulled the silk cord and a bell echoed faintly from the back of the house. 'I'll get Sarah to put some in a basket, but I warn you, don't overstay your welcome and don't walk home in the dark.'

'I won't.' Shanni was excited. Seeing Pedr would give her the chance to find out exactly what had gone on at the Dwr Coch, or the Red Gate. She waited in a fever of impatience until the maid brought in the basket, covered with a pristine white cloth. The girl bobbed a curtsy and handed it to Shanni.

Madame Isabelle accompanied Shanni to the door and gave her directions to Farmyard Lane. 'Be sure to act like a lady, now,' Madame Isabelle said. 'Use the fine speech I've taught you and make us all proud of the way you conduct yourself.'

'Don't worry, I won't let you down.' Shanni set out from the smart area where Madame lived, feeling like a lady bountiful with the basket over her arm. Pedr would be surprised to see her at his door and she only hoped she would have the chance to talk to him alone.

The streets of Llanelli were unfamiliar but Shanni was as at home there as she was in Swansea. The sound of the Welsh tongue was all around her, the people were friendly and some called a greeting to her. It was a bright day, a day when she should remember the debt of gratitude she owed to Mrs Mainwaring as well as to Madame Isabelle.

As Shanni left the leafy suburbs and made her

way to where the kilns of the Llanelli pottery shimmered against the sky she realized, perhaps for the first time, how far she had come from her days in the slums of Swansea. She had almost forgotten the poverty, the grime, the lack of food. She had become used to good clothes, to folk waiting on her, bringing her well-cooked meals. She had grown used to privilege and saw how easily she could lose it if she stepped out of line.

The potter's house was one of a row of crouched, small-windowed cottages. The narrow doors and the low lintels revealed how cramped living conditions must be. Even so, compared to the place where Shanni had been born the pottery cottages were respectable, grand, even. The doorsteps were scrubbed, the windows cleaned until the glass shone, and Shanni knew that the women fought a constant battle with the clay dust from the pottery.

Mrs Morgan turned out to be a white-haired lady but with a glow in her dark eyes that reminded her of Pedr.

'I hope I'm not intruding, Mrs Morgan,' Shanni said pleasantly. 'Madame Isabelle heard that Pedr was poorly and asked me to bring a few goodies for him.'

'Oh, *Duw*, so come in, Miss.' Mrs Morgan bobbed a curtsy and Shanni wondered afresh at how far she had come from her roots. Now she spoke in the cultured tones of the gentry. She was dressed in fine linen and her shoes were made of well-seasoned leather. All the trappings of a well-brought-up young lady had made her respectable in the eyes of the poorer people.

She handed the basket to the old woman. Poor Mrs Morgan would never realize that working people were as good as the gentry any day. The rich had just grasped at life for themselves.

The inside of the house was sparkling clean. The small front room was furnished with a polished mahogany chest of drawers and a worn sofa. A small table stood near the window holding a vast plant that threatened to overflow and fill the tiny parlour.

'Pedr, there's a young lady to see you. Are you decent, *boy bach*?'

Pedr was seated in an armchair in the tiny kitchen. He wore only a flannel vest and working breeches. His arms were bare and muscular and covered with curling dark hair.

'*Dewch i mewn*,' Pedr said. 'Come in, I won't bite.' He smiled painfully with swollen lips. 'Shanni, sit down and, Mam, stop dithering and get us some of that tasty blackcurrant cordial you made, won't you?'

'*Siaradwch Cymraig, boy bach.*'

'Mam wants me to speak in Welsh. She doesn't understand much English,' Pedr said.

As soon as Mrs Morgan left the room, Shanni sat close to Pedr. 'Tell me what happened. By the look of your poor face you got a fine beating.'

'Let's say a gate accidentally fell on me, Shanni.' His smile was cheerful in spite of his bruises; one eye was almost closed. 'Gates have a funny habit of falling down when you take an axe to them.'

'And Mr Ceri Buchan was there, that was unexpected. What happened to him?'

'*Darro!* Mr Buchan should never have been there. We weren't to know he would be passing the gate at the very time we meant to do the business.'

'Will he be all right?'

'Aye, he'll survive. He's got plenty of money for doctors, hasn't he?' He sighed. 'Still, Dafydd won't like it that his brother got hurt, and he'll blame us for going ahead without him.'

'Where was Dafydd, then?'

Pedr gave her a dark look. 'You don't know?'

'No! I wouldn't be asking you if I did.'

Pedr leaned closer and as his lips brushed her ear Shanni resisted the temptation to pull away from him. 'Our Dafydd has been fishing in another man's stream,' Pedr whispered. 'He's having what you posh people would call "an illicit affair with a married woman".'

'What?' Shanni was startled. A pain spread from her heart to encompass her entire body. 'Who with?'

'Mrs Mainwaring. Who else? Don't tell me you didn't know – and you living in the same house as her? Everyone is saying her husband's left her over it, and who can blame him?'

'No!' Shanni moved away from Pedr as his mother returned to the room carrying two cups of cordial. Shanni took one, but her hand was trembling. It could not be true. Dafydd and Llinos Mainwaring lovers? It was impossible.

'Thank you, Mrs Morgan. *Diolch yn fawr,*' she repeated in Welsh. But her mind was racing. 'She's too old for him,' she said to Pedr. 'It must be a mistake. What would Dafydd see in a woman

191

of her age?' But the more she thought about it, the more she realized Pedr was telling the truth. Mrs Mainwaring was a woman of taste and culture, and Dafydd would be more her sort of man than Joe Mainwaring, who was half Indian. 'No wonder Mrs Mainwaring is giving me so much freedom,' she said. And no wonder there was a bloom about Mrs Mainwaring, these days.

'Haven't you noticed anything wrong between husband and wife, then?' Pedr said, and he was laughing at her.

'Well, I thought they had quarrelled over something because Mr Mainwaring came home from America and then, after a few days, he left the house again.'

It all added up, now that she thought about it. How could Mrs Mainwaring cheapen herself by having an affair with a man so much younger than herself?

'Sinking in now, is it?' Pedr winced. 'Damn my eyes!' he said feelingly, touching his face lightly. 'Trust me to be in the wrong place at the wrong time.'

'Well, I'd better get back to Madame's house.' Shanni hoped Pedr did not notice how agitated she was. 'She told me not to be out too long.' She suddenly felt ill, and the more she thought of Dafydd with Mrs Mainwaring the more angry and hurt she became.

'Ah, Madame Isabelle is a wise woman. She knows I have my eye on you, my girl.'

Shanni made a half-hearted attempt to smile: it would not do to let Pedr see how upset she was.

'Don't try to fool me, Pedr Morgan. I know you have your eye on half the girls in Llanelli!' She moved to the door. 'When do you think you'll be able to work, Pedr?'

'In a day or two,' he replied. 'As soon as I can see to put a piece of clay on the wheel I'll be there.'

Mrs Morgan showed Shanni out. 'Thank you kindly, Miss,' she said, in halting English. 'And tell Madame I am . . .' she hesitated, trying to find the word in English '. . . grateful.'

Shanni walked rapidly away from the narrow streets. The clay dust in the air made her cough, and it was difficult to keep back the tears – she was so angry! How could Mrs Mainwaring be so sly, so immoral? She was cheating her husband and it did not seem to bother her one bit. She went about her everyday tasks as though nothing had happened.

Shanni was glad to return to the more pleasant area where Madame lived, where trees grew fresh and green and where flowers coloured the hedgerows. She enjoyed a fine standard of living now, she reminded herself, and angry though she was, she must do nothing to jeopardize her position. Still, it would not be easy to disguise her feelings of disgust. Mrs Mainwaring was supposed to be a lady born yet she was carrying on like a loose woman. Money and position did not make a lady of anyone.

Shanni clenched her fists; she would be going home to Swansea in the morning. Graves would come to fetch her and take her back to the big house, to the luxury she had grown accustomed to. But Shanni would never forgive Mrs Mainwaring for what she'd done. She had taken away the only man Shanni would ever love.

'Dafydd, don't blame yourself. You couldn't have known any of this was going to happen.' Llinos sat up in bed with the silk coverlet pulled over her breasts. Outside the hotel the rumble of carriage wheels and the calling of street vendors heralded the morning. 'The men acted without your permission and your brother was unfortunate enough to be hurt. I don't suppose anyone meant to fire a gun – indeed, I'm surprised any of the protestors would be in possession of one.' She paused. 'But, in any case, you can't blame yourself for anything that happened when you weren't there.'

'Perhaps I should blame myself, though,' Dafydd said edgily. 'I should have been there. You are distracting me from my objectives, Llinos. I should have my mind on other things instead of lusting after you.'

'Oh, and is that how you think of your involvement with me?' Llinos was cut to the quick. 'Just another woman to take to your bed. I had hoped I meant more to you than that.'

Dafydd returned to the bed. 'Of course you do!' He took her face in his hands. 'I could take my fill of women who would offer me the comfort of their body,' he kissed her lightly, 'but you, my Llinos, are special. That's why I came back so early this morning to be with you.'

She knew he meant it. Dafydd was a well-to-do, intelligent man. He was also very good-looking.

As he rightly said, he could have his pick if all he wanted was a woman in his arms.

'I must go.' Dafydd left the bedside and took his coat from the large cupboard. 'I still have work to do. We can't all sit back in luxury and allow the pottery to run itself.'

He was teasing and she knew it. 'Ah, you slaves to industry, how difficult your lives must be.' She threw back her head and laughed, her happiness restored.

Dafydd stopped at the door. 'I don't think you understand how very beautiful you are,' he said softly, 'with your hair tumbling over your white shoulders and the look of a woman fulfilled in your eyes.' He opened the door abruptly. 'If I don't leave now I never will. Until later, Llinos.'

Llinos washed and dressed at her own pace. Later she would walk to the shops and treat herself to some new undergarments. She felt the colour rise to her face as she imagined Dafydd removing her shift and her corset and laying her on the bed so that he could gaze at her body. He loved her so much. He would never stray, not in the way that Joe had.

Joe. The thought of him was like a knife wound. 'Oh, Joe!' Llinos sank on to the rumpled bed and put her hands over her face. 'I never meant to be unfaithful but you hurt me so much, Joe. Our love turned sour when you took another woman to your bed.'

Swallowing her tears, Llinos stood before the mirror and brushed her hair into place. At the door, she stood for a moment looking round the hotel bedroom. Was this a shallow illicit affair? Or did Dafydd really love her?

The thought of going back to her home in Pottery Row held no appeal for her yet soon Graves would be fetching Shanni from Llanelli, they would meet in the large emporium in town, and after their shopping was complete Graves would drive them home. Home. It seemed an empty word and, all at once, a great sadness filled her heart.

Shanni was already seated behind the ornate glass windows of the emporium tea-rooms when Llinos arrived. She glanced up as if sensing Llinos's presence and, though she made a pretence of smiling, there was something mutinous about her expression. She looked like a child who had been denied a treat.

'Mrs Mainwaring, I'm glad you've come. The waiter has been giving me odd looks, wanting me to give an order or something,' she said at once.

Ah, so that was the problem. 'I'm sorry, am I late?' Llinos allowed the man to draw out a chair for her. She glanced up as she peeled off her gloves. 'Thank you, Wesley.' She took her seat and accepted the menu he held at a deferential distance from her face. 'I think I'll just have a pot of tea and some lightly toasted bread. What will you have, Shanni?'

'The same, if I may, Mrs Mainwaring.'

As the man walked away Llinos leaned forward. 'I think the time has come when you could be less formal. Please call me Llinos. Being addressed as

Mrs Mainwaring makes me feel a hundred years old!'

'Oh, I don't know if I could get used to that.' Shanni did not meet Llinos's gaze. 'You are much older than me, even older than my mother was. It would seem disrespectful to call you by your Christian name.'

Llinos sat back in her chair feeling as though she had been slapped. She swallowed her anger and forced a light note into her voice. 'Tell me, how did your visit to Madame go? Did you learn a great deal of music and shall I hear the results of your tuition when we go home?'

Shanni's mouth twisted into a grimace. 'I'll never be really good at the pianoforte, not like Madame.'

The waiter brought the pot of tea along with a tiny milk jug and sugar bowl. He placed the silver tea strainer beside Shanni and smiled. 'Would you like to pour the tea for your mother?' he said kindly.

Llinos was as shocked as if water had been thrown in her face. Only this morning she had lain in her lover's arms, listening to his compliments, and had felt reborn. Now this man was assuming she was Shanni's mother.

'I am the young lady's aunt,' she said, forcing a smile. She leaned back in her chair, feeling all of her forty years. To most people she was a woman past her prime: she was the mother of a son a little older than Shanni – why was she trying to fool herself into believing she was young and beautiful? 'Come along, Shanni.' Llinos tried to lighten the mood of the moment. 'Did anything unusual or exciting happen while you were with Madame?'

'Well,' Shanni hesitated, 'there was an incident.'

'What sort of incident?' Llinos had heard what Dafydd had told her about the fracas at the gate but it would be interesting to discover what Shanni knew of the business.

'Well, it was the servants gossiping.' Shanni seemed evasive. 'One of the maids said someone got shot. I think Mr Ceri Buchan was injured, though I'm not sure.'

'I see.' Llinos had the distinct feeling that Shanni knew more than she was telling. 'Are his injuries serious?'

'I don't really know, Mrs Mainwaring. Madame doesn't encourage gossip.'

'But Isabelle is very friendly with the Buchan brothers, is she not? Surely she would be concerned about one of them being injured.'

'If she was she wouldn't tell me. She is a very forceful lady. She has warned me about gossiping. She says it's dangerous at times like these.'

There was a note in Shanni's voice that troubled Llinos. 'Let's have this tea, shall we?'

Even though her heart was not in it Llinos spent an hour in the emporium buying materials for day and evening gowns. As the seamstress measured Shanni it became apparent how much the girl had grown since she had lived at Pottery Row: her skin had a healthy glow and her figure was maturing rapidly. She was at least an inch taller than she had been even a few months ago. It was clear that she had matured in every way. Somehow, Llinos found the thought disconcerting.

Llinos was relieved when at last Graves drove the carriage into the yard at the back of the house. As she stepped down to the ground, Llinos saw the groom was leading Joe's horse in the direction of the stable. Her heart sank. So he had come home, had he? Now she would have to make excuses to go out, and Joe would see right through her lies.

She gave herself a mental shake. He had been the first one to break their marriage vows so why should she feel guilty? She lifted her head defiantly. She had nothing to reproach herself with.

She became aware that Shanni was staring at her and when she turned to look at the girl there was a definite gleam of malice in her eyes. It was almost as though Shanni knew of her discomfort and revelled in it.

'Come along, let's get indoors,' Llinos said briskly. 'I can't spend all day on you, girl, I do have other things to do.'

She strode into the hall, feeling a mood of depression darkening the day. It had started badly and, by the look of it, was going to get worse.

CHAPTER FOURTEEN

'So, Buchan is your lover, then?' Joe was standing near the fireplace in the drawing room, his elbow resting on the ornate marble mantelpiece. He looked every inch master of the house and tears welled in Llinos's eyes for all she had lost.

'Shanni thought it her duty to tell me. The poor child is worried about your reputation while you, clearly, are not. Do you love him?'

For a moment Llinos was angry with Shanni. How dare the girl interfere? 'I suppose Pedr Morgan told Shanni about us. Why couldn't he keep a still tongue in his head?'

'Do you love him?' Joe repeated.

'I don't know.' She sank into an armchair and wrapped her arms around herself. 'I don't really know what I feel for Dafydd, but I do know I can't give him up.'

She glanced at Joe. He was as handsome as ever, his body lithe and slim as the day they first met. She ached for the time when they had shared a beautiful untarnished love. That innocent time before Joe broke his marriage vows.

'You've come here to see Lloyd, not me, I

suppose?' she asked. 'You know he'll be home some time today, don't you?'

Joe nodded, and Llinos looked away from him feeling a deep disappointment: Joe still had the power to hurt her.

'Perhaps we should try to share the same room, for Lloyd's sake,' Llinos said, but as soon as she had spoken she regretted her words. She saw Joe smile ruefully.

'That would be asking too much, Llinos,' he said. 'How could I lie in the same bed as you and not touch you?' His voice hardened. 'And how could I lie with you knowing you had come straight from the arms of another man?'

Llinos sat up straight, anger making her heart pound. 'The same way I put up with you when you came from the arms of Sho Ka!' She stood up abruptly and walked to the door. 'Joe, how do you think I felt when you went off to live with another woman? Do you think I was happy about it? No. I was furious, humiliated. I felt old and unwanted. You have a lot to answer for, Joe, believe me!'

She expected him to say that his affair had been different, that men were different, but he remained silent. Joe was a fair-minded and sensitive man, and he knew how much he had hurt her.

'At least I am making a pretence of respecting our marriage.' There was an edge of bitterness in her voice. 'I haven't moved in with my lover and shamed you before the world.'

'Ah, so that is the crux of the matter.' Joe's voice was raised. 'Your pride was damaged because I took another beautiful woman. Is that it?'

Llinos wanted to hit him. She took a deep breath. 'I suppose that was part of it. Do you think I wanted other women pitying me, ridiculing me because I was a woman who could not keep her man?'

'Most of the men of Swansea have mistresses.' Joe moderated his tone. 'Their wives accept it – indeed, some are grateful for it.'

'And I thought you were different,' Llinos said. 'I thought our marriage was made in heaven. Like a fool I believed in you, believed you would be faithful, come hell or high water. I can't believe how stupid I was.'

She left him and went into the hall, not seeing the sunlight casting shadows on the mellow wood of the floor, not even glancing in the mirror as she passed, perhaps because she could not face herself. She walked slowly up the stairs. She felt old and tired.

What was she doing with a man so much younger than herself? Was she searching for her lost youth? But no, her feelings for Dafydd went far deeper than that. In any case she was not old. Women of forty often married and lived a long and healthy life.

And, in any case, Dafydd wanted her, needed her. The thought brought a flush to her cheeks. Dafydd was such a wonderful man, such an ardent lover that he made her feel desirable, even beautiful.

But her moment of happiness was transient. In her room she sank on to the bed and put her head in her hands. What would Lloyd think of her if Joe chose to tell him the truth? He would doubtless take the stand that any man would take, even a young man, that men were entitled to their comforts but wives were expected to remain chaste.

Perhaps for everyone's sake she should stop seeing Dafydd. She rejected the idea even as it formed. She could not give him up. Dafydd had given her back her joy in life and, more, he had given her back her confidence.

Llinos heard the sound of carriage wheels outside and her spirits rose. Lloyd was home. She went to the window, looked down and saw her son. Graves retrieved the luggage then led the horses away to the stables.

Llinos hurried downstairs and met Lloyd in the hallway. '*Cariad!*' She hugged him, having to reach up to put her arms around his neck. 'My darling, you've grown so tall I hardly know you.' She kissed his cheek and the scent of him reminded her of Joe. She had loved Joe so much . . . and perhaps she still loved him.

'Hello, son.' Joe opened the door. 'I've poured you a good measure of whisky. I expect you need it after your long journey.'

In the drawing room they sat and talked together. To any outsider they would have appeared to be an ordinary happy family. They talked about Lloyd's education, about his love of sport, about the time when he would leave college to make his way in the world.

'And how are you, Mother?' Lloyd was staring at her. 'You look a little pale. Aren't you well?'

Llinos forced a smile. 'I am very well, Lloyd, but I'm getting to be an old lady, remember.'

'Never! Not my mother!' Lloyd said loyally. 'You look like a girl, without a hint of grey in your lovely hair.'

'You are not the only one to think your mother beautiful, son,' Joe said. His eyes met hers and Llinos sent a message to him not to say anything about Dafydd – at least, not yet.

Shanni came into the room like a whirlwind, bringing with her the scent of the outdoors, of the early roses, and Llinos smiled at her in gratitude.

'Lloyd!' Shanni hugged him then settled herself on the sofa beside him. 'How was college, and have you found a lady-love yet?'

'Oh, here we go.' Lloyd's expression spoke volumes. 'You're just like a sister, teasing me about my love life before I've even unpacked my bags!' He tilted his head on one side. 'Mind, you've grown up a bit. I might even take a fancy to you – what do you think of that?'

Shanni pushed his shoulder playfully. 'Oh, yes? You're so handsome I expect all the girls fall into a faint when they see you, don't they?'

'I don't really know.' Lloyd was smiling. 'We college boys don't get many young ladies falling at our feet.'

Llinos glanced up at the clock. She had only an hour before she must leave to meet Dafydd. Should she send one of the maids to tell him she could not see him? No, Lloyd would have his own interests. He would not sit indoors, not on such a fine evening.

'Any plans for tonight?' Joe had caught her glance and read her thoughts.

Llinos faced him defiantly. 'I have as a matter

of fact,' she said. 'I have arranged to visit a friend. Do you mind, Lloyd?'

'Of course I don't mind. Do you think I want to sit around like a child tied to Mother's apron strings?'

Llinos swallowed her guilt. 'I should hope not. Your father and I have brought you up to be a man, and so far you haven't disappointed us.'

'Well, that's a relief! Do you hear that, Shanni? I'm not in danger of being cut off without a penny, not yet at least!'

He rubbed his hand through his hair in a gesture reminiscent of Joe, and Llinos wished the clock could be set back to when they were a happy family.

'Well, parents, I'm going to wash the dust of the journey away and change into fresh clothes.'

He pulled Shanni's hair as he walked past her, and she smacked his hand playfully. 'Stop that, Lloyd, I'm not a child any longer.'

He smiled. 'Oh, sorry. For a moment I forgot you're all grown-up.' He winked at her as he left the room.

'I'd better go upstairs and change, too,' Llinos said. 'I didn't realize how late it was.'

She hurried from the room and lifted her skirts to climb the stairs. Her head was spinning. Part of her wanted to stay at home with her family yet she could not bear the thought of disappointing Dafydd. Once in the privacy of her room the tears flowed again. Llinos lay on the bed, wondering if she would ever be truly happy again.

Some time later she left the house and climbed into the carriage without a backward glance.

Lloyd was quite happy to sit and eat a light meal with his father and Shanni to keep him company.

Dafydd was waiting for her in the hotel bedroom. He opened the door and immediately took her in his arms. 'I was so afraid you wouldn't come.' He kissed her passionately, his tongue probing, his hands warm on her back as he pressed her closer.

She closed her eyes. Whatever happened, she had to keep seeing Dafydd or she would fade away and die.

'Let me make love to you.' Dafydd undressed her slowly and, when she was naked, loosened her hair. 'Perfect,' he said. 'You are a perfect woman. Do you know that, Llinos?'

He quickly stripped off his own clothes and stood before her, his arousal clear to see. His skin was not bronzed like Joe's but lightly tanned. His body was young and strong, his shoulders broad, his hips slim. He was not as tall as Joe but he gave an impression of strength that, if once unleashed, would move mountains.

'Come here,' he said, in a throaty voice. She went into his arms and closed her eyes as he trailed his hands across her breasts and down along the flat of her stomach.

'So lovely, so very lovely.' He bent and kissed her neck, then tenderly pressed her back against the bed. He bent his head and took her nipple into his mouth. Llinos moaned softly. She wanted him so much, wanted him to possess her, to fill her and drive away pain and guilt and anger.

As he entered her, Llinos cried out in pleasure.

He was so strong, so powerful; he aroused feelings she had thought were dead. He was a more vigorous lover than Joe: Dafydd took her with abandon but with great skill. He moulded himself into her. Surely all this joy could not be wrong? Llinos cried out as waves of delight raced through her loins and to her breasts and filled her head with nothing but sensation.

When they lay quietly together, entwined in each other's arms, Llinos wondered if, in the heat of passion, she had forgotten that the heart must be touched as well as the senses. With Joe everything had been perfect. He was as skilled as Dafydd but with a finesse that Dafydd did not yet possess, Joe had touched her very soul as well as delighting her body. And yet she had not been enough for him.

'You're very quiet,' Dafydd said softly, his breath ruffling the curls around her face.

'I'm sated with passion,' she whispered. 'I am too exhausted by lovemaking to think of anything else.'

He held her close. 'And love – do you love me, Llinos?'

She felt a stirring of unease. How could she answer Dafydd honestly when she still did not know the answer herself?

'Dafydd, am I not with you every minute we can spare?' she said. 'My son came home this afternoon and I've left him to be with you. Isn't that enough?'

He kissed her gently. 'How would it be if I bought us a little house, a place where we could meet without fear of intrusion?'

Llinos was suddenly frightened. She had not envisaged anything as permanent as a love retreat. Yet Dafydd was being more sensible than she was. In the hotel there was always the danger of meeting someone who would recognize them. 'Leave it just for now, Dafydd,' she said. 'I don't want to make any big decisions on the spur of the moment.'

'You don't have to decide anything,' Dafydd said. He raised himself on one elbow. 'Look, my little darling, my *cariad*, I know this love between us might not last. You are married and have responsibilities, but allow us to be together in comfort for as much time as we have.'

'As you wish, Dafydd.' Llinos clung to his strong shoulders, pressing her face into the warmth of his neck. 'Find us a house, if that's what you really want.' And even as she spoke the words, she wondered if she had gone one step too far.

'Well, Lloyd, tell me about your conquests then,' Shanni teased. 'How many girls have you taken into secluded spots to make love?'

She was sitting beside him in the sunlit conservatory. The warmth of the spring sunshine was pleasant and the green of the plants hid them from view.

'Mind your own business.' Lloyd tweaked her nose. 'Good thing my parents are both out otherwise you would shock them.'

'Don't you believe it,' Shanni said. 'Your parents are wiser than you think, Lloyd.'

'Never,' Lloyd insisted. 'My parents are from

old stock. They have stronger principles than people of our generation.'

'Oh, Lloyd, you must know your father kept a squaw woman some time back. Everyone in Swansea knows about it.'

'I hope you don't gossip about my family, Shanni.' Lloyd's jaw tightened. 'What my father does is his own business.'

'And your mother?' Shanni felt a devil of mischief inside her. She knew she should be careful not to goad Lloyd too far but his smugness was beginning to annoy her.

'My mother is above reproach,' Lloyd said, in a hard voice.

'Do you think so?' Shanni saw the colour rise in Lloyd's face and knew he was really angry with her. It would be wise to leave the subject of his mother well alone. 'I expect you're right,' she said mildly. 'Now, talk to me about your love affairs. There must have been many.'

'What about your love affairs?' Lloyd's good humour returned. 'How many young lads have you rolled in the hay with?'

'None!' Shanni was shocked. 'I'm a good girl, Lloyd Mainwaring, not a loose woman.'

'Well, I hear a great deal about the behaviour of the young courting couples.' He pinched her cheek. 'I have heard that they share a bed even before the wedding bells ring.'

'Well, that might be true of some girls, Lloyd, but I've never met a young man I'd share anything with, let alone my bed.'

'And when you do?'

'And when I do I will keep my own counsel just as you are doing.'

Lloyd sighed. 'Look, Shanni, enough of this silly talk. What exactly has been happening here in Swansea since I've been away?'

For a moment Shanni wondered if he had heard rumours about his mother but on reflection decided to take the easy way out. 'Well, there's been a lot of talk about rebelling against the toll prices,' she shrugged, 'but then, that's nothing new, is it? People always object to paying out money, especially money they can ill afford.'

'From what I hear there's been more than talk,' Lloyd persisted. 'Come on, Shanni, I know you've been mixing with Dafydd Buchan's protestors so don't play the innocent with me.'

'How did you hear of this?' Shanni demanded.

'That is not important,' Lloyd replied. 'What is important to me is your safety.'

'I'm safe enough.' Shanni frowned. How did he know so much about affairs of the town yet not that his mother had taken Dafydd as a lover? But folk were guarded about that sort of thing. The Mainwaring family was wealthy and even though the townsfolk did not approve of Joe Mainwaring they accepted that Llinos was born and bred in Swansea so had a right to be respected.

'No-one is safe when pistols are used indiscriminately.' Lloyd took her hand. 'You know I'm aware of the injustice suffered by the farmers, Shanni, and perhaps more aware than you realize.'

Shanni swallowed hard, thinking of the pistols she had borrowed. Well, they were safely back in place now. 'So,' she said, 'are you willing to see good men ruined by the greed of the land-lords?'

'No, but neither am I raising my voice and losing my head over it.' There was a hint of reproof in Lloyd's voice.

'I'm sorry, you're right, of course. And let me reassure you that Dafydd Buchan is a sensible man. He is also a fine, brave man. I admire him tremendously.'

'I can see that. And the young potter, Pedr, do you admire him as well?'

He was teasing her again and Shanni's shoulders relaxed. 'That is my business, Lloyd Mainwaring. And you are not my father so don't try to lecture me about the company I keep.'

'I am your brother, by choice if not by blood. I care about you, Shanni. I have seen your intelligence, your spirit, and I don't want you to throw everything away on a man who is not worthy of you.'

'I don't know what you mean.' Shanni avoided his eyes.

'Yes, you do, you know very well.' Lloyd sat back in his chair. 'Don't lie to me, Shanni, I can read your mind. You've fallen in love.'

'I like Pedr, of course I do, but as for love, I don't know what that is any more.' She did not fool Lloyd, but it was easier to let him think she had a fancy for Pedr. He was hardly likely to approve of how she felt about Dafydd Buchan.

'Now, to serious matters. When is the next meeting?'

'Why do you want to know?' Shanni could have

bitten back the words even as they were spoken. 'What meeting are you talking about?'

'You know very well, and if you don't tell me I'll go and see Pedr. Or maybe I'd better speak directly to Dafydd Buchan.'

'How would you find him?'

'I happen to know he is spending the night in an hotel in the town.' He smiled wickedly. 'With a lady-love, so I've been told. There is nothing stopping me seeking him out, is there?'

Shanni caught her breath. She could not allow Lloyd to intrude in Dafydd's private life. Lloyd would have murder in his heart if he caught Dafydd with Llinos.

'All right, I'll tell you.' She sighed heavily. 'But I don't want anyone else knowing. Do you understand?'

'I am not a child, Shanni,' Lloyd said evenly. 'I am not simply curious either. I want to help fight injustice, just as you do.'

Shanni nodded. 'I know you mean well so, if you must, you can come with me tonight.' She looked over his well-cut coat and the straight woollen trousers. 'You'll have to borrow some clothes from the stable-boy, otherwise you'll be taken for a landowner and shot.'

'I agree to your terms, madam. And I won't mention Buchan or Madame Isabelle outside this room.' Lloyd bowed his head then looked up and met her eye.

Shanni realized then that Lloyd knew more than she had imagined. It seemed that the only thing he did not know about was his mother's affair with the leader of the rebels.

When he did find out, would he still be so keen to fight for justice with the Daughters of Rebecca? Well, it was all in the hands of the fates now, but Shanni had the feeling that Lloyd's presence did not bode well for the cause. She stared at him, her feelings mixed. Should she warn him now about his mother's involvement with Dafydd? But her mouth was dry and the words would not come.

The spell was broken when Lloyd took her hand and pulled her to her feet. 'Come, let's go outside and enjoy the lawns and the lovely sunshine. For heaven's sake, take that worried look off your face. Everything is going to be all right, you'll see.'

Somehow, Shanni doubted it.

CHAPTER FIFTEEN

'I was only trying to help, Dafydd, I hoped to prevent bloodshed.' Ceri was lying against the pillows, his face ashen. 'I don't know how you could allow yourself to mix with the rabble that call themselves Rebeccarites, troublemakers to a man.'

'Others call it fighting for justice.' Dafydd concealed his irritation. He had already felt the sharp edge of Hilda's tongue. Ceri's wife was a martinet and her personality had provided Dafydd with a good enough reason to move out of the house and find one of his own. He felt warmed by the thought of the house where he and Llinos could be private, could indulge in their romance without prying eyes watching them.

'In any case,' Dafydd said, 'the men are usually more restrained. The use of firearms is rare.'

'No-one was restrained at the Dwr Coch.' Ceri spoke wryly. 'It was razed to the ground, and if I had not intervened the toll-house would have been burned down with the keeper in it.'

Dafydd patted his brother's hand. 'I know you mean well, Ceri, but do try to think of the rights of the poor wretches struggling to make a living out of the land. Times are hard enough for them as it is because of the Poor Law.'

Ceri waved a dismissive hand. 'The Poor Law! The blame for anything and everything is placed squarely on the back of the Poor Law.'

Dafydd was tempted to tell his brother that people like themselves suffered no hardship from such laws but he took a look at Ceri's face, shadowed with fatigue, and got to his feet. 'I'd better be going,' he said, with forced joviality. 'Things to do, you know.'

He moved towards the door and Ceri's voice halted him in his tracks. 'Some foreigner came looking for you. Did Hilda tell you?'

'No, she didn't. What did he want?'

'Hilda didn't ask. She felt he didn't look best pleased, whatever his mission.' Ceri frowned. 'You haven't been playing with the wrong lady again, have you? I certainly wouldn't like to think of you with a foreign woman.'

'Don't you think it better if I decide for myself on that sort of thing? I wouldn't want you and Hilda to be involved.'

'It seems we *are* involved.' Ceri's tone was dry. 'You've dragged me into more trouble than any of my children ever did.' He smiled suddenly. 'But you're not a bad brother for all that. Go on with you now. See to the pottery, make sure everything is running smoothly. And, Dafydd, look after yourself. I don't want you killed by an irate husband.'

Dafydd lifted his hand in farewell. 'Ceri, my man, you worry too much.'

He left the house and walked round the back of the rambling building to the stables. The groom was waiting for him, talking softly to the horse, smoothing the animal's powerful neck. It whinnied softly into the darkening night. 'Thank you, Cradoc.' Dafydd took the reins, mounted with one easy movement and settled himself comfortably in the saddle. 'And good night to you.'

As he rode away along the curving pathway that led to the ornate gates of his brother's property, he felt a thrill of happiness. Soon he would see Llinos, he would hold her perfect body in his arms, he would kiss her lips, her full breasts, and then he would take her, as he always did, with unbounded joy and the knowledge that this lovely woman was his.

A cloud passed over the moon, obscuring the light. Dafydd frowned, remembering his brother's remark about the foreigner visitor. It had to have been Joe Mainwaring, Llinos's husband. What had he thought he could achieve by going to Ceri's house? Well, whatever it was, he would not be allowed to interfere in Dafydd's life. There could be no question of him giving up Llinos, he loved her far too much for that.

As Dafydd guided his horse through the gates a figure on a white mount confronted him. The long hair and the strong features, illuminated in a brilliant glow of light as the clouds glided away from the face of the moon, identified the man as Joe Mainwaring.

'Mainwaring, what are you doing here?' Dafydd

was unafraid. He might be bedding the man's wife but Mainwaring did not deserve her. He had been neglecting Llinos and he had a bastard child by an American-Indian squaw. It was an insult to a beautiful white woman. 'You want to talk to me, I presume?' he asked. His voice had a hard edge to it. 'You have involved my brother and I don't like it. Say what you have to then leave the property.'

'I would have come directly to you but I might have met my wife.' He paused. 'It's about Llinos I'm here. I want you to leave her alone.'

The man's voice was surprisingly gentle, and Dafydd peered at him trying to read his expression. 'And if I don't?'

Dafydd heard Mainwaring sigh. 'One day, in the not too distant future, Llinos will be devastated by the pain of losing you. The shock will be far greater for her than if you made a clean break of things right now.'

'You're talking rubbish, or is that a threat?' Dafydd edged his horse closer to the mare and her rider. 'If it's a fight you want then I'm more than happy to take you on. Pistols or swords?'

'I don't wish to fight you. If I wanted to harm you I have enough methods at my fingertips to make a very good job of it.' Mainwaring spoke gently but the conviction in his tone assured Dafydd that he meant every word. 'All I want is for you to think of Llinos. She will lose you, and one day soon, so why not end it now?'

Dafydd shuddered. He was not usually superstitious but something in the appearance and the voice of Mainwaring was unnerving. Before

217

Dafydd could ask any questions the pale horse and the man with the long hair had vanished.

Dafydd sat for a long time until his horse, unsettled by the inactivity, began to paw the ground. 'Come on, then, girl, let's get home.' He urged the horse to gallop, as if he could outrun the feeling of dread that had come with the foreigner's words.

'Damn you, Mainwaring!' he shouted into the wind. 'I want Llinos as my own, and to hell with the likes of you!'

'So you dared to go and see him?' Llinos walked across the carpeted room then back again twisting her hands together. 'How could you, Joe?'

'I wanted to warn him.' Joe spoke levelly. 'He will come to a bad end and I don't want you involved in any rabble-rousing.'

'I have asked you to leave this house and to leave me in peace.' Llinos sank into a chair. 'I simply won't have you interfering in my life making threats to Dafydd as you did.' She looked up at him. 'At least I didn't threaten your woman, did I?' The edge of bitterness was still there in her voice, and in her heart.

Joe came towards her and took her hands in his. 'So my faithlessness still has the power to hurt you? That shows you still feel something for me, Llinos, doesn't it?'

'Don't read too much into my words. I can't give Dafydd up just as you couldn't give up Sho Ka.' She pushed herself up from the chair and moved to the door.

Joe remained standing before the fire, his head

held proudly and his eyes following her every move. 'You are going to him now, tonight?'

'Yes,' Llinos said. 'Don't try to stop me.'

Joe did not speak. He simply stared at her as, with anger in her every movement, she strode out into the hall.

Later, as the coach jogged its way towards the small house in the Strand, which Dafydd had rented as their love-nest, Llinos thought about Joe, about the stricken look on his face and, in that moment, guilt was a heavy burden on her heart.

But she reminded herself that he had left her, abandoned her time after time, and rushed off to his mistress. He had betrayed her with every day he had spent with Sho Ka. Llinos had had no-one to lean on: when she had most needed love and support Joe had been away on yet another trip.

When the coach stopped outside the house Llinos stepped down eagerly. The young maid ushered her into the drawing room where Dafydd was waiting for her. Before the girl had even closed the door he took Llinos in his arms and buried his face in her neck.

'I thought he would stop you coming to me,' he said, and his voice was gruff with emotion. 'I prayed to all the saints that you would be strong.'

'What did he say to you?' Llinos touched Dafydd's cheek. 'Did he threaten you?'

Dafydd released her and led her to the plump sofa. He shook his head and sat beside her, his arm around her shoulders. 'In a way I suppose he did. He practically told me that my days are numbered and if our love continues you will be badly hurt.'

Llinos shivered. She knew that Joe had not been threatening Dafydd but seeing into his future. 'Forget Joe!' She took Dafydd's hand. 'Take me to bed and make love to me as if we will never part.'

'And we won't, I promise you that.'

Shanni sat in the softly lit parlour with Madame Isabelle and listened as the older woman played a delicate tune on the piano. The music was soothing, beautiful, and Shanni relaxed against the soft cushions on the sofa. She was grateful that Madame Isabelle had allowed her to stay with her in Llanelli, especially after Mr Ceri Buchan had been shot in the riot.

A flutter of excitement went through her as she glanced at the clock, anticipating the moment when Dafydd Buchan would walk in the door.

Madame Isabelle stopped playing as the sound of the bell echoed through the house. He was here, Dafydd was only moments away from her, and Shanni took a deep breath, telling herself to be calm but all the time listening to the sounds in the hallway as the maid took Dafydd's outdoor coat and hat.

And then he was in the room, standing tall and imposing, bringing in with him the freshness of the evening breeze. He took Madame Isabelle's hand and kissed it, then held Shanni's hand tightly in his. Was the way he looked at her special? Wasn't he leaning closer to her than necessary, holding on to her hand for longer than was proper?

'Please take a seat, Dafydd.' Madame Isabelle gestured towards the sofa, and as Dafydd sat beside Shanni, his sleeve touched hers, and Shanni was happy she had manoeuvred things so that she would be close to him.

'How is your brother?' Madame Isabelle asked. 'I do hope his injuries are not going to prove serious.'

'He is recovering slowly,' Dafydd said quietly. 'It was unfortunate that he happened to ride past the gate on that particular night, though, because he is not in sympathy with the cause and he was a fool to have interfered in something that was not his business.'

'His intentions were good,' Madame Isabelle said. 'Now, Dafydd, where do we go from here? For all our efforts the tolls keep rising and the farmers are almost ruined.' She paused. 'I certainly don't want an escalation of violence. There's been enough bloodshed as it is.'

Glancing at Dafydd, Shanni saw that he was shaking his head. 'I don't see how we can avoid it. So far we've got nowhere in the fight for justice and the patience of the people is wearing thin.'

'I know you're right but isn't there another way to tackle this?' Madame Isabelle asked.

'Such as a letter to the Queen?' Dafydd smiled. 'Her Majesty, like her government, does not wish to know of our problems. Face facts, Isabelle, we are on our own in the fight for justice. What we need to do now is discuss our next move.'

The doorbell rang and Dafydd looked up quickly. 'Are you expecting visitors?'

'No. I'll go and see who it is.' Madame Isabelle swept out of the room, and Shanni risked a quick look at Dafydd. He was so handsome. His hair curled around his strong-jawed face and to Shanni he looked every inch the hero from the history books she had read.

He caught her glance and smiled. 'What are you thinking about, little girl?'

Dimples showed in his cheeks, and Shanni ached to throw herself into his arms. She felt her colour rising. 'I'm not a little girl. I'm grown-up, mature. The place of my birth saw to that.' She spoke in a low voice. 'And if you want to know what I'm really thinking it's that you're fine and handsome and I'd follow you to the ends of the earth.'

He pinched her cheek. 'I know you would, and I'm grateful to you for your loyalty. But, in spite of what you think, you have a lot of growing up to do yet. You must meet people your own age, the right people.'

'I'm happy to be here with you. And with Madame Isabelle, of course,' she added hastily.

The voices from the hall came nearer. The door opened, and when Madame Isabelle came into the room Shanni was puzzled by her manner. She was flushed, her eyes sparkling; a curl had become unpinned and hung beguilingly down her neck. In that moment Shanni saw that Madame was not only an excellent teacher but a beautiful lady into the bargain.

'Allow me to introduce my visitor.' She spoke

breathlessly. 'Eynon Morton-Edwards, please meet Dafydd Buchan, and Shanni Price, my pupil.'

Eynon shook hands with Dafydd. 'We've met,' he said curtly. He turned to Shanni and smiled. 'Ah, we are old friends, aren't we, Shanni?'

She was relieved that Mr Morton-Edwards did not enlarge on his statement. For some reason she did not want Dafydd to learn that she had once been a humble maidservant. He knew she had been penniless but, then, even high-born ladies were sometimes without a fortune.

The talk became general, pleasantries were exchanged, and Shanni knew that the secret meeting was at an end. She felt in her bones that soon Dafydd would leave; he was not here to be sociable though he put on a good show for Madame's sake.

'I hear you used to own the large pottery on the banks of the Tawe.' He smiled at Eynon. 'I'm trying to make a success of a pottery I've opened here in Llanelli. Perhaps you could share your knowledge of the business with me some time.'

Mr Morton-Edwards seemed cool. 'I hear you already have an adviser in Mrs Llinos Mainwaring,' he said. 'You could find no finer person to instruct you in the art of potting and all it entails.'

Dafydd rose to his feet, glancing at the clock. 'I think it is time I was on my way.' He bowed over Madame's hand. 'If you will excuse me, Isabelle.'

'Of course, Dafydd. You have much to attend to with your brother sick.'

'Ah, I heard about the fracas at the Dwr

Coch gate,' Eynon said, 'and my sympathies to your brother. His attempt to prevent violence is laudable.'

'Quite so.' Dafydd smiled at Shanni. 'See you soon, little lady.'

When he had left, the room seemed very quiet. Shanni was sensitive to atmosphere, and she knew that Madame Isabelle wished to be alone with her visitor.

'I think I'll go to my room, Madame, if I may.'

'Of course, Shanni.'

Shanni closed the door of the sitting room behind her, resenting the intrusion of Mr Morton-Edwards with an intensity that made her heart pound. Because of him Dafydd had left earlier than he had intended, depriving Shanni of his company.

Madame Isabelle was happy to see him, that much was obvious. It was not within the bounds of possibility that she fancied herself in love with him. In her room, Shanni sank on to the bed and stared into the fire, the embers flickering towards extinction. She decided that soon the room was getting cold and that it would be wise to wash and climb into bed as soon as she could.

From downstairs she heard the sound of muted voices and frowned. Why, oh, why had Mr Morton-Edwards chosen this very night to visit Madame and without an invitation? It was unpardonable.

She smiled suddenly at her reflection in the mirror then grimaced. 'You, my girl, are turning into a snobbish little horror,' she said. 'It's about time you remembered the slums whence you came, instead of worrying about the petty manners of the gentry.'

She climbed into bed, pulled the blankets up to her chin and snuggled down to dream about Dafydd.

'You don't mind me calling unexpectedly?' Eynon said, and Isabelle took both his hands in hers.

'You, my darling, can call on me any time you wish but please be discreet and come on a night when I am without visitors.'

He gripped her hands and slid on to one knee. 'To hell with being discreet. I want to marry you, Isabelle.'

Her heart began to thump so loudly she thought he would hear it. 'What do you mean, Eynon?'

'I'm asking you to be my wife.' He took a small calfskin purse from his pocket and opened it. A diamond slipped into the palm of his hand, the glow from the fire shooting flames of colour from the stone.

'But, Eynon!' Isabelle clasped her hands together. 'I'm so far beneath you in station. I am a humble teacher of the pianoforte and you, well, you are a rich, respected businessman. You could have your pick of any of the eligible young women living in Swansea.'

'So I could.' Eynon leaned closer to her and his lips briefly touched hers. 'But I don't want any of them. I want you.'

'But I am older than you. I can't have your children, Eynon. To marry you would not be fair.'

'Will you stop raising objections to a perfectly logical proposal?' Eynon took her hand and slipped the ring on to her finger. It sparkled up at her like the promise of eternal love.

As she stared at it, Eynon drew her to her feet and held her against him. 'I want you so much, Isa. I love the way your hair curls and I love your fine, intelligent mind.' His hands slid from her waist to cup her breasts. 'And I love the sensuousness of you. Please, Isa, say you'll marry me.'

Uncharacteristically, Isabelle found herself throwing caution to the winds. She wanted to marry Eynon more than she had ever wanted anything. To hell with the world and what the people in it would think! Life was passing her by and she had to grab at her chances with both hands. As their lips met, Isabelle knew herself to be the happiest woman in the world.

CHAPTER SIXTEEN

Llinos sat in the window-seat so that the slant of sunlight fell on the letter she was reading. She was hardly aware of Shanni, who was tucked up on the sofa reading her book. The letter was from her old friend Binnie Dundee: he was planning to visit Britain, and he hoped he would be welcome to call on her.

She felt a stab of pain as she thought of Binnie and Hortense, so in love with each other. She imagined the life they shared in the sun, with no complications, no infidelity, no secrets from each other. The secrets from Binnie's past had been exorcized long ago.

It hurt to think that it was Binnie who had comforted Joe when he lost his Indian woman and her child. It somehow seemed to be a betrayal of their friendship that Binnie should sympathize with Joe but, then, men stuck together where matters like infidelity were concerned.

Llinos glanced unseeingly through the window, her thoughts bitter. Joe should have come back to her sooner. Then, perhaps, she would never have been tempted to sleep with Dafydd.

She forced her mind back to the matter in hand and reread the letter. She should be anticipating Binnie's visit with joy not sadness; he was like a big brother to her, so uncomplicated, so sensible.

She folded the letter away. She would reply at once, tell Binnie that he and Hortense were welcome to stay with her for as long as they wished. Impulsively, she kissed the paper. 'My old friend Binnie is coming home. It will be so good to see him again,' she said.

Shanni looked up from her book. 'Did you say something, Mrs Mainwaring?'

Llinos felt a sudden chill. The fickle sunshine had vanished. Clouds hovered threateningly over the Mumbles Head, and then the rain began to fall. She felt her spirits sink. 'No, Shanni, I think I must have been talking to myself.' She realized at once how petty she must seem. She held out the letter. 'Come, take this from me and read it aloud. I want to see how you've progressed.'

Shanni stretched her slim legs and flexed her dainty feet. '*Duw!* I'm getting stiff, sitting with my legs tucked under my skirt.' She took the letter, glancing at the address with a flicker of excitement.

'It's all the way from America!' she said. 'Who do you know out there, then?' She put her hand to her mouth. 'I'm sorry,' she mumbled. 'Your husband is American, isn't he?'

'American-Indian,' Llinos replied. 'And this letter is nothing to do with Joe. Binnie is a friend of mine. He worked here once, helped to build up the pottery to what it is today.'

'Oh, I see, he's quite old, then?' Shanni lost

interest in the letter and dropped it on to Llinos's lap. 'And it's not very well written, is it?'

Llinos hid her irritation. 'Binnie is a dear friend. He saved me from disaster more than once.' Llinos stared out of the window, not seeing anything but her memories of the past. Binnie had tried to help her the day her stepfather had cornered her in one of the sheds and had been beaten half to death for his pains.

Llinos loved Binnie as a dear friend. There had never been any hint of a romance between them.

'Binnie is a rich man now,' she said proudly. 'He owns a pottery in a place called West Troy. He has a magnificent house and three lovely sons. I'm so proud of what he's achieved because Binnie, like you, grew up in poverty.'

Shanni ignored her last remark. 'And he's coming here to visit? How old are his sons?'

'Dan is the eldest. He's probably about your age, perhaps a little older.' She smiled at Shanni's open curiosity. 'Looking for a sweetheart, are you?'

'Not me!' She looked up at Llinos. 'Can I confide in you?'

'Of course you can.' Llinos sat near her and took her hands. 'What is it? Have you fallen in love already?'

'In a way.' Shanni did not meet her eyes. 'I've met a most wonderful man. He's older than me, and I think he sees me as a child but I mean to win him over.'

Somehow, Llinos felt uneasy. There was a look in Shanni's eyes that could almost be described as spiteful. It was as if she was holding some secret in her heart, something she knew would hurt Llinos. Her instincts were not wrong.

'I'm in love with Dafydd Buchan,' Shanni said. 'He's handsome and brave and, oh, I admire him so much!'

Llinos was frightened. Her mouth was dry when she tried to speak. 'That's silly. He's so far too old for you, Shanni.'

'But, then, you are much older than Dafydd,' Shanni said quickly. 'In any case, you were in love when you were my age, weren't you? You do still love Mr Mainwaring, don't you?' She was challenging Llinos. Her attitude was one of defiance. She knew. Somehow she had found out that Llinos and Dafydd were lovers.

'Would you advise me to tell Dafydd how I feel?' Shanni persisted, her expression bland.

Llinos took a deep breath. 'I don't think so. In any case, I'd rather not talk about it.' Llinos swallowed hard. 'Just don't do anything you might regret.'

She was silent then, wondering how Shanni had found out about the affair. Every move she made, every word she uttered spoke volumes. She wanted to take Dafydd away from Llinos.

'Look, Shanni, you will meet many young men, suitable sweethearts, more your own age. You will soon get over your infatuation.'

Shanni shook her head. 'No, I won't. From the moment I set eyes on Dafydd I wanted him. I suppose you think he's above me in station, that I'm not good enough for him, is that it?' Her voice was edged with anger.

'No, I'm not saying that at all.' Llinos got up

and turned her back on the girl, her mind racing, jealousy searing her. How close had they been? Had Dafydd given Shanni so much attention that she thought she had a chance with him?

Outside the rain was dripping from the trees, the sky was heavy. There would be no break in the weather for some time to come.

Llinos rubbed her eyes, knowing she must tread carefully. 'Never think you are unworthy of any man. You are an intelligent young woman. Just don't love unwisely, that's what I'm trying to say.'

'Is it all, though, Mrs Mainwaring? I think you are angry with me and I don't understand why.'

Llinos spun round to face Shanni and the disgust in the girl's eyes was almost tangible.

'Mind how you talk to me, girl!' Llinos said. 'Remember why you are here in my house and who is paying for your education. Now, you're due a lesson with Isabelle soon. In any case, I can't stay here gossiping. I have work to do.'

She left the room and crossed the hallway, clasping her hands to stop them shaking. The clouds parted and, for a moment, pale sunshine highlighted the coating of dust from the clay that settled afresh on the glass panes every day.

Llinos sat at her desk and took out her drawing pad. It was time she thought up some fresh designs – at least she could still contribute something to the pottery. But her mind was not on her work: Shanni's words still echoed in her mind. Silly girl, how could she think that Dafydd would be interested in her? Had he encouraged her in any way? The thought nagged at her.

Llinos rested her chin in her hands and stared out into the garden. The rain had started again and beat down with a vengeance. She was filled with uncertainty. Shanni probably saw as much of Dafydd as she did. Every time Shanni stayed with Isabelle it seemed Dafydd was there too. Was he flattered by the attentions of a young and lovely girl?

She would be meeting Dafydd later that night and, at the thought, her heart fluttered in nervous excitement. Should she talk to him about Shanni's infatuation for him? That was all it was, of course – Shanni was too young to be truly in love. Llinos could see wherein the attraction lay: as well as being handsome Dafydd was a man of courage, a hero. But there was no way he would look at Shanni as anything other than a child. Would he?

She forced her concentration back to her drawing but it was pointless: her pencil refused to move across the page. The sound of voices in the hall came as a welcome distraction. She lifted her head, her senses alert, as she recognized Joe's tones.

Before she had time to rise from her chair he was in the room. 'I want to talk to you,' he said, closing the door firmly behind him.

'Really?' Llinos said, sarcasm evident in every nuance of her voice. 'Should I be flattered?'

'You have to stop this affair.' Joe's arms were folded across his chest. He was barring her way as though worried she might try to make her escape. 'You are becoming the talk of the town.'

'Fancy that!' Llinos turned her back on him, unable to bear the hurt in her husband's eyes. 'That makes two of us, doesn't it?'

'Look, Llinos,' he said, 'I did you wrong and I am sorry for it, but it's one thing for a man to have a mistress and quite another for a married woman to take a lover. You will have not one shred of reputation left if you continue to flout the rules of society.'

Llinos turned to face him. 'How dare you tell me how to behave? You are the worst sort of philanderer. You are a man who makes excuses so that he can enjoy bedding another woman with an easy conscience.'

Joe sighed heavily. 'Sho Ka never meant anything to me, not in the way you did.'

Llinos felt anger flare at the mention of the Indian's name. Joe had lived openly with her on Llinos's own doorstep, and now he was adding lying to his list of crimes.

'I told you, I spoke to your lover.' The words hung in the air and Llinos felt her shoulders tense. 'I asked him to end this affair.'

Llinos rose quickly and walked over to where Joe was standing, exuding righteous indignation. She raised her hand and slapped him hard across the face. 'How dare you!' She was so angry that her voice came out as a croak.

'You are my wife, or have you forgotten that?' Joe's words fell like chips of ice.

'And you were my husband,' Llinos said. 'And I respected you until you killed my respect by taking that Indian squaw to your bed. You even bought a house to keep her and your bastard child

233

in. What more could you do to betray me, Joe? Answer me that.'

He took a deep breath. He looked mighty and strong, and so very handsome. Why had he ruined everything between them?

'Are you forgetting that you are speaking ill of the dead?' His voice was husky.

'No.' Llinos sank back into her chair. 'But I am very much alive, Joe, and I need love and comfort, and I need to know that the man I am with is faithful to me.' She looked up at him. 'I need that like parched ground needs water. You failed me, Joe. I want nothing more to do with you.'

She picked up her drawing pad and her hand was trembling. 'Close the door on your way out.'

He left the room silently, like a whisper of the breeze, and as Llinos stared at the carved wooden panels of the door she grieved for all she had lost when Joe had given his body, perhaps his soul, to another woman.

But now she had Dafydd, and her heart rose at the prospect of seeing him, of lying in his arms feeling young again. She frowned. What would he think of Joe's visit? Would he end their relationship? Would he be worried about the scandal if Joe challenged him openly? No. Dafydd was as brave a man as Joe. He would fight to the death for what he wanted.

She threw down her pencil. All the joy of the morning, of Binnie's letter and her excitement at the prospect of seeing Dafydd that evening, had vanished like a puff of smoke. Between them, Joe and Shanni had taken away her peace of mind.

*   *   *

'But you cannot let this affair of yours interfere with our plans.' Isabelle sat in her drawing room staring up at Dafydd Buchan with indignation in every line of her body.

'Isabelle, you enjoy having a lover, don't you? Your Eynon Morton-Edwards courts you and you lie in his bed, so how can you blame me for wanting the love of a woman?'

'There is a difference,' she said, in a hard voice. 'Neither Eynon nor I are married. Are you forgetting that?'

'I'm forgetting nothing,' Dafydd said mildly. 'You are a single woman, as you point out, and you are intimate with a man who is not your husband. Not the behaviour of a lady, if you'll pardon me saying so.'

He had a point and Isabelle inclined her head, conceding that he was right. 'Let's not argue about this,' she said at last. 'I have told you my opinion, and now we have far more important matters to consider.'

'I know. Do you mind if I sit down?'

'Of course not.'

The maid knocked and entered the room, holding a tray. The aroma of hot chocolate came with her and Dafydd sniffed appreciatively. 'Something smells good.' Isabelle returned his smile, knowing she was forgiven for intruding into what was, after all, his private life.

'I think the next move is to attack the gates along the stretch of the Nant y Caws,' he said quietly. 'There are three gates in an area of only a mile. It's disgraceful.'

'But hopefully we can avoid a violent confrontation,' she said, though in her heart she knew that violence was inevitable. She saw Dafydd's raised eyebrows. 'I know, it's an impossible thing to ask. Knocking down and burning gates is bound to arouse protest from the keepers.'

She glanced at the clock, noting that she had barely an hour to get ready for dinner.

Dafydd saw her look. 'Expecting visitors?' he asked innocently.

'That's right.' Isabelle smiled suddenly. 'I'm expecting Eynon, as well you know. In any case, I'm sure you are in a hurry to meet your, your . . .' Her voice trailed away into silence.

'My lady-love,' Dafydd supplied, his face sombre. 'I'm in love with Llinos, I want her for my wife but that's not possible while her faithless husband is alive.'

Isabelle rose and touched his shoulder. 'Be careful, Dafydd. You're a good friend and I would hate to see you hurt. Now, drink your chocolate and be off with you. I need at least an hour to make myself presentable.'

Dafydd drained his cup and rose to his feet, studying Isabelle with fresh eyes. She was a statuesque woman, her abundant hair fashioned into a bun at the back of her head with small tendrils hanging around her face. 'No need for paint and powder, my dear Isabelle, you are lovely as you are.' He kissed her cheek and made for the door. 'I can see why your Eynon is so adoring.'

'Go on with you and stop your flattery! And take care, Dafydd.'

She watched him ride away along the lane and

her heart lightened. Soon she would be with her lover and she would put out of her mind all the ills of society. At least for the time being.

Llinos lay in Dafydd's arms, staring through the window at the night sky. He had made love to her as always with a deep passion yet she felt unsettled. For the first time she wondered if what she and Dafydd had was simply a transient dream that would one day vanish as quickly as it had come.

'You're far away, Llinos.' Dafydd brushed her long hair from her face and kissed her mouth lightly. 'Not worried about that husband of yours, are you?'

'I am. Just a little,' she admitted. 'What if he became violent?'

'I can handle him.' Dafydd spoke with the arrogance of the young. He had little knowledge of Joe's prowess, his speed of foot, his strength. Dafydd was a brave man but he would be no match for Joe.

'Still,' Llinos said, 'Joe's not a violent man. I can't think he would resort to pistols at dawn.' Her voice was light, but who was she trying to convince? Herself or Dafydd?

'Forget Joe.' He kissed her lips, aroused once more, and Llinos turned into his arms determined to enjoy the sweetness of his touch.

He took her more gently, his hands caressing her naked skin, his mouth warm against her breasts. 'I love you, Llinos,' he said hoarsely, and she trembled, wondering at the power of the emotion she kindled in the man at her side.

Later, she leaned on her elbow and looked down into his face. He had the dreamy look of a man who had made love, and she adored him for it. How long was it since Joe had looked like that?

She touched his face lightly with her lips, aware of the responsibility she had for his happiness. She believed him when he told her he loved her. Dafydd was not the sort of man who used pretty words to flatter a woman.

'Where are we going, Llinos?' he said, sitting up and leaning back against the brass head-rail of the bed. He was so handsome but so completely the opposite to Joe.

'What do you mean, my love?' she said, but she knew exactly what he meant. Was she ready to face it? That was the question that worried at her in the still moments of the night.

'I mean, when are we going to stop this pretence and set up home together? I don't mean hurried visits but for us to live as man and wife.' He smoothed her hair as she snuggled into the warmth of his shoulder.

'I don't know if I could do that to Lloyd,' she said gently. 'He still believes his father and I are in love.'

'And are you?'

'Dafydd, please don't. I'm so confused with anger and uncertainty, I don't know how to think straight any more.' She frowned. 'Am I standing in the way of your finding a good wife?' she asked softly. 'I can't have any more children so we could never have a family of our own. You would be sacrificing a lot to be with me. We would have to move right away from Swansea, you know that, don't you?'

'So what?' he said. 'We could find a little farm in Carmarthen somewhere.' He smiled. 'Then I could still work the pottery and carry on my campaign with the rebels.'

Llinos watched the pale dawn poke fingers through the drapes, patterning the room with light and shade. Outside, the world would be waking, folk would be breaking their fast and preparing for work. It was strange how life continued normally around her while she was in turmoil.

'Why don't we wait until you have won the battle of the gates fairly and squarely?' she suggested. 'Perhaps then we should move away from Wales. We could even go to America, live near my old friend Binnie Dundee. He's a potting man too.'

'Ah, Llinos, I see you are not ready to make the final break from Joe,' he said softly.

'It's not that!' But even as she denied it she knew it was the truth. Was she ready to admit even to herself that her marriage to Joe was well and truly dead? If it was, why did she keep thinking about him?

When Dafydd had left her, she watched from the window as he rode his horse along the lane that led to the road to Llanelli. He needed to give more of his attention to his pottery, and they both knew it. The venture was still in its infancy and with Ceri Buchan still ill from his wounds it fell on Dafydd to make sure that nothing was left to chance.

Llinos asked the maid to boil water for a bath. Her nerves were taut and she felt she would fall apart into little pieces unless she managed to calm her mind. Later, as she luxuriated in warm water she studied her still slender body. The only change was that her breasts were fuller, standing proud now as the cold air touched her skin. She began to feel more optimistic: not only had she proved a passionate lover to Dafydd but she had helped him a great deal in his business. She had emphasized the need for good oven workers: the men who worked on the kilns needed knowledge and experience to build just the right temperatures for the successful firing of china.

She dressed slowly and sat before the mirror, brushing her hair into some sort of order. It was still thick and strong, curling on her shoulders and, in that moment, in the half-light, she looked like a young girl.

But she was no young girl. She was a middle-aged woman, and she should have more wisdom than to waste the life of a younger man, tying him to her when he should be looking for a wife.

Shanni's declaration of love for Dafydd had shaken her. Several times she had almost broached the subject, hoping Dafydd would laugh it off, but in the end she had kept quiet, frightened that he would see the girl in a different light. He might realize that Shanni was no longer a girl but a beautiful young woman. 'Damn!' she said aloud. 'Why is life so complicated?' She stared at herself in the mirror. Suddenly she looked old, with shadows beneath her eyes and worry lines around her mouth.

She rose from the stool and took a deep breath. It was time she went home – and high time that she did some serious thinking about her future.

CHAPTER SEVENTEEN

Shanni looked up at Dafydd, her heart thudding with happiness. He was illuminated in a flash of the fading sun and he seemed exalted, a man with great things on his mind.

She was glad of the moment alone with him: Madame Isabelle was in the other room talking to Eynon Morton-Edwards. Shanni knew from experience that she would return flushed, looking like a woman in love. She wondered if the same expression of softness and joy was on her own face as Dafydd talked to her. She longed to declare her love for him, to beg him to treat her like a woman, but something told her this was not the time.

'Pedr has been asking after you,' Dafydd said. 'I think he has a soft spot for our little rebel girl.'

Shanni bit her lip. Dafydd was treating her like a child again. 'Well, I haven't got a soft spot for him!' she said sharply. 'I think Pedr is a nice enough boy but rather immature,' she added, feeling proud of her new awareness of language.

'Really?' Dafydd sounded amused. 'I can see

you're a fine lady, very grown-up and beautiful too.'

Was he flirting with her? Greatly daring, she leaned closer. 'I prefer the more mature man. A man like you,' she said, then blushed and was embarrassed by her own forwardness. She must learn to be subtle, to be more tactful.

'Well, then, I'm flattered!' There was a hint of laughter in Dafydd's voice.

'Don't make fun of me!' She turned and looked at him, determined to change the line of the conversation. 'Anyway, what's more important is when the next attack on the gates will be.'

'Tonight.' He glanced at his pocket watch, which gleamed gold in the light from the window. 'I'd better be going if I'm to get to Efailwen in time to join in the action.'

He rose to his feet and Shanni followed him to the door. He turned and she almost cannoned into him. He put his hands on her shoulders, and Shanni felt a thrill of sheer pleasure run through her body. 'Tell Isabelle I'm sorry to leave without seeing her.' He listened to the voices across the hallway. 'It seems she's still busy with her guest.' He winked at Shanni, and then his lips touched hers softly, like the brush of a petal. 'See you soon, little one.'

Shanni watched from the window as he rode away, a magnificent figure on his silky-coated horse, man and beast touched by the rays of the dying sun.

'Efailwen,' Shanni murmured to herself. She envied the men their right to be at the scene when the gates were destroyed. The excitement of tearing down the gates, a symbol of authority, was something she longed for. She lifted her head and stared at the clock. She could follow Dafydd if she acted quickly.

She ran up the stairs and pulled on the dark riding habit Llinos had bought her. She needed something to cover her head – a shawl would do.

She went through the wardrobes and at last, in the maid's room, Shanni found an old, worn shawl and a discarded bonnet. She dressed in them quickly and hurried back down the stairs.

'Madame?' Shanni called, as she knocked on the door of Madame Isabelle's study. 'I'm going over to see Pedr. I shan't be long.'

Without waiting for a reply, she hurried outside, closing the front door with a snap of finality. She was not lying, she told herself, she *was* going to visit Pedr, but with the sole purpose of making him take her with him to the gate at Efailwen.

She felt as light as air as she hurried through the fields towards the roadway. She was going to have some excitement and surely Dafydd would applaud her actions. She thought of the touch of his hands on her shoulders, the lightness of his mouth against hers, and she laughed in sheer joy.

Llinos was restless. She was not seeing Dafydd tonight and she knew only too well the reason why. Dafydd was riding with the rebels, the Beccas, they called themselves. The men were going to storm another gate, incensed by yet another rise in the tolls. It now cost a farmer twelve shillings and sixpence to travel a distance of thirteen miles. It was a disgrace, and something had to be done about it.

Llinos felt lonely. The house seemed to close in around her. Strangely, as a child she had never felt lonely, not even when her mother died. But then she had been young and resilient, a girl with ambition and drive. What was she now?

Even though she and Shanni were not the best of friends, Llinos wished the girl was not staying with Isabelle for the night. If nothing else, Shanni was lively company.

The doorbell jangled, breaking the silence, and Llinos looked up, her heart thumping. Had Dafydd changed his mind? Had he come for her after all?

But it was Joe's voice she heard in the hall and she sank back in her chair, unwilling to face yet another scene.

He came into the room quietly, as he always did, and he looked big and handsome, with a proud arrogance to his features. His long hair hung to his shoulders and the streak of white could be seen clearly in the light from the candelabra.

'I have to talk to you.' Joe sank into a seat, without waiting for invitation. 'It's about Lloyd.'

Llinos put her hand over her heart. 'Is he ill? What is it, Joe?'

'No – at least, not in body. In spirit he is troubled by the problems facing his parents.'

'How does he know?' Llinos asked, alarmed.

'You need to ask when Lloyd is my son? He's well aware of the friction between us. He is also aware you have a lover. The boy is not stupid.'

'And he is well aware that you had a mistress by whom you sired a son,' Llinos retorted. 'He knows only too well how many times you were absent with your whore when I was in trouble and needed you.'

'Llinos, in the name of all the saints, stop saying that,' Joe said. 'Every time we argue you go over old ground.'

'What do you expect?' She was furious. 'I have been humiliated for years by your faithless ways. You have only yourself to blame for losing me.'

'*Have* I lost you, Llinos?'

'I don't know what to think any more!' Llinos put her hand to her head. 'I can't trust you, Joe. Every time you go away I'm wondering if there's another woman tucked away somewhere.'

'We must forget our feelings for the moment,' he said. 'All this is upsetting Lloyd's studies. He is determined now to abandon college and come home.'

'I know better than you what Lloyd feels,' Llinos said. 'And if he had seen more of his father when he needed him things might be different.' She paused, rubbing her brow. 'You must tell Lloyd it's out of the question to leave college. He must not give up his chance of a good education.'

Joe raised his eyebrows. 'And do you think talking will do any good? Lloyd is almost a man. You can't order him about as if he was a child.'

'To me he *is* a child,' Llinos said. 'And I tell you this, Joe, if you think you will force my hand, make me give up Dafydd, you can forget it!' She took a deep breath, trying to be calm. 'If you allow Lloyd to come home I will move out and live openly with Dafydd, do you understand me?'

'Certainly, and so do half the people of Pottery Row!' He smiled grimly. 'They are all quite acquainted with your affair.'

'Oh, get out!' Llinos turned away from Joe's bitterness. 'I will go to see Dafydd tonight. I will stop him visiting me here. I will just stay with him more frequently.'

Joe left the room on silent feet. He moved like the breeze, and in that moment her heart ached. Llinos put her hands over her face. 'I loved you so much, Joe,' she said softly.

Shanni stared up at Pedr, her heart singing in triumph. She had argued fiercely about her right to ride with him and, at last, he had agreed. She reminded him of the pistols she had managed to get, and how she had sneakily returned them to their rightful place.

'You are a stubborn, obstinate girl!' he said, swinging her up on his horse. Shanni wrapped her arms around his waist, resting her cheek against his broad back, enjoying her power over him. He was falling in love with her, and she knew it.

The chill night air lifted her hair away from her face.

'You're a lovely boy, Pedr,' she said. She could charm him, that much was obvious, but things would be better still if she could charm an experienced man like Dafydd.

The sound of the horse's hoofs on the rough road sounded like a heartbeat, and Shanni felt excitement flow through her. She was in charge of her own life, she would run it as she saw fit, and not bow to anyone's wishes – certainly not those of Mrs Llinos Mainwaring.

Pedr slowed their mount as the lights from the toll-house came into view. Shanni, peering around his shoulder, saw the shadowy figures of the Rebeccarites massing for the attack.

The man who called himself Becca was at the front of the crowd. He was wearing a horsehair wig and skirts billowed around his long legs. She knew it was Dafydd, of course, everyone in the movement knew who the leader was, but no-one would ever talk of it, not even under pain of death.

Shanni slipped from the horse and watched as Pedr tied the reins loosely around an overhanging branch of the sheltering trees. He caught her arm, his finger to his lips warning her to be silent.

The men were shouting abuse at the keeper in the toll-house, and the sound echoed into the clouds above her head. Shanni pulled away from Pedr in alarm. She put her hands over her face, the noise reminding her again of the way her mother had been dragged from the house by the *Ceffyl Pren*.

The gate was in pieces, and a shadowy figure held a torch to the dry timber. It blazed into life, sending a shower of sparks into the night sky. The men cheered the noise, animal-like in the silence of the night.

Shanni saw again her mother's stricken face. She heard screaming from inside the toll-house and she almost turned to run. A woman rushed out from the building holding a lantern above her head. In the wash of candlelight she appeared ghoulish, her eyes deep caverns like those of a skull, her mouth an open tomb as she screamed at the rioters. She drew nearer the men, brandishing a broom. 'Why are you doing this to me, you snivelling cowards?' she shouted. 'Why pick on a defenceless woman? Tell me that.' The men fell back uneasily.

'My Twm is a coachman and he's away, as well you know. Are you men or mice that you attack a woman alone?'

The leader stepped forward, the toes of his boots incongruous beneath the calico petticoats he was wearing. 'We are not against you, woman.' His voice was scarcely recognizable: it was gruff and sounded ill-bred, as though he was a peasant, not a landowner. Shanni was shocked. Perhaps the leader tonight was not Dafydd after all.

She felt angry and disappointed, wished she had stayed at home. Perhaps even now Dafydd was with Llinos Mainwaring. The thought made her bite her lip in despair.

The woman had the attention of the crowd. 'You men disgust me! You come dressed as women to terrify and destroy the living of a family who is as dirt poor as you.' She moved closer to the blaze.

'Do you want to burn me and my few possessions too?' She could be seen more clearly now, and in the light she looked young and pretty with flowing dark hair hanging loose to her waist.

One of the men leaped across the burning timber and felled the woman with one blow. He knelt over her and lifted her nightgown.

'How about a little kiss and cuddle, then, girl?' He slipped his hand along her thigh, and the woman screamed like a wounded animal. She struck out at him, trying to pull away. He knelt over her, fumbling with his buttons. His intention was obvious to everyone watching yet no-one moved.

Shanni thought again of the humiliation her mother had suffered, naked and shamed, tied to a post, while the people who should have been her friends reviled her.

As the man pressed forward the woman screamed in terror. Shanni could not stand it. She rushed forward throwing herself against the man catching him off balance. 'Leave her alone, you *mochyn frwnt*!' she shouted. 'You are nothing but a dirty pig!'

The man leaped to his feet and faced Shanni, anger suffusing his face. The woman from the toll-house scrambled to her feet and rushed back inside the house, crying with fear and shame. Shanni heard the door slam and the bars fall into place.

'Don't you call me a dirty pig!' She was caught and held, her arms twisted cruelly behind her. 'You've stopped me havin' a bit o' fun this night, my girl, so you'll have to do instead.'

He threw her to the ground but before he could do anything else, Pedr was standing over her. 'Get off, man. This has gone far enough,' he said easily. 'This girl is with me and we're going to be wed, so I'll thank you to let me be the one to take her maidenhead!' He laughed, pulling Shanni close to him.

There was silence for a moment. Then Becca stepped forward, towering head and shoulders above the rest. He shook Pedr's hand then kissed Shanni, the horsehair wig rough against her face.

'Congratulations, young Shanni,' he said. Gone was the rough accent: the voice was cultured and she knew that the man under the wig was Dafydd after all. Now he thought she was betrothed to Pedr, which was the last thing she wanted.

She did understand the pressure of his hand on her arm, though, and nodded almost imperceptibly before putting her arms around Pedr's waist.

'Shall we let young Pedr take his bride off into the trees to do a bit of courtin', then, boys?' His voice was harsh again. Shanni looked anxiously at Pedr, then at the group of men staring at her.

One threw back his head and laughed, and soon everyone was joining in, making crude jokes.

Becca held up his hand. 'I say Pedr should give her a lesson this night.' He rested his hand on Pedr's shoulder. 'See, Pedr boy, don't let the maid keep you at a distance now. Get her bundling and plant your seed, lest some other man get there first.'

The men laughed loudly, the tension released. The timber from the gate crackled into embers, and now the men would be ready to disperse. But she was wrong and before Shanni knew what was happening she was being lifted shoulder high. Her heart was pounding and she felt as though she would choke. What was going to happen to her?

She struggled to look round and saw that Pedr was being carried along with her. The men took them through the wood to a clearing and she was put down on her feet again. In front of her was a shack. She watched with dread as one of the men pushed open the door and gestured for her to go inside.

Shanni looked around for Dafydd but he had gone. Pedr was at her side then, pushing her into the hut. He closed the door and the darkness was intense, with just one window revealing a pale streak of moonlight. 'Better lie down in case anyone looks in,' Pedr whispered.

'I'm not going to lie down anywhere with you, Pedr Morgan!' Shanni said fiercely.

'Then take your chances with them out there, girl.' He caught her hand and drew her on to a makeshift bed. 'Now, look, this is just pretend, right? I mean you no harm, you know that. Once the men have gone we'll be away from here.' He pressed his mouth against hers effectively stopping her protest.

Shanni knew he was talking sense. She could hear the men singing a lewd song about a couple in love, and shuddered. Pedr put his arms around her and she felt the bristle of his unshaven face against her own. She was tense, her heart thumping. This was not what she wanted. She put her hands against Pedr's chest and attempted to push him away.

'Get astride the girl, lad!' A raucous laugh close to the window made Shanni realize that they were being watched. 'Get on with it! If taking a young girl's maidenhead is too much for you, step aside and let a man show you how.'

'I'd rather do this in private, if you don't mind,'

Pedr said harshly. 'I don't want to hurt my sweetheart and put her off for life, do I?'

Shanni felt for his face in the dark. It was hot beneath her fingers. She became aware that Pedr was trembling. She smiled suddenly. 'You've done this sort of courting before, haven't you?' she whispered. She felt like giggling. She was in no danger from Pedr so she might as well enter into the spirit of the charade.

'Darling Pedr,' she gasped out loud, 'you are so wonderful, such a strong man.' It was strange how easily the Welsh tongue came back to her. She put her arms around Pedr and held him close, planting loud kisses on his face. Suddenly she thought the whole thing hilarious. 'Oh, my love, can't we marry straight away? I can't live another day without you.'

'That's it.' Pedr had caught her mood and clasped her to him gasping with laughter. 'If they really knew what we were up to, they'd all pee their trews!' he whispered. He rested his hot face against hers and turned to speak to her. Their lips touched and, in a moment, laughter fled. Shanni was aware of him as a man, aware of his thighs pressing against hers. He kissed her again and she felt him harden against her.

'Pedr,' she said breathlessly, 'don't get carried away now, *boy bach*.'

'That's the trouble, though, girl. I'm not a little boy, I'm a man, and I want to make love to you with every bit of me.'

'Well, you can't!' Shanni said. 'Now, get off me. The men have all gone from the sound of it.'

Pedr released her and peered warily through the

window. 'There's no sign of anyone. I expect they've gone home to pester their wives after all this excitement.'

As Shanni moved towards the door Pedr caught her and held her close. 'I'm going to have some reward for my trouble,' he said. He pressed his mouth to hers in a passionate kiss.

Shanni felt a mixture of emotions run through her. She wanted to push him away, but something stopped her. Then, abruptly, she was released.

'Now then, Shanni, that will teach you to come to a burning with me,' Pedr said. 'From now on you'll stay safe at home, won't you?'

She knew Pedr was right. Had he been less of a gentleman he would have taken advantage of her. She touched his cheek. 'Thank you, Pedr,' she said softly.

'For what?'

'Just for being you. Come on, let's go home.' She held his hand as they walked out of the shed into the light of the moon.

CHAPTER EIGHTEEN

Llinos sat opposite Shanni and stared angrily at her across the drawing room. Shanni's head was bent but Llinos could see that her face was flushed and her red hair hung in rough tendrils around her shoulders. 'What on earth were you doing riding out at night with a crowd of rebels?' Llinos remonstrated. 'Are you foolish or downright wicked?'

'I didn't do anything wrong,' Shanni said defensively. She looked up at last. 'I promise you I did nothing wrong. It was just . . .' She shrugged. 'I wanted to go with the men, to see what happened when a gate was being burned down.'

'Wanted to see Dafydd Buchan is more like the truth, isn't it, Shanni? Answer me.'

Shanni's eyes gleamed. 'I have as much right to be in Dafydd's company as you do!' she said.

'So you end up in a hut with Pedr Morgan. Is that proper behaviour for a lady, do you think?'

'I'm embarrassed about that.' Shanni pushed back her hair. 'We had to pretend we were courting. I was only safe because they thought I was Pedr's sweetheart. We didn't do anything wrong, though. Can't you believe me?' She stared defiantly at Llinos. 'Pedr thought it best if he brought me back here. Madame Isabelle would have been so angry if we'd gone to her house.'

'So, in his wisdom, Pedr brought you home to me when day was breaking. It wasn't very clever of him to let the whole of Pottery Row know you were out all night.' Llinos got to her feet. 'I still can't believe you have been so stupid.' She rubbed her temple. 'As if I haven't enough to worry about, without you causing me grief, too.' She stood at the window gazing out at the morning. The air was still and clouds were gathering, threatening a storm. She believed the girl was telling the truth, that she had not slept with Pedr Morgan. Shanni was no liar and, in any case, it was Dafydd she wanted, not one of his workers.

'Well,' Llinos said at last, 'there will be no more visits to Madame Isabelle's house, do you understand? I am appalled that she allowed you to associate with such people.'

'Those people included Dafydd Buchan.' Shanni smiled as if she had scored a point. 'In any case, Madame knew nothing about it.'

Llinos swung round to face the girl. 'Didn't she? Well, I expect this is not the first time you have acted the wanton and gone out riding at night. No, Shanni, you will be kept indoors for a month until you learn some self-control.'

Shanni did not reply. She stared down at her hands, twisting them in her lap, and Llinos wondered what she was thinking. Was it true that bad blood was carried through successive generations? If so, Shanni was liable to lose her head over a man just as her mother had.

A dreadful thought struck her. Had Shanni stayed with Dafydd? Had Pedr brought her home to cover the truth? Llinos turned back to the window. The shimmer of heat that rose from the bottle kilns hung like a haze over the yard.

Llinos glanced at Shanni and saw spots of red on the girl's cheeks. Suddenly, Llinos felt like a monster. Shanni was beholden to her, but that did not give her the right to think the worst of her or to treat her so harshly. 'Let's forget all about last night,' Llinos said. 'I shall call for Graves to take us into town. We'll get some dresses made for you, ready for when the fine weather comes.' She smiled as Shanni looked up at her. 'I'm sorry for venting my anger on you but the truth is that my own life is not running as smoothly as I would like. Come, let's go and get ready. A trip out will do us both good.'

Shanni nodded, but refused to meet Llinos's eyes. She was still angry, her colour high. Shanni had an unforgiving streak in her, and who could blame her? Until Llinos had taken her in, Shanni's life had been one of misery and poverty.

Later, as the carriage rolled into Swansea, Llinos felt her spirits lift. The sun was breaking through the clouds and the Stryd Fawr was crowded with people. Vehicles jostled for space outside the large emporia and it seemed that the whole world had come shopping.

Llinos stepped out of the carriage, catching the sense of excitement of the moment. She would buy some pretty dresses ready for summer, when she and Dafydd could lie in the sweet grass and make love under the skies. There were many problems to be sorted out but for now Llinos intended to enjoy herself.

With Shanni following her, she went through the doors of Jefferson's Emporium. She allowed Shanni to choose her own bolt of material in green satin for evenings, and soft muslin for the hot summer days. 'We shall have to find time for fittings with the seamstress.' Llinos was making an effort to be pleasant. 'I should think the material you've chosen will make up very well, and the green will suit your lovely red hair.'

Shanni did not reply. Llinos frowned: she was fast losing patience with the girl's truculent attitude. 'Very well, let's forget the fittings,' Llinos said. 'I've had enough. I want to go home.'

As she stepped out into the pale sunshine Llinos came face to face with Dafydd. She stopped, her heart thumping.

'Mrs Mainwaring, this is indeed a pleasure.' He took her hand and kissed it formally. 'Are you keeping well?' He did not even glance at Shanni, and Llinos knew her fears had been groundless.

She clung to Dafydd's hand longer than was necessary. 'I am very well indeed,' she said breathlessly. 'Are you in town for anything in particular, Mr Buchan?'

'I was visiting one of the stores,' he said. 'Bagshaw's, at the top of the high street.' His smile widened. 'I'm happy to say that the directors of the company have given me a repeat order for china ware.'

'That's excellent!' Llinos said. 'Oh, Dafydd,

I'm so happy to see you making a success of your business.'

'You are not angry with me for stealing a march on you, then?'

'Of course not! Bagshaw's is large enough to take supplies from both of us.'

Llinos became aware of Shanni fidgeting at her side. 'I suppose we'd better be going,' she said reluctantly.

'No, don't go. What if I take you ladies for a cup of chocolate or perhaps some coffee? How about going to the Grand? I hear they provide excellent service.' His eyes twinkled with laughter. The Grand was where they had first made love and was a special place to both of them.

'What a good idea,' she said. 'Shanni, I'm sure you would enjoy a drink.'

'If you like.' The girl sounded sulky. She stared down at her feet, her hands twisting the folds of her skirt. Llinos knew it was mean to feel a moment of triumph but she was so happy that Dafydd had scarcely looked at Shanni. He was wishing they could be alone, and even Shanni knew it.

'Right, then,' Llinos said. 'The Grand it is.'

The coffee-room was filled with the sound of tinkling china and muted voices. The pale sun dappled the tables with patches of brightness.

Dafydd held the chair for Llinos to sit down then turned to Shanni. 'How wonderful it is to have two lovely ladies for company.'

He sat as close to Llinos as he could, without being indiscreet. He had eyes for no-one but her, and Llinos marvelled again that at her age

259

she had the love of a young, handsome man like Dafydd.

'You are looking very beautiful today, Mrs Mainwaring,' he said, as he made love to her with his eyes.

'Thank you kindly.' Llinos flirted with him, longing to touch him, to curl his dark hair around her fingers and draw his lips to hers. She was besotted with Dafydd and, in that moment, she did not care if the entire population of Swansea knew it.

The coffee arrived and the waiter put the pot on the table with a flourish. From the tray, he deftly took the dainty china cups and saucers and placed them in front of Llinos.

'Shall I pour?' She did not wait for a reply, and as the coffee streamed hot and fragrant into the cups, she felt she had never been happier in her life. 'There, Dafydd.' She handed him the cup and as his fingers touched hers she smiled, staring into his eyes, offering him more than coffee, much more.

'It smells delicious,' he said, 'and served by such a beautiful woman. I am a fortunate man.'

Llinos coughed, deciding to move the conversation on to safer ground. 'I have been designing new patterns for the china ware,' she said. 'I thought perhaps a dinner set decorated with the four seasons might be attractive.'

'So,' Dafydd said, leaning towards her, 'you would have a winter set, then spring, summer and autumn. What an excellent idea. You would sell four sets of everything. Capital!'

'Well,' Llinos said doubtfully, 'I had thought

of putting all the seasons in one set of table-ware but I suppose it makes sense to sell them separately.'

'Of course it does!' Dafydd touched her hand. 'You would market much more china that way.'

'That's a very good idea. Thank you for suggesting it.'

Dafydd laughed. 'Well, I didn't really suggest anything. It's what I thought you had in mind. I think you need taking in hand, my dear Llinos.' He winked at her and a smile lit her face.

'I think you're right,' she said, knowing exactly what was on his mind. She imagined them rolling naked on the softness of a bed, thought of Dafydd's firm young body possessing hers, and a blush of desire spread over her neck and face.

She sensed rather than saw a movement from Shanni. 'Excuse me!' the girl threw down her napkin and got abruptly to her feet. 'I see I am playing the gooseberry here. I will leave you two alone.'

Llinos watched open-mouthed as Shanni stormed across the room and disappeared through the wide doorway.

'Oh dear!' she said. 'I do believe we've annoyed Shanni. I think she's just a little jealous.'

Dafydd caught her hand. 'Nonsense! She's taken by one of my potters. I believe they are betrothed to each other. In any case, I love you, Llinos, and I don't care who knows it.'

'You don't realize, do you?' Llinos said, happiness flooding through her. 'Poor little Shanni is in love with you.'

'No!' Dafydd's expression of surprise was

almost laughable. 'I knew she admired me but, then, she probably sees me as some sort of romantic hero.'

'I'm telling you, she is in love with you,' Llinos insisted. 'I only hope she can keep her feelings under control.'

'Never mind Shanni. Let's just enjoy the moment,' Dafydd said softly. 'I can't get enough of you, Llinos, you know that, don't you?'

'And your eyes have never strayed in Shanni's direction? She's young and beautiful, don't you think?'

'I have eyes only for you,' he said, with conviction.

Llinos believed him. It was wonderful how eager he was for her love. Dafydd was a man overwhelmed by his passions. His dedication to his cause and his unshakeable love for her was as much part of him as the colour of his hair and the darkness of his eyes.

She swallowed a sudden feeling of fear. Was she too deeply enmeshed with Dafydd ever to extricate herself? Would it all end in disaster? The questions ran through her mind like a chill wind.

'You're far away, Llinos.' His voice penetrated her thoughts and she forced a smile.

'A goose just walked over my grave. It's nothing,' she said. 'But, Dafydd, do you have to keep attacking the gates? It's dangerous to flout the law. I want you to give up riding with the Rebeccarites.'

Dafydd looked away across the sunlit tea-rooms and Llinos wondered if he was angry with her. He was an adult man: he did not have to sit there and have his actions questioned by a woman, however much he might love her.

'I'm sorry!' she said. 'It really is none of my business. I shall stop Shanni visiting Isabelle's house, though. There, she has too much freedom and is able to get into mischief.'

'You have no real need to worry,' Dafydd said. 'These days, Isabelle is more engrossed in her lover than the cause. It will be worse when she marries.'

In spite of herself, Llinos was intrigued: Isabelle, so stiff and upright, was human after all. 'So Eynon has bedded her, then? In that case, does he really mean to marry her? I know it's not nice of me to say so but he has had many women and was not serious about any of them.'

'Oh, I think Morton-Edwards is serious because the wedding is being arranged even as we speak. He might be against the Beccas but he doesn't realize how deeply Isabelle is involved in it all.' He lowered his voice. 'Our Isabelle has even killed a man in the name of justice. Thomas Carpenter was going to expose our plans to the constable and Isabelle shot him. We covered it up, of course, we had no choice.'

Llinos sat back in her chair. 'Oh, how awful! Eynon wouldn't want anything to do with Isabelle if he heard what you've just told me.'

'Well, he won't know from me or from you, Llinos,' Dafydd said firmly.

'But Eynon and I, well, we're old friends and if he means to go through with the marriage perhaps he should know the truth.'

She poured more coffee. Somehow she just could not picture a marriage between Eynon and Isabelle: they were so different. Eynon was one of the richest men in the country and Isabelle, well, she had killed a man. It was all most disturbing. At best it showed Isabelle's lack of breeding.

'You are upset by this, aren't you?' Dafydd said. 'Don't worry about your friend. He and Isabelle are old enough to know their own minds, don't you think?'

'You're right, of course.' Llinos looked into Dafydd's eyes and realized afresh how lucky she was to have a man like him as a lover. Then she became aware that she and Dafydd were holding hands openly and that people were staring. 'I'd better go home,' she said. 'You know we shouldn't be sitting here holding hands in public, don't you?'

'I think it's a bit late to worry about that,' Dafydd said. 'Let me see you tonight, please. I know it wasn't what we planned but being with you now I can't wait to hold you in my arms, to make love to you and to make sure you still love me.'

She heard the uncertainty in his voice with a feeling of awe. Dafydd, young, handsome, rich, was afraid of losing her.

'I want to be alone with you as much as you want to be with me,' she said. 'I'll come down to the house tonight as soon as I can get away.'

As she left the tea-rooms, Llinos glanced back to where Dafydd was sitting. He was watching her, his eyes hungry. His naked expression of love was there for everyone to see. She left the hotel as if she was walking on air. Tonight she would lie in Dafydd's arms, in their little love-nest, and all would be right with her world.

CHAPTER NINETEEN

'I hate her!' Shanni was walking with Pedr near the river, which flowed swiftly past the pottery. 'How could she behave like that, throwing herself at Dafydd like a harlot?'

'Hey!' Pedr took her hand. 'Mrs Mainwaring has been good to you. Look how she let me visit you. And who can blame her for liking Dafydd? They are in the same business after all.' He stared at her. 'I won't listen to a word against Dafydd. He fights for the rights of the poor and not many rich folks do that.'

Shanni took a deep breath, intending to say more, but the expression on Pedr's face stopped her. She walked to the edge of the water, hugging her warm shawl around her, and sat on the bank to watch the ever-increasing circles made by fish looking for food.

Winter was almost over now but the weather was still chill. The riverbanks were dotted with the white of snowdrops. Once the winds of March came in, the daffodils would spread like a carpet of sunshine through the grass.

Her eyes were full of dreams. Surely in spring,

when she was wearing her new gowns, Dafydd would notice that she was a woman? He would see that she had matured in every way but until then she would not allow anyone to know her secret. It was one she would hug to herself for now.

Then she thought of Llinos, the way she had flirted with Dafydd, eating him up with her eyes, and anger made a bitter taste in her mouth. Why did Llinos have to step in and take Dafydd's attention? She had her own husband to love and care for. What sort of woman was she?

'You've got a look on your face that bodes ill for someone,' Pedr said quietly. 'You don't fancy our Dafydd yourself, do you?'

Shanni swallowed her anger and made an attempt to smile. 'Don't be silly! Why would I want a man old enough to be my father?'

Pedr shrugged, and Shanni realized her protest had not convinced him. She slipped her arm through his and drew him closer. 'Would I be sitting by here with you if I wanted Dafydd? Tell me that, Pedr Morgan.'

He turned to her at once and she saw the intent in his eyes. He was going to kiss her. She leaped to her feet and ran laughing downriver, her hair coming loose and flowing to her shoulders. He caught her easily. 'Now, my girl, what are you going to do?' He wrapped his arms around her, and before she could move, his lips were on hers.

She tried to push him away but he held her fast. She relaxed. Perhaps it was wise to let Pedr believe she liked him. He might be useful to her. In any case, the feel of his lips parting hers was strangely exciting. It was only when his hand touched her breast that she jerked away from him. 'No!' she said, as he released her. 'I am a lady, Pedr Morgan, and I will not allow anyone to take liberties with me.'

'Sorry, Shanni.' He looked anything but sorry. His eyes were bright, his breathing ragged, his strong mouth curved in a smile. 'You're so beautiful I can't resist you.'

'I'm sure you say that to all the girls in Swansea,' Shanni said, 'but I'm not easy. Just you remember that.'

Her mother had been easy, foolishly giving herself to a married man, and she had been harshly punished for it. The thought of the *Ceffyl Pren* made Shanni shudder.

'Shanni, what's the matter?'

'Nothing.' She lifted her hair and twisted it into a knot behind her neck. She could still see her mother struggling to give birth to her poor dead baby, and Mrs Mainwaring at her bedside, ministering to her like an angel.

Her conscience smote her. She had no right to be bitter against Llinos. If it were not for her Shanni would be living in poverty in the backstreets of Swansea. Still, her stomach churned as she thought of the love in Dafydd's eyes, love for an older woman, a woman already married, and her anger returned.

'We'd better get back home,' she said at last. 'I don't want to be called a slut, do I, Pedr?'

'You are a lady and no-one could say different.' He smiled. 'Mind, you're a bit wilful. You would need taming if you were my wife.'

She laughed, glancing up at him through her eyelashes. 'And who says I would think of marrying you, Pedr Morgan? You're just a potter. I want a rich man for a husband, someone who has plenty of money and a fine house and . . .' she waved her hands '. . . well, everything.'

'I'd get you all that if I could,' Pedr said, but his eyes were merry. 'I would climb mountains and sail the seven seas if I could have you for my wife.'

'I'm sure!'

Her sarcasm was not lost on Pedr. 'Well, I could at least work hard for you and give you a comfortable living,' he said reasonably.

'But you're not being serious, are you, Pedr?'

'Course not!' He caught her hand and forced her to run back along the riverbank towards the pottery. 'Me? Married? What a terrible fate.'

He walked with her by the river below the pottery just as the Sunday bells rang out in the clear morning air. 'See you tonight down at Madame Isabelle's house, if you're allowed to visit her again,' he said.

'I'll be allowed,' she said. 'I can get round Mrs Mainwaring any time I choose.' She touched her lips with her hands and threw him a kiss. And then she turned to take the river path and promptly forgot him.

'Well, Binnie, it's lovely to see you again.' Llinos stood in the hall hugging her old friend. 'And you haven't changed a bit.'

Binnie held her away from him. 'And you, my dear Llinos, are as beautiful as ever.' He glanced towards his wife, who was waiting patiently, a smile on her face, and Llinos smiled. 'Hortense, you are welcome in my home. Where are your boys? Didn't they come with you?'

'No, they think they're far too grown-up to travel with their parents, don't they, honey?' Hortense said.

'They surely do!' Binnie shrugged. 'They have their own friends, their own lives to lead, and I'm glad. I don't want my sons to be tied to their mother's apron strings.'

'I know what you mean,' Llinos said. 'Lloyd already thinks he knows better than his parents ever did. Come in, let the maid take your coats – and, Graves, get Merfyn to take Mr Dundee's bags upstairs, please.'

When they were seated in the drawing room, Llinos studied Binnie carefully. He was older, of course, and although his hair was as thick as ever it was touched with grey at the temples. Hortense looked well, her skin fresh, her eyes bright. Clearly, she was happy with her lot.

'What's this I hear about the rioting that's been taking place?' Binnie's voice held a trace of an American accent. 'Burning gates and tearing down buildings.' He paused. 'It reminds me of old times when the folk of Pottery Row blew up the riverbank and flooded the area.'

Llinos remembered it too: she had been trapped, locked in a shed at the waterside. She shivered.

'Aye,' Binnie continued, 'old Mr Morton-Edwards lost his life that night and his new wife drowned with him when the river took away their carriage.' He turned to his wife. 'That villain antagonized the workers, alienated his son and almost killed Llinos into the bargain, all in the name of greed. Anyway, enough of the past. What's this rioting all about now, Llinos?'

'The people are incensed that so many toll-gates are being erected,' Llinos replied. 'It's costing the farmers so much to bring the lime to their land that it's ruining the trade.' She looked quickly at Hortense. 'I'm sorry, Hortense, we don't want to talk about anything controversial today, do we?'

Llinos arranged to have tea, small sandwiches and cakes served in the conservatory. The weather had improved a little, spring was on its way and the wind blew in more kindly from the sea. In the conservatory, it seemed like summer.

'It sure is as beautiful here as you said, honey,' Hortense laid her hand on her husband's knee, 'but everything seems so small!'

Binnie smiled fondly. 'Aye, my love, compared to America everything does look small but, for all that, Wales is a wonderful place.'

'Where's Joe, Llinos? Not off on a trip again, is he?' Binnie spoke awkwardly, aware that some subjects were best not talked about in Llinos's company.

'I'm sorry, but Joe is away seeing to his estates,' Llinos said quickly. 'Still, Lloyd will be coming home from college any time now and I know he'll be glad to see you.'

'You have only one child?' Hortense asked conversationally.

Llinos smiled. Binnie's wife was honest and

direct, someone she felt she could talk to. 'I lost my daughter at birth,' Llinos said. 'I have become guardian of a young girl, Shanni. She's an orphan but so intelligent. You'll meet her when she gets home.'

'So good-hearted of you, Llinos,' Hortense said, but she had a faraway look in her eyes.

Llinos smiled wryly. 'Joe had another family in America but, then, you know about that, of course.'

The sudden sound of hoofs in the courtyard startled Llinos; she was not expecting visitors. She half rose from her chair to peer through the conservatory windows but subsided, her heart sinking as Joe came into view. She hoped that he was not going to be difficult in front of guests.

'Joe's come home,' she said flatly. 'I'm sure he'll be happy to see you both. You were very kind to him in his loss.' The sarcasm in her voice was not lost on Hortense, who rested her hand briefly on Llinos's arm. The look of under-standing in her eyes made Llinos want to weep.

A few minutes later, Joe came into the house and stood in the doorway of the conservatory. 'Hello, my dear friends. I'm so happy to see you.' He smiled and shook hands warmly with Binnie, kissed Hortense on both cheeks and brushed Llinos's cheek with his lips, like a dutiful husband.

He had tied back his long hair and the streak of white was evident. He looked so distinguished, and if her head had not been full of Dafydd Buchan, Llinos would have flung herself into his arms.

Joe took a seat, appearing very much master of the house. Llinos felt aggrieved: it was she who had built up the pottery into a thriving business, she who had added extensions to the house. Joe had cared for his own business but never very much about hers.

'You both look well,' Joe smiled at the visitors, 'and we meet in happier circumstances today.'

Llinos tensed. In referring to his last visit to America, Joe had reminded her and everyone else that he had other interests, personal interests, abroad.

'We are both well, thank you,' Hortense said quickly. She glanced worriedly at Llinos, sensing the atmosphere.

'I've made a special trip to welcome you to my home as warmly as you welcomed me to yours,' Joe said easily.

'Joe, hadn't you better bathe and change?' Llinos said sharply. She resented his proprietary attitude to the house, referring to it as 'his' home. Since when had he contributed anything to it?

'Llinos, leave the poor man alone,' Binnie said playfully. 'We are all used to dust and the smell of horses, remember?'

Llinos watched as Joe accepted a drink from the tray the maid held towards him. When his eyes met hers it was she who looked away. She sank back in her chair, worry tugging at her mind. What would Joe do if Dafydd turned up unexpectedly? It was one thing for him to know that his wife was being unfaithful and another for him to face her lover on home territory. Would he cause a scene? Damn him! Why had he come home now?

'So how's the business doing, Joe?' Binnie asked, as he realized at last there was an air of tension in the room.

Joe got to his feet. 'Let's go down to the river and talk, perhaps?' He glanced at Llinos. 'The women can gossip to their heart's content without us around.'

Llinos watched as the two men walked away, Binnie the shorter man, stocky and strong, and Joe tall, elegant even in his dusty riding clothes. They seemed easy in each other's company, friends and colleagues, and it dawned on Llinos that there was still a great deal about Joe that she did not know. Who were his other friends and colleagues? Were they the businessmen of Swansea or was he like a wolf and always walked alone?

'You seem troubled, honey.' Hortense spoke softly. 'Is everything all right between you and Joe?'

Llinos looked down at her hands. She had no idea what to say. It would be impossible to tell Hortense the truth, that she had not slept with her husband for a long time or that she had a lover who might come calling at any moment.

'I'm sorry, honey, I'm prying.'

Before Llinos could think of something to say she heard the bell ring through the house, shattering the quiet. She knew without being told that she had a visitor and that that visitor was Dafydd. Her worst fears were realized when the maid brought him into the conservatory.

Dafydd stood in the doorway. He only had eyes for Llinos and smiled lovingly at her. Llinos felt the heat of desire burn in her heart. 'Mr Buchan,' she moved towards him quickly, holding out her hands, 'do come and join us. You must meet one of our friends from America.'

Dafydd looked at Hortense. 'I'm charmed to meet you.' He bent over as Hortense held out her hand.

'This is Hortense Dundee, Binnie's wife,' Llinos said quickly. 'Binnie and Joe have wandered away to gossip about boring business things.'

She was warning him that Joe was at home and he nodded. 'Well, I can't stay too long, I'm afraid. I was just passing through Swansea and thought it rude not to pay my respects.'

'Oh, please, Mr Buchan,' Hortense stumbled over the unfamiliar name, 'do sit with us for a time and talk to us. I don't want to drive you away.' Dafydd glanced towards Llinos but Hortense spoke again. 'Just for a few moments. You surely can't refuse a visitor from so far across the sea a little of your time.'

Reluctantly, Dafydd took the chair Joe had vacated a few minutes earlier. He accepted a drink of cordial from the tray and held the cup in his hands, studying the contents as though the rosy liquid might contain poison.

Llinos became aware that Hortense was watching him. She was nobody's fool and it was obvious she was intrigued by the tension in the air.

'Oh, look, the menfolk are coming back.' She pointed to the edge of the garden. Llinos held her breath and Dafydd sat rooted to his chair. He could not, would not run away. Llinos knew he was made of sterner stuff than that. She felt her colour ebb as her husband drew closer.

'We have another visitor, Joe.' Llinos heard her voice crack; she was very conscious that Dafydd had come to stand beside her.

'So I see.' Joe stood for a few minutes as Binnie took his place beside his wife. 'Mr Buchan, how good of you to call,' Joe said evenly.

Dafydd took a step forward and the two men stood sizing each other up, as if about to lock horns in combat. Llinos held her breath, then Joe spoke again. 'I won't take your hand, sir,' he said, in a clipped tone. 'I fear there is too much between us to make a mockery of any show of civility.' He moved to the door.

'Excuse me, Hortense, Binnie, I'd better change out of these dusty clothes. I will see you both at supper, which we will take in the dining room. Goodbye, Mr Buchan.'

Joe was dismissing Dafydd, asserting his right to be master in his own house. Llinos looked up at Dafydd, trying to read his reaction. His face was expressionless but his eyes burned with anger. Llinos took his arm. 'Let me see you out, Mr Buchan.' When they were out of sight of the house, she put her arms around him and held him close.

'Don't be angry and upset, Dafydd,' she said softly. 'Joe might intend to stay in the house and I can hardly forbid him, but I will not be sharing his bed, you can be sure of that.'

'Can I?' Dafydd put his hands on her cheeks.

276

'I hadn't noticed before how handsome your husband is, how magnetic his personality. How can I compete with him?'

Llinos stretched up to kiss him. 'You don't have to compete, my darling,' she said. 'My passion is all for you.'

'I have to go away tomorrow,' Dafydd said. 'I need to do business in Bristol. I hoped we could spend the night together.'

They remained locked in each other's arms for a long moment. Then Llinos drew away. 'Go home, Dafydd. As soon as I can I will make my excuses and come to you.'

'Promise?' He seemed filled with uncertainty, and Llinos felt her heart contract.

'I promise, Dafydd. The devil himself wouldn't keep me away.'

She watched him mount his horse, stared at his strong legs in his riding breeches with a rush of tenderness. What joy he brought her, what pleasure. He lifted his riding crop and wheeled his horse away from her. Its hoofs threw up dust as Dafydd rode at great speed towards the front gates of the pottery. Llinos bit her lip in fear for his safety: he was riding like a man possessed.

She returned to the house reluctantly. Perhaps later she could plead a headache and say she intended to retire early to bed. Then she would go to see Dafydd. She had to reassure him that nothing had changed. And, if she was honest, her body burned for his touch with a fire that needed to be quenched.

At supper, Hortense talked pleasantly about her sons and Joe leaned forward as though he was listening intently, but Llinos knew he was aware of her every movement. The next few hours were going to be difficult.

Later, when supper had been cleared away, Llinos made her apologies. 'Will you forgive me, Hortense? I must go to my room.' She smiled ruefully. 'I'm afraid that being in the heat of the conservatory so long has given me a head-ache.'

Hortense looked at her for a long moment, then nodded. 'Of course, honey. You are looking a little pale, I must say.'

Llinos felt sure that Hortense understood the situation and was making things easy for her. 'I will see you in the morning – you too, Binnie.'

She glanced at Joe but he rose and, avoiding her gaze, refilled the glasses with the ruby port, which shimmered like blood in the candlelight. Llinos felt cold. Was it a portent of the fate that would meet one of them? But she was being foolish. Joe placed the glasses on the table and the illusion vanished.

Llinos went upstairs to her room. Her head was a whirl of chaotic thoughts. Could she slip out unnoticed? Perhaps she had better wait until the house was quiet. She did not want to answer difficult questions.

She lay rigid for what seemed hours then heard footsteps outside the bedroom, the sound of muted voices. The door handle turned and Llinos sat up quickly as Joe came into the room, closing the door behind him.

'We have to talk,' he said. He sat beside her and she bowed her head ashamed to look into his face.

He put his arm around her shoulder, kissed her cheek and then her mouth.

She pulled away from him. 'No!'

'You refuse me what is my right?' he asked quietly.

'You forfeited the right when you took a mistress,' she said abruptly. She tried to slip off the bed but Joe drew her into his arms. 'Don't go. Stay with me just for tonight. It's not much to ask, is it?'

She thought of Dafydd waiting for her, she thought of the joy she would find in his arms. Then she looked at Joe. Tears were glinting on his dark lashes. How could she leave him now without making a scene? After all, she would have the rest of her life to live with Dafydd.

'I'll stay for tonight, Joe.' She undressed swiftly, remembering the time when Joe was sick, how she had climbed into bed with him knowing he needed the comfort of her arms. She had tried to force the incident from her mind, refusing to accept that she had betrayed Dafydd, but now the thought of Joe's lovemaking set her pulses beating. When she climbed into bed she kept as far away from him as she could.

At last, the warmth of the bed and the closeness of Joe's body eased the tension. On the edge of sleep she relaxed against the familiarity of her husband. She knew so well the scent of his skin, the silk touch of his hair against her cheek.

'I love you so much, Llinos.' His whispered words brought her wide awake. 'I never stopped loving you, you must know that.' His mouth covered hers, burning with need, and for a moment she remained quiescent. Then he touched her breast, his fingers teasing her nipple.

'No!' She pushed him away. 'I can't do this!' She put her hands over her face as hot tears ran down her cheeks and between her fingers.

'I can't, Joe. I can't sleep with the two of you. What would that make me?'

He pulled her close to him. 'You want me as much as I want you,' he said. 'I ache for you, Llinos. Please don't turn me away.'

Slowly, sensuously, he began to kiss every part of her body. She tried to resist him, she held herself away from him, but he would not leave her alone. He kissed her again and again, and at last her fingers tangled in his hair and she felt the old desire flood through her. Joe was so dear, so familiar. She knew every part of him. She traced the outline of his muscled arms with her fingertips, she breathed in the scent of him, of the open air, the fresh spring grass, and she wanted him.

As he lay above her she drew a ragged breath. She could not think rationally any longer for this man was her husband and she loved him. The truth was like a blow. But if she loved Joe then what was it she felt for Dafydd?

At the thought of her lover, she tensed, trying to ease herself away from Joe's arms. But it was too late, she had allowed him too close. She could not push him away now. In any case, she did not want to push him away.

She moaned as Joe entered her. He teased her with the old sweetness, bringing her to the brink then drawing away like the outgoing sea. She heard her own murmurs of pleasure and abandoned herself to him. He was once again the young, eager Joe, full of love for her soul as well as her body. All that had happened between them seemed to vanish in the heat of their passion. At last the shuddering climax of passion flooded through her. She clung to her husband's strong shoulders, pressing him into her. At last, she fell away from him exhausted, sated.

She lay back against the pillows hearing Joe's breathing in the silence. Neither of them spoke. All at once, shame engulfed her. She had betrayed Dafydd and herself. She was no better than a woman of the streets or the animals of the field who mated indiscriminately. Softly, she began to cry.

CHAPTER TWENTY

'It was wrong of me, Joe, and please don't read too much into last night.' Llinos watched as Joe closed the bedroom door behind them. The smell of breakfast hung on the air, the rich bacon, the devilled kidneys and the platter of eggs. The meal that had been provided for the visitors was over.

'I'm sorry, Joe, it's all my fault and it was a mistake,' Llinos said quietly. She moved over to the window, and saw Binnie and Hortense in the garden, walking together, hand in hand. Her throat ached with unshed tears.

'You are my wife,' Joe said softly. 'How can you say it's a mistake to sleep with me?'

She held up her hand. 'Just leave me alone until I sort out my feelings, Joe, please.' She had promised Dafydd she would go to him last night and she had broken her word. How could she live with herself? 'I'd better go downstairs and talk to the cook about lunch.' She sighed. 'Americans seem to enjoy hearty appetites. I suppose that comes from long days spent outdoors.'

She was talking to Joe as if he were a mere guest, someone to whom she had to be polite.

Llinos wanted nothing more than to run away, to go straight to Dafydd and explain why she had not come to him, but he would have left for Bristol by now and, in any case, what would she say?

She left Joe alone in the bedroom and went to the drawing room where Shanni was sitting in her usual seat, her shoes abandoned on the carpet, her feet tucked up under her skirts.

'The Americans seem very nice people,' Shanni said. 'They met Dafydd, then.' Her tone was heavy with innuendo. 'I saw him ride away as I was coming back from my walk. Dafydd seems keen to be with you, doesn't he?'

'I'll ask you to keep your nose out of my business, young lady,' Llinos said. 'Remember that you are a guest in my house and behave accordingly.'

'So he did call. How awkward.' Shanni returned to her book, her eyes downcast, but a smile turned up the corners of her full young lips. Llinos wanted to slap her.

The day seemed to pass in a haze of pain and doubt, and Llinos felt she needed time alone to gather her thoughts. The presence of Binnie and Hortense made everything more difficult, but she could hardly be rude to her guests. Otherwise she would have gone to the house she and Dafydd shared, and there she would have waited for his return from Bristol. She would have had time alone to think of a way of explaining to him what had happened.

It was a relief when, later in the day, the carriage rolled up outside bringing Lloyd home from college. Llinos hoped his presence would add a touch of normality to what had become a nightmare.

'Lloyd, my lovely boy, you're taller than ever!' Llinos hugged her son then held him at arm's length. He was as tall as Joe, with Joe's startlingly blue eyes but otherwise he favoured her family. 'Come into the drawing room and meet our friends,' she said, pinching his cheek.

'Mother, behave.' Lloyd was smiling good-naturedly. 'I'm not a little boy now.'

Binnie greeted Lloyd warmly, and Hortense hugged him then kissed both his cheeks. 'Seeing you sure makes me pine for my own boys.' She sounded just a little tearful.

'Getting homesick already, honey?' Binnie teased, and Llinos envied the rapport between husband and wife. They had an inner peace, something she and Joe once enjoyed but which was now lost for ever.

That night, Llinos made up a bed for herself in her study. She had no intention of sharing a bed with Joe again. She needed to clear her head, to decide just what it was she wanted. And what did she want?

She could not deny that she had enjoyed Joe's love-making – he was her husband, he knew what thrilled her. But, she reminded herself, he had shared his passion with Sho Ka, had given the Indian the love he should have kept for his wife.

She lay for a long time staring through the window at the moon and the brightness of the stars against a velvet sky. Somewhere out there was the God she worshipped in her church.

Out there, too, was Joe's Great Spirit. Why did neither of them answer when she prayed for guidance?

The next day it was decided that Llinos would take Hortense on a shopping trip. She dressed with little enthusiasm, wondering dully if Dafydd was home yet. What would he have been thinking when he was away? That she had let him down, betrayed his trust.

In the coach, Llinos made an effort to talk pleasantly to Hortense. She knew the other woman was alert to the tensions in the house. She wanted to confide in Hortense: there was a wisdom about her that was encouraging yet Llinos hesitated. It was hardly right for a hostess to burden her guests with her problems.

It was Hortense who provided the opening she needed. 'What's gone wrong, honey?' she said softly. 'I know your Joe was not always faithful but he loves you very much. Anyone can see that.'

'Is that enough, though?' Llinos said. 'I am still bitter that he gave his love to another woman, that he even had a child by her. It's hard to get over a betrayal like that.'

'It was a betrayal,' Hortense agreed. 'But men think differently from us women. They don't look on intimacy with another woman as a betrayal. If you ask any man, he'll tell you the wife is important and the other woman . . . well, she's not.'

'And would you stand for that with Binnie?' Llinos challenged.

Hortense shook her head. 'I would not.' She laid her hand on Llinos's arm. 'But I nearly broke up my marriage because Binnie didn't tell me the truth about his past. In the end he was honest with me. So long as there is honesty a woman can cope with most trials and tribulations, don't you think?'

'Maybe,' Llinos said. 'But have you forgiven Binnie for not being honest with you in the beginning?'

'I came to understand that he kept things from me out of fear. If he'd told me he had a wife at home I wouldn't have given him a second glance.' She smiled. 'And now I would be alone, with no-one to love me.'

'The trouble with me is I don't know what I want,' Llinos said. 'I do know I can't give Dafydd up.' She glanced quickly at Hortense. 'You knew he and I were lovers, didn't you?'

'I knew the minute I saw you together,' Hortense said. 'And I can't tell you what to do or feel. All I can say is that Joe loves you more than life itself.'

The coach drew to a halt outside the large emporium in the high street, and as she stepped out into the sunlit street Llinos felt a flutter of excitement. What if she met Dafydd by accident? Would he stop and talk, or would he walk right past her? It would be no more than she deserved.

Still, she was clear about one thing: she needed to see Dafydd soon. She wanted to be with him, to talk to him, to tell him she loved him.

'This looks a fine store.' Hortense was staring up at the huge window display. 'I've never seen the like of it before. Just look at the fine china. The place must be a wonderland inside.'

'Let's go in and see.' Llinos forced a light note into her voice but there was a constriction in her throat: the china Hortense had admired was made at the Llanelli pottery. She followed Hortense, who walked eagerly to the double doors of the emporium. Then she saw it: a sign in bold lettering inviting customers to step inside and meet the pottery owner, Mr Dafydd Buchan.

So Dafydd was home from Bristol and he was here in Swansea. Her mind was racing. Why had he not sent her a note? She struggled for composure.

The store was dim after the brightness of the street, and Llinos narrowed her eyes, peering into the gloom. The porter touched his hat. 'Which department, ladies?' he asked.

Hortense smiled. 'All of them, of course! My goodness,' Hortense turned to Llinos, 'West Troy is a backwater compared to Swansea. I'm surprised Binnie ever wanted to leave here.'

Llinos smiled absently but her eyes were searching the faces in the crowd for Dafydd's. Her heart was thumping. What would he say to her?

The china department was thronged with shoppers; some of its wares were being sold at knock-down prices, a good plan designed to promote the more expensive dinner- and tea-sets.

She saw him then, and Llinos was almost afraid to move. Dafydd was seated at a large table, explaining to a young girl how the painting on the dinner plates was executed by hand.

Llinos stood as though frozen, staring at him, wanting him so badly it was like a pain. How could she ever think of giving him up? He glanced

287

towards her, as though drawn by her thoughts, and stared straight into her eyes. It was as if they were suddenly alone. The sound of voices grew dim and Llinos could see no-one but Dafydd. He was rising, coming towards her, taking her hands. 'Excuse us for just a moment.' He bowed politely to Hortense. Without waiting for a reply, he led Llinos into a small back room and put his arms around her, holding her tightly as if he would never let her go.

'I love you, God help me!' His tone was pained. 'When you didn't come that night I was devastated. As soon as I returned from Bristol I came to Swansea and to the house to see you.'

'But I was there all the time. Did Joe stop you speaking to me?' Llinos said breathlessly.

He kissed her cheeks, her eyelids, her mouth. 'No, not Joe. I tried to stay away, to be honourable, but I can't live without you, whatever your son says.'

'My son?' Her voice was strained. 'You've seen Lloyd?'

'He talked to me. He's a very wise young man,' Dafydd said. 'He begged me not to ruin your life and I tried to listen but seeing you now, well, I don't care about anything, not honour, not even the plight of the poor. Without you my life is meaningless.'

She clung to him, burying her head in his shoulder. 'I know, my love, I know.' So what if Lloyd knew? The boy had to learn about life sooner or later. She loved her son, she loved Joe, but she wanted to be with Dafydd.

'Come home with me now, please!' His voice

was urgent. 'You can't run away from me, Llinos, you just can't.'

'I'll come with you,' she said, 'but first I must tell Graves to take Hortense safely home.' As he led her out of the store Llinos clung to his arm, weak with the need of him.

Graves was waiting at the roadside and Llinos gave him instructions to fetch Mrs Dundee from the store and take her home. Then, holding Dafydd's hand, she allowed him to lead her to his own coach and pair at the back of Bagshaw's Emporium.

She leaned against his broad shoulder as the coach jerked into motion and closed her eyes. She was mad, out of her mind. She was leaving Joe, leaving her son, running away with her young lover. But she could not help herself.

He tilted her face up to his. 'I love you so much, Llinos, my lovely.' He kissed her tenderly. 'I've missed you, my darling. I thought I'd lost you for ever.'

'That night,' she said, 'I just couldn't get away. I wanted you so much but I just couldn't come to you. I'm sorry, Dafydd, but I just . . .'

He stopped her words with his lips, kissing her passionately, rousing feelings of happiness and hot desire. Llinos clung to him, wanting to tell him what she had done but words failed her. 'I'm sorry, so sorry,' she said.

'Never mind, we're together now, and I'm never going to let you go again. I love you with all my heart and soul, Llinos. I'd give up everything if I could marry you.'

'And I love you, Dafydd.' She did love him but

she loved Joe too. All she knew now, all she could sort out from her tangled thoughts, was that she had to be with Dafydd.

Hortense looked at the large clock on the wall and knew in her heart that Mrs Mainwaring was not going to return. She sighed. Poor torn woman. The look in her eyes when she saw Dafydd Buchan had spoken volumes.

She left the store and stood outside on the pavement. She recognized Graves the coachman, who bowed politely before speaking to her. 'Mrs Mainwaring says I'm to take you home.'

'Oh, thank you, Graves. I thought I had been abandoned.' She allowed him to help her into the coach, wondering what on earth Llinos was up to. She stared out of the window as the broad streets narrowed into hedgebound lanes. What would she say to Binnie, to Joe? It was going to be difficult to explain why she had returned alone. Should she lie and say she had become parted from Llinos in the crowds? But was Llinos ever going to come home? Somehow Hortense doubted it.

When she alighted from the coach, Joe was waiting on the doorstep. He helped her down and looked at her with his deep blue eyes. 'She's gone to him, hasn't she?' he said, without preamble.

Hortense nodded, her throat taut. 'I'm sorry, Joe. I couldn't do anything to stop her.'

'It's not your fault.' He led her indoors. 'Come and tell me what happened.' The drawing room was empty. Hortense looked round, as if hoping Binnie would come to her rescue.

'Binnie and Lloyd have stayed at the park.' Joe had read her mind. Hortense sank into a chair, feeling desperate. 'We are alone so just tell me exactly what happened.'

'Well, I only saw them leave the room,' she said, 'and after a time I realized that Llinos was not coming back. When I left the store the coach was waiting for me.' She shrugged. 'That's all I know, Joe, but I don't think she'll be coming back. I'm so sorry.'

Hortense felt Joe's pain. His eyes were clouded, his shoulders hunched, as if he had been dealt a physical blow.

'Was their meeting arranged?' He could hardly speak.

'No, I don't think so.' Hortense cleared her throat. 'There was a sign in the window of Bagshaw's saying the Llanelli pottery owner was in the store. I think it shook Llinos to the core when she saw him.'

'So, she's chosen him above me, then.' Joe sat down abruptly, his head in his hands. 'How could she?'

Hortense was silent. How quick men were to blame and how blind they were to their own faults.

'It's not only you who has been hurt, though, Joe, is it?' Hortense said at last. 'How do you think your wife felt when you were visiting another woman in America?'

Joe looked up. 'I suppose you have a point.' He got to his feet. 'Will you excuse me, Hortense?'

As he left the room she wondered where he was going but she was helpless to do anything. She was a visitor in a strange world, and suddenly what Hortense wanted more than anything in the world was to board a ship and sail back across the Atlantic to her home.

'May I come in?' Watt could smell baking, and the aroma of fresh bread was mouthwatering. He had been seeing quite a lot of Rosie lately and felt she was warming to him. Maybe one day she would believe he loved her. He had told her so often enough.

'Of course you can.' Rosie was looking beautiful, her face flushed, eyes bright, and Watt's heart leaped with hope. Could it be that she was happy to see him? He felt instinctively that she was, but he knew better than to rush things. He sat quietly at the polished table in the parlour and waited as she washed the flour from her hands.

'Any gossip?' Rosie pushed the heavy kettle on to the fire, not looking at him. Some of the water spilled from the blackened spout and hissed against the hot coals.

'You shouldn't be lifting that thing,' Watt said. 'Couldn't you find a smaller kettle?'

Rosie bustled into the pantry, bringing milk from the cold slab and cups from the hooks on the shelves. 'It was here,' she said. 'It was left by the previous owner, I suppose, and it seems a waste not to use it.' She smiled. 'Old habits are hard to forget.'

'But you are not poor now, Rosie, you are a woman of means, you don't need to penny-pinch any more.' Watt sighed. 'And perhaps that is the problem.'

As the kettle began to sing on the fire, Watt rose and took the brown teapot from Rosie's trembling hands. 'Sit down,' he said quietly. 'Let me make the tea. I'm well used to it, you know.'

She did know. Watt had cared for her brothers for a long time, nurtured them until they were old enough to fend for themselves. He had been wonderful to her entire family and she should be grateful to him.

He made the tea and she watched his strong hands replace the kettle on the side of the hob. He was a handsome man, perhaps more handsome now than when she had first married him.

'I know you're well off now but I'm not without money myself,' Watt said. 'Now that your brothers are working and independent I have nothing to spend my wages on.'

'Look, Watt,' Rosie said, 'none of this is to do with money, you must know that.' She studied his face. He was a strong-featured man, a man who had worked hard all his life, a man who had suffered. He was a man any woman would be proud to call her husband. But how could she be sure that he loved her?

She drank some of her tea, uncertain of herself and her feelings. She and Watt were married; he was bound to her by law. Perhaps he simply thought it easier to live with her than to form a new relationship.

Still, it was pleasant sitting opposite him in the small, bright kitchen with the fire crackling merrily, the warm flames leaping upwards. The little house was fine during the daytime and when the sun shone, but when night came and the winds roared down the chimney she felt lonely.

She still loved Watt, she was sure of that. She had never stopped loving him, not for one minute. But she had been hurt and perhaps the pain would linger and blight their marriage, even if she did take him back.

She looked up. He was watching her face as if trying to read her thoughts. She sighed heavily. 'It's about love, Watt.'

'But I do love you, Rosie.' He spoke urgently. 'Just give me a chance to persuade you of that.'

She pushed back her chair and got to her feet. 'And how can you prove it?' She was suddenly angry. 'You can speak the words until you are exhausted but that is not proof.'

'Rosie!' He sounded wounded.

'Don't Rosie me!' she exclaimed. 'I was so in love with you and you threw that love in my face.'

She wrapped her arms around her body. 'You can never go back, Watt, don't you realize that? Nothing will make me the innocent, loving girl I once was. I have grown up. There are no stars dazzling my eyes, not any more. Any naïve worship I had for you died when I found out that you had never loved me.'

She stood with her back to him. 'Just go. I can't think straight, not with you sitting staring at me like some sick animal.'

She heard him rise, heard his footsteps cross the small space to the door and then he was gone. She looked around. His tea was untasted. She remembered how he had held the heavy kettle and poured the steaming water into the teapot. How protective he was of her.

But why did he do things for her when all she wanted was for him to take her in his arms, to beg her forgiveness, to kiss her and promise that he would never desert her? Well, if Watt could not humble himself enough to find the words perhaps it was better for them to remain apart.

The rapid knock on the door made her heart leap with hope. Had Watt come back? She hurriedly lifted the latch and stepped away from the door, the words of welcome dying half formed. It was not Watt but a stranger who stood at her door.

'Excuse me coming here like this, Mrs Bevan.' The man was clearly a farmer: he wore muddy trews and his boots looked as if they had never been cleaned. He smelt of sheep and grass and the open air, and Rosie found herself smiling at him.

'I know we haven't been introduced,' he said awkwardly. 'I'm your neighbour, Iori Thomas. That there behind us is my farm.' He gestured across the fields. 'I am no tenant, I own my land and my folks have farmed here for many a long year.'

'Oh, Mr Thomas, how good of you to call,' Rosie said, bewildered by the visit. 'Is there anything I can do for you?'

'Well, no. I know you live alone with only a girl coming in to help, and I saw a stranger come up here and wondered if the man was bothering you.'

'No, of course not,' Rosie said. 'Please, Mr Thomas, come inside. There's a pot of tea on the hob, fresh and hot, perhaps you would like some?'

He glanced down at his muddy clothes. 'I don't know 'bout that,' he said. 'I saw that man here before and I wondered,' he shrugged, 'well, as I said, if he was bothering you.'

'No, he was not bothering me at all. Be easy in your mind about that, Mr Thomas, and never mind the boots, just come in.' She held the door wide and smiled, liking the open, honest face of the farmer.

'My wife said I should have come over before this to pay our respects, like, but I didn't want to be a bother.'

Mr Thomas was a man of few words and limited vocabulary but he meant well, Rosie had no doubt about that. 'Well, perhaps you and your wife would like to come over for tea on Sunday,' she said warmly. 'I'm sure you'd be most welcome.'

'That's very kind, Mrs Bevan.' He sat awkwardly on the kitchen chair, and stared longingly at the pot.

Rosie brought a clean cup and poured the tea. 'You know my name, then?'

He smiled slowly. 'Oh, yes, we all knows your name, missus. We know most things about you.'

'Oh, do you now?' Rosie said. 'And what do you know?'

'In a small place like this news travels like fire. We all know you're a well-to-do widow.' He frowned. 'And there are some wicked men about.'

'It's very kind of you to worry about me, Mr Thomas, but I—'

He held up his hand. 'Call me Iori, I'm not

used to being Mr Thomas.' He drank his tea in one swallow. 'Best get back to my wife, then.'

At the door he stopped, his hand on the latch. 'But we're here, girl. We're neighbours, right?'

'Thank you, Mr . . . Iori.' Rosie stood on the step and waved as the farmer plodded out of the garden and along the grassy bank. ''Bye, Iori!' Rosie smiled. It was good to be treated like a little girl. She had become so used to being grown-up, in charge of her own destiny, and Alice's, too, that she had forgotten what it was like to be carefree, young. And she was young. She felt the breeze in her face, smelt the softness of the evening air and suddenly felt good.

It was then that she saw Watt. He was standing a little way off in the shelter of the trees. He stared at her for a long moment, and Rosie realized how Iori Thomas's visit must look to her husband.

Watt shook his head, turned and walked swiftly away.

CHAPTER TWENTY-ONE

'Well, Joe, things are not looking too good for you, then?' Binnie was seated opposite Joe in the gentlemen's lounge of the Castle Hotel. Joe looked thinner, worry lines were etched around his eyes, and Binnie felt sorry for him.

'You've taken a bit of a beating lately, what with your native woman and the baby dying like that, and now Llinos walking out on you.' He wondered if he was making things worse for Joe by talking about his troubles but once started he felt he could not stop mid-flow. 'Terrible thing that plague killing off those Indians like that. Just to be on the safe side we went away to the coast, took the boys with us, though the three of them protested they were all grown and didn't need us to look out for them.'

Joe stared across the room as if he did not even hear him. Binnie picked up his glass of whisky. He had developed a taste for it in West Troy and now thought it rather girlish to drink port. Not that Joe could ever be accused of being feminine; he was more man than anyone Binnie knew.

Still, steeped as he was in the folklore of the Indian nation, Joe had betrayed the solemn vows of the marriage he had made to Llinos. Much as he respected Joe, Binnie's sympathy was for his dear friend.

Aloud, he attempted to mitigate Joe's crime. 'I suppose you were brought up in a different way from the rest of us,' he said slowly. 'Women like Llinos take their marriage vows seriously.'

Joe looked at Binnie then, his clear blue eyes penetrating Binnie's very soul. Startled, Binnie leaned back in his leather chair as if to distance himself from Joe. 'What I mean is, women are strange creatures and don't look on infidelity the way we men do.'

'You don't know Llinos as well as you think.' Joe's words were loaded. Through the smoke of the room, his eyes gleamed unnaturally bright and Binnie felt a moment of horror as he grasped that Joe was deeply distressed, so much so that he was on the point of shedding tears.

'Joe, what do you mean?' The implications of Joe's stark expression burst into his mind. He remembered the atmosphere when that young chap Buchan had called at the pottery. He frowned, thinking of how flustered Llinos had been, how she had rushed Buchan out of the house.

'You don't mean Llinos is having an affair?' Binnie picked up his glass and swallowed the whisky neat, not bothering to add the water placed strategically in the white china jug at his side.

Joe looked down into his drink, picked up the

glass and swirled the port into flurries of bright colour. 'That is exactly what I mean.'

He sounded like a man defeated. All his fighting spirit seemed to have left him. Binnie stared at him, remembering the first bright days of the love affair between his dear friend Llinos and Joe. How could such promise have been dashed into the dust?

He ran his hand round his collar, thinking of his own indiscretions. Hortense had been devastated when she learned he had lied to her about his first marriage. That had been the biggest mistake of Binnie's life.

He went hot and cold even now when he thought about the awful time he had gone through when Hortense threw him out. He had been a married man when he met her, and the father of a child, but he had still gone through a ceremony with Hortense, afraid of losing her.

Now that his first wife and daughter were dead, Hortense was his wife in law, the second service conducted in secret. But sometimes, even now, Binnie would see a faraway look in her face and he would feel that she was still angry and hurt by his betrayal. To a woman, physical love between a man and his woman was a sacred thing to be treasured. What pressures then must have been brought to bear on Llinos to make her turn to another man?

'I suppose I can understand Llinos's feelings,' he ventured. 'She adored you, Joe. She worshipped you and she must have been devastated when you brought an Indian squaw home to Swansea.'

'But how could she go to the arms of another man?' The words were torn from Joe. He was suffering the torments of hell and there was little Binnie could say to ease his mind.

'I don't know,' Binnie said. 'It's not like Llinos to stray – she always had such high principles.'

'Well, those principles have vanished,' Joe said, in a low voice. 'She's with the man even now, lying in his bed, letting him . . .' His voice trailed away.

'Come on, Joe!' Binnie urged. 'It's not like you to give up. Perhaps if you bide your time she'll see the error of her ways then everything can return to normal.'

'You think so?' Joe looked up, his eyes shadowed. 'Haven't you sensed the unease in the house, the air of deceit and betrayal?' He took a little of his drink. 'I think your wife knows how badly wrong my marriage is. Hortense is a sensitive woman.'

For a moment Binnie resented the implication that he was insensitive but then, looking at Joe's face, the feeling of acute pity returned. But there was nothing he could do. Interfering in someone else's marriage was dangerous. Perhaps it was time to leave Swansea and take Hortense home. He could do no good by staying here.

'Have another drink?' he asked, but Joe shook his head. He had never been much of a drinking man; he had always been strong, with an inner peace Binnie had envied. Now, though, his strength seemed to have deserted him.

'Go on!' Binnie urged. 'A drink of alcohol often takes the edge off pain, haven't you found that?'

'I suppose so.' Joe accepted another drink and then another. Binnie matched him, glass for glass. But Binnie was used to it. It did not affect him, not any more.

Binnie looked at Joe and realized the other man was drunk. 'I think we'd better get back to the house,' he said. 'I'll get the horses brought round to the front. Just you sit there and leave everything to me.'

Binnie went out into the night and looked up at the sky studded with stars. How he longed to be home in America, where everything was more impressive, where the moon almost touched the earth, and where the open spaces were vast and he could breathe.

The horses were brought and Binnie gave instructions to the stable-boy to hold the animals there while he fetched his friend. For a moment, he hesitated, stroking the strong neck of the animal nearest to him wishing himself anywhere but here in the streets of Swansea with a man drunk and sunk into misery.

Taking a deep breath, Binnie went back into the hotel and stood at the door of the lounge looking for Joe. There was no sign of him.

Llinos lay in the darkness, looking up at the moon-dappled ceiling. Beside her, Dafydd slept peacefully, his bare chest naked, his arm still under her head. They had made love and, though the passion was still there, her fascination for Dafydd still as strong as ever, Llinos knew in her heart that she had tarnished their love by sleeping with Joe. She had not brought herself to tell

Dafydd the truth – how could she when he had so much trust in her? Dafydd believed implicitly that she loved him, would never be with her husband or any other man ever again.

Hot tears formed in her eyes and her throat ached. She was so confused – and so angry with herself for being weak. She turned to look at Dafydd and saw the outline of his face against the white of the pillows. He was so young, so precious to her. Was that it? Was she just trying to recapture her youth?

She was just drifting off to sleep when she heard a pounding on the door. The small house Dafydd had rented for them boasted only one maid, and Llinos sat up, clutching the bedclothes to her as she heard the sound of footsteps then of the door being opened. Loud voices in the hall roused Dafydd, and at once he was slipping out of bed, pulling on a gown.

He was like an animal sensing danger but before he had taken the first step towards the door it was flung open and Joe stood in the doorway, tall and menacing, a candle held aloft in his hand. His hair hung around his face, his arms were outstretched and in the darkness he looked like a demon of destruction.

'What the hell—' Dafydd said. 'How dare you barge into my house?' Dafydd stood facing Joe, his young, lithe body taut, his shoulders tense. He was a man who felt he could tackle anything and anyone, but Llinos knew that this was a time for diplomacy not violence.

'Please, Joe, go downstairs while we dress. At least afford us the dignity of wearing clothes.'

'I won't be here long.' Joe's voice was harsh. 'I just came to tell you, Buchan, that Llinos still loves and desires me. Yes, that's right, she came to me eagerly enough, a woman who needs a real man to make her feel good.'

'Liar!' Dafydd said. 'I'll kill you for that, you bastard!'

'No!' Llinos stood between the two men, her heart thumping with fear. If the men fought it would be to the death, for neither of them would countenance defeat. 'No, Dafydd, don't let Joe provoke you. That's what he wants. Can't you see it?'

Dafydd put his arm around her and, with his other hand, dragged the quilt from the bed and covered her with it.

'Do you think I have never seen my wife naked?' Joe's voice was edged with sarcasm. 'Tell him, Llinos, tell him how you came to my bed the other night. Tell him I know how to make you weep with pleasure.'

'He's goading you, Dafydd,' Llinos said desperately. 'Get out, Joe. If you ever intend even to speak to me again you'll get out of here now, before I open the window and scream for the constable.'

'I won't go until you tell him!' Joe said. 'Tell your lover how you betrayed him with me. You can't deny it, Llinos.' His voice had softened. 'Tell the man, he deserves the truth.'

Dafydd looked down at her. 'Is it the truth, Llinos?' His voice shook with uncertainty and Llinos felt her heart plummet. 'Speak to me.'

'Dafydd, I was forced into it.'

'You mean, he forced himself on you?'

'No, but when we had visitors we were obliged to sleep in the same room. It just happened, Dafydd. I'm sorry in my heart!'

Dafydd released her and began to pull on his clothes like a man possessed. 'You whore!' He stared at Joe. 'Take her. You deserve each other!' He rushed from the room and Llinos heard him racing downstairs, then the front door slam.

She whirled on Joe, her eyes wide. 'Are you happy now?' She wrapped the quilt more tightly around her. 'Get out, Joe. You've done your worst and I will never forgive you, never.'

'Llinos, he's not the man for you. One day he will look at your face, really look, and then he'll see how much older you are than he is.'

'Get out before I kill you,' Llinos said. 'And move your belongings out of my house in Pottery Row. I won't return there until you do.'

He stared at her for a long moment. Then, defeated, he left the room. Llinos crawled back into the bed and began to cry, loud, heartrending sobs that racked her body. How could Joe have done this to her? How could he confront Dafydd in his own home?

'I hate you, Joe Mainwaring!' she murmured into the pillow. 'I never want to see you again.'

At last, exhausted, Llinos fell into an uneasy sleep. When she woke it was morning. Light filtered into the room and streaks of pale sun dappled the ceiling. She opened her eyes slowly, not wanting to think or feel. She stared at the indentation in the pillow where Dafydd's head had been, and a terrible fear gripped her. How could she live without him? She turned her face into the pillow again and wept.

'How could she do it to me, Isabelle?' Dafydd was unwashed. His hair, uncombed, clung around his face in tight curls. 'I trusted her and she betrayed me. How can I ever forgive her?'

Isabelle sat beside him, still dressed only in her nightclothes. 'Dafydd, she is a married woman. It must be difficult to tell your husband you no longer want any intimacy with him. As her husband he has the right to take her when he pleases.'

Dafydd looked up at her. 'Isabelle, you of all people! I know you don't agree with that!'

'Well, if she wanted to keep the peace – and with visitors in the house, what else could she do? – she couldn't fight off her own husband and make a scene, could she? It would be so humiliating. Many married women give in to their husbands for the sake of peace. Think about it, Dafydd.'

'She could have said no.'

'But could she?' Isabelle challenged him. 'What was she to do? Scream out in the night? Shame herself and her husband by causing a fuss? Sometimes it is easier to let a man have his way and be done with it.'

Dafydd looked up. 'But he said she cried out in delight, that he knew ways to please her. How can I live with her now knowing that?'

'He might have been fantasizing,' Isabelle said. 'Ask yourself, would she be so uninhibited as to cry out with guests in the next bedroom? I doubt it.' She smoothed back Dafydd's hair, as though he were a child. 'As I said, sometimes it is easier to give in and get the thing over.'

Isabelle's words were throwing a new light on the whole sorry episode with Joe. He had been making a last-ditch stand to get his wife back, and who could blame him?

'Llinos did say he forced her into it.' He looked at Isabelle. She was a rational woman and her first loyalty would always be towards him.

She continued to talk softly: 'This man, Llinos's husband, he came to you like a braggart, exaggerating everything. Don't you think this was a plan of his to separate you?'

The more Dafydd thought about it, the more he could see the happenings of the night from a different perspective. Mainwaring had come in bragging about his prowess, taunting Dafydd to the point of madness. And had Llinos stood by her husband? She had not.

He looked up. 'Thank you for talking to me, Isabelle,' he said. 'You have made me see things in a much different light.' It still pained him like a knife wound to think of Llinos in bed with Joe, but now he could accept that it had not been entirely her fault. 'I'll go home.' He got to his feet and hugged Isabelle. 'Thank you for making me see sense.' He almost smiled. 'And I apologize for dragging you out of your bed like this.'

'We are friends and that's what friends are for. Still, this passion, this urge to conquer that men have, it takes a great deal of understanding, especially for an independent woman like me.'

'You are a wise old owl.' Dafydd felt a glimmer

of humour. After all, Mainwaring had stolen only one night with Llinos while he had her for ever.

Llinos was waiting for him, standing at the window of their bedroom, her face puffy with tears. Without a word, Dafydd took her in his arms and she clung to him, weeping afresh.

'I hate Mainwaring,' he said, in a low voice, 'and I hate what he made you do, but as God is my judge, I can't live without you, Llinos.'

She held his face in her hands and kissed his lips. She spoke through her tears. 'And I can never let you go, never.' She swallowed hard. 'I will stay here with you always. I'll never go back to the pottery. I won't risk losing you, Dafydd, even if it means changing the whole pattern of my life.'

Dafydd buried his face in her neck and they clung together like drowning souls.

As the carriage drove away from the heat and smell of the pottery Binnie glanced back along the row, where doors stood open and women fought a constant battle against dust, and was happy to be leaving.

Hortense was at his side, her hand resting on his thigh, her eyes bright with happiness because she was going home. Binnie had been lucky: a ship had been leaving the docks at Swansea to cross the Atlantic with room for passengers. Soon, the shores of Wales would be left behind. Out of the harbour, the sails would be unfurled and the wind would take the ship through the Bristol Channel and out to the open sea.

'That was a strange visit, honey.' Hortense

stroked his thigh, and he was acutely aware of the warmth of her hand.

He swallowed hard. He loved her so much, his Hortense, his wife. 'I love you, Hortense,' he said. 'It's strange how the troubles of others makes a soul realize that good fortune has smiled on them.'

'I'm so sad about Joe,' Hortense said. 'I have never seen him so despairing, not even when he came to us after his woman and child died. How could Llinos leave him for another man?'

'I don't blame her,' Binnie said defensively. 'Joe was the first to stray, remember? He even brought the Indian woman here with him to Swansea, set her up in a house in the valley somewhere and sired a child on her. How did that make Llinos feel? Ask yourself that.'

'No need to leap to Llinos's defence,' Hortense said mildly. 'I am quite aware how she must have felt betrayed.'

Her words were uncomfortably close to home and Binnie changed the subject. 'I hope we have calm weather across the Atlantic,' he said, glancing out of the window, as if the heavens could give him an answer.

Hortense concealed a smile. She knew when Binnie was shamefaced about his own past behaviour. Simple soul that he was, he pushed it away from his mind, acting as though he had been a perfect husband all his life.

She leaned against him and, without another word, he put his arm around her, his hand straying to her breast. Triumph flared through her. She might be a mature woman with grown sons, but she still had the power to arouse her husband.

She snuggled closer to him. 'I'll sure be glad when we're back on American soil again, honey,' she said softly.

'Why?' he asked, with a hint of laughter in his voice.

'Because, Binnie Dundee, then I can ravish you to my heart's content.' She sighed softly. She was going home and all was well with her world.

CHAPTER TWENTY-TWO

'So what really happened, then, Isabelle?' Eynon was seated in the neat parlour in her house.

She looked at him with admiration. He was so handsome, so much a gentleman. His long legs were stretched towards the fire and, in spite of his own opulent surroundings, he appeared completely at ease in her house. 'There was some sort of confrontation. Joe Mainwaring created a scene and, from what I gather, it almost came to blows.'

'So Joe caught them in bed together?'

'Of course.'

'But if he knew they were lovers what made him suddenly boil over? In any case, after what he's been up to he has no right to complain.'

Isabelle looked at Eynon long and hard. 'Llinos slept with her husband at least on one occasion after becoming intimate with Dafydd. Is that fair to either man?'

Eynon was frowning. 'No doubt she was coerced into sharing Joe's bed. She wouldn't have gone to him willingly – she was so hurt by the way he treated her.'

'I know that you and Llinos have been friends

for a very long time but I sometimes wonder if your feelings go beyond friendship.' Isabelle was aware that her voice held a touch of asperity. 'You seem to think Llinos can do no wrong.'

'Look, Isa, I'm sad for both Joe and Llinos. Their love was so beautiful once, but it was Joe who wrecked the marriage and he must accept his responsibility for that.'

Isabelle thought it politic to change the subject. 'Have you seen anything of Shanni?'

'No.' Eynon shook his head. 'I don't know what the girl is going to do now that Llinos has moved out of the house.'

'Is she living openly with Dafydd then?' Isabelle was curious in spite of herself.

'It seems so.'

'Oh dear. Poor Shanni, she's caught betwixt the devil and the deep blue sea, then. I worry about that girl.'

'Why don't you have her here for a while?' Eynon said. 'If it's a question of money I'm sure I could help.'

'You make everything sound so simple, and thank you, but it's nothing to do with money.'

'Well, then, it's not very complicated just asking a pupil to stay, is it?'

'Llinos thinks I'm a bad influence. I don't think she'd like the thought of Shanni living here permanently.'

'I shouldn't think any of that matters now, if Llinos has left home.'

He was right, of course. If Llinos had gone to live with Dafydd she would hardly care what Shanni did with her life. 'You may have a point.'

There was silence in the room, except for the shifting of the coals burning low in the grate. Isabelle looked at Eynon, who met her gaze and smiled. But was it the smile of a friend or a lover? Isabelle could not tell.

Sometimes when they lay in bed satiated with love-making she believed he cared about her very much. But at other times, like today, she wondered if Llinos was his real love and she a poor second best.

'When are we going to set a date for the wedding?' Eynon asked.

Startled, Isabelle looked down at her hands. Perhaps she should allow some time to elapse before she committed herself. She cared deeply about Eynon but she certainly did not want to tie him down if he was not sure of his love for her. 'Soon, Eynon,' she promised. She was older than Eynon by only a few years, but just then she felt ancient, as though she had the wisdom of the ages in her blood. She changed the subject again. 'I think I'll take your advice. If I write a letter inviting Shanni to stay, will you deliver it for me when you ride back to Swansea?'

'Of course,' Eynon said. 'But I was hoping I might stay with you tonight. See? It's growing dark, the rainclouds are closing in. Riding home to Swansea in such weather would be the death of me.' He winked.

She glanced up at him, happy to play the coquette. 'Is the inclement weather the only reason you want to stay?'

He came and knelt at her feet, his head resting against her breast. She touched his golden hair, tinged now with threads of silver, and her heart swelled with love. She must marry him because she could not bear to live without him.

'Of course you can stay.' She tipped his face up to hers. 'And, Eynon, I will marry you as soon as ever you can make the arrangements.'

She knew she was throwing caution to the wind but all her fears vanished as she bent and kissed his lips. His response was so warm, so passionate: surely she could not doubt that he loved her. Even if she should turn out to be second best wasn't that preferable to living her life without love and the comfort of a man's arms around her in the night? She kissed him again. 'How about a little rest before supper?' she whispered intimately in his ear. His hands were on her breasts, his mouth hot against her throat. Desire for him burned suddenly like a flaming beacon in the darkness. She wanted him, and he wanted her with equal urgency. Surely that was enough for any woman.

'Mr Mainwaring.' Shanni was hesitant about intruding into the study where Joe was packing a bag with papers. 'May I speak to you?'

'Of course you may. What is it?'

'I've had an invitation to stay with Madame Isabelle, and in view of the situation here I think it wise I should go.'

'You are probably right.' Joe did not look up and his voice was casual, but Shanni knew he was not listening to what she was saying.

'The thing is,' Shanni hesitated, 'I can't get to

Llanelli on my own. May I ask Graves to take me?'

Joe waved his hand. 'As you like.' He looked up then. 'I'm sorry, Shanni, I'm being thoughtless. Of course Graves must take you.' He smiled but his eyes were shadowed. 'You are a fine young lady now, and how would it look if you travelled alone?'

Shanni stared down at her feet, suitably modest. If he knew of half the things she was up to he would hardly call her a lady. 'Thank you very much, Mr Mainwaring.'

She hesitated, and Joe looked at her questioningly. 'Was there anything else, Shanni? I am in rather a hurry. I have a journey to make.'

'I only wanted to say that you have my sympathy, Mr Mainwaring. How your wife could leave you for a man half her age I don't know.' Some of her bitterness erupted into her voice.

Joe looked at her carefully. 'Setting your cap at the man yourself, were you, Shanni?' He was no fool, she realized. Mr Mainwaring was a man who could see into a woman's soul. 'If that is the case, I think you are better out of it. The man has no moral values.' He regarded her steadily. 'Another thing, Shanni, you would not enjoy a long and happy marriage to Buchan even if he did fall in love with you.'

She was afraid to ask what he meant. Was Joe Mainwaring going to kill Dafydd? Panic rushed through her, and all at once she was anxious to be gone. 'Thank you, sir, for your kindness.' She hurried to the kitchen and told one of the younger maids to have Graves bring the carriage round.

'It's on Mr Mainwaring's orders,' she said, as the maid looked daggers at her.

Upstairs, Shanni packed a few of her nicer clothes into a bag and glanced around the bedroom. She had come to think of it as her retreat, her own place where she could be alone. She would miss it.

She felt a moment of sadness – she could not deny that Llinos had been good to her but all her kindness faded into insignificance against the fact that she had stolen Dafydd's love. Llinos had no right to it, she was married, she should have left him alone. Then Dafydd might have seen that Shanni had grown up, had turned into a well-bred young woman.

It was strange riding down Pottery Row not knowing if she would ever see it again. She was moving out of Swansea, perhaps for ever, and in spite of herself, she felt a tug at her heartstrings.

As Graves drove through the streets of the town, Shanni drank in the familiar sights, the busy market where vendors offered their wares in raucous tones. She leaned out to see the cockle-women, baskets swinging from plump arms, black hats marking them out from the more elegant shoppers. She felt tears burn her eyes and rubbed them away impatiently. She was young, with her whole life before her: she should look to the future and be happy.

Soon, the busy roads petered out to be replaced by narrow, hilly lanes. Shanni sank back in the coach, tired of watching the passing countryside, and closed her eyes. She thought of Dafydd, of his fine figure, his dark hair curling round his strong features, and in spite of her anguish she felt a thrill of pride that she knew this man who would one day set the world to rights.

She must have dozed because she was suddenly conscious of the carriage jerking to a halt. She heard hoofs pawing the ground then Graves was opening the door and helping her out on to the dusty road.

Isabelle was waiting in the immaculate hallway. She took Shanni in her arms and hugged her. 'You are very welcome here, Shanni,' she said. 'Stay as long as you like. I'm pleased to have you.'

For the first time it occurred to Shanni that she was throwing herself on Isabelle's mercy. Shanni had no money of her own, no skills to equip her to earn her keep. She would be entirely dependent on Isabelle's charity. It was a most unsettling feeling.

Graves was taken to the kitchen for refreshment and Shanni watched his familiar figure as he walked away from the front door towards the back entrance. She felt a sense of loss – pain was not too strong a word for it. She had left behind all she had known and thrown herself on the charity of a woman who needed to work for a living. Was she being fair to Madame Isabelle?

'Come in, Shanni,' Madame smiled, 'and, for heaven's sake, take that glum look off your face. This isn't the end of the world, you know.'

'I'm not ungrateful, Madame,' Shanni said quickly, 'and I do realize that I'm imposing on you. I can't live on your charity for ever. I'll have to find an occupation and earn my own living.'

317

Shanni had no idea what sort of work she was suited for. She would hate to be in service as a maid-of-all-work, especially after the luxury she had enjoyed in the Mainwaring household. A shop, then? That idea did not appeal either.

Madame's voice broke into her thoughts. 'We can think about all that later. Now you must settle yourself in, hang up your clothes and make sure you have water in the jug on your table.' She smiled. 'I'm afraid you won't be able to live to the standards you've come to expect in Swansea, though.' She shrugged. 'I'm not rich, as you know, but what I have I will share with you wholeheartedly.'

On an impulse Shanni hugged her. Madame smelt of lavender and fresh roses. She returned Shanni's hug then released her.

'Right, enough of this sentimentality. Come and sit down. We'll have tea in a moment – I'm sure you're hungry.'

'Have you seen anything of Dafydd?' Shanni asked. Madame Isabelle looked at her, eyebrows raised.

'He is rather too busy with his lady-love to spare the time to visit old friends.' There was an edge of bitterness in her voice. 'I am a little worried he'll neglect the cause for which we have fought long and hard.'

'Surely he won't do that!' Shanni said. She wondered if she should tell Madame about Joe's strange remark. He had insinuated that Dafydd would not remain long on this earth to enjoy Llinos's company. Almost at once she dismissed the idea. Joe was going away. He was probably very angry, and angry men said things they did not mean.

'Dafydd is very wrapped up in himself and his love for a married woman just now,' Isabelle said. 'You do know that he and Llinos Mainwaring are living together, don't you?'

'Of course I do! I've known for a long time they were involved with each other.' She remembered the day as if it were yesterday. She had been shopping with Llinos and they had met Dafydd by accident. Or perhaps it had been by design?

'We had tea together,' she said. 'I was so embarrassed by the way they were staring into each other's eyes that I just walked out and left them to it. I can't understand how a woman like Llinos Mainwaring could be so lacking in moral scruples.'

'Don't be so quick to judge, and keep your voice down.' Madame Isabelle put her finger to her lips as the maid rapped on the door and entered almost immediately with the tea tray.

'Put the tray there, Sarah,' Isabelle said. 'Shanni, will you pour, dear?' Isabelle waited until the maid had left the room then leaned forward in her chair. 'Anyway, let's talk about happier topics, shall we?' She smiled, and in that moment Shanni realized that Madame Isabelle was very beautiful for her age. 'I have had a proposal of marriage. What do you think of that?'

'Oh, Madame, I am so pleased for you!' Shanni did her best to appear happy at the unexpected news, but she could hardly help wondering what would become of her when Isabelle took a husband.

'I shall be very happy to be Mrs Eynon Morton-Edwards.' Madame's eyes were misty. 'I will have to buy some new clothes, a bridal dress – a discreet gown, of course. You must come with me and advise me, Shanni.'

Shanni stared at her. It was strange that a woman of her mature years would want to marry at all. 'Have you set the date for the wedding yet?' Shanni asked, a little anxiously.

'Not exactly, but it won't be for a few months yet, I shouldn't think.' Isabelle appeared to hug herself. 'But I hope I will not have *too* long to wait.'

Shanni wondered if Madame would forget the cause of the poor farmers once she was Mrs Morton-Edwards. The problems of the toll-gates seemed to have been washed from her mind.

This was the very accusation she had levelled against Dafydd, and here she was, acting in exactly the same way, putting herself first.

Madame Isabelle seemed to pick up on her thoughts. 'Dafydd has been persuaded to come over tonight, Shanni. Perhaps then we shall get some sense out of him. I want to know what his plans are. We must still fight to reduce the price of the tolls.'

Shanni's heart missed a beat. Just the mention of Dafydd's name was enough to make her tremble. Perhaps one day he would come to his senses and realize that Llinos Mainwaring was far too old for him. All at once she was filled with resentment. Here she was, a young and by now well-educated young lady, with no suitable beau to come calling on her, while older women like

Llinos Mainwaring and Madame Isabelle seemed to have everything they wanted.

'Why so glum?' Madame Isabelle asked, taking a muffin from the plate. 'Not worrying about your own chances of marriage, are you?'

'Well, yes, I am.' Shanni thought it best to tell the truth. 'The only one who seems to like me is Pedr, and he isn't really suitable, is he?'

Madame Isabelle looked steadily at her plate. 'Why do you say that?'

Shanni was aware of the strange note in the other woman's voice and knew that she had sounded disparaging. 'It's not that I don't like him but he wants different things from life.'

'I see.'

Shanni had the feeling that she saw all too clearly. 'Apart from which I'm in love with someone else, someone I can't have.'

'I know.' Madame Isabelle smiled then. 'But you are very young. The young fall in and out of love a dozen times before they settle.' She took another bite from her muffin and the butter spilled on to the front of her gown. 'Damn!' She brushed at the stain ineffectually. 'Now I'll have to change. And so will you.' She looked at Shanni's dusty boots. 'After tea you must go to your room and find yourself something nice to wear. We must look our best by the time my guests arrive for supper.'

She leaned back in her chair. 'And in the morning we shall do some shopping for my trousseau.'

Shanni put down her cup and stared long and hard at Madame. 'You're wrong,' she said. 'I won't ever love anyone else. I know my own mind and nothing will change it.'

Before Madame Isabelle could make any comment Shanni left the parlour and hurried up the winding stairs. She was conscious that the house smelt of beeswax and lavender, and the homely aroma of bread baking in the oven. Despair possessed her. Was she doomed to spend her days alone, never to have a home of her own? Would she be unloved for the rest of her life?

Shanni heard the rattle of wheels outside and realized that Graves had left for Swansea. Here she was in Madame Isabelle's house, and here she would have to stay. Suddenly there were tears in Shanni's eyes. Her whole life had taken a turn for the worse and her future was uncertain. Llinos Mainwaring had a lot to answer for.

CHAPTER TWENTY-THREE

Joe sat in the large, airy drawing room of the house his father had left him and stared through the window at the rolling green countryside. Out there, somewhere on the horizon, was the border between England and Wales. Swansea seemed a million miles away.

He missed Swansea: it had become his home; it was where he had married and where his legitimate son had been born. Now, miles away from all he loved, life seemed meaningless. He had once had a wife and a mistress, a legitimate son and a love-child. Now he had nothing but ghosts and memories.

Joe was honest enough to recognize that the fault was his: Llinos had been so hurt when he had taken another woman. Like a thoughtless fool he had moved Sho Ka into the house in Neath, in close proximity to Swansea. In doing so he had ground Llinos's pride into the dust.

Joe was racked with pain whenever he thought of his wife in bed with Dafydd Buchan. It had been like a knife twisting inside him when he saw them together. Llinos had been flushed with the joy of it, her features softened by passion. Once that passion had been his. Now he had thrown it away, and Dafydd Buchan had stepped in to take advantage of the situation.

The man was brave enough, and Joe gave him due credit for that: Buchan had stood his ground even though Joe was acting the outraged husband, bursting into the house and threatening him. Buchan was the sort who would defend himself and Llinos to the death, and it might well come to that.

Joe glanced at his pocket watch. Lloyd would be arriving soon. He wanted to talk to his father, to find out exactly what was happening. How would he take it when Joe told him that Llinos had left him?

But, whatever happened, Lloyd was finished with college. He had made that perfectly plain in his letter. He wanted to travel the world, to see different nations, his father's nation of American-Indians. Lloyd was searching for his roots, which Joe understood.

Joe was eager to see his son again, but dreaded telling him about his mother living with another man. It was agony to think of it. Had Llinos suffered like this in imagining him with another woman?

Joe could not deny that he had enjoyed making love to Sho Ka. She was beautiful, exotic. She had shown him great passion. Perhaps he even loved her a little. But to admit that was the ultimate betrayal. And, in the end, it had all been for nothing. Joe remembered how he held Sho Ka in his arms until the big sleep took her. And then their son had drifted into another, remote world. Now there was no heir to take up the leadership of the Mandan tribe, no great chief to fight for the survival of the few remaining people who had escaped the terrible plague. Had it all been in vain? Had his entire life been in vain?

Joe felt desperate. He stood up and squared his shoulders: sitting in the large empty house feeling sorry for himself did no good at all. He would go out and walk, see the fields and rivers, and feel the cool breezes bathing his brow.

A heavy rain had begun to soak the fields and gather on the leaves of the strong English oaks, which bent under the weight. It was as if the whole world was encased in grey, a tearful world where only misery had free rein.

Perhaps he should shake the dust of England from his feet and go back to the plains of America. There, the hills towered above deep rivers; there, a man had space to breathe. And yet, in his heart, Joe knew he had unfinished business in Swansea. He could not walk away from his wife. He must at least make an attempt to win her back. But was it a hopeless task? Had he lost her for ever?

That night Joe ate no supper. Not even the cajoling of the rheumy old cook, hired for the duration of his stay, could make him enjoy the hot soup and the roly-poly pudding soaked in wine.

He took a drink of port to his bed, and sat up against the pillows, staring into the darkness beyond the windows and wondering if his spirits could possibly sink any lower. At last he slept, but it was a restless sleep where images taunted him.

He saw the ghosts of his mother and Sho Ka. He felt the pallid skin of his dead baby son. And through the long hours of the night he felt as though fire consumed him.

It was in his bed of sickness that Lloyd found him the next day. Joe heard his voice: he spoke low as a man does in the presence of sickness. A cool hand rested on his brow and he saw Llinos, her dark hair tangled about her face, her eyes wide with fear. Had she come to him in a dream?

'Come, Joe,' she said, her face floating before him, 'you are a brave, strong man, you must fight the fever.' She crept into bed beside him and he held her close. He made love to her with the last of his strength and then, spent, he slept. He woke briefly and saw her beside him. He clung to her, knowing that with the coming of morning she might disappear, but in his heart there was hope that Llinos still loved him.

One morning Joe woke to find the sun washing palely through the bedroom. He felt very weak, could barely lift his head from the pillow, but his mind was clear.

'Llinos?' He murmured her name and she was there, her hand on his cheek.

'Joe, you're awake. The fever has broken!' She sat at his side and held his hand close to her breast. 'Oh, Joe, you've been so sick, I thought we were going to lose you.'

'Llinos,' he whispered, 'my life is meaningless without you.'

'Hush, I'm here now and so is Lloyd.' She forced a smile. 'Our son took charge. He hired a nurse then came to Swansea to fetch me.'

'You came willingly?'

'How could I not come when you needed me so badly?'

Joe felt his eyes begin to close but he knew that a healing sleep was claiming him. His wife was there, at his side, and that knowledge gave him the strength to face life again.

'So.' Lloyd stood in the drawing room, his hands thrust into his pockets. 'You are going back to him, aren't you, Mother?' Lloyd's face was filled with anxiety. 'Buchan, I mean.'

Llinos swallowed hard. 'Lloyd, I don't know what your father has told you but . . .'

Her voice trailed away as Lloyd held up his hand. 'Father told me nothing, at least not intentionally.' Lloyd sighed. 'My father ranted in his fever about another man, Dafydd Buchan, who had taken you away from him. How could you, Mother? How could you betray my father with another man like that?'

'I can't begin to justify what I did, Lloyd.' Llinos rubbed her eyes tiredly. 'I was so beaten when Joe took Sho Ka as his mistress and even had a child by her. I felt I was no longer a real woman. I felt that no man would ever love and desire me. Then Dafydd came into my life.' She shrugged. 'I can't give him up, Lloyd, I just can't.'

'But you will stay with Father for the time being.' Lloyd spoke forcefully. 'We will take him home with us to Swansea. There we can nurse him back to health. He's a broken man, Mother. Can't you see that?'

'What about me, Lloyd?' Llinos was suddenly angry. 'What about *my* feelings? I suffered the humiliation your father inflicted on me. I died a thousand deaths thinking of him in another woman's arms, loving her, giving her his baby when I could no longer conceive. Was I supposed to take all that without protest?'

'Most women do,' Lloyd said mildly.

'I am not most women!' Llinos was on her feet. 'I wrested a livelihood from clay. I dragged my father's business out of poverty and fought back against fate with all my strength. I am not cut from the same mould as the spoilt, rich wives who turn a blind eye to their husband's infidelities.'

'I know you are a proud woman, Mam,' Lloyd spoke to her now in Welsh, his voice softening, 'but if he can forgive, can't you?'

'I can try,' Llinos said. 'But I won't give Dafydd up. I can't give him up. If you don't understand, then so be it.' She paced across the room. 'How do you think he feels with me running off to nurse my sick husband? Dafydd is not happy with my decision to come here, but he supports me in it.'

'You can't expect me to condone what you are doing, Mother,' Lloyd said. 'I can see how it's affecting Father. I saw how sick he was, all because of you. He might have died of the fever.'

'That's why I came.'

Lloyd stared moodily out of the window and Llinos saw that his upper lip sported a moustache and that on the strong curve of his chin a beard was growing.

'Of course, the real reason for Father's sickness

is a broken heart. He can't bear it that you have left him.'

'I told you, your father has no monopoly on broken hearts. I had a broken heart and spirit when your father left me for another woman,' Llinos said. 'Lloyd, this is not revenge. I just have to be with Dafydd, that's all.'

'Don't you love Father any more?'

'Yes! I don't know. Oh, just leave me alone, Lloyd, please. My head is reeling with all these questions.'

Without another word, Lloyd disappeared through the door soundlessly, the way Joe did. Llinos sank into a chair and shut her eyes. Behind the lids, she saw Dafydd's worried face, heard the fear in his voice when she said she was leaving. She had hugged him to her and promised faithfully she would be back. And she *would* return to him, but when?

Another week had passed before Lloyd decided that his father was well enough to undertake the coach journey back to Swansea. Joe accepted his son's decision with unaccustomed meekness, grateful to let Lloyd take charge. He appeared, as Lloyd had claimed, to be a broken man.

As she sat beside him in the coach, Llinos looked out at the rolling green countryside. The Marches were the no man's land between England and Wales and to Llinos meant separation not only from her home but from her lover.

She felt Joe reach for her hand beneath the woollen rug and her first instinct was to draw away from him. Then she relaxed. What harm could it do to give him a little comfort on the long journey? And long it was. The overnight stops at coaching inns were a nightmare, Llinos forced to share a bed with him. The first night, she put as much distance between herself and her husband as was possible, but when she woke in the morning, she was curled up in Joe's arms.

'Dafydd, my love!' Llinos could not believe she was home at last. As soon as she stepped through the door of Dafydd's house he was there, waiting for her. And then she was in his arms, breathing in the scent of him, wanting the fit young hardness of him against her.

She pressed her lips to his and his tongue probed hers. Desire flamed through her. 'Take me to bed, Dafydd,' she whispered. 'Make me your own again.'

The house was silent as they went upstairs, even the cook and the maid were absent. Dafydd had planned it that way so that he and Llinos would meet for the first time in weeks with no distractions.

'Let me undress you. I need to look at your perfect body. I can't wait to make love to you again.' He buried his face in her neck. 'I was so afraid you wouldn't come back to me. I can't believe it even now with you here in my arms.'

His hands were gentle, untying ribbons, opening buttons but his need was great. Llinos could see the urgency in his eyes, feel it in the tautness of his body. She lay naked before him, praying she would be beautiful in his sight. She was a mature woman and Dafydd was a young man. How could he love her so much?

He kissed her lips, her neck, and then his mouth was hot on her breasts. She closed her eyes feeling as if she was melting in the intense heat of their desire. He moved into her easily – she wanted him as much as he wanted her.

Llinos arched against him. Sensations of pleasure ran through her thighs and belly and seemed to reach to her very heart. Dafydd's hands were beneath her, lifting her even closer. He needed to possess her and she understood that need because she felt it as much as he did.

They rode together on waves of love and delight. Llinos risked looking up at him and his eyes were bright, shining down into hers, loving her with every glance. Every movement of his body was a message of love, and when the shuddering moment of release held them both in its spell Llinos cried out his name.

Afterwards, they lay entwined in each other's arms. He smoothed Llinos's tangled hair away from her face and kissed her brow. 'My girl has come home to me,' she could hear the tears in his voice, 'my sweet girl is here in my arms. I must be the happiest man in the whole world.'

Later, when they had bathed and dressed Dafydd took her to a coaching inn and ordered a meal of sizzling beef steaks stuffed with oysters. He filled her cup with fine wine and, content, they sat together silent and sated like an old married couple.

The wine loosened Dafydd's tongue, and he leaned even closer to her as they sat side by side on the oak settle near the fire. 'You haven't slept with *him* again, have you, Llinos? Please tell me the truth.'

'I made a mistake once and I won't do it again,' Llinos said softly. 'I didn't allow Joe to touch me, not even to rest his hand on my shoulder, and I can swear that on the Bible, if you like.'

He touched her cheek. 'I believe you, my little girl,' he said softly. 'I saw the love and joy in your face when you came to me. I know you are mine now, and only mine. I will hold you like the greatest treasure on earth and I will never let you go, not until death do us part.'

Llinos shivered. It was as if a shadow had fallen over her heart. She reached for him. 'Hold me close, Dafydd,' she said softly. 'Just hold me close.'

CHAPTER TWENTY-FOUR

Shanni could see the difference in Dafydd as soon as he came into Madame Isabelle's house. He stood in the hall, happiness shining from him like a beacon, and all because Llinos Mainwaring had come back to him. Anger and pain warred within her. She was young, she was much prettier than Llinos Mainwaring, and she was free. She had no husband, no lover, and if Dafydd came to her he would find her a virgin.

'Isabelle!' Dafydd took Madame in his arms and kissed her on both cheeks. 'More lovely than ever. Do I hear wedding bells by any chance?'

'You do indeed, Dafydd.' She spoke in a low voice. 'And you are looking much better. You've been going around like a man ready to throw himself off a cliff. I presume your love life has taken a turn for the better?'

He tapped his nose playfully. 'You can be so nosy, Isabelle,' he teased. 'And you, Shanni, can put your eyes back into your head now because there's no gossip to relate.'

A moment before, Shanni had congratulated herself on being young. Now she felt her youth was a disadvantage. She allowed Dafydd to hold her lightly in his arms and breathed in the scent of him – the freshness of the evening air, the aroma of tobacco – and her heart lurched. She would have Dafydd for her own, even if she had to wait for ever.

He released her and she smiled up at him. He was so tall, so handsome, such a brave, strong man. Dafydd was her hero, he was everything her heart desired, and she would fight Llinos Mainwaring to the death for him if she had to.

'How is Pedr, these days? Behaving himself, is he?' Dafydd waited until the ladies were seated then took a seat himself.

Shanni made an effort to smile but she resented the implication that Pedr and she were involved with each other. 'I suppose he's fine,' she said. 'I haven't seen anything of him for ages.' She folded her fingers together and sat back in the shadows of the big armchair, unaware of the mutinous look on her face.

'Your brother is well now?' Isabelle broke the silence that followed Shanni's petulant words. 'I saw Ceri out riding the other day and he looked well. It seems he's fully recovered from his injuries.'

'He is well enough,' Dafydd said. 'He's still furious with me, of course. He thinks I should be on the side of law and order. Ceri pays lip service to the plight of the farmers but he is, first and foremost, a businessman.' Dafydd shook his head. 'And as such he believes it to be in his best interest to stay away from political debate.'

'I can't say I blame him.' Isabelle leaned

forward. 'However, it's left to people like you and me to do something to right the wrongs of this world. If you are not too busy, shall we begin to map out our plans?'

Dafydd rubbed his chin, and his head was bent so that Shanni could not see his expression. She felt, rather than saw, that he would rather speak of his foolish, disgusting affair with Llinos Mainwaring than think of the wrong done to the farmers. 'Well, I suppose we should think up a strategy.' He spoke almost reluctantly. 'It must be something big, though. What if we plan for the middle of summer? That would give us plenty of time and lull the authorities into believing we have given up the fight.'

Shanni saw him glance at Madame Isabelle as if waiting for her approval. He did not even think to seek Shanni's opinion.

'With the element of surprise working for us,' he went on, 'we can strike hard and swift at the structure of the law.'

'You could be right,' Madame Isabelle said quietly. 'But the men are getting restless. I've arranged a meeting here for tonight. I thought you would want that.'

'Oh, yes, you did right, of course.' Dafydd did not look very pleased. He had probably arranged to be with his married woman. Shanni waited, with bated breath, until Dafydd spoke again.

'Tonight it is.' He got to his feet abruptly. 'I'll have to alter some of my plans. I'd better go and see to things at once.'

Shanni felt a flood of triumph. Dafydd would have to make excuses to Llinos Mainwaring for his absence. At least tonight he would be here with Shanni and not with *her*. The thought gave Shanni a feeling of pure satisfaction.

Dafydd took his leave with what Shanni could only describe as indecent haste. He was frowning, clearly expecting a scene with Llinos Mainwaring. Well, serve him right: perhaps now he would grasp what it meant to be entangled in an illicit affair.

'Well,' Madame Isabelle looked at Shanni, 'that was a sudden departure.'

Shanni was silent: she was imagining Dafydd's halting explanation about tonight and Llinos's reaction. She would be furious that she was being set aside for a meeting with what she would describe as a group of rabble-rousers.

'You look rather like the cat that's caught a mouse,' Madame said. 'What are you thinking, Shanni?'

'I'm thinking that Dafydd is very foolish to get mixed up with a married woman.' The words were spoken before Shanni had time to examine them, and she saw Madame Isabelle frown.

'Judge not that ye be not judged,' she said darkly. 'It is not your place to criticize the private lives of the people who are my guests.'

Shanni knew she had made a mistake in speaking so frankly. As far as Madame Isabelle was concerned Dafydd's affair was a private matter and nothing to do with the cause. Sometimes Shanni wondered how Madame could allow herself a love life, so committed was she to setting right the wrongs of the world.

Still, for tonight at least Dafydd would be here,

336

and she would see him again, look into his eyes, try to make him realize she was a woman, not a little girl. She had too much pride to be a mistress, and that was all Llinos would ever amount to: the mistress of a younger man.

The pottery was running smoothly, the output of brightly decorated tea- and supperware stacked neatly on shelves ready for the final firing. Dafydd breathed in the smell of paint, watching as the artists splashed colour and light on to the surface of the plain white china. The brushwork was loose, flowing but beautiful, and he congratulated himself on securing the services of an excellent artist. Dafydd had a good team of workers and he was fortunate enough to enjoy a close working relationship with them.

Some of the men fought alongside him in his role as leader of the Rebeccarites. He smiled. How Llinos would laugh if she saw him dressed in his horsehair wig and his long petticoats. His heart missed a beat. He would have to let her know that he would be out for the best part of the evening. He was worried that she might take the opportunity to go and see her son.

He hated the thought of it, of Llinos in the same house as her husband. Joe Mainwaring was powerful, handsome in his exotic way. He had an inner strength that spoke of great self-knowledge. He was a dangerous adversary.

Dafydd left the painting shed, stepping out into the warm sunshine. He stood aside to watch the tail end of the retinue of wagons being drawn towards the gates. Ceri had stipulated that only one horse be used per wagon as a means of economy. Dafydd had disagreed: he thought it would slow down the journey but in the end Ceri had had his way.

Ceri had risen from his sickbed with a new energy. He asserted himself more often and Dafydd, occupied as he was by other matters, allowed his brother to take charge. One of Ceri's decisions was that when winter came, the carpenters and millwrights were to work until six o'clock, even when it meant using candles. Dafydd frowned. Anyone would imagine that the Buchan family were impoverished, the way Ceri carried on. He had even objected to Pedr Morgan earning more than some of the other workers. He paid no mind to the fact that Pedr was a good potter, swift and talented into the bargain.

As Dafydd walked through the yard the unmistakable smell of tobacco drifted towards him. He walked silently around the pile of broken pottery and into the clay yard. A man was slouched against the wall. His head was turned away but a thin trail of smoke gave him away. 'Smoking, Barratt?' Dafydd said quietly. 'If I were you I'd put away your pipe in case my brother decides to walk around the place.' The man hesitated. 'You don't want a fine imposed on you, do you?' Dafydd's voice had a stern edge to it. 'You can ill afford it, not with your brood of young ones.'

Sulkily, Barratt tapped his pipe against the wall. 'Right, sir.'

'Now, I suggest you get back to work while you still have work to do. And if I catch you smoking in working hours again you'll be dismissed, do you understand?'

Dafydd watched the man walk away. He knew his ill humour was all to do with the meeting Isabelle had arranged. He would much rather be with Llinos tonight. He still could not believe his luck in getting her back. He cursed under his breath. Even thinking about her, her perfect body, her wonderful eyes, the way she loved him, was enough to arouse him. 'Damn the meeting!' he said softly.

'So this is only a visit, Mother?' Lloyd watched as Llinos stood in the hallway pinning a hat on to her curling hair. 'You just sail in, pick up some more things and sail out again without thought for me or Father.'

Llinos treated him to a blast from her beautiful eyes, and Lloyd felt his courage desert him. 'Please stay. I've invited Jayne for the evening but when she leaves we can talk to each other, can't we?'

'There's nothing you can say, Lloyd. As for Jayne, well, she's your guest and you must entertain her.' His mother spoke in a way that was unfamiliar to him. She was besotted by this man Buchan, bewitched. How else could she do this to them?

'So you are never coming home again?' Lloyd was trying to speak reasonably, but he felt as if he could shake his mother. 'You know he is sick at heart thinking of you and that man? You can't throw everything away, Mother, not for a man like Buchan.'

His mother turned to face him. 'Please don't speak to me in that tone of voice.' Her eyes flashed fire and Lloyd knew, even though he towered above her now, that his mother demanded respect.

'You were at college when your father carried on with Sho Ka so you didn't realize he was never here. He left me alone day and night and no-one was around to comfort me when I cried myself to sleep. You never saw the hours of anguish I suffered.'

Lloyd knew she had a point. His father had been the one to break the marriage vows first but, still, he had thought his mother had more self-control than to become involved with any other man.

'I will not give up my lover, and if you or your father will not accept that then it's just too bad. Do you understand me?'

'So you are choosing him over Father and me?' Lloyd asked.

Llinos picked up her bag. 'Give my regards to Jayne, won't you?'

He watched as his mother was helped into the carriage by Graves. The man was old, he should have been pensioned off by now, but he would be loyal to Llinos to the death. In any case, the young man trained to take over had suddenly left his position so Graves had stayed.

Lloyd watched until the carriage had rolled out of sight along the bend in the road at the end of Pottery Row. His mother was a changed woman: she had left her home and her family for good, and there was nothing Lloyd could do about it.

'Why, Dafydd, not another meeting?' Llinos said. 'That's the third in little over a week. Not growing tired of me, are you?'

Dafydd held her close. 'You know I love you with every fibre of my being, my sweet girl.'

She touched his mouth with her fingertips. 'But this meeting is important, I know that, and I do understand. You've been neglecting your business and your friends because of me.'

Dafydd kissed her tenderly. 'I would give up everything I own to be with you, and if you don't want me to go tonight then I'll stay at home.'

'You go to your meeting,' Llinos said. 'I will sit and wait until you come home and then, my darling, I'll tear off your clothes and ravish you!'

'Is that a promise?' Dafydd tipped her face up to his.

Llinos leaned her head on his chest. 'It's a promise,' she said.

'I'm glad you managed to make it.' Madame Isabelle did not look too pleased as Dafydd walked into her parlour a great deal later than planned.

'I was detained,' he said. 'Business, you know.'

He became aware that Hayden Jones was staring at him from across the room. His eyes were narrowed and the expression in them was evil. He blamed Dafydd for the death of his brother-in-law, shot in this very house. Nothing would ever convince him that the shooting had been an accident.

'Come, sit here beside me,' Isabelle said

quickly, sensing the tension between the men. 'We've been discussing an attack on the town hall, the workhouse too. What do you think?'

'I think we should be careful,' Dafydd said. 'So far we have confined ourselves to legitimate targets, like the toll-gates themselves.'

'Aye and a fat lot of good it's done us so far!' Hayden Jones said angrily. 'We are like a fly swatting at an elephant. We're getting nowhere.'

'I'm just advising we exercise a little caution,' Dafydd said evenly. 'We can't risk jeopardizing our position by taking the protest into Carmarthen Town.'

'It wouldn't be that you're losing your nerve, would it?' Jones's voice was hard. 'Handy with a firearm when there's no danger to yourself, aren't you? Not so brave out there where the real trouble is.'

'Please,' Isabelle said, 'let's keep to the point, shall we?' She consulted her notebook. 'We won't have the cover of darkness until late in the evening, so perhaps we should talk about the advantages and disadvantages of the summer weather.'

Hayden Jones did not give up easily. 'I 'spect you're worried about that pretty face of yours, Buchan,' he said. 'Afraid your married lady will go off you.' He smirked. 'But she's no lady, is she, or she wouldn't be bothering with you in the first place, would she?'

Dafydd moved swiftly. His fist connected with Jones's jaw and the man went down as if felled by an axe.

'Dafydd, please!' Isabelle was agitated but he did not even hear her.

He picked Jones up and frogmarched him out through the narrow hall. 'Get away from here and don't come back, do you understand?' Dafydd pushed him out of the door.

Jones staggered a little on the uneven cobbles. 'You're going to meet your match one of these dark nights, Buchan,' he said, 'and I'll be there to see it, don't you worry.' He stumbled off into the darkness and Dafydd slammed the door. For a moment, he leaned against the stout wooden panelling, fighting for control. He wanted to kill the man for putting his tongue to Llinos's reputation.

Then he straightened his shoulders and returned to the meeting. 'Right, let's get on, shall we?' he said, glaring around the room.

There was silence, and Isabelle rang the bell for the maid. 'I think we'll all have some tea and take control of ourselves, shall we?' She stared meaningfully at Daffyd.

He sank back into a chair and wished he had never become involved in the struggles of the farmers. He was a rich businessman, he should be at home minding his own business, living his own life, not sharing it with trash like Jones.

He glanced at the clock. He had a feeling that this was going to be a very long evening.

CHAPTER TWENTY-FIVE

'So, Isabelle, the date is set for our wedding. Are you happy?' Eynon took her hand and she looked up at him, knowing he would read his answer in her eyes.

It was warm in the conservatory. Trails of vines dripped moisture on to the flagged floor. He had built the conservatory for her – that proved his love for her, did it not? He had asked her opinion before building it on to the back of his house. It was his gift to her.

From the windows the splendid view was a delight. Green fields sloped down to the beach, and beyond the trees, the sea sparkled as if with a million diamonds. Once Isabelle was installed in his home, she would come to love it as he did, though she might find the grandeur strange, a little awe-inspiring at first.

'I can see you're happy.' He bent to kiss her lips lightly. She clung to him, holding him tightly, as though afraid of losing him, and not for the first time, Eynon felt misgivings about the step he was taking. He enjoyed being with Isabelle. He found her an attractive, intelligent woman. They had become intimate, and she thrilled him with her passion. But even though he listed her qualities to himself he knew that in his heart she would never match up to Llinos.

But Llinos did not return his love. Bitterness rose in his throat like bile. Even when her marriage vows were broken, it was not to Eynon she had turned but to a young upstart.

Dafydd Buchan might be rich, successful and undoubtedly handsome, but he was not all he appeared to be. Rumour had it that he was closely involved with the rioters, the hooligans who burned down gates and broke the law without a qualm.

Eynon had some doubts, too, about Isabelle's involvement with the rioters: she knew the Buchan family well. Dafydd Buchan was a troublemaker, involved in the rioting. His brother Ceri was the complete opposite: a law-abiding, honest Christian gentleman, and he was well respected in the area.

Isabelle drew away from him. 'What are you thinking?' She spoke lightly, but she was troubled by his long silence.

'I wondered if we should wed in Swansea or Llanelli.' He quickly gathered his thoughts. 'Not that I mind where we get married, so long as you are happy.'

'What about St Mary's Church in Swansea?' Isabelle's face was bright with happiness.

'That suits me but it's your day, after all.'

'I'm very happy with St Mary's,' Isabelle said. 'It is one of the best churches in Swansea.' She clutched his hand, and he felt irritated: she

345

seemed to have changed from the confident, self-controlled woman he had first known and had become too dependent on him.

'What about your friends? Will they be happy to travel to Swansea for the day?' he asked.

'I have few friends,' Isabelle said quietly, 'but there is another issue we have to discuss.'

'Oh dear, this sounds serious. Let's sit down and talk.' He smiled, as he released himself from her grip. 'I'm sure there is nothing we can't resolve.'

'It's about the Buchan brothers,' Isabelle said. 'I would like to invite Ceri and his family to the wedding.' She held up her hand. 'I know your views on Dafydd's politics but I want him there, too. Please try to understand.'

'Well, I'm not keen on the idea. He's a hot-head by all accounts and I don't like the man's lack of moral scruples either,' Eynon said.

'He's not all bad, I assure you.' Isabelle's tone was more than a little pained. 'Dafydd is a gentleman, remember. His manners are impeccable.'

'And he's running around with a married woman, ruining her life.'

'That's not fair,' Isabelle said. 'I think two are to blame in that situation but, of course, you would take the side of your dear friend Llinos.'

'Are we bickering already?' Eynon said. 'Have Buchan there if it means so much to you. Now, let's talk about bridesmaids, shall we?'

'We'll have Jayne, of course,' Isabelle relaxed, 'and I would like Shanni too.'

'There, then, that's settled,' Eynon said. But

nothing was settled in his mind. He was in a quandary: it would be unthinkable to marry without Llinos being present, but if Buchan was there could he bear to see them together? In any case, what about Joe's feelings? He was the cuckolded husband.

'What's the matter?' Isabelle asked. 'You're still thinking of Llinos, aren't you?'

She was more perceptive than Eynon had given her credit for. 'Well, yes. How will Joe react if they both come to the wedding?'

'You must invite Llinos whatever happens. Remember, they are all adults and surely know how to conduct themselves in public. And there's the son, too. I know Jayne wants him to be at the wedding.'

'I want Lloyd to be my best man as it happens.' Eynon shook his head. 'Look, we'll invite Joe and Llinos, and leave them to decide what they want to do.'

'So we'll set the date as June the tenth, then, shall we?' Isabelle asked, her head on one side. A tendril of hair was coming loose from the pins. She looked adorable, a lovely, intelligent woman. He was a fortunate man to have won her love, so why did he feel he was locking himself in a prison and throwing away the keys?

'June the tenth it shall be.' He slid his arm around her shoulders enjoying the feel of softness against him. He was doing the right thing: he had no intention of living out his old age as a lonely man. Isabelle would give him everything he desired, warmth, affection, love. She could not give him children but he had his Jayne: she was enough to fulfil all his needs in that direction. Yes, Isabelle was giving him all she had, but what was he giving her?

He rose and opened one of the conservatory windows. The sound of the sea filled his ears. In his mind's eye he could see her, Llinos, his love, with her dark tumbling curls, her eyes from which fire flashed when she was angry. He had never held her, never made love to her, yet he felt as bound to her as though she was his wife.

'What does she see in him, Isa?' he asked, unaware of the bitterness in his voice.

Isabelle was silent for a moment. 'I imagine you're referring to Llinos Mainwaring.' She spoke in a hard tone. 'How can I answer for the foolishness of women? Perhaps I am one of them, believing that you are marrying me out of love.'

'I *am* marrying you for love,' he protested quickly. 'I think you are wonderful, beautiful, talented. I am lucky to have you.' He kissed her fingers, then her mouth.

'And with that, I will have to be content,' Isabelle said. She smiled suddenly. 'Let's have a picnic, shall we?'

He was amazed by the turn in the conversation, but relieved that Isabelle had let the uncomfortable matter of his feelings drop. 'That's a wonderful idea. When shall we go?'

'At once,' Isabelle said. 'You have plenty of staff. They can rustle up a meal for us with little notice, can't they?'

'I'm sure they can. I'll ring for the maid now.' He was happy again, sure he was doing the right thing with his life. He needed stability, needed a wife on his arm before he was too old. He needed a woman's company, someone to take to elegant balls at the Assembly Rooms, a woman to respect. He looked at Isabelle: she was all of those things, and with that he must be content.

'I've been invited to a wedding.' Llinos lay beside Dafydd in the large bed, naked except for the sheet thrown over her. It was unbearably hot. Even the breeze drifting in through the wide open windows gave little relief.

'If you mean Isabelle's wedding to Morton-Edwards, then so have I.' Dafydd was languid, his arm lying across her abdomen, his eyes closed against the glare of the sun. 'I think it must be a mistake, though. Isabelle and I are not seeing eye to eye at the moment, are we?'

Llinos did not want to dwell on the problems of social engagements. She was sated, luxuriating in the euphoria of the moment. Still, there were decisions that must be made.

'I don't know how I am going to get through it,' she said softly. 'My son will be there and so will Joe. Perhaps I should plead sickness and not go at all.'

Dafydd rose up on his elbow and stared down at her. 'We can't go on like this.' His voice was thick with emotion. 'We can't go hiding around corners as if we are criminals. We will go to the wedding together, as a couple.'

'Is that wise, Dafydd?' Llinos asked slowly. 'I don't want to embarrass my friends or my son.'

'Well, you have to make up your mind, Llinos. You must choose between me and your family.'

'But, Dafydd,' Llinos said softly, 'how would you face people if you admit openly that we are lovers? The respectable houses wouldn't accept me, and you would be ostracized as well.'

'Of course I wouldn't! Even the great kings of England had mistresses. You would soon be accepted by my friends and certainly by my family.'

Mistress. The word hung heavily in her heart. 'Very well,' Llinos said. 'Ask your brother to invite us to tea one day. Let us see how he deals with the situation.'

'My brother?'

'Yes, your brother, Ceri.'

'He is very straitlaced and so is his wife.'

'That's what I thought.' Llinos smiled ruefully. 'This house is in a sort of no man's land where we can be private without people gossiping about us. But once we are seen together in public everything will change.'

'No, it won't. I love you, Llinos, I would make you my wife tomorrow, if only you were free.' He paused. 'Why don't you divorce him? He can hardly protest, can he?'

'Oh, Dafydd!' Llinos put her hands on his cheeks. 'Divorce is so scandalous that the news of it would reach out beyond Swansea and the business might suffer.'

'I don't care, Llinos. All I want is you. I would give everything up for you. We could go away, leave Wales – leave Britain, come to that. We could live on the Continent, where people are more tolerant in matters of love.'

'Your brother needs you here, Dafydd. You

have obligations and you can't just walk away from them.'

'I know you're right, my love.' He held her close. 'But I'm so afraid of losing you. Say you'll always love me and that you'll never leave me.'

'Hold my hand,' she said softly. Dafydd took her hand. 'I will be with you until death us do part.'

His eyes were alight. 'And I'll make the same vow. Till death us do part.'

Llinos entered the tea-rooms of the Grand Hotel and stared around her, looking for Eynon's familiar figure. He waved and Llinos hurried across the room towards him. 'Eynon, how lovely to see you again.' She hugged her old friend, and Eynon kissed both her cheeks.

'Sit down, Llinos, I've ordered tea.' He held the chair for her to be seated.

'You're looking well, Eynon, and Jayne is more beautiful than ever. You look so cool in this hot weather, Jayne, how do you do it?'

'We've been busy choosing material for my gown,' Jayne said. 'I've no time to feel the heat. I've decided on a gorgeous pale blue satin. I know it will suit me, and it will be just right for a summer wedding. I'm so excited I can't wait for the big day to come.'

Llinos sat back in her chair as the waiter served the tea. A plate with tiny sandwiches was placed on the table along with a stand of mouthwatering cakes. 'And Isabelle? What is she wearing?'

'Oh, something in ivory, I think.' Jayne was scarcely interested in the bride.

'You will all look splendid. Congratulations, Eynon, and I hope you will be very happy.'

He kissed her cheek again, his lips lingering near her ear. 'Why don't I feel happy?' He held her away from him, and his eyes were dark with sadness.

'You are doing the right thing, Eynon, my dear friend,' Llinos said. 'I couldn't bear to think of you alone at your fireside when old age comes along.'

Jayne selected a cake. 'What colour wrap shall I wear, Aunt Llinos? Do you think a deeper shade of blue would be in good taste?'

Llinos glanced at Eynon, who was smiling. 'Go on, Aunt Llinos, tell the girl what you truly think.'

'I think any colour would suit you, Jayne. Your skin is clear and beautiful, and your hair is shining in the sunlight. We'll be finding you a suitor before too long, I dare say.'

Jayne beamed: she had always been susceptible to compliments. 'I am going to have such an exciting year,' she said. 'There's dear Daddy's wedding, and then I'm going to London for the season.' She had a dreamy look in her eyes. 'I should meet some fine young gentlemen there, don't you think?'

'Of course. You are a very eligible young lady. Your father is a wealthy man and your grand-mother had friends at court, I believe?'

It was Eynon who replied. 'Elizabeth had friends everywhere.' His tone was dry, and Llinos smiled, remembering that Jayne's maternal grand-mother had been wont to offer her favours readily to any man of position who propositioned her.

'It helps to have friends in high places, Jayne,' Llinos said softly, 'and I'm sure you will be pursued by gentlemen vying for the honour of your hand in marriage.'

'I do hope so!' Jayne's eyes lit with anticipation. She turned to look round and Llinos followed her gaze, her heart contracting with pain. Her son was crossing the room; he was studiously ignoring his mother.

Lloyd stopped at the table and smiled at Jayne. 'I thought I'd track you down here. A fine friend you are, sneaking off when I was looking at new boots.'

'Don't grumble, Lloyd,' Jayne said. 'You know you are my dear friend but I can't bear looking at men's clothes. They're so dull.' She caught his hand and pulled him closer, kissing his cheek. 'Why don't you do the London season with me? It would be such fun to be together. Come, sit down, for goodness' sake, you're making me dizzy.'

'Thank you, I am honoured.' Lloyd took a seat beside her. 'But, you see, it might be that my destiny leads me beyond our shores. Who knows?'

Llinos gave him a sharp look. What had her son meant? 'You are not going all fey like your father, are you, Lloyd?'

'I don't know what you mean, Mother.' He spoke smoothly but was still avoiding her eyes. 'I was just making a general remark about the future. None of us is able to see far into it, and who knows what fate has in store for us?'

Lloyd's talk made her uneasy. It had been Joc's insistence on destiny that had ruined their

353

marriage. His excuse for bedding Sho Ka had been that he must fulfil his so-called destiny. The thought still hurt her.

'If I can get a word in edgeways,' Eynon said, 'we have set the date for the tenth of June. I hope that is convenient for you and Joe, of course.' He looked at her meaningfully.

'I will make it convenient,' Llinos said. 'I wouldn't miss your wedding for the world, Eynon.'

'Lloyd has agreed to be my best man,' Eynon said. He winked at Lloyd. 'And no flirting with the bridesmaids, mind.'

Llinos swallowed hard, remembering her conversation earlier with Dafydd. He would hate it if she was seated with Joe at the wedding breakfast. He had been right: to be free they would have to go away, begin a new life, make new friends. It would be wonderful to be accepted as a couple, committed to each other for life. Once, she had believed her future was with Joe. Now she knew that life was never that simple.

'I enjoyed having tea with you, Llinos, but we really must be getting home.' Eynon rose from his chair. 'Isabelle is coming to supper.' He grimaced. 'She and Jayne will be talking gowns and veils and such things all night, and I'll be half asleep by the time they've finished.'

'You are forgetting that Isabelle is bringing Shanni.' Jayne's tone was edged with spite. 'That girl will have no taste at all, coming from her background.'

'Don't be such an arrant snob.' Lloyd pulled Jayne's hair playfully.

'Do you mind that Shanni's a bridesmaid?' Eynon asked. 'I've heard that you two don't get on these days.'

'Why should I mind?' Llinos said. 'I have no quarrel with Shanni. I did my best to educate her, to make a lady of her. I fulfilled my duty to her mother's memory and now it seems that Shanni is more than capable of taking care of herself.'

'Everyone knows how kind you've been to the girl,' Eynon said quickly, sensing she was hurt, 'and you've made a fine job of fitting her for a better life.'

Llinos looked down at her hands, at the gleaming gold band that now seemed to imprison her. She wished that Eynon had not decided to marry just at this time. It was a complication she could do without.

She kissed him goodbye and watched as he and Jayne left the room. Lloyd was still sitting beside her, his brow furrowed. 'Have you quarrelled with Shanni, then?'

'The row was not of my making.' Llinos spoke in a low voice. 'She was impertinent and ungrateful. I suppose I do feel a little hurt that she hasn't tried to make things up. A brief note would have done.'

'You know what's wrong with the girl, don't you?' Lloyd said. 'She's in love, or thinks she's in love, with Dafydd Buchan.'

Llinos felt her colour rise. 'She'll fall in love many times before she settles down to marriage,' she said sharply. 'Thanks to me, she's now an eligible young lady.'

She became aware of a shadow falling over her, looked up and saw Joe standing beside her.

'But, Llinos,' he said, 'there is more to being a lady than meets the eye, isn't there?'

Llinos felt a surge of anger. 'I should ask Sho Ka if I were you.'

'Unfortunately I can't do that,' Joe said. 'Sho Ka is dead. Have you forgotten that?'

'I have forgotten nothing, Joe.' She picked up her bag. 'I have to go.' She touched her son's cheek gently. 'I am sorry your father and I are airing our differences in front of you, Lloyd.'

She brushed past Joe without another word but the scent of him was so familiar, so very dear, that tears came to her eyes. How could she love him even now? Was it possible to be in love with two men at the same time?

She returned to the house. On the way she felt as if everyone was staring at her, the scarlet woman. She hurried the last few steps and let herself into the sun-splashed hall.

She took off her coat and went upstairs. In her room, she sank into a chair and stared out into the darkening blue of the evening sky.

Perhaps she loved Joe and was *in* love with Dafydd. Suddenly her head was spinning and nausea overwhelmed her. She tried to rise to call the maid but then she was falling into a dark abyss in which there was no glimmer of light.

CHAPTER TWENTY-SIX

Rosie sat on the riverbank staring into the water. She seemed at ease but her calm face concealed the knot of tension inside her. She glanced at Watt and knew that the moment of decision had come.

'Watt,' she said slowly, 'I'll agree to give our marriage another go.'

His eyes brightened. 'Rosie, do you really mean it? Last time I came up here, when I saw you talking to that farmer, I thought . . . Well, you know what I thought.' He took her hand. 'Rosie, I've been such a fool, I married you thinking I was doing the right thing for your family but now I know I must have been falling in love with you all along.'

Rosie was silent. She wanted to believe him, but there would always be an element of doubt in their relationship. She wondered if *she* had done the right thing. She was giving up her freedom – was that wise?

And there were practical considerations to be taken into account. Would Watt come to live in her little cottage? He was a man of property now.

Once her brothers had left home for good, Watt had been free to buy himself a large house on the western slopes of Swansea.

'We'll have to see how we get along,' she said. 'We mustn't jump to any hasty decisions.'

'What do you mean?'

'Well, I don't think I'd like to move out of my house, Watt,' she said slowly. 'Shall we keep both our homes for the time being, see how things work out between us?'

He put his arm around her shoulder and drew her close. 'I don't care if we live in a shack so long as we're together.' He tipped her face up to his and kissed her. She felt as though she was coming alive. It had been a long time since she had made love to Watt. Since she walked out on him she had spent endless nights alone in her bed, pining for what she could not have.

'I do love you, Rosie. Please try and believe me. I've had other women, I can't deny that, but I always wished it was you.'

She closed her eyes. 'Don't tell me anything about your past,' she said quickly. She could hardly bear to think of him in the arms of another woman. Still, she must make allowances for him: a woman could control her feelings but men were cut from a different cloth.

'Have you had other men?' Watt sounded almost frightened to ask.

Rosie took his face in her hands. 'No, I have not.' She pressed her mouth against his, and a shock of desire ran through her. She moved away from him. Perhaps she was not as controlled as she believed she was.

'And you never hankered after another man, not even in your dreams?'

'I never wanted anyone but you, Watt,' Rosie said. 'I suppose that was my trouble all along. I fell in love with you as soon as I set eyes on you and my love has never changed.'

He stood up and drew her to her feet, his eyes shining. 'Let me take you home to your little cottage by the sea.' He held her close in his arms, his cheek against her hair. 'Let me show you how much I love you.'

Rosie pushed aside her doubts as, hand in hand, they walked away from the river. The summer sun shone down hotly and it seemed to her that their love was blessed by the gods.

'It's not possible!' Llinos stared up at the doctor in disbelief. 'I am too old to have a child and, anyway, I was told a long time ago that there would be no more babies for me.'

The doctor smiled. 'Whoever told you that was wrong, Mrs Mainwaring.'

'Are you sure this sickness is not caused by my age?' Llinos asked. 'In middle years women suffer strange symptoms, don't they?'

The doctor sat on the bed. 'How long is it since you saw your last monthly courses?'

Llinos frowned, trying to think. It was about three months ago when she and Dafydd had laughed and commiserated with each other because they could not make love.

'About three months, I think,' she said.

'And your breasts are tender, the veins standing

proud. Has there been some feeling of sickness in the mornings?'

'Well, just a little, perhaps.' She tried to concentrate. She had been off her food lately but she had thought her loss of appetite was the result of being torn between her husband and her lover. 'It surely can't be true!' The implications of her condition suddenly became alarmingly clear. 'I can't be having another child. I just can't, not now.'

'You can and you are.' The doctor rose and snapped shut his case. 'I have dealt with too many pregnant ladies to be mistaken. I know you probably look on me as a new young doctor but, I assure you, I trained in the best London hospitals.'

'I'm sorry. I don't doubt your ability – but a child at my age and when I thought I would never have another one . . . It's just too much to take in.'

'Who told you there would be no more children? Some well-meaning midwife, I suspect.'

He was right. It had been Mrs Cottle, the woman who had delivered her stillborn daughter years ago told her there would be no more children.

Her head was spinning with questions, questions she hardly dared ask herself. 'Thank you, Doctor,' she said. 'And, please, can we keep this to ourselves for the moment?'

'I quite understand.' He moved to the door. 'My lips are sealed, Mrs Mainwaring. What is said between doctor and patient is sacrosanct.'

He left the room and she heard him go downstairs. Then voices spoke in the hall and Dafydd was running up the stairs. 'What did he say?' Dafydd looked worried as he sat beside her on the bed and Llinos felt her heart melt with protective love.

'I might have eaten something that disagreed with me, that's all. Cheer up, I'm not about to expire.'

'But, Llinos, it's not like you to fall sick. Are you sure you're being honest with me?'

She looked away from him quickly. 'Please, just have a glass of hot milk sent up to me. I think all I need is a good night's sleep.'

'If that's what you want, but we can always get the doctor back here if you don't feel better by tomorrow.'

She waved her hand at him. 'Go on! Stop fussing over me, I'm fine.'

When Dafydd left the room, Llinos fell back against the pillows and closed her eyes. A baby at her age! She just could not take it in. She heard light footsteps on the stairs and the maid came into the room, carrying a tray. 'Here we are, madam, you'll soon feel better.' She was looking at Llinos oddly, as if she guessed what was wrong but that was ridiculous: it would be difficult for anyone to imagine that a middle-aged woman had fallen for a baby.

When she was alone, Llinos put aside the glass and stared out into the night. It was now completely dark: the last of the light had vanished from the sky and the moon was obscured by cloud. Tomorrow it would probably rain.

She sighed and put her hands over her face, but

however she tried to marshal her thoughts they came back to the same thing: she was expecting a child and she did not know who its father was.

Had she conceived on her one night with Joe? But surely it was more likely that she was carrying Dafydd's child. Would she be glad or sorry if she was?

'Oh, God, help me!' she said, as hot, bitter tears welled in her eyes.

She scarcely slept. At her side Dafydd stirred a few times and she tried her best not to disturb him. She woke in the morning, heavy-eyed, and contrary to her expectations, the bright light of the sun was filtering between the curtains. It was going to be a beautiful day.

Llinos turned to look at the empty bed beside her, Dafydd had probably been up at first light: he was a strong young man, eager to get on with the business of the day.

She felt an overwhelming urge to talk to someone about the baby, but whom could she confide in? She had no close women friends, no confidante who would listen and keep her counsel.

By the time she went down to the dining room Dafydd was half-way through his meal. He held her chair for her and smiled; he seemed to have forgotten all about her fainting spell. She hoped he would not notice that much of her breakfast was pushed aside.

'And what are you going to do with yourself today?' he asked, as he put down his napkin.

'I'll have to go up to the pottery, collect a few more things,' she said, attempting to appear as lighthearted as he was. She would need the larger clothes she had worn for her first pregnancy – it was wasteful to buy more. In any case, she could imagine the speculation if she were to have fittings for clothes suitable for an expectant mother.

'I don't like you going back there. Anything you need you can buy new, can't you?'

'Of course, my love, but there are drawings and other personal things that I want to bring here.'

'I see.' Dafydd looked thoughtful. 'Perhaps I should come with you, then.'

'No, really, I'm not a silly child, Dafydd. I promise I won't stay there a moment longer than necessary. Look, I'll be home before you, you'll see.'

'If you're sure.' Dafydd took her in his arms and kissed her lingeringly. 'And remember, whatever Joe says you are with me now.'

It was almost noon by the time Llinos felt ready to go out. Dafydd had alerted the groom, who was waiting with the coach and pair. Llinos climbed into the seat and arranged her skirts.

The carriage jerked into motion and Llinos stared up at the blue of the sky, wondering fearfully who was the father of her child: her husband or her lover? Her hands lingered wonderingly on her stomach. It was flat still, with no sign of her condition. She felt a sudden glow of happiness. Whatever happened, whoever proved to be the father, she was going to bring a new life into the world. Perhaps when they knew the truth neither of the men in her life would want her but if necessary she would bring up her child alone.

It was strange riding along Pottery Row. Doors were open, as always, and neighbours waved to her as she drove past. There was a catch in her throat. Was she leaving her home for ever?

Joe was sitting in the drawing room. He looked a little better than when she had seen him last, but he was still far too thin. There was no sign of her son.

Joe looked up at her. 'Come in and make yourself comfortable. This is still your home.'

'Where's Lloyd?' she asked, pulling off her gloves.

'He's gone riding with Jayne. He is taking every opportunity to get out of the house these days, upset by the friction between us.'

'Then he must have been upset long ago, when you went to Sho Ka's bed.' Llinos heard the waspish tone in her voice with a feeling of sadness and shame. 'I'm sorry, Joe. This is no time to be sniping at each other, is it?'

He stared at her long and hard. 'Are you going to stay with him?'

'You know I am.'

'Llinos, don't leave me, I'm begging you.'

'I have to. Don't ask the impossible.' She left him with his head bowed and there was nothing she could say to comfort him.

In her room, she sank on to the freshly made bed. She had to stay with Dafydd: it was as if some invisible cord was drawing her to him. She could not explain her feelings when she did not understand them herself. Joe was wealthy: he could return to his luxurious house on the Marches if he wanted to.

She opened drawers and cupboards, pulling out the clothes she needed, then rang the bell for the maid. 'Tell the coachman I'm ready to leave,' she said briskly, aware that Flora was staring at her wide-eyed. 'Go on, girl, don't just stand there gawping!'

She closed her bag. She was eager to leave the house and its memories behind her. She looked out for a moment at the shimmering bottle kilns. Why was life so complicated? Why had Joe ruined their love, ruined the trust she once had in him because of what he called 'his destiny'? She saw now it had been an excuse to justify his infidelity. What a fool she had been to believe his lies.

He tried to speak to her before she left, but she waved him away. She climbed into the coach. 'Drive on,' she said. As the wheels clattered on the drive, and the horses headed away from the pottery, Llinos stared straight ahead, leaving her home without a backward glance.

One day she would have to decide what to do with the pottery. She might sell up, or leave Watt to take care of things. If Watt was reconciled with Rosie they could live in the house in comfort, bring up children there. She thought briefly of her son. Would he live with his father from now on?

Llinos brushed her eyes impatiently. This emotion, the tearing apart of her spirit, was too much for her. She rested her hand on her stomach and tried to take in the reality of her situation. She was expecting a baby. What would happen if the child looked like Joe? Would Dafydd desert her?

She spanned her waist with her fingers, it was not as slim as it had been. She was feeling the urge to hold a new life in her arms again.

Part of the pain of Joe's betrayal had been the child he had sired on his mistress when he thought his wife was barren. He had loved that child, and every time he sent money or wrote letters to America, it had been like a knife thrust in Llinos's heart.

She breathed a sigh of relief as she let herself into the house she shared with Dafydd. She breathed in his scent; the aura of her young, vigorous lover permeated the house. Surely Dafydd's child was growing within her. But did she want it to be Dafydd's? That was the question she found impossible to answer.

Llinos was in the drawing room when she heard the front door open and the sound of voices in the hallway. She rose to her feet as Dafydd came into the room with Madame Isabelle and Shanni beside him.

'Llinos!' Dafydd took her into his arms. 'My love, you kept your promise to be home before me. You still look pale, though. Are you sure you're all right?'

'I'm fine. I've just a bit of a headache, that's all.'

Dafydd remembered he had company. 'Come and make yourself comfortable, Isabelle – you too, Shanni.' He kissed Llinos again and whispered in her ear, 'Sorry about the visitors. I would much rather be alone with you.' Aloud, he said, 'I'd better check that the horses are stabled. I won't be long.'

When he left the room, the three women sat in uncomfortable silence. It was Isabelle who spoke first. 'Are you sure you're feeling well, Mrs Mainwaring? You look rather peaky.'

'I'm perfectly all right, really. How are the plans for the wedding going?'

'Well enough,' Isabelle said, 'but I didn't realize how much work was involved. I wanted a quiet affair but it seems that's out of the question.'

Llinos wished they would go and leave her alone with Dafydd. She needed to talk to him, to tell him about the baby. 'I expect you have bought the material for your gown.' She forced a note of enthusiasm into her voice.

'As a matter of fact I could do with your opinion on that.' Isabelle sat forward in her chair. 'At my age, I feel white to be a little unsuitable. Do you think cream will serve as well? Shanni thinks I'm being silly, that I should wear white like any other bride.'

'Cream would be beautiful with your colouring,' Llinos said. 'What does Eynon think?'

'He doesn't seem to mind what I wear. I think he wants the whole thing over and done with as quickly as possible, but all the arrangements seem to have run away with us.'

Shanni was taking a great interest in the conversation. 'Do you know,' she said, her voice smooth, cultured, 'I always thought Mr Morton-Edwards was in love with you, Mrs Mainwaring?' Shanni's eyes were narrowed and Llinos felt as if she had been slapped in the face. 'He seems to light up when he's with you.'

'We are old friends, nothing more.' Llinos spoke more sharply than she intended. She felt Isabelle's eyes on her.

'Are you sure?' Isabelle said softly.

Llinos met her gaze. 'I can only speak for my own feelings.' She glanced towards Shanni. 'And you are both well aware of where my affections lie.'

'He's too young for you!' Shanni said. Immediately her colour rose. 'I'm sorry,' she said. 'I know I should be grateful for all you've done for me but I think you are behaving very badly.'

Llinos stared at the girl in astonishment. She knew Shanni disapproved of her relationship with Dafydd but how dare she speak out so rudely?

'My own mother was dragged out of the house, out of her sick bed, as you well know.' Shanni seemed unable to stop. 'She was humiliated, beaten for what you are doing now. Is there no justice?'

'That's quite enough!' Unnoticed, Dafydd had entered the room. He glared at Shanni. He was more angry than Llinos had ever seen him. 'You are a guest in my house and you use insulting language to a lady who has shown you nothing but kindness.' He stood in front of the fire. 'I will have to ask you not to come here again. I'm sorry, but I have no other choice.'

'Does that include me?' Isabelle asked. 'For Shanni is only saying what everyone else is thinking.' She rose to her feet. 'I'm sorry, Dafydd, but your attention has been anywhere but on the cause. You have neglected meetings, let us down when we expected you to be leader and I for one am concerned for your reputation.'

'You should be concerned for your own, Isabelle,' Dafydd retorted. 'Your own behaviour hasn't been impeccable, has it?'

'Eynon is unmarried and, in any case, what I do is my own business,' Isabelle said hotly.

'I couldn't agree more,' Dafydd said, 'I'll stop interfering in your private affairs if you'll stop interfering in mine.'

'Stop this!' Llinos said, rising to her feet. 'I never wanted any of this ill feeling. I have enough to worry about without listening to such petty spite, especially from you, Shanni.'

She crossed the room and, with her hand on the door, looked back at Isabelle. 'I thought you were a woman of compassion but I was wrong. I regret ever bringing you into my house in the first place, you with your subversive talk.'

'It is not subversive talk,' Isabelle said. 'I only want to speak up for people who have no voice.'

'I don't think Eynon would take too kindly to your views.' She turned to Dafydd. 'Perhaps I should leave you alone to sort things out with your guests.'

'No, Llinos, we need to talk. In private.' He looked pointedly at Isabelle.

'Don't trouble yourself about us, Dafydd. We were going anyway,' Isabelle said. 'We'll leave you and Mrs Mainwaring well alone in future.'

Dafydd glared at her. 'The bitterness of some women makes me fear for the future. You, Shanni, are simply a jealous little girl who needs to grow up, and, Isabelle, I thought you of all people would be more tolerant.'

'Well, I'm not tolerant!' Isabelle's voice was raised. 'I won't stand aside and say nothing while you ruin your life, Dafydd. You can't do this, give everything up for a married woman.'

'Stop this, for pity's sake!' Llinos hurried from the room. Outside, the coachman was brushing down the horses. Llinos spoke quietly to him. 'Please harness the horses again. I need to go out, to visit a friend of mine.' She would go to Rosie. There was no-one else she could think of.

Her eyes were wet with tears as she sank back into the warm leather seat of the coach. Dafydd must be still quarrelling with Isabelle. And Shanni would be putting her spoke in the wheel too. How dare Shanni speak to her like that, as if she, Llinos, was little more than a cheap hussy?

She tried to think of some excuse to make to Rosie for her sudden appearance so late in the evening, but she need not have worried. When she arrived at the little cottage an hour later, she was greeted with a warm welcome and a cheerful fire.

'Can I stay here tonight, Rosie?' Llinos noticed a man's coat hanging on the door. 'I hope I'm not intruding.'

'Of course not! You gave both my mam and me a job. You've always been kind to us. Please, come in and let me make you a hot drink.'

'Can I just go to bed?' Llinos asked tiredly. 'I'll explain everything to you in the morning.'

'No need to explain anything to me,' Rosie said. 'Now let me stir up the fire in the bedroom and push a bottle into the bed just to make sure you don't catch a chill.'

'Thank you, Rosie,' Llinos said. 'I think you

must be the only person in the whole of Swansea who still thinks of me as a friend.'

Then Llinos sank into one of the kitchen chairs and, laying her head on her arms, let the bitter tears flow.

CHAPTER TWENTY-SEVEN

'You shouldn't have spoken to Llinos Mainwaring like that.' Isabelle was angry with Shanni, but more angry with herself for joining in what she now saw as a spiteful attack on an unhappy woman.

'I know, I'm sorry.' Shanni was sitting up in bed, her long hair tied back from her face, her eyes shadowed. 'I just got carried away.'

'I know what it is. You're jealous of her.' Isabelle held up her hand to stop Shanni as she tried to speak. 'No, don't interrupt, listen and learn. Dafydd Buchan is a man, and you are a child. Dafydd could be taking advantage of your obvious hero worship, but he is too decent for that, and thank your lucky stars that he is.'

Shanni looked down at her hands, fumbling with the sheets, patting out imaginary creases. Her face was white. Isabelle felt sorry for her. She sat on the side of the bed, her anger vanishing.

'Shanni, I know you think you're in love with Dafydd but you're not ready for the grown-up world. If you let a man take advantage of you, you'll end up just like your mother, destitute and abused. Haven't you learned your lesson from the past?'

'My mother was taken by a wicked man!' Shanni said defensively. 'What happened to her will never happen to me.'

Isabelle saw that she was wasting her time talking: the girl would never learn except by her own mistakes. Still, it would not hurt her to listen to good advice sometimes. Shanni would have to learn tolerance but it would probably take some hard knocks to make her see that other people had a point of view too.

'Put it this way, then, Shanni, if you are in love with Dafydd, can't you see why Llinos would love him just as much as you do?'

'But she's a married woman!' Shanni protested. 'She has a husband and a son. Why can't she be content with what she's got?'

'Aren't you forgetting something?' Isabelle was becoming irritated by Shanni's attitude. 'Llinos took you out of poverty and did her best to make a lady of you. From what I see before me she failed miserably.'

Isabelle left the bedroom before more angry words came tumbling from her lips. Shanni was still a child in many ways; she had a great deal of growing up to do before she could reason as an adult.

When she returned to the parlour, she saw that the fire was burning low in the grate. She toyed with the idea of calling the maid to fetch more coal but it was late, time she went to bed.

However, she was not ready for bed. She sank into a chair and watched the embers fade and die.

She told herself she should be thinking about her wedding day, not troubling herself over the ranting of a silly young girl.

When she did think of her wedding, her mind was teased with doubts. Was marriage what Eynon really wanted? Isabelle could not shake the feeling that she was only second best. Eynon had never really told her he loved her. He heaped compliments on her, promised to take care of her always. He could offer her money and position, but was that enough?

Isabelle's mind was racing. She wanted a respectable marriage and any woman would be eager to have a man like Eynon Morton-Edwards as a husband. He was good-natured and wealthy but all of that meant nothing compared to the fact that she loved him.

When the last cinder fell and died in the grate, Isabelle got to her feet and glanced wearily at the clock. It really was time she went to bed because tomorrow she had some decisions to make about her life.

'Llinos, did you sleep well?' Rosie was stoking up the fire. The smell of bacon filled the kitchen and the kettle steamed cheerfully on the hob. Rosie stacked Watt's plates and put them into a bowl, happy that he had gone to work early that morning so that she and Llinos could talk privately. Rosie didn't think the time was right to tell Llinos that she and Watt were back together.

'Sit down here. See? I've put a cushion there to make you comfortable.' Poor Llinos, she looked so pale and weary and seemed a little unsteady as she groped for a chair. 'What's wrong? Are you ill?' Rosie was concerned. When Llinos had arrived the night before in tears, Rosie had tucked her into bed, talked soothingly to her and made her feel that dealing with an unexpected visitor was no trouble at all. Llinos had looked ill then, but this morning she seemed worse.

'What is it?' she asked. 'Have you quarrelled with your husband?' Rosie knew the marriage had been faltering ever since Joe had installed his foreign mistress in the house in Neath. 'We all have rows from time to time. It's only human.'

She poured the tea. 'Look, drink this. It will make you feel better.'

She sat at the table opposite Llinos. 'Come, it might help to talk. Have you had bad news?' Rosie did not want to pry but she felt instinctively that Llinos needed to confide in someone.

'I'm pregnant.'

The words fell into the silence, and Rosie swallowed hard. From the look on Llinos's face this was a tragedy and not an occasion for celebration.

'Is that so bad?' Rosie ventured. 'I mean, it might bring you and Joe together again.'

'The trouble is, Joe might not be the father.'

Rosie looked down into her cup, her mind was racing. 'You mean you've had . . . ?' Her voice trailed into silence. She felt unable to say out loud what was patently obvious: that Llinos Main-waring was having an affair.

'I've been with another man, yes,' Llinos said. 'And, Rosie, I don't even know what I want any more. *Who* I want, if it comes to that.'

Rosie was out of touch in her small house on the hill and scarcely saw anyone except Watt, and he was the last one to spread gossip about Llinos. She was silent. What could she say? She had no advice to offer. It had taken her years to make her own husband love her.

'Are you shocked, Rosie?' Llinos picked up her cup and sipped the tea, her eyes filled with tears.

Rosie saw her pain and knew that Llinos did not know which way to turn. 'You can stay here for as long as you like,' she said quickly. 'You can have your baby here if you like. I'm used to caring for babies – I had plenty of experience with my brothers.'

Llinos wiped her eyes impatiently. 'You're so kind, Rosie, and I know crying won't help but I feel so miserable.' She hesitated. 'Could I stay for just a few days?'

'Of course you can.' Rosie picked up the pan of bacon and eggs. 'I'll move this. When Mam was expecting she couldn't bear to smell food in the mornings.' She smiled. 'Shall I just make you a piece of toast?'

'I couldn't eat anything,' Llinos said.

'Yes, you can. A piece of toast will get you started for the day. It's no good starving yourself, not in your condition.'

Llinos's smile was wan. 'You are sweet, and very wise for your age, too, do you know that, Rosie?'

'I've been through a lot myself. Nothing like bad times to make you appreciate other folk's troubles.' Rosie cut a thick slice of bread and stuck it on to the long-handled fork. She sat on the stool before the fire and held it close to the flames. 'I've watched my mother die, I rushed into marriage and regretted it, and I nursed Alice, who I came to love as a sister, as she faded away in the prime of her life.'

'And now I'm adding to your burden,' Llinos said.

'Not a bit of it!' Rosie slid the toast on to a plate and dug a knife into the pat of butter. It melted as soon as it touched the hot bread and sank deliciously into it.

'Here, eat some of this. I promise it will make you feel better.' Rosie made several more pieces of toast and returned to her seat at the table. 'It's very nice to have a woman's company,' she said. 'I hadn't realized how isolated I've become, living up here on the hill like some old recluse.'

'How are things between you and Watt now?' Llinos asked.

'They're much better,' Rosie said tentatively. 'We've agreed to try again to make our marriage work.' She blushed. 'If I'm lucky, I might be in the same condition as you before too long.'

'Oh, Rosie, I'm so happy for you,' Llinos said softly. 'Watt is a proud, stiff-necked man but he does love you, I know he does. He's told me often enough.'

'I'm doing my best to believe that.' Rosie brought her chair closer to the table. 'But what about you? Do you want to talk about what's happened?'

Llinos put down her cup. 'I don't really know what's hit me,' she said. 'I met a man, younger than me, not married, and I'm besotted with him. I want to be with him all the time.'

'But?'

'But I think I still love Joe. I'm crazy, aren't I?'

Rosie had no glib reply. She had only ever loved Watt. 'No, you're not. You're only doing what men have always done, including your Joe.'

'Maybe so, but I know what I'm doing is wrong, immoral, sinful, all the things the preachers warn us against, but I can't help it.'

'So what happened last night to make you come up here to me?' Rosie asked. 'Not that you aren't welcome, mind.'

'I was in his house. He had brought home company, Madame Isabelle and Shanni Price, the young girl I took in. Well, the atmosphere was strained and things got out of hand. Anyway, it ended with a scene and I had to get away from there. What can I do now, Rosie?'

'Your life is your own, Llinos,' Rosie said softly. 'No-one can tell you what to do with it. The only thing you can think of now is what's best for the baby you're expecting.'

Llinos rubbed her eyes tiredly. 'I know you're right but I can't seem to think straight, not just now.'

'Well, stay here a few days, longer if you want, just until you sort yourself out. By the look of you, you need a good rest.'

'I feel as if I could sleep for a week. Thank you, Rosie, I will stay for a while, if you really don't mind.'

'It's decided, then,' Rosie said. 'Now, today I'm going to the market in Swansea. How about if

I take messages to your . . . well, to whoever you want?'

'Tell Lloyd he mustn't worry about me, but don't tell him where I am,' Llinos said. 'As for Joe and Dafydd, let them both stew for a while.'

She took a sip of her tea and Rosie held out the pot to refill the cups. 'When I'm out you just rest and enjoy the peace.'

'It is peaceful here,' Llinos said, 'not even a maid about the place. What's happened to the girl you had in to help?'

'She's gone home for a few days to look after her mother but I don't mind, really. It's good to manage my own little house, to bake when I want to and to sit in the sun without anyone standing over me. Now, take my advice and while I'm out just rest. Will you promise to do that, Llinos?'

'I promise I'll be good.' Llinos smiled. 'And, Rosie, I'm so grateful to you.' She looked down at her crumpled dress. 'Do you think you could bring me some clothes from Pottery Row? I know it will be awkward for you, but I haven't brought anything with me.'

Rosie picked up her shawl – the winds could be fierce here on the hill. She hesitated in the doorway. 'Are you sure you are going to be all right? I won't be too long anyway.'

'Go on, Rosie. Have a good day out, and put any shopping on my account.'

Rosie smiled. 'I'm not short of money, thanks to Alice. Now, if you're sure you'll be all right I'll be on my way.'

Rosie left the house and stood for a moment at the gate looking back. Llinos appeared in the window and Rosie waved before turning into the lane.

What a dilemma! A lady like Llinos Mainwaring expecting and not knowing who the father was. It was almost unbelievable. Still, whatever anyone else thought, Llinos was a good woman. Watt had always loved her, she was like the family he never had, and what was good enough for her husband was good enough for Rosie.

When Rosie had left, Llinos sank into a chair and listened to the birdsong outside. Through the open window a soft breeze brought in the scent of roses, and Llinos closed her eyes, revelling in the peace. It was so good to be alone: she never seemed to have any time to herself any more.

It seemed only a short while ago that she had little to keep her occupied, but since she had met Dafydd all that had changed. Now, why did she have to go and think of Dafydd? She should close her mind to everything, just do what Rosie suggested and rest. She tried to relax but there was a restlessness inside her, a feeling that she would lose everything she loved if she did not act soon.

Llinos stacked the breakfast dishes and decided to wash them, anything to keep her mind from going over the same ground. She found a bowl in the pantry; the enamel was somewhat chipped but it would do.

In the garden, the sun was hot on her face; Llinos breathed in the silence of the countryside. This was a beautiful spot. Behind Rosie's cottage, the hills rolled away into the distance, and below her, to the south, Llinos could see the sparkling waves gently lapping the shore. There was a spring just outside the garden fence and Llinos used the bowl to scoop up some water, which gushed cold and refreshing over her wrists. Up in the trees a blackbird began to sing, the sweet notes carrying on the soft air. To Llinos, who was used to the bustle of Pottery Row, the place seemed like Paradise.

In the kitchen, she poured hot water from the kettle into the bowl to heat the spring water and slowly, enjoying the task, she washed the breakfast dishes.

Perhaps she should buy or rent a small house in the country and have her baby there alone. Well, not completely alone, that would be impractical, but she could well afford a maid and a cook, and a midwife to deliver the baby when her time came.

Suddenly Llinos felt tired. She was getting old, especially to be carrying a child, so it might be a good idea to lie down for a while.

It was warm in her room, the polished wooden floors splashed with sunlight. She kicked off her shoes and stretched out on the bed, closing her eyes. She would keep her confused feelings at bay at least for the moment. She slept.

She woke to a sound in the kitchen and sat up, bewildered by the unfamiliarity of her surroundings. Then she remembered where she was, and the reason why she was here in Rosie's house. Depression swept over her. She wanted Dafydd, wanted to be in his arms, to look into his eyes and hear him tell her how much he loved her.

The sounds downstairs were repeated, and Llinos realized she had been sleeping quite a while. Rosie must have come back from town ages ago.

She slid off the bed and stood at the washstand, splashing water into her sleepy eyes. The sun was still hot, the room filled with brightness.

Llinos patted her hair and smiled wryly at her own foolishness. Here she was in a crumpled dress and she was attempting to make herself look neat. It was ridiculous. Who was she going to see? No-one, except Rosie.

She made her way carefully down the small twisting staircase into the hallway. 'Rosie, I'm sorry I've been asleep and I . . .' Her words trailed away as she saw a man standing with his back to the sunlight. She recognized him at once but for a long moment she could not speak.

'Dafydd, what are you doing here?' she said at last, her voice thin with shock.

'Llinos, my lovely!' He took her into his arms holding her close to him murmuring sweet words into her ear. 'How could I live without you, my darling?'

He embraced her, kissing her eyes, her cheeks, her mouth. She held him away and stared up at him, her heart thumping. 'Dafydd, how did you know where to find me?'

His reply was indistinct. She felt his tears against her face and her heart swelled with love for him. She clung to him kissing him eagerly. He had come to find her and to take her home. 'Tell me, Dafydd, how did you know I was here?' Her voice trembled.

'I went up to Pottery Row looking for you,' he said. 'I saw Watt and he told me you were staying in Rosie Bevan's house.'

Dafydd drew her close again, and she closed her eyes, thankful he had come for her. It was not her husband who had found her, she thought bitterly, but her lover.

'I want to take you home,' Dafydd said. 'Please say you'll come with me. I can't bear to be without you, not for another moment.'

'What about Isabelle? Is she still angry with you?'

'Never mind Isabelle or anyone else. We are talking about our own future. We are not accountable to anyone.'

'We'll have to wait for Rosie,' Llinos said. 'We must tell her where I'm going, otherwise she'll be worried.'

'No, she won't.' Dafydd smiled. 'Don't be angry, but Rosie was up at the pottery talking to Watt. She's told me about the baby, Llinos! My darling girl, how could you keep it from me? Didn't you know I'd be thrilled about it? A baby is the best gift you could give me.'

'Rosie told you?' Llinos felt alarmed. What else had Rosie said?

'She meant it for the best. She said you needed me now more than ever. Oh, my love, I never believed I could be so happy.'

She looked up at him, trying to find the words to tell him the baby might not be his. She opened her mouth to speak but the clatter of hoofs on the sun-baked ground outside stopped her. Rosie had returned.

'Oh, Llinos, have I done the right thing?' Rosie hurried into the house. 'I'm sorry, my tongue just got caught up in my words. I never was much good at lying.'

'It's all right, Rosie, but what else have you said?'

Rosie met her eyes. 'I just blurted out about the baby and then I realized I had already said too much so I stopped.' Rosie looked anxious. 'Please don't think I want you to leave. You can stay here as long as you like.'

'It's all right.' Llinos felt a sense of relief. If Dafydd was to be told the truth, all of it, it would be better coming from her own lips.

'Thank you for your kindness,' Dafydd said, 'but I'm taking Llinos home, Rosie.'

Rosie's eyebrows rose questioningly. 'As I said, if Llinos wants to stay, she's very welcome.'

'Rosie,' Llinos hugged her, 'thank you for all you've done, for putting up with me at such short notice. But you and Watt need time to yourselves, and Dafydd and I need to talk.'

'I suppose it's for the best, then,' Rosie said, 'but my door is always open to you, Llinos, never forget that.'

Dafydd took Llinos's hand, and as they stepped out into the sunshine she looked up at the blue bowl of the sky and sent up a silent prayer. 'Please, dear Lord, show me what I must do.'

Dafydd helped her into the carriage. 'Come, Llinos, tell me everything. When did you find out you were expecting and how long will it be before our baby is born?'

Llinos looked out of the open carriage and

stared down at the sea sparkling below. 'The doctor thinks I'm three months gone, so the baby should be born early in spring.'

'We must think of some good Welsh names for our child. What do you think it will be? A son or a daughter?' Dafydd was as excited as a child himself. How could she break his heart by telling him the truth?

She leaned against his shoulder. 'I don't know, Dafydd. I'm just happy that I'm with child.' She suppressed a sigh. Now the thought of her baby was the only certainty in her life. All else was confusion.

CHAPTER TWENTY-EIGHT

Joe sat among the sand dunes and stared out at the wide expanse of sea along the curve of Swansea Bay. Over the Mumbles Head storm-clouds were gathering. The air was heavy – there would be thunder tonight, if he was any judge.

The atmosphere around him echoed the feelings within him. Llinos had left him and there was nothing for him in Swansea, not now. His bag was at his side, he was ready to return to the Marches, but he had stopped to linger near the sea he had grown to love.

The small country of Wales was so different from his homeland. He had been born near the shores of a wide river, his mother had taught him the American-Indian folklore and his father had educated him as an English gentleman. Now he felt rootless, as if there was no place on earth where he truly belonged.

Joe rubbed his eyes tiredly. Llinos, his firebird, had made her decision. She had run to Dafydd Buchan and there was nothing Joe could do about it.

'Father?'

Lloyd had come up silently behind him and Joe smiled. 'You're walking in the footsteps of your father, such silent footsteps. I didn't know you were there.'

'I'm like you in many ways, Father, and I'm proud of that.' Lloyd sat in the sand beside him.

'I'm proud too, son.' Joe looked at Lloyd. He was a fine young man, handsome and strong with the fire of his mother in his belly. 'I've always loved your mother, you know,' Joe said, 'but I can't blame her leaving me for another man, can I?'

Lloyd picked at a stalk of tough sand grass and chewed it. 'Don't you see into your own future? Surely you know, as you always do, what's going to happen to Mother and that man.'

'I can't trust my instincts now,' Joe said. 'I was wrong about Sho Ka and the child. I might be wrong about everything else.'

Lloyd sighed. 'I don't know what to say, Father. I do know I'm worried about you. It's not like you to be beaten.'

'I'm helpless, Lloyd, I can't do anything until your mother realizes that Buchan is not the man for her.'

'Isn't it strange,' Lloyd said slowly, 'that infidelity in a man is accepted but an unfaithful wife is called a harlot?'

Joe shrugged. 'It's just the way of the world, son. I suppose part of it is that a man needs to know that the children his wife bears are his.'

'I find it all so strange,' Lloyd said, 'that this thing called love can build or destroy. Is that what the good Lord intended?'

'No-one can answer that, son. All we know for sure is we're born, we love and we die,' Joe said. 'Our lives should be simple but they seldom are.'

They sat in silence for a while. The soft sea breeze came in on the lapping tide. The smell of salt air and the rustle of shells as they tumbled in the waves seemed like music to Joe, haunting, painful music.

'What are you going to do now, Father?' Lloyd rested his hand on Joe's shoulder. 'I see you have your bag packed.'

'I thought I'd pay a visit to my estate on the Marches,' Joe said. He looked at his son, sensing Lloyd's reluctance to move away from Swansea. Perhaps Joe was selfish, but he could not stay and watch Llinos being happy with another man. 'I may stay there for good, and you know you are welcome to join me any time you please.'

Lloyd shook his head. 'My life is here, Father. I was born in our house in Pottery Row. My roots are here.' He smiled a soft smile, and Joe knew without being told what his son was about to say. 'In any case, I think I've fallen in love.'

'With Jayne Morton-Edwards?' Joe said.

Lloyd nodded his head. His curling hair, just touching his collar, shone like silk in the brightness of the sun. He seemed so happy, but life played cruel tricks sometimes. How could Joe spoil the boy's dreams by telling him that, though?

Joe stared out towards Mumbles Head. 'Take things one step at a time, Lloyd,' he said at last. 'You have the wisdom of the Mandan in you. Use it.'

'And what about you, Father? Where is your wisdom? Do you think you'll win Mother back by running away?'

'This is a fight I can't win, Lloyd. The affair must play itself out and then, only then, will I have a chance of renewing my marriage vows. I treated your mother badly, son, when all she did was love me.'

'Your life together hasn't been exactly an oasis of peace, has it, Father? I can remember you and Mother shouting at each other, and the row was always about Sho Ka.' He paused to choose his words. 'Mother hated the fact that you had another son. I suppose it was a bitter pill to swallow when she couldn't have any more children herself.'

'I do realize that, son.' Joe was silent, reflecting on the past, on his life with Sho Ka. He had truly believed that it was his destiny to provide an heir to the Mandan tribe. His own mother had told him so on her death-bed. But, if he was honest, he had embraced the prospect of sleeping with another woman with great enthusiasm.

When he had taken Sho Ka to his bed, with her dark, exotic beauty, he had been as excited as a young buck. His blood was hot, his urges strong. He could not deny even to himself that being with Sho Ka had become more than just his duty.

Could Llinos be feeling the same urges now as he had felt then? Loving her husband yet wanting another man so badly it was like a sickness?

'Will you ever come home, Father?' Lloyd's voice brought Joe out of his reverie. He looked up at the blue sky spread wide above him. He loved this coast – he enjoyed the feel of the sandy beach beneath his bare feet. He loved the river Tawe, loved the people who inhabited Pottery Row.

'Of course I will. I can't leave Swansea for good – your mother might need me.' He touched his son's arm. 'In any case, I have a dear son whom I love very much indeed.'

'We'll all be together one day, I feel it in my bones.' Lloyd pushed himself to his feet and brushed the sand from his clothes. Joe stood up too, and realized that he was a good inch or two shorter than his son.

Lloyd took Joe's hand. 'This is goodbye, then, but just for now.'

'Just for now, son.' Joe pulled him close and hugged him. 'Take good care of yourself, Lloyd, and if you're ever in trouble, I'll be here.' Joe looked up at his son. He was a man to be proud of. 'God go with you.'

Lloyd picked his way through the dunes, walking swiftly, his footsteps cushioned by the sand. Joe shaded his eyes from the sun to watch him and his heart warmed with love, Lloyd was a good son, a loving son. He did not for one moment presume to judge his father. There was no need for anyone else to pass judgement for Joe knew only too well that he had been a fool. Now he was the one feeling rejected, passed over for another man.

He had a sudden mental picture of Llinos in bed with Buchan, and the pain withered his soul and his spirit. This was how Llinos must have felt every time he left her for Sho Ka. Joe stood facing the sea; his long hair drifted across his face and he felt tears on his cheeks. 'Llinos, my firebird, come home to me soon,' he said, but the words were carried away on the wind.

'So your mother is staying with that other man, then, is she?' Jayne was seated in the grassy garden of her father's house, her skirts spread around her. She looked like a beautiful flower, with her hair coming loose and tendrils drifting across her face.

'That's the way of it,' Lloyd said, 'and I can't blame her. It was my father who was first to stray.'

Jayne reached out for his hand. 'We will never be like that, will we, Lloyd? Promise me.'

He curled her fingers into his palm. 'I promise you that I will never look at another woman. Why should I, when I have the most beautiful woman in the world at my side?'

Jayne blushed with happiness. 'You wait until you see me dressed for Papa's wedding. I will be as beautiful as if I were the bride instead of a bridesmaid.'

'You are beautiful to me whatever you wear.' He pulled her close to him and kissed her full lips. He could understand his father's eagerness to taste the love of a beautiful woman: Lloyd knew only too well the feeling of fire in the belly, the urge to conquer and possess. He longed to throw Jayne down in the grass and make her his own sweet love. But the niceties had to be observed. He would have to wait until they were both older, more mature and, as Jayne's father said, until they knew their own minds. Well, he knew his own mind right now. 'It's not long now to your father's wedding,' he said, wondering if Eynon would give Jayne more freedom once he had a woman to care for.

'I know,' Jayne said, 'and there's so much to do. I must have my hair curled and see if my shoes are fitting properly and, oh, I don't know, a hundred and one things.'

Lloyd smiled indulgently: Jayne was so girlishly delighted with the thought of dressing herself up and being on show as a bridesmaid. He stared at her, loving her. Her complexion was so smooth, her hair shining in the sun; she needed no gilding to make her beautiful.

'So, this is where you two have got to.' Eynon came around the corner of the house and stood, hand over his eyes, shading them from the sun. 'Is she still talking about the wedding?' He sat beside Lloyd on the garden bench. 'If she's like this about my wedding, goodness knows how she'll be about her own.'

Lloyd felt comfortable with Eynon, who had been a constant visitor to Pottery Row since Lloyd was a small child. Eynon was one of Mother's best friends and Lloyd had always been able to see that Eynon's feeling for her went much deeper than friendship. But he must have given up all hope of winning Llinos now because he was marrying Madame Isabelle, a rather stern-looking woman, though lovely in a moody sort of way.

'Your wedding day is what everyone seems to be talking about,' Lloyd said. 'I think it's a grand occasion for everyone in the town, especially as you are one of the richest men in Swansea.'

'I suppose that's true,' Eynon said. 'About everyone loving a wedding, I mean. The townspeople will be waiting for me to throw coins in the street, a good old custom that causes quite a stir. In that way, rich and poor alike can share in the festivities.'

In that instant Lloyd's conscience was stirred. He remembered how Shanni had introduced him to the sights and sounds of poverty at first hand. He had been appalled, wondering how people survived in such squalor. No wonder the festivities of the rich had such an impact on the people who inhabited the dark courts and backwaters of Swansea. A coin thrown carelessly could mean a week's food for some families.

Lloyd looked around him at the opulent splendour of the garden, the well-kept shrubs and the ancient trees. If he was to spend his life in Swansea, he should be doing something to improve the lot of the people. Not in the way that Dafydd Buchan did, by flouting the law, but something constructive that would improve conditions in the town.

'What are you thinking about, Lloyd?' Jayne's voice filtered through his mind and Lloyd smiled at her.

'Lots of things, Jayne, but mainly I was thinking about you, how beautiful you look with your skin touched by the warmth of the sun.'

Eynon smiled. 'You have your father's silver tongue, Lloyd, and your mother's determination. You will do well in life.'

It was the first mark of approval Eynon had shown, and Lloyd felt a warm response to the

393

man who had always befriended his mother but had never taken advantage of her loneliness. Suddenly he was so angry with Dafydd Buchan that he wanted to kill him. How dare the man beguile Mother into sharing his bed?

'Why are you looking so cross, Lloyd?' Jayne rested her hand on his arm, and he felt the warmth of her fingers through the cloth of his shirt.

'I'm sorry, I was thinking of my mother and that man.' He rubbed his eyes. 'I can't bear to think of them together. It makes me want to—' He stopped abruptly. 'But, then, it's not up to me, is it? I can't govern the way my parents run their lives.'

'It's called growing up, my boy,' Eynon said slowly, 'when we realize our thoughts, our words, can do little to alter the course of other people's lives.'

'But you love my mother, what do you think of her behaviour?' Lloyd asked, the edge of pain and anger still in his voice.

Eynon patted his shoulder. 'I *do* love her. We have been friends since childhood, but I wouldn't presume to tell Llinos how she should live her life.'

'Has my father made her so unhappy that she's willing to give up everything to be with a man like Buchan?'

'It looks that way,' Eynon said. 'Llinos took it very hard when Joe left her to live with the Indian girl. How do you expect her to feel, Lloyd? She is only flesh and blood, and she thought her marriage to Joe would last a lifetime.'

'I know. I'll make sure I never live like that. Once I marry it will be for all time.'

'I hope so, son,' Eynon said. 'But nothing stays the same. When I married Jayne's mother I had no idea she would die a young woman. Do you blame me now for taking another wife?'

Lloyd shook his head. 'No, of course not.' Eynon was a good man and he should not live out his life alone. 'But what happened to you is different.' Lloyd continued, 'You are not betraying your first wife. You have shown her every respect by waiting this long to take another woman.'

'Maybe so, son.' He turned to his daughter. 'Jayne, be a good girl and ask one of the maids to fetch us a drink. It's so hot out here.'

Jayne looked surprised: it was rare for her father to ask her to run an errand. She nodded. 'Of course, Papa, but I know you just want to get me out of the way so you can talk man talk.'

'Wise girl.' Eynon tugged at her hair. 'Go on with you then, let me talk to Lloyd in peace.'

Jayne took her time, skirting around the flower beds and walking between the trees as she made her way back to the house.

'Lloyd,' Eynon said, 'I could not say this while Jayne was here but I'll say it now. A man has needs and don't fool yourself that I have remained faithful to my wife's memory all these years.' He shook his head. 'Oh no! I have had many women, some respectable, some not. But they filled a need, an emptiness. Do you understand?'

Lloyd stared at Eynon in surprise. He had

thought of Eynon as an ageing man, not someone with hot blood running in his veins. 'I suppose I do,' he said reluctantly.

'And that's not all.' Eynon stared up at the sky and Lloyd noticed the way the sun touched his hair with gold. 'I never intended to marry Jayne's mother. I only agreed because she was having my child.'

Lloyd digested Eynon's words in silence. It was hard to credit that Eynon, who appeared to be a pillar of respectability, had led the life of a rake.

'Nothing is neat and tidy in life, Lloyd, just you remember that. Passions run high in men and in women and love is a cobweb that breaks at the first suggestion of a breeze.'

They were wise words and Lloyd digested them in silence. 'I do realize love has to be nurtured,' he said. 'But I can't imagine being unfaithful to Jayne.'

'I hope not,' Eynon said. 'And here she is returning with the maid and a tray of cooling drinks. Now remember, not a word of this to my daughter. I want her to think of me as a good old father.'

Lloyd smiled. 'One thing, sir, I will never think of you as Jayne's good old father again. Thank you for talking so honestly to me.' He watched as Jayne approached, her hair drifting back from her face in the summer breeze. She was so beautiful, so innocent. Lloyd smiled. Whatever Eynon said, he would never betray his love. Lloyd knew in his heart he would be a faithful and loving husband for ever.

* * *

'I'm so glad you're back, Watt.' Rosie stood away from the door and allowed Watt to come into the kitchen. The cottage was filled with the warmth of evening. The soft light illuminated the whole room and Rosie blinked as the dying sun filled her eyes. She put her arms around Watt and rested her head against his shoulder.

'Dafydd Buchan came here, took Llinos away with him. I hope we did the right thing, telling him everything.'

'It was the only thing we could do,' Watt said. 'Now forget other people's troubles. You can't solve them all. Anyway, what's to eat? I'm starving.'

'The maid's still away nursing her sick mammy and I haven't baked anything. I'm sorry.' She studied his face, wondering how he really felt about her. She and Watt had fallen into a pattern: some days Watt spent time at the cottage with Rosie and occasionally she stayed with him in his elegant house.

'Don't worry,' Watt said quickly, 'I'll take you out for a meal. Would the Castle suit you?'

'I would rather stay here with you. We can have some bread and cheese later,' she said softly. 'Come on, let's go into the parlour. It's cooler in there.'

They sat together on the plump sofa and Rosie touched Watt's hand. 'Is something wrong, Watt?'

'No, not wrong, not really,' Watt said. He leaned forward, his face earnest. 'I've been thinking and I've come to the conclusion I can't sit on the fence any longer. I've joined the Rebeccas.'

'Oh no, Watt, you'll be in danger riding with that gang of outlaws. Please don't do it.'

'I must, love. Look, we're planning to burn the gates at Carmarthen as soon as it can be arranged, but no-one will get hurt, I promise you.'

Rosie felt fear clutch at her heart; this was the last thing she had expected to hear. She twisted her hands together, trying to think of the right words to stop him from putting himself in danger.

'It's not going to be very pleasant, I know that, but I have to show my support. Everything will be just fine, you'll see.'

Rosie turned her head to stare sightlessly at the window. 'I don't want you to go. I can't lose you, not after finding you again.'

He put his arms around her. 'Don't worry. I'll be all right, I promise, and I'll be back home with you before you know it.'

She clung to him. 'What if you got shot? I've heard that the landowners are carrying guns to repel the rioters.'

'I won't get shot. Half the stories you hear about the riots are blown up out of proportion.' He kissed her hair. 'Look, everything I possess is yours, Rosie. You'll be well taken care of even if something did happen to me.'

She stared at him. 'I don't want more possessions. Alice Sparks left enough for my needs. I just want you to be safe.'

'But you're my wife, Rosie. Whatever has happened between us, nothing changes the fact that we are still married and you are my legal heir.' He took her hand. 'Don't look so frightened. I'm telling you, it will be all right.'

Rosie swallowed hard, her mind racing. She looked up at Watt's dear face and knew she would always love him. Whatever differences they had in the past, she had always been glad he was still there, still alive and well.

'Do you love me, Rosie? Please let me hear you say it.'

'Of course I love you!' The words burst from Rosie's lips. 'I've always loved you. Many nights I've cried myself to sleep thinking of you.'

'And I wanted to be with you so much, my love,' Watt said. 'But I couldn't rush you into coming back to me. You were very young when we married, too young perhaps. You were a beautiful girl full of romantic dreams and I was the biggest fool on earth to destroy those dreams. Now come on, no more gloomy talk. I want to smother you with kisses and I want to take my wife to bed. What do you say?'

'I thought you were starving!'

'And so I am, but not for food any more.'

Watt smiled and Rosie's heart was full of happiness. Perhaps, just perhaps, they might be able to breach the gap that had grown between them over the painful years. One day they might become the happy married couple Rosie had believed they could be. It might be a dream but it was a dream she would cling to for ever.

CHAPTER TWENTY-NINE

Jayne woke early to the sound of birds singing in the trees outside her window. The sun was slanting in through the chink in the heavy curtains, dappling the floor with light, and Jayne sat up, excitement fluttering in her stomach. Today was Father's wedding day.

She slid from between the sheets and padded across the room to the window. Outside, the garden was in full flower; the grass, touched by dew, shone with life. The fountain sprinkled diamonds of light into the waiting bowl and Jayne sighed with pleasure. This was going to be a beautiful day, a day when Lloyd would see her in all her glory. Surely, then, he would declare himself.

Jayne hugged herself. He loved her, he had made that very plain, but he had never said he wanted to marry her. She was still very young but Lloyd was a man now, a tall, handsome man, and he had inherited all the best features from both his parents.

The maid knocked and entered the room with a tray of tea. Jayne climbed back into bed and accepted the tray on her lap. The appetizing smell from thinly cut slices of toast made Jayne feel hungry. Not hungry enough for a huge breakfast with her father, she had given up that practice long ago when she realized she was inclined to plumpness, but this morning she needed sustenance, something to fortify her for the long day ahead.

'Morning, my love.' Her father came into the room smelling of soap. 'And are you ready for the big day?'

'I'm really looking forward to it,' Jayne said through a mouthful of toast. 'It's glorious weather, the sun is shining and that means you are going to be a very happy groom, Papa.'

'Does it indeed? Well, that's good to know.'

Eynon planted a kiss on her cheek and Jayne studied him thoughtfully. He was getting old, his hair was tinged with white, and to her it was a wonder he would even think of remarriage at his age.

'Did you have a lovely day for your wedding to my mother?' she asked curiously.

'Yes, of course, the sun shone so brightly and your mother was very beautiful in her wedding gown.' Something in her father's words rang false.

'Were you madly in love?'

Eynon took her hand. 'I was very happy, especially when you were born. I adored you from the start.'

'I was born prematurely, wasn't I?'

'Yes, that's right.' There was an edge to his voice that Jayne did not quite understand. Jayne stared at him but he was avoiding her eyes. Suddenly everything fell into place.

'My mother was expecting me when you got married. That's it, isn't it, Father?' she said accusingly. Of course that was it, there had been veiled hints from her grandmother on more than one occasion and the facts surrounding Jayne's birth had always been shrouded in mystery.

'You are an intelligent girl, Jayne, and I suppose you are old enough to know the truth. You're quite right, your mother was expecting before we were married.'

'And you wouldn't have married her if it wasn't for me?'

'I don't know!' Her father stood up and rubbed his eyes. 'I don't want to talk any more about this now, Jayne. I'm getting married to Isabelle in a few hours' time and there's a great deal to do.'

'Yes, of course, Father. Come here and give me a proper kiss.'

Jayne hugged him. He had always been good to her, very loving. Some men would have denied responsibility for an illegitimate child but not him.

'Papa, you're a good man. Now go and get ready, you don't want to be late for your own wedding, do you?'

When Eynon left the room, Jayne put down the tray and slipped out of bed. It was time she began to dress. She wanted to look her best, to be Eynon Morton-Edwards's beautiful daughter. She stared at her reflection in the mirror. 'Lloyd, my boy, I'm going to dazzle you out of your senses today, you just wait and see.'

*   *   *

'You look beautiful, Shanni.' Isabelle tugged a fold of Shanni's dress into place. 'My bridesmaids will outshine me if I'm not careful.'

'I don't believe that for one minute, you look gorgeous,' Shanni said. 'Mr Morton-Edwards is a very lucky man.'

Isabelle turned to be inspected. 'What's the bow like, and the ribbons, are they hanging properly?'

'The back of the gown is as lovely as the front,' Shanni said. 'The dressmaker did you proud.'

Isabelle did look splendid. The gown of old gold suited her tall figure and the veil of coffee-coloured lace seemed to bring more colour into her face. Isabelle's eyes sparkled with happiness and Shanni knew that she could not wait to be married; to have a gold ring on her finger telling the world she was a wife at last.

'There's no fear of anyone outshining you,' Shanni said. 'You are so lovely I think your groom will fall in a faint when he sees you.'

'I do hope not!' Isabelle chuckled. She was so happy, so full of joy, so beautiful that Shanni held her breath. Was it good for anyone to be so happy? Would a spiteful fate swoop down and steal the happiness away?

'It will be time to leave for the church soon,' Isabelle said, 'but before we go I want you to know I'm very fond of you. And I'm very pleased with your progress. Your reading is equal to that of any fine lady and your command of language can't be faulted. And remember, Shanni, I will always be here if you need me.'

Shanni realized quite suddenly that everything would change once Isabelle was married. She and Eynon Morton-Edwards would be living together and that meant Jayne would always be present too. Jayne had never liked Shanni and the feeling was entirely mutual.

'Can I ask you something, Isabelle?' She spoke quietly. 'I know it's selfish of me to think of myself on your wedding day but will I be living with you when you move into Mr Morton-Edwards's house?'

'Of course you will.' Isabelle was staring in the mirror, tucking a stray curl into place. 'I have taken you under my wing and you will naturally come with me when I move.'

Shanni felt a sense of relief mingled with some misgiving. She did not relish the idea of sharing a home with the stuck-up Jayne. She watched as Isabelle looked around at the small parlour.

'It will be strange leaving here but I no longer need the house so I'm giving it to you.' She smiled. 'I've made sure you will never be homeless again.'

'I don't understand.' Shanni frowned. 'How can this be my house?'

'Because I signed it over to you. It's all done legally, Shanni. You will need your own home sooner or later and if you grow tired of living in luxury in Eynon's wonderful home you can escape back to this little place.'

Shanni sank down into a chair. 'I really have a house all of my own?' She was awestruck. 'You mean I can live here for ever and ever?'

'That's right. I saw my solicitor a month ago and signed the deeds.' She turned from the mirror to face Shanni. 'I was fortunate enough to have modestly well-to-do parents. This was their house and when they died it passed to me. In law my property should belong to my husband but Eynon does not need or want it.'

She moved to the small desk in the corner of the room and took out an envelope. 'These are your deeds, Shanni. Put them away safely because some time, perhaps in the near future, you will marry and need a place of your own.'

'Me married, never!' Shanni's tone was emphatic and Isabelle smiled indulgently.

'Oh, you will, when the time is right. But in any case you will always be independent. You won't have to marry anyone if you don't want to.'

Shanni took the envelope and stared at it in disbelief. 'I actually own a house all to myself, I can't believe it.' She hugged Isabelle. 'Thank you so much for all you've done for me. I'll always be grateful to you not only for the house but for all the rest of it, for the education and the fine manners you've taught me.'

'But never forget that your improvement began with Llinos Mainwaring. If she hadn't taken you in you would be living in poverty in one of those dreadful courts in Swansea.'

'I know you're right. I shouldn't hate her.'

'But you do hate her because she's stolen Dafydd's affections.' Isabelle rested her hands on Shanni's shoulders; she was a tall woman and towered over Shanni. She had a troubled expression on her face.

'Dafydd would never have been yours, Shanni. Face it, my dear, he is not the man for you.'

Shanni hung her head. 'You saying that doesn't make it any easier for me to accept.'

'You are very young, Shanni. You have youth on your side. You must have your fun before you settle down to marriage, so don't pine for a man who's not meant for you.'

'All right, I'll try to be sensible.'

'He'll be at the wedding and Mrs Mainwaring will probably be with him,' Isabelle said. 'When you see them together you must pretend not to care. Hold up your head and show the world you are a proud young lady.'

'I promise to try,' Shanni said meekly.

'Now put your deeds away and remember, you are Miss Shanni Price, property owner. Be strong and brave and look to the future, my dear girl.'

'I will.' Shanni was overcome at Isabelle's generosity. It seemed a long time since anyone had cared about her.

'I can't thank you enough for all you've done for me.' Shanni swallowed the constriction in her throat. 'Now I'd better finish getting ready for your big day.'

She went upstairs to her room and stood for a moment studying her reflection in the mirror; she was small of stature and her satin gown clung to her slender body like a second skin. How would she look to Dafydd? Would he still think of her as a little girl?

She pinned up her hair and put on the coronet of flowers Isabelle had chosen for her. She looked like a lady born to luxury and the thought pleased her. She drew herself upright, her eyes bright as she stared at herself in the mirror; she was a woman of property now and a catch for any man, even Dafydd Buchan.

She locked the deeds to the house in a drawer for safe keeping until she could read the impressive handwriting at her leisure. She would be coming back here this evening to stay with the small staff of servants because Isabelle was going to travel for a week or two with her new husband. Both she and Isabelle thought it would be a good idea to wait until Isabelle came home before moving into Mr Morton-Edwards's house. Perhaps she could even stay here for ever.

Shanni shook her head in despair. There was one glaring drawback to living on her own: how would she support herself? She had no skills to speak of. Her only option would be to find a post as a governess. She discarded that idea at once; she had no intention of living in someone else's house with a family she did not even know. Her future was far from certain, for she needed a great deal more than a house to make her completely independent. She stared at her image in the mirror, checking that everything about her appearance was perfect. She would enjoy the day; why be troubled about the future? Thanks to Isabelle, she was far better placed than she had ever thought possible. Shanni lifted her head and straightened her back. She would show the world she was a person who commanded respect. After one last look in the mirror she left the room.

* * *

The church bells rang out a joyful message on the clear summer air. Isabelle looked up at Eynon, her heart overflowing with love. But he was not looking at her. She followed the direction of his gaze and saw Llinos Mainwaring standing close to Dafydd. Her joy vanished.

Isabelle was aware of friends and strangers wishing her well, throwing flower petals over her, and she responded with her usual aplomb. She smiled though her heart was breaking. She knew the moment she looked up at her husband that he loved Llinos Mainwaring in a way that he would never love another woman.

She glanced at the gold band glinting on her finger. She was a wife, a married woman. She would have luxuries such as she had never dreamed of. She would lie in the arms of the man she loved, but she would never see that love returned.

'Are you happy, my sweet?' Eynon was leaning close, whispering in her ear. For a moment she wondered if she should speak out honestly, tell him she knew that his vows to love her were a sham. She took a deep breath and forced a smile.

'Of course, why wouldn't I be happy? This is my wedding day.' If there was an edge to her voice, Eynon failed to notice.

From the corner of her eye Isabelle saw Llinos making her way towards them. Isabelle steeled herself to behave as a new bride would behave.

'Congratulations, both of you!' Llinos said. Eynon took her in his arms and when he kissed her it was the kiss of a lover, not a friend.

Then Dafydd was beside Isabelle kissing her

cheek. 'You look very lovely, Mrs Morton-Edwards,' he said playfully.

'And you should be more careful, Dafydd.' Isabelle glanced anxiously over her shoulder.

'Why, what do you mean?' Dafydd looked genuinely puzzled.

'You are with a married woman, Dafydd! You are here with her in the public eye and the scandal of it could ruin you.'

'Nonsense!' Dafydd said. 'All eyes are on you today, who cares if I'm in the company of Mrs Mainwaring? No-one will even notice.'

'Can't you see this parading around with a married woman will damage your credibility as well as hers? It's a good thing her husband did not put in an appearance, otherwise there might have been trouble here today.'

Dafydd was frowning. 'You're making too much of it. We arrived separately and we will leave separately. Not even Joe Mainwaring could complain, we have been very discreet.'

Isabelle shook her head; it was pointless to talk to Dafydd. He was blind to everything but his love for Llinos Mainwaring. And he did love her, Isabelle had no doubt about that. It was no passing fancy, no hole-in-the-corner affair: Dafydd was as committed to Llinos as if they were man and wife.

'Come along, Isabelle,' Eynon said, 'we'd better attend our own wedding feast or what will everybody think?' He smiled mischievously and Isabelle took his arm. She might as well carry the day with dignity and forget about Dafydd's problems. She had enough of her own.

She did her best to be bright and happy as any

bride should be, but in her heart was a deep despair. Eynon did not love her, would never love her. She had just taken her marriage vows but had she made the biggest mistake of her life?

The day was full of sunshine, the birds were singing in the trees and a great sense of peace filled Rosie's heart. She walked along the familiar path at the side of the river Tawe and wondered if Watt would be home early. He would be busy at the pottery, supervising the business, running it as smoothly as if it was his own.

She sat on the grass and, greatly daring, showed her legs to the sun. Around her, bright daisies looked up as if they were smiling at her. She was happy, so happy that she felt like a rainbow dazzling the sky. She had wanted to be with Watt for so long and she could hardly believe it had really happened.

The peace was suddenly shattered by the sound of hoofs on the pathway above her. The Mainwaring carriage was heading along the path that led from the heart of Swansea. She caught sight of Lloyd Mainwaring and he was alone.

Poor young man, the town was alight with the scandal of his mother's affair. The gossip that had simmered quietly beneath the surface, spoken of in lowered voices by maid and mistress, had burst into vociferous outrage when Llinos Mainwaring had chosen to live openly with her lover.

Rosie leaned against the comforting bark of a tree, remembering the happy days when Llinos had loved her husband, had stood by him in the face of dreadful opposition from the townsfolk.

Rosie had thought the couple would never part and yet now the marriage was lying in the dust.

Times were changing; today, Mr Morton-Edwards had married a woman from the lower orders. If that were not scandal enough, Llinos Mainwaring had attended the wedding of her friend on the arm of her lover. How the gossips would talk!

Well, there was nothing she could do about it; she had enough difficulty running her own life. Watt wanted them to buy a house together, to live as they should, man and wife. It sounded idyllic but was it what she wanted? Was she wise to consider giving up her independence?

'Rosie, wait!' It was Watt's voice and her heart lifted with joy. She turned and saw that Watt, tall and broad-shouldered, was striding towards her. He had such an expression of love that tears came to Rosie's eyes. How could she not believe him when he said he loved her?

He had remained faithful to their marriage vows even when Rosie kept turning him away every time he begged her to come back.

'Watt!' She waved to him, her heart leaping with happiness. 'Watt!' Her voice carried on the breeze. 'Watt, I love you!'

He burst into a run, his features transformed with joy. 'Rosie!' He stopped, breathless, a few feet away from her. 'Rosie, my sweetheart, did I hear you right, did you say you loved me?'

It was she who made the first move. She took his face, his dear face, in her hands and kissed him.

'Come on, husband,' she said softly, 'let's go home.'

CHAPTER THIRTY

'Dafydd, I'm frightened, please don't join the rioters in this mad scheme of theirs.' Llinos sat on the sagging chair in the window of the coaching inn and stared up at him anxiously. Her instincts told her that Dafydd would be walking into grave danger if he rode as Rebecca into Carmarthen.

'I can't back out now, Llinos. I've let them down before and I won't do it again. The men are meeting at Nantgarredig and I gave my word I'd be there. It's about time the greedy rich realized they can't get away with squeezing the farmers any longer.'

Llinos knew she was wasting her time: she would never persuade Dafydd to give up the fight against the toll rises. This was the reason why she was here in the unfamiliar surroundings of a country coaching inn.

'I've got a bad feeling about this whole venture.' She stared down at her hands. A strong voice inside her was telling her that she would lose Dafydd if he left now.

'Don't worry so much, my lovely girl.' Dafydd

drew her to her feet. 'Once this is over we'll go home, I promise.'

'And you will make this the last time you act as Rebecca?' Llinos asked quietly. 'Because I can't live with the fear, Dafydd. I hate the whole idea of violence. Whenever men gather in an angry mob there is bound to be trouble.'

He led her towards the bed. 'Come on, let's make love. I can't wait to hold you in my arms, you beautiful witch!'

'Dafydd.' Llinos stopped him, her hands against his chest. 'There is something I must tell you.'

'I know what you're going to say – that you love me to distraction, that the very sight of me fires the blood, that you can't wait for me to possess you,' he teased.

'No.' She looked up at him. 'Dafydd, this is very difficult to say.' She took a deep breath. 'The baby might not be yours. Do you understand that?' She searched his face, trying to judge by his expression what his reaction would be. He held her at arm's length and stared at her in disbelief.

'I'm sorry, Dafydd, but I thought you would have realized that the night I slept with Joe, well, I might have fallen pregnant then.' She sank on to the bed. 'When I was with Joe, when he was sick and I went to care for him, and I—' She saw the happiness drain from Dafydd's face and her voice faltered.

'So the baby might be Joe's?' There was disbelief in Dafydd's eyes and he turned away from her, his shoulders hunched. 'I never thought . . . I don't understand . . . How could I have been so dense?'

He strode back and forth across the room. 'Llinos, how could you let me go on believing we were to have a child between us? You should have been honest from the start.'

'I'm so sorry. Dafydd, don't get angry, please.'

'How am I supposed to feel?' The words seemed dragged from his lips. He turned to look directly at her and it was as though he had never seen her before.

'You might be the father, Dafydd, I just don't know. I only slept with Joe that one night, so the baby is probably yours.'

Dafydd's face set in hard lines. 'Oh, thank you! Am I supposed to be grateful that you only slept with him once?'

'Dafydd, don't take it like that.'

'How am I supposed to take it?' She had never seen him so angry. 'The thought of you and Joe being together was just bearable, but how can you expect me to be father to a child by another man?'

His forehead furrowed. 'What sort of woman are you, Llinos? I don't know what to think any more. Have you ever truly loved me?'

'Of course I have! Dafydd, I'm so sorry.' Tears welled in her eyes and she made no attempt to wipe them away. 'I've behaved badly, I don't need anyone to tell me that.'

'Well, your apology doesn't put anything right, not for me.' His voice was low. 'I think I hate you, Llinos, do you know that? How can I bear the humiliation of it all? Tell me that.'

Llinos stared at him miserably. He was a proud

young man and she was causing him such grief. Or was it pride talking when he berated her, the silly male pride of possession, of needing to be in control?

He moved towards the door. 'I'm going out. I have never hit a woman and I don't intend to start now.' He paused, his hand on the latch. 'Do you know, Llinos? I realize now what it's like to have murder in your heart.'

Suddenly Llinos was as angry as he was. 'Dafydd, you have murder in your heart every time you go to a meeting of the Rebeccarites!' she said. 'You can't deny it. You need the excitement of the fight.' And he did. He was a rebel because he liked the feeling of power it gave him. He could have lived his life as a respectable businessman but that was too tame for him.

'I'm going out.' His voice was hard. 'Don't be here when I get back.' He left the room, and Llinos heard him clattering down the stairs. She stared through the window, trying to catch a glimpse of him. She was heartsick and confused. Should she follow him?

There was a knock on the door and Llinos felt a glimmer of hope. Had Dafydd come back? But it was Shanni Price who pushed her way into the room, and Llinos looked at her in startled surprise.

'Shanni, what on earth are you doing here?' Llinos's voice was hard as she tried to swallow her tears.

'I'm not going to bed with a lover, not like some people.' Shanni was white with anger, her small hands were clenched into fists.

'Why have you travelled to Carmarthen?' Llinos retorted angrily. 'Are you following me?'

'I've just come to tell you to leave Dafydd alone before it's too late.' Shanni stood against the door and it was clear she intended to have her say. 'You are putting Dafydd in danger. The men are turning against him because of you.'

'I don't understand.' Llinos tried to gather her wits, confused by the turn of the conversation. 'How am I putting him in danger?'

'He has let the men down more than once just to satisfy you. It was because of you that Ceri Buchan got injured. Dafydd should have been leading the men that night, he would have kept them in check. But, no, he had to be with you.' There was a world of scorn in Shanni's voice as she stared at Llinos with cold dislike. 'That's all I wanted to say. Keep out of Dafydd's life. Stay away from him before it's too late.'

Shanni flung open the door and Llinos heard her quick, light steps on the stairs. She closed the door, her heart beating so fast she felt breathless. She sat on the bed, her legs suddenly refusing to support her. She knew Dafydd was in danger every time he rode with the Daughters of Rebecca but she had never considered that she was making things worse for him.

She got up from the bed, and forced herself to think calmly. She must find Dafydd and convince him that the venture was too dangerous. She took her cloak out of the cupboard and swung it round her shoulders. She would go after him, stop him going into Carmarthen, even if it meant begging him on bended knee.

She stared at her reflection in the mirror. What a mess she had made of her life. Here she was in a shoddy room, sharing it with a lover. She was pale, her eyes wide with fear, and her pride was in the dust – but she knew she would do anything for Dafydd if only he would say he still loved her.

She opened the door and paused, taking one last look around the room where she and Dafydd had made love, perhaps for the last time, and her heart was heavy.

'Where on earth have you been, Shanni?' Madame Isabelle's face was white. 'This is no time to go missing. We're strangers here, remember, and in any case, I am not comfortable sitting alone in a coaching inn. Where's your sense, Shanni?'

'I've just been to the privy,' Shanni said, afraid to tell her the truth. The landlord's son had been eager to talk to her, and what he had to say had been most interesting. It was because of him that she knew Dafydd had been here, and that whore Llinos Mainwaring with him.

'Thank goodness Eynon brought me back from the trip sooner than we had intended,' Isabelle said. 'I'm only away for a few days and all hell breaks loose. It's madness! The men must be out of their minds to think of attacking the Union Workhouse.' She glanced over her shoulder. 'I heard the landlord say that the militia have been alerted. The men will all be killed.'

Shanni stared at Isabelle, her heart thumping

with fear. She had always known that Dafydd was involved in a dangerous struggle but now the danger was a reality.

'That long coach ride from Swansea has given me bone-ache,' Isabelle rubbed her back, 'and I still don't know if I was wise to bring you along. I don't even know if we'll do any good by being here.'

'We will, you'll see, and you had to bring me,' Shanni said. 'I remember how I used to talk when I lived in the slums and your voice would give you away at once.'

'Quite so,' Madame Isabelle said. 'Oh dear! What my husband will make of my absence I don't know, but I have to try to stop this madness.' She rubbed her brow. 'Look, we'll try to head the men off, warn them they might be ambushed. Cover your hair, Shanni, so that no-one can recognize you.'

Shanni leaned closer to her. 'Do you see that boy over there? Well, I talked to him when I was outside. He was saying that five hundred men are riding on horseback into Carmarthen and many more are on foot. He thinks they're making for the workhouse.'

She sat back against the warm wood of the oak settle, feeling smug. She knew more about the riot than Madame Isabelle ever would. She knew how brave Dafydd was. He was a man she would be proud to have as a husband – she would love him all her days. But he was way above her in social position and she knew it. Even now, as a property owner, she was not cut from the same mould as Dafydd Buchan. He was a gentleman born and bred and she was a child from the slums of Swansea.

Shanni felt downhearted. She knew in her gut that Dafydd would never be hers. 'Curse Llinos Mainwaring!' she said, under her breath. 'If anything happens to Dafydd, it will all be her fault.'

'Stop muttering and pay attention,' Madame Isabelle said. 'I think we'd better be leaving.'

Shanni pulled up her hood and tried to be calm, but it was impossible. Excitement and fear burned within her, and she knew that this was going to be the most important moment in her life.

CHAPTER THIRTY-ONE

Llinos left her room and picked her way carefully down the stairs of the inn. She had spent a sleepless night searching for answers. Could Dafydd forgive her enough to bring up the child even if it was Joe's? Somehow she doubted it.

She would have to find him, though, talk to him again, tell him she loved him. She must try to convince him that attacking the workhouse was a lost cause, that it might damage the efforts of the Rebeccarites, not further them.

She paused on the rickety stairs, trying to sort out her thoughts and feelings, but she found it difficult to come to any sensible conclusions about her future and the future of her child. How foolish she had been to burden Dafydd with her doubts. He was so upset he might rush headlong into the fray not caring if he lived or died. She should have waited until the time was right to tell him. But she had the dismal feeling that the time would never have been right.

As she neared the public rooms she heard the sound of a familiar voice and realized that Shanni was still at the inn, but who was with her? Llinos peered round the door and saw Shanni seated with Madame Isabelle at one of the beer-stained tables.

As Llinos watched, Isabelle stood up and Shanni tugged at her hood in an effort to cover her bright hair. They were going to leave, and Llinos knew at once where they were going. She followed them outside into the brightness of the day. The sun was hot, though a cooling breeze rustled the leaves on the trees. Overhead, light clouds raced across the sky with the promise of rain to come.

Ahead of her, Isabelle paused to loosen her cloak and Llinos took her courage in both hands. 'Isabelle, wait,' she called. 'I'm coming with you.'

She caught up with Isabelle and clung to her arm. 'Please, I have to come with you.'

Coolly Isabelle disengaged herself. 'Dafydd's mind hasn't been on the cause since he began his affair with you.' She spoke icily. 'Had he been his usual sharp self he would know his plan had been discovered.'

'Discovered? What do you mean?' Llinos felt as though a heavy weight was pressing on her chest.

'I mean that the dragoons will be riding into town with sabres at the ready.' Isabelle's tone sharpened. 'You've done enough harm, and I don't think this is the place for you, Mrs Mainwaring. Why don't you go home?'

'I can't go home,' Llinos said. 'I feel in my heart that Dafydd will need me before the day is over, and your words have only added to my fears.'

'I haven't time to argue with you, so come if

you must,' Isabelle said. 'But on your own head be it.'

Shanni's mouth was tightly closed. She stared mutinously at Llinos, hostility in every line of her slender body. Llinos tried to talk to her. 'Shanni, we must work together to save Dafydd, don't you understand that?' Shanni turned away without replying. Damn her! Llinos was worried enough without Shanni venting her spleen on her.

The walk to town was a short one and soon Isabelle led the way through Water Street gate. Faintly at first on the summer air came the sound of drums and Llinos's heart missed a beat: Isabelle was right, the soldiers were on the march against the rebels.

Llinos pushed her way through the crowd, trying to keep up with Isabelle. The roadways thronged with people; the procession of rioters was already under way. She glanced up at the sun: it was overhead – it must be almost noon.

'Well,' Isabelle paused to speak to Llinos, 'there are lots of people about but no sign of violence. Hopefully the attack has been called off. Why don't you go back to the inn, Mrs Mainwaring? Wait there. You are in no condition to be walking about town.' Isabelle's voice was more kindly and Llinos bit her lip.

'I just have to be with him, whatever the outcome.' Llinos took a deep breath. She wanted to believe that everything was going to be all right yet in her heart she knew that the day boded nothing but ill. 'I can't wait on the sidelines, not knowing what's happening.'

Suddenly, the throng of spectators began to

run. 'Come on!' Shanni cried. 'We mustn't get left behind.'

Llinos followed Shanni and Isabelle through Red Street to where the grim walls of the Union Workhouse stood out from the rest of the buildings. Her heart sank: some of the rioters were already hammering on the wooden doors with pickaxes and stout oak branches.

Llinos looked frantically around for Dafydd. He would be dressed in the clothes of Rebecca, wearing a horsehair wig of ringlets. His face, like that of most of the rioters, would be blackened with coal dust. Her heart was pounding and she lost sight of Isabelle, but Shanni's red hair was visible just ahead.

There was a sudden crash as the gates gave way, then the throng were in the workhouse yard screaming, waving cudgels and pushing aside anyone who stood in their way.

The matron came bustling out of the door, her face red. 'Stop this, you men!' she called, but she was pushed up against a wall and Llinos could hear her protests as her keys were snatched from her.

'Please, you men, leave the little ones be,' the matron begged, as the children screamed in fear.

'We are here to set them free,' one man shouted, above the crowd. 'Let the children go, boys.'

'They have no homes to go to!' the matron protested, but she was forced away from the doors and Llinos lost sight of her.

'That's Pedr's voice I can hear.' Isabelle was suddenly close to Llinos, straining to see above the heads of the crowd. 'That means Dafydd is not far away. This is a dreadful day for all of us, Mrs Mainwaring, and you have to take some of the blame for it.'

Before Llinos could reply a voice rang out above the crowd. 'Stop this!' She saw a man climbing on to a bench, his hands held aloft. Her heart missed a beat as she recognized the tall figure and stern face of her husband.

'Joe!' His name escaped her lips like a sigh.

'Listen to me, men!' he shouted. 'Your cause might be just, but if you turn these children loose they will starve to death in the streets. Can't you understand that?'

'Get out of the way or you'll be killed!' One of the rioters raised a stick, but Joe stood his ground. Llinos gasped in fear. Joe had come all this way and she knew that even now he wanted to protect her.

'What good would it do to kill me?' Joe shouted. 'I am here to help you. The dragoons are in town! Run while you can!'

Some of the men were hesitating, mumbling among themselves, but a strange silence fell as Joe spoke again.

'I am speaking the truth. The military have been warned of the riot, they will be here any minute now. I beg you to go home before any blood is shed.'

One of the protestors cheered him. Several men on horseback turned to leave the workhouse yard. Llinos leaned against the wall, gasping for breath. She was in no condition to be rushing about, pushing her way through the crowds.

'Don't listen to him, men! Fight on, I say!' Dafydd's voice cut through Llinos like a knife and she looked up, startled. Why did he want to continue with the battle? Could he not see that all was lost?

'We can't give up! We've got a long way to go yet!' Dafydd climbed up on the bench to stand beside Joe. Llinos stared at them, the two men in her life, facing each other in open enmity. Dafydd was still dressed in the clothes of Rebecca. Now he tore aside the wig and bonnet and rubbed away the soot on his face. 'Clear off, man,' he said to Joe. 'You don't belong here, you're not one of us.'

'Oh, my God!' Llinos tried to push her way through the crowd towards her husband. She must reach him before Dafydd tried to kill him. Suddenly she heard a blood-curdling scream and stopped abruptly. She glanced round fearfully to see the men of the Light Dragoons bearing down on her, cutting a way through the throng with raised swords. One man had his hand raised to save himself and his arm was severed. He fell to the ground, writhing in agony.

Llinos found a pathway through the crowd, desperation lending her strength, but both Joe and Dafydd had disappeared from sight. As Llinos drew nearer to the workhouse door she saw Isabelle standing there, rooted to the spot, her eyes wide with fear.

'Isabelle! Look out!' Llinos screamed. One of the rebels was standing over her, a thick stick in his hand, his face a mask of hatred. He brought the stick down on Isabelle's head, and blood began to run down her cheek.

'Murderer! You killed my brother!' The man was hysterical. 'You shot Thomas Carpenter dead and got away with it. Well, now is the time for me to avenge him.'

He raised the stick and hit Isabelle again and again, battering her to the ground. Her still body lay spreadeagled against the workhouse wall.

'Oh, Isabelle!' Llinos tried to reach her but she was thrust aside as the crowd surged forward, trying to escape the dragoons.

'No!' Llinos cried, but there was nothing she could do as Isabelle was trampled beneath the pounding hoofs of the horses. She turned away, feeling sick.

Abruptly, Shanni was beside Llinos, tugging at her arm. 'Come on, we've got to get away.'

'No, leave me alone,' Llinos said. 'You run if you must.'

'I've no time to argue but, believe me, Dafydd wants you to be taken to a place of safety. Pedr's got some horses. He'll take us away and then come back for Dafydd.'

'No, I can't leave, not until I know what's happened to Joe.' Llinos was cold with fear. 'I can't go, I just can't!'

Pedr reached down and lifted Shanni on to the saddle in front of him. 'Isabelle's dead,' he shouted, 'and the dragoons are killing everyone in sight. Get out of here, Mrs Mainwaring, while you can.'

'No, I can't.' Llinos stood there, shaking her head, and Pedr did not wait any longer. He urged his terrified horse on through the crowd and rode at high speed around the grim walls of the workhouse.

Someone pushed Llinos forward and she fell on to her knees. She began to sob. She would never find Joe and they would both die here in the workhouse yard with a mob of rioters. He might even now be lying injured, even dead, somewhere. 'Oh, dear God, spare him!' she whispered.

She tried to rise but there were people all around her, rebels and dragoons fighting to the death. 'Llinos, my little love.' She was dragged to her feet and turned to look into Dafydd's face. A sense of deep disappointment filled her, and she knew in that moment she loved Joe in a way she would never love Dafydd.

'You must get away,' Dafydd said. 'Come on, I'll lead you out of here. Just cling on to me.'

'Dafydd, thank God you're all right.' She stared at him. 'Get out of those ridiculous clothes.' He looked ludicrous in women's petticoats. 'And for pity's sake, Dafydd, think of yourself. Run before the dragoons take you.'

He ripped off the petticoats, throwing them into the crowd. 'I'll be all right. Go, Llinos, you have to get away from all this before you're hurt. This is no place for a woman with child. Go quickly, while you can!'

Over Dafydd's shoulder Llinos saw a dragoon riding towards her, his sabre held aloft. She was going to die here for a pointless cause, here in the workhouse yard, slaughtered like some dumb beast. Llinos pressed her hands to her stomach and felt the flutter of new life. A life that would be over before it began.

Dafydd shielded her with his own body and Llinos screamed as the sabre cut into his arm. 'Dafydd, no!' She looked up. The dragoon was lifting his arm to strike again. 'Don't you know this man is Dafydd Buchan, owner of the pottery? He's here to stop the riot, you fool!' She screamed the lie, and it stopped the dragoon in his tracks.

Dafydd staggered to his feet, clutching his wound, as the dragoon stared down at him doubtfully. 'Don't look like a pottery owner to me.'

'I assure you I am Dafydd Buchan. I own the Llanelli pottery,' Dafydd said. 'Now, get out of here before I report you to a higher authority.'

The dragoon seemed uncertain what course to take, but after a moment he turned his horse away and headed for the heart of the fray.

Dafydd sagged against Llinos and she struggled to hold him. How would she get herself and Dafydd through the crowd? He swayed against her and Llinos began to despair. 'You must help me, Dafydd, I can't do it alone,' she said. And then, miraculously, Joe was there. He came as silently as always, like a shadow against the sun, and took control.

'Come on, Buchan,' he said firmly. 'Follow me through the back gate. Young Pedr Morgan is waiting there for you.'

He turned to Llinos and lifted her in his arms. Wearily, thankfully, she rested her head on his shoulder. He carried her around the workhouse to the streets beyond. Pedr was waiting with two horses and his face lit up when he saw Dafydd.

'Mr Buchan, man, I thought they'd got you.'

He helped Dafydd on to the back of one of the horses. 'I'll take you to my mam's,' he said. 'She'll know how to patch you up.'

'Go with your God, Buchan,' Joe said, 'and leave my wife alone in future. You owe me that much.'

Llinos clung to Joe, her face turned away from Dafydd. 'Goodbye, Llinos, my love.' Dafydd's voice was hoarse. 'I'll never forget you.'

Pedr whipped the horses into action and Llinos heard the hoofs clattering along the hard, sun-baked earth.

'I've got the carriage waiting,' Joe said softly. 'Come on, my firebird, no tears, not now.' Joe lifted her into the seat and climbed in beside her. He touched her face tenderly. 'Forget Buchan. You and I must think of ourselves and of our future. We are meant to be together, you know that, Llinos.'

Llinos looked at him, her husband, so wise, so forgiving. She put her head against his shoulder. 'I know.' She hesitated. 'But I'm with child, Joe. What if it's his?'

'Then we will bring up the baby as our own, and I will be proud to call him my son.'

Llinos began to cry. Her whole body was racked with the pain of losing Dafydd but she knew, deep down inside her, that he never would have been as generous as Joe. Dafydd was not a big enough man to bring up a child that was not his.

'I do love you, Joe,' she said softly. She understood now how Joe had loved her even while he lay with another woman. It was a madness that had possessed him just as a madness for Dafydd had possessed her.

One day, perhaps, they could both forget the wrongs they had done each other. One day, if the Great Spirit willed it, they would be happy again.

THE END

SWEET ROSIE
by Iris Gower

Rosie – eighteen, beautiful and vivacious – is in love with Watt Bevan, the manager of the famous Mainwaring Pottery where her mother Pearl works. But Watt is mourning the loss of a former love, and when Pearl falls ill and Watt becomes the protector of the family Rosie realizes that her feelings for him are not returned. Meanwhile Llinos Mainwaring's romantic marriage to Joe, the American Indian who stole her heart all those years ago, seems to be in trouble, and Llinos – hurt and bewildered by Joe's apparent neglect – finds the ownership of her family pottery to be increasingly burdensome.

Into all these lives intrudes the troublesome Mrs Sparks, voluptuous wife of the local bank manager. Her scheming involves Llinos, Joe and Watt – and when she enmeshes the innocent Rosie in her net the whole future of the pottery looks threatened.

In this powerful novel Iris Gower continues the romantic story of the South Wales potteries, begun in *Firebird* and *Dream Catcher*.

0 552 14449 5

A SELECTED LIST OF FINE NOVELS
AVAILABLE FROM CORGI BOOKS

14058 9	**MIST OVER THE MERSEY**	*Lyn Andrews*	£5.99
14712 5	**ROSIE OF THE RIVER**	*Catherine Cookson*	£5.99
13915 7	**WHEN NIGHT CLOSES IN**	*Iris Gower*	£5.99
13631 X	**THE LOVES OF CATRIN**	*Iris Gower*	£5.99
13686 7	**THE SHOEMAKER'S DAUGHTER**	*Iris Gower*	£5.99
13688 3	**THE OYSTER CATCHERS**	*Iris Gower*	£5.99
13687 5	**HONEY'S FARM**	*Iris Gower*	£5.99
14095 3	**ARIAN**	*Iris Gower*	£4.99
14097 X	**SEA MISTRESS**	*Iris Gower*	£5.99
14096 1	**THE WILD SEED**	*Iris Gower*	£5.99
14447 9	**FIREBIRD**	*Iris Gower*	£5.99
14448 7	**DREAM CATCHER**	*Iris Gower*	£5.99
14449 5	**SWEET ROSIE**	*Iris Gower*	£5.99
14537 8	**APPLE BLOSSOM TIME**	*Kathryn Haig*	£5.99
14770 2	**MULLIGAN'S YARD**	*Ruth Hamilton*	£5.99
14820 2	**THE TAVERNERS' PLACE**	*Caroline Harvey*	£5.99
14868 7	**SEASON OF MISTS**	*Joan Hessayon*	£5.99
14603 X	**THE SHADOW CHILD**	*Judith Lennox*	£5.99
14772 9	**THE COLOUR OF HOPE**	*Susan Madison*	£5.99
14822 9	**OUR YANKS**	*Margaret Mayhew*	£5.99
14659 5	**WHAT BECAME OF US**	*Imogen Parker*	£5.99
14753 2	**A PLACE IN THE HILLS**	*Michelle Paver*	£5.99
10375 6	**CSARDAS**	*Diane Pearson*	£5.99
14715 X	**MIDSUMMER MEETING**	*Elvi Rhodes*	£5.99
14747 8	**THE APPLE BARREL**	*Susan Sallis*	£5.99
14813 X	**YEAR OF VICTORY**	*Mary Jane Staples*	£5.99
14845 8	**GOING HOME**	*Valerie Wood*	£5.99